Christmas in Paris

BOOKS BY TILLY TENNANT

TILLY TENNANT

Christmas in Paris

Bookouture

Published by Bookouture in 2022

An imprint of Storyfire Ltd.
Carmelite House
50 Victoria Embankment
London EC4Y 0DZ

www.bookouture.com

ISBN: 978-1-80314-770-3
eBook ISBN: 978-1-80314-769-7

For best friends everywhere

CHAPTER ONE

In the shadow of Ely Cathedral, Brooke waited, as she did every Saturday afternoon, for Johnny. There was a wedding at the cathedral, as there often was. Brooke sat on a wall with the sun on her face, watching the bridal car arrive. There were excited gasps of approval as the vintage Rolls-Royce slowed to a halt and the bride emerged, smiling. Brooke could see why. She liked to see the brides arrive, and she especially liked to see their gowns. Some she loved more than others, but she'd never yet seen one that didn't look exactly right for the woman wearing it, and today's diaphanous ivory number, finished with hair piled in a casual up-do with flowers pinned into it, was no different. The bouquet was refreshingly informal; more like a posy of wildflowers plucked hastily from a meadow than anything created by a florist – as if the bride might have stopped the car on the way to the cathedral and rushed out to pick them – though it was also immediately obvious that this supposed informality had probably been very deliberately and expensively designed. Usually, the less it looked like you had bothered, the more it cost.

As Brooke watched she tried to imagine if it was something

she'd wear… should Johnny ever get round to popping the question. Three years down the line there hadn't been much progress in that regard, and every month that passed had Brooke convinced that it would have to happen soon. Surely he'd want to make things more permanent before too much longer? They'd discussed moving in together as an alternative to marriage and he'd said yes, eventually, but told her that he had too much else to think about right then. Brooke wouldn't push it; he'd asked her to be patient, to wait until he was in the right place in his life to think about it, and she'd respected that.

But she didn't want to wait forever.

A smile hovered at the corners of Brooke's mouth as she watched the scene unfolding – the bride's gown being straightened out by the bridesmaids ready to go inside, the guests who'd waited to see her arrival snapping photos on a forest of mobile phones and tiny digital cameras, and the official photographer getting a few of his own, the mini-drama set against the resplendence of the cathedral, all gleaming sandstone in the afternoon sun.

Brooke loved this old building – she never tired of looking at it. Whatever light characterised the day held the power to make the cathedral look entirely different, so every day and every season presented a new aspect to admire. Without a doubt, this would be the venue for her own wedding. She'd say as much when Johnny turned up, as she often did, and as he often did he'd probably nod and smile vaguely and then change the subject. In fact, his usual response was to ask a question, mostly what pub she wanted to go to, though it seemed a pointless one because they always spent their Saturday afternoons at the same one – The Coxon, overlooking the sparkling broads of the River Great Ouse. They'd sit on the shaded patio in the spring and summer and some of the autumn months, only heading inside for a window seat when the weather turned cold. Johnny had beer and Brooke's usual G&T would slide down nicely as they watched the pleasure cruisers and barges glide by. Brooke's life wasn't complete by any means, but she could do a great job of convincing herself she was content with a glass in one hand, Johnny sitting across from her, and white clouds reflecting on the blue of the river that ran past their favourite pub.

With a last deep breath, the bride turned to the huge wooden doors of the church – wide open and ready to welcome her to her brand-new life. She nodded briefly to three corn-flower-blue-clad adult bridesmaids who attended her and then began the walk down the path. Brooke felt in her bag for her phone, eyes still trained on the figures of the women going inside. When they'd gone in she'd get a cheeky photo of the wedding cars decked out in their ribbons and flowers in front of the cathedral for her Insta.

As she rummaged, she knocked the smoothie she'd been sipping and had just set down on the wall next to her with her elbow and sent it flying.

'Shit!'

She bent forward, chestnut hair spilling down as she hurriedly retrieved it. The lid had come off, of course, and most of it was now soaking into the grass. Annoying as hell, but there was little she could do about it.

Seeing there was the smallest drop left but still enough for one more slurp, Brooke put the lid back on and stuck the straw in. As she straightened to retake her seat, a shadow was cast on the ground in front of her and she looked up to see Johnny.

'Hey,' he said.

Brooke smiled, putting her cup down to smooth her hair. He was wearing her favourite shirt, a soft denim one that brought out the blue of his eyes, teamed with fitted midnight jeans. She'd bought the shirt for him the previous Christmas, but he hadn't worn it as much as she'd hoped he would. She worried that he didn't like it because she'd bought it second-hand and he didn't share her vintage shop fetish, so it was good to see him in it today. 'I was almost ready to give up on you,' she said. 'Held up?'

'Yeah...' Johnny rubbed at the back of his neck as he gave a vague shrug. 'Sorry about that. I had... well, I couldn't get away.'

'That's alright.' Brooke stood to kiss him. 'You made it in the end.'

Johnny nodded, but he didn't smile, and he barely returned her kiss.

Why wasn't he smiling? And why had Brooke's stomach suddenly dropped? Something wasn't right here.

'Where do you want to go today?' she asked, hoping that she was wrong and the moment would pass.

'The usual,' he said listlessly.

'Yeah.' Brooke forced a small laugh. 'I mean, I didn't think there was any point in having an in-depth discussion about it, because we know we'll end up at The Coxon anyway. I just thought I'd go through the motions... you know...'

'No, no point at all.'

'But we could go somewhere else...' Brooke replied uncertainly.

'I'm too tired to think about anywhere else.'

'Well, if you're tired we don't have to go to the pub at all. We can skip it today. Go back to mine, watch something on TV, get a takeout, some cans... I'm sure The Coxon can manage without us for one weekend.'

Johnny stared at her. Or rather, he seemed to stare through her. It was unnerving, and Brooke was about to say so when he spoke.

'Look, there's no easy way to say this so I'm just going to say it.' A pause. 'I think we should split up.'

Brooke grabbed for the wall, the roughness of the stone beneath her fingers strangely apparent for no reason at all. 'What?'

'Come on – even you have to admit it's got stale.'

'Stale?'

'You and me... all this...' He wafted a hand from her back to himself. 'Monday nights at mine, Wednesdays at yours, curry nights Friday, Saturday afternoon sessions... it's the same, week in, week out.'

'But I thought you liked it!'

'I did... for a while anyway. But we never change it up.'

'You never asked to change it up! And I've wanted different... I wanted us to move in together – you know that!'

'So we could repeat the routine, except in one house instead of two?'

'It wouldn't have been like that! You could have said if you wanted it to be different!'

'Brooke,' he began in a withering tone that cut her to the core, 'if I'd ever suggested we did curry on a Tuesday I think you would have combusted with the stress.'

'Don't be stupid! If you'd said you wanted curry on Tuesday I'd have gone along with it!'

He shook his head. 'You're not really getting it.'

'Then explain better.'

The wall was still rough beneath her fingers and it was then Brooke realised she was gripping it. She took a breath, steadied herself against it, tried to relax her grip, but she couldn't. She looked for the same signs of stress in Johnny's face, but there was nothing. It was like he didn't care about the words that were coming from his mouth. But he was ending this... he was ending *them*! How could he not care? How could he be about to destroy her life and be so cold about it? Hadn't it been good for him like it had been for her?

'How long have you been feeling this way?' she demanded.

'I don't know... it's not important now.'

'Of course it is.'

'I think we've come to a natural end, that's all. Things do that sometimes. We had fun in the beginning, but we ran out of steam a while ago... please don't ask me when because I can't tell you to the hour or day or even month – we just did. And if we're both being honest, it was never going to go the distance, was it?'

'I didn't think that! We talked about the future!'

'No, *you* talked about the future. I was forced to listen.'

Brooke's expression darkened. The shock she'd been near paralysed with up until now was slowly being replaced by anger. 'And you didn't see fit to say any of this before I wasted all that time on something that was going nowhere? Instead, you let me witter on about houses and marriage and you didn't think to put me straight? I must have looked like such a loser to you. I hope you enjoyed the spectacle.'

'It wasn't like that. I thought if I gave it time things would settle and I'd feel differently. I thought I might want those things eventually, but... well, here we are, and I don't.'

'What's changed? Something must have changed. You don't let a relationship go on and on and then one day, out of the blue, suddenly decide to do something about it.'

'Nothing's changed.'

'You're lying.'

He glanced around the grounds. The wedding party had gone into the cathedral, but there were still plenty of tourists and locals milling around, and as Brooke's voice had risen, one or two had stopped what they were doing to pay attention. 'I don't think this is the place for—'

'Then where is the place?'

'Brooke, people can hear you.'

'I don't care! Tell me, where is the place? Let's go there right now, because I'm not letting you walk away from this without proper answers!'

'Brooke, I've told—'

'Three years! You don't stick around for three years hoping it will come good! If you're bored you do something about it long before that, so cut the bullshit, Johnny. What's really going on?'

He stared at her, his expression, at last, showing signs of regret and maybe a little guilt. There was something satisfying about it that Brooke seized on in a moment of savagery. *Good. Let's see you squirm.*

'You really want to know?'

'That's why I asked.'

'Even though you might regret asking?'

'What you actually mean is that you're too spineless to come clean and you know it's going to make you feel like a total shit saying it.' Brooke's mouth set in a hard line. She sat on the wall and folded her arms. 'OK. Who is she?'

'I don't know what you're talking about.'

'Don't make any more of a fool of me than you already have please. You've strung me along for all this time, surely one last bit of honesty is the least I deserve?'

'If you put it like that...' He let out a heavy sigh.

'I knew it,' she said tersely.

His expression told her the truth and he didn't need to say anything more. All was now clear. What was less clear was why she hadn't seen this the moment he'd told her he wanted to end things. They'd been coasting for the last year, maybe even two, sure, but they'd been fine. They'd been content and there had been a future... at least Brooke had always been certain of that much.

'I'm sorry.'

'How long... Who is she? Do I know her?'

'No,' he said. 'You don't.'

The shock which had been replaced by anger was now replaced by a sense of defeat. Brooke sniffed back tears. 'The last three years meant so little to you? You weren't happy at all? Not even for some of it? You must have been for it to last so long.'

'We were something,' he said. 'We were... well, we were *us*.'

'That counts for something, doesn't it? Did you ever love me?'

He gave the most infuriatingly vague shrug. Suddenly, in the face of such indifference, Brooke itched to slap him. Her fingers went back to the wall as she fought to resist the urge.

'Do you love her?' she asked in a very deliberate voice. This was not up for debate – Brooke needed to know, and she would have her answer no matter how it might make him squirm.

'Brooke, don't—'

'*Do you love her*? Or are you going to spend the next three years pissing about with her only to drop her one day? Or is that royal treatment only reserved for me?'

'Yes,' he said finally. 'I love her.'

'Huh...' Brooke nodded vigorously. 'Well, how about that. And how long have you been cheating on me? Actually, how long have you been cheating on us both? And do you intend to tell her about me, or were you hoping by dumping me now you could sweep away your skeletons before she found out?'

'I haven't cheated on either of you. I didn't mean for this to happen – you have to believe that. I met her last week and I haven't been able to stop thinking about her. I'm sorry, I've been—'

'You went to see her this morning, didn't you? That's why you were late.'

'I went to tell her how I felt and she said she felt it too. I was honest about you and she said I had to deal with this first before she'd go out with me.'

'*Deal with this*? Oh, right, thanks. What am I? A case of the clap that you need to get rid of before she'll sleep with you?'

'Brooke, don't be like this—'

'Like what? Like the only person here talking any sense? You said you met her last week and you haven't even been out on a single date yet – how can you be in love with her? How could you throw away three years with me for a girl you've literally just met?'

'I can't explain it. I know it sounds mad, but this feels so right. I feel like I already know her. I feel like she's... well, she's the one.'

'That's the biggest pile of crap I've ever heard. I've read more convincing motives in a Mills and Boon.'

'Probably,' he said. 'But then, you always were too sensible for things like love at first sight.'

'Because it doesn't exist!'

'Yes, and you'd say that too.'

'What the hell does that mean?'

'It means whatever you want it to. We're going round in circles here, and I think we're done. I've said what I need to say and the rest... it's getting us nowhere.'

'I suppose you have to go because your new girlfriend is waiting somewhere around the corner for you to have done the dirty deed so you can skip off together with your "love at first sight". Probably be married next week.'

'I'm honestly sorry it came to this.'

'No you're not.'

'Believe what you want, Brooke. Believe whatever makes you feel better. I don't wish you ill—'

'*I* do!' she fired back. 'I wish you shit! If I could curse you, I bloody would! In fact, I might go and learn how to do it!'

'You don't mean that.'

'Try me.'

'Whatever you say, I have a lot of fondness for what we had, and I'd like to think that when all this has blown over we can still be friends. Or at least say hello on the street like civilised people.'

'Spoken like a man who has shat on someone from a great height and feels ever so slightly guilty about it, but not enough to stop himself enjoying the shit.'

Brooke stood up and yanked her handbag onto her shoulder. 'The old friendship card – always guaranteed to make you feel like the bigger person, gracious in victory and all that. Think what you want of me, but I have no intention of being gracious, because grace is easy for the winner, isn't it? Not so easy for the person who has to try and put their life back together. So no, *Johnny*, we can't be friends. The only reason I haven't thrown the rest of this smoothie at you is because there isn't enough left to make any discernible difference to your shitty appearance, and because what *is* left is too good to waste on you. But if I do see you on the street after today, I will punch you in the face – and if the love of your life is with you, I'll do her too for good measure.'

She turned to leave, but his hand closed over her arm.

'You have to know, I didn't mean to—'

Brooke rounded on him. 'I don't have to know anything except I hate you, and I'll never, ever forgive you for this!'

'I'm sorry to hear that,' he said in such an even tone that Brooke felt that urge to slap him again so strongly she wasn't sure she could stop herself this time. Perhaps it was a good thing that his hand was still on her arm. 'For what it's worth, I wish it could be different.'

'If you wished it that much you could have made it different.' Brooke prodded his chest. 'You've chosen this – it's what you want. Don't pretend it's some destiny you can't fight. *Your* actions have made this happen, nothing else.'

Shaking her arm from his grip, she stood to her full height and took a deep breath. 'I'm going home. Have a nice life. See you never, if I'm lucky.'

CHAPTER TWO

Thank God for Felicity, Brooke thought – and not for the first time. Thank God for a best friend who always knew exactly what Brooke needed before Brooke even did. No sooner had the SOS gone out than Felicity had arrived at Brooke's door in a taxi to take her out for a stiff drink. And nowhere near The Coxon, thank goodness. They were in a quiet bar on the high street. It was nothing special – the usual relaxed and understated comfort of a mid-price establishment with parquet floors, inoffensive but unremarkable artwork on the walls, perfectly nice chrome fittings and big old windows that offered glimpses of the Saturday shoppers as they hurried past, umbrellas turned against the sleet beating against the glass.

Summer had turned to autumn, which was now well on its way to winter proper. In just over six weeks, in fact, it would be Christmas Day. It had felt like a long five months since Johnny had dumped Brooke so coldly in the grounds of Ely Cathedral and while everyone else had been doing the usual rounds of garden parties and barbecues and long evenings at the pub by the river, as she and Johnny had done for the past couple of summers, Brooke had moped at home, barely noticing whether the sun was out or not and certainly not caring. Now, gradually and almost timidly, she'd begun to venture out into society again.

Felicity had been the one constant through it all, the one person who'd refused to make herself scarce when Brooke had requested it, the one person who understood that the solitude Brooke had asked for wasn't what she'd needed. She'd turned up at Brooke's house and insisted they talk it over, had got her drunk so that she'd open up, had held her when she'd cried, had forced her to make plans for the future. Eventually she'd suggested that they amalgamate their separate businesses – hers making jewellery and Brooke's textiles – insisting that they could grow them more effectively together. Brooke suspected the real reason was so that she could lend her support in more than just a personal capacity. The only thing Brooke had left worth anything was her business, but she'd been so distracted by events that even though she'd known how important it was to keep that afloat, she'd struggled to focus.

Finally, as autumn arrived, Brooke had felt as if she was coming out of the other side of a very long and dark tunnel.

And then she'd heard about Johnny's wedding.

At first she'd tried to ignore her feelings of shock and upset. She had no right to them, she'd told herself. Johnny was no longer her concern; neither was what he got up to. If he wanted to marry a girl he'd known for less than half a year then that was his lookout. But the feelings grew the more she heard about it, until they were too big and hurt too much to ignore.

She'd be in a shop and bump into a mutual friend and they'd ask if she'd heard about it. Why did everyone insist on doing that? What made them think she'd want to hear it from them, even if she hadn't already known about it? What made them want to be the person who broke the news? Was there some sort of sadistic, perverted pleasure to be gained from the deed? Then she'd overheard a conversation in a bar while out with Felicity between two girls who knew the bride but obviously didn't realise that the woman who'd been there before the bride was within listening distance.

It was going to be lavish and beautiful, the bride was stunning and the groom handsome and there were going to be bridesmaids galore, and the reception was going to be on a river cruiser, and – possibly worst of all – the service was due to take place at Brooke's beloved cathedral, the place she'd stood outside so many Saturdays watching other people getting married and dreaming of the day it would be her turn. Johnny knew only too well her feelings about that place. She felt sure he wouldn't have deliberately planned it that way, and perhaps he hadn't even remembered the dreams Brooke had regularly told him about at all, but it still stung. Finally, he would be a groom standing at the altar of that beautiful old building, but the bride walking down the aisle towards him wouldn't be her.

'I suppose I didn't really think he'd go through with it.' Brooke stirred her raspberry gin fizz with a paper straw that threatened to buckle with the pressure of doing anything other than transporting the drink to a waiting mouth.

Felicity put her peach Bellini down and raised her eyebrows. 'So you went to spy on another woman's wedding hoping to see her humiliated at the altar?'

'Of course not! It's just... seeing is believing, isn't it? I suppose I knew Johnny fully intended to go through with the wedding, but after three years of avoiding the merest mention of marriage with me, to see him walk down the aisle with someone else after literally five months...' Brooke gave a weak shrug. 'I couldn't get my head around it. I had to see for myself it was actually happening.'

'OK,' Felicity said slowly. 'And now that you've seen it?'

Brooke was transported, momentarily, back to the scene outside the cathedral. She was beginning to wish she hadn't gone now. She'd stood across the road from the grounds in the shadow of a bakeshop and had watched the wedding party arrive, hoping no old mutual friend of hers and Johnny's would recognise her or even notice she was there. How many weddings had she stood and watched from afar over the years? How many times had she passed by the cathedral on a Saturday only to find a ceremony in full swing and stopped to take a look. Being witness to someone's big day had always made her smile in the past, had always given her a warm feeling. It had been like seeing the happy-ever-after of a romantic film, only better, because this was real life and real people.

That was before Johnny had soured everything, of course. Since he'd dumped Brooke, she hadn't stopped to watch a single wedding, and had never imagined that the first one after her hiatus would be his. Spying on it was pathetic and creepy and lots of other negative things, and Brooke knew all that only too well but still hadn't been able to stop herself from going along.

Johnny was there first, of course, looking tall and heart-breakingly handsome in his morning suit. She hated him and longed for him all at once, and then hated herself even more for wanting him at all. It had been five months. She hadn't even seen him on the street to keep her promise of punching him, she hadn't allowed herself to phone or text, and when she'd been tempted to peek at his social media, she'd found he'd blocked her. All those months without contact should have been enough to get him out of her system, surely? But then she'd seen the wedding announcement on the notice board of the cathedral as she'd passed one day and something in her just couldn't let the day go by without coming to see it, no matter how much it might hurt.

She could handle it, she'd told herself as she'd paid special attention to her make-up that morning. She could be the bigger person. But as soon as she'd seen him, she'd realised she wasn't over him at all. This was meant to be *her* wedding venue. This was the day she'd planned and wanted, and here she was, hiding in the shadows of a bakery across the road like some mad old Miss Havisham while some other woman married Johnny in her place. She should have left then, but she was glued to the spot, determined to see this ultimate masochistic act through.

A vintage Daimler pulled onto the gravel next and out clambered two adult bridesmaids in emerald green. It wouldn't have been Brooke's choice of colour, but she had to grudgingly approve of the jewel palette. And then the bride herself arrived in a full silk gown with a high neck and long lace sleeves. It was a bit traditional for Brooke's more bohemian tastes.

Erin. That was her name. Brooke hadn't wanted to know, but it had been impossible to avoid finding out. She'd been mentioned in brief conversations with people who'd come up to Brooke on the street or in the pub or the supermarket to express their condolences that she and Johnny had split. Brooke hadn't asked how he was doing but they'd told her anyway. She hadn't asked who the woman was, but they'd offered the name whether she wanted it or not. They'd asked how she was and she'd pretended not to care. It had crossed her mind to invent a new boyfriend, but Ely was a very small place, despite its city status, and it wouldn't take long for her to be found out. She might have been desperate, but she wasn't stupid.

Erin's bridesmaids fussed around her while she laughed in the last of the autumn sun, smiling, radiant, loving every second of the attention. The day was crisp, the trees in the cathedral grounds glowing tangerine, russet and saffron, the last of the wasps buzzing drunkenly amongst their branches. The usual onlookers gathered at the gates to see the spectacle, hoping to catch a glimpse of the bride before she went in. They were tourists mostly, who'd come to see the cathedral and had stumbled onto the pleasant and unexpected bonus of a wedding in progress. Some took photos of the cars or the scene as a whole – most too respectful to take photos of Erin and her bridesmaids, though it was obvious they were itching to. For once, as she watched them, Brooke was thankful that her home town was so popular with visitors because at least the crowds were a shield between her and the grounds so she could watch, relatively unnoticed, by the rest of the onlookers.

A few months ago she'd have sobbed to witness the end of her own hopes for marriage to Johnny. At first she'd refused to believe it was over and she'd convinced herself that it was only a matter of time before he realised his mistake and came back to her. She'd play hard to get, make him sweat, but she'd have taken him back in the end. To act as he'd done... well, he must have taken temporary leave of his senses – it was the only explanation, so it followed that he'd realise eventually that love at first sight wasn't a thing, or that his infatuation with the new barista of his favourite coffee shop had made her seem far more perfect than she actually was. Perhaps it was just the coffee that was good and not her.

Here today, however, seeing that dream die, Brooke didn't sob. Instead, she was overwhelmed by a sense of melancholy and foolishness. What an idiot she'd been to imagine for one solitary second that he'd change his mind. This had all happened for a reason, and if Johnny had been nothing else, he'd never been less than honest about that. Brooke had asked him, as he'd dealt the final blow, if he'd ever loved her, and he hadn't been able to reply. That had been the only answer, in the end, that mattered. She'd loved him, and she had to wonder now how a one-sided love like that could ever have worked. Could one person be in love if the other wasn't? Didn't it have to be some sort of reciprocal arrangement for it to be real, proper love? So what was it, exactly, that Brooke had felt if it wasn't love? How had she missed the gaping hole at the centre of their relationship for so long? How had she not recognised it in his deeds and words?

However it had escaped her, Brooke had to suppose that it didn't matter now. Johnny was married to someone else. In the time it had taken her to search her soul for answers, he'd emerged, smiling, Erin on his arm.

So that was that, the end of the chapter. For her, at least. For Johnny it was the opening page of a whole new book.

'Now you've seen it,' Felicity repeated, pulling Brooke from her memories and back to the room, 'are you finally going to drop this crazy notion that there might still be a chance for you and him?'

'I dropped it months ago,' Brooke said quietly. 'I just couldn't admit as much.'

Felicity's face was full of genuine empathy. 'It's for the best, you know. You might not see it that way now, but you will one day. If you and Johnny had ever been meant for each other then you'd be together, but you're not, so you can't have been.'

Brooke took a sip of her drink. 'I wish I could be that philosophical about it.'

'Boo, philosophical is all you can be. The deed is done, and nothing you think or say is going to change that. It sounds cruel, I know, but I think cruelty is what you need right now. I don't honestly know why you forced yourself to go and see the bloody thing. Wasn't it bad enough knowing it was the day without going to watch?'

'Well, I suppose I was dealing out my own kind of cruelty to myself,' Brooke said ruefully.

'You certainly did that. So that's it now? The end of the saga?'

'The end of the saga... that's one way of putting it.'

'Right...' Felicity straightened up, her tone brisk. It signalled the end of the conversation. This was how Felicity worked – she allowed only so much time for Brooke – or anyone for that matter – to wallow, and when she'd run out of patience for such behaviour she'd make it obvious. To people who didn't know her it seemed cold and unfeeling, but Brooke understood it differently. It was a way of nudging her along, pulling her out of unhelpful and destructive emotional spirals, of channelling her thoughts into something more productive and healing. 'Now that's out of the way, we have bigger fish to fry.'

'Do we?'

'Seriously, Boo? Of course we do! I know it's a working trip but you've got to be getting a little bit excited about Paris now that we've finally confirmed the pitch?'

'I wish I could be. I'll be honest, I've barely thought about it this week.'

'Then you'd better give it your full attention from now on. I can afford to indulge you as your friend, but as your business partner I really can't cut you the same sort of slack. We're way behind on prep. We've still got raw materials to source and until we get that we're going to be far too short on stock. And by *we*, I'm afraid I mostly mean you. You need to get printing and sewing – and fast.'

Though she understood her friend's concerns, Brooke was wounded by her tone. 'Have I ever let you down?'

'No, but we've never tackled anything this big before. If you think about it, this is the first real test of our business partnership. And before you start going on about how you said at the beginning that you thought mixing business and friendship was a bad idea, I'm not saying that I think any less of you as a person when I tell you this stuff. You'll always be my best mate, Brooke, and that will always be a separate thing from our business. I'd also like to think, regardless of anything else, that our friendship is strong enough that I could say this sort of thing without you getting all weird and offended anyway.'

'You know you can, but it's not that straightforward, is it? People can't help their feelings.'

'Oh, come off it, I'm not trying to hurt your feelings. This is a kick up the arse that comes from a place of love and you know it.'

'As all of them have over the past five months – I know,'

Brooke said ruefully. 'But I did warn you I might drag you down with me if you got this involved.'

'And I said that if you really wanted to you could stop that from happening. Your life isn't so out of control as you might think, and this working trip to Paris will prove it. You are worth more and you are capable of more than recent circumstances have made you believe. I can see that – I just wish you'd try to.'

'I *am* trying.'

'You keep saying that but I need to see it with my own eyes, Boo.'

Brooke's gaze went to the window, where the rain was beating against the glass with even greater ferocity than before, bouncing off the pavements and umbrellas, sending shoppers scurrying for cover wherever they could find it. She had to admit that Felicity had stuck her neck out where this trip to the Paris markets was concerned. Before they'd become business partners, their separate enterprises had ticked along, but Felicity's had been far more profitable than Brooke's. Her custom-made jewellery items from recycled materials were extremely cool and, more importantly, she'd tapped into a market that was rapidly growing and ever more relevant. Her selling points of unique design, sustainability and care for the planet went down well both in her online shop and at the regular markets, festivals, student events, fayres and exhibitions she attended. Brooke, while relying on much the same ethos for her products – which included tote bags from recycled fabrics and sustainable cotton – didn't have the same cutting-edge flair for design – at least, she never thought so. Her goods were cute and colourful, but alternative types weren't desperate to own them in the same way. In fact, Felicity had grown quite a social media following and often sold out of new creations within hours of their photos being posted.

As far as this Paris venture was concerned, Felicity had stuck her neck out, calling in many favours to get them there. It was the next big step, a whole new pool of customers, a chance to test their products in the wider world and gauge where the business ought to go next. Felicity had driven it all. She'd got her Paris-based cousin Fabien to secure their permits to trade, and the opportunity was too big to squander. It almost felt like make or break for them; they could stay as they were, selling bits here and there in the local area or online, or they could spread their wings and sell far and wide. As she looked across at Felicity now – calm and assured, but her expression silently asking Brooke not to let her down – she could see why her friend needed her to be on the ball, and why Felicity might fret that she wasn't.

'Don't worry,' she said quietly. 'You're right and I'm sorry. I promise it'll get done.'

'In time?'

Brooke nodded solemnly and crossed her heart with her fingers. 'Absolutely.'

Felicity relaxed into a smile. 'I know you'll pull it off. Don't mind if I get a bit jittery from time to time but—'

'God, don't even apologise! If I was dealing with me, I'd be getting jittery too!'

'But I needn't be, I know that. I know you wouldn't let me down.'

'Never,' Brooke said. 'I know how important this is to you.'

'And to you too, I hope.'

'Of course, but you've done most of the legwork to make it happen, and you're right – the least I can do is to make sure my stock is ready. It will be, I promise. I suppose you're on track?'

'I've got about three quarters of what I think I'm going to need. I've got to source some more plastic pellets and I'm waiting for some glass beads to arrive, but I'm fairly confident all my stock will be ready to go. I only hope the fashionable Parisian of today is willing to splash out on recycled and upcy-cled jewellery.'

'Oh my God, are you kidding? They're going to lap that stuff up. And you know your designs are amazing.'

Felicity grinned. 'OK, maybe I do a little. But selling that stuff on a street corner in Ely or Cambridge or St Ed's is different from selling it in Paris. I mean, *Paris*! The fashion capital of the world!'

'Don't let Milan hear you say that.'

'Milan Schmilan. They can fight me. I'm half French so I'm always going to side with my people.'

A grudging smile spread across Brooke's face. It was hard not to be cheered up in Felicity's company. 'I suppose there could be far worse places to be spending Christmas.'

'Way worse! And who knows? Maybe you'll find yourself a hot Frenchman to take your mind off Johnny-no-brains. I'll make sure it's all over social media too – let's see how he likes it when the shoe's on the other foot!'

Brooke let out a short laugh. 'While I appreciate the sentiment, I'm not planning on going near another man for... I don't know – about fifty years ought to do it. I don't care how hot or French he is.'

'Not even if he looks like that Lupin guy?'

'Not even if he *is* that Lupin guy! No, no, no... absolutely not! In all seriousness, you were right the first time – I need to concentrate on the business, especially now. It's make or break – at least, it feels that way, doesn't it?'

'Well, I don't know about make or break exactly, but we have invested a lot of time, money and energy. Nobody can say we haven't put our all into being there. So I suppose it is a big deal when you put it that way.'

'No pressure then.'

Felicity laughed. 'No pressure.'

'You know what, though,' Brooke continued, more pensive now. 'I don't feel as stressed as maybe I ought to. Part of me thinks all we can do is be as ready as possible, turn up, set up, get everything looking lovely and the rest... well, it's in the lap of the gods, isn't it? People will buy or they won't, and there's not a great deal we can do about it, so why stress?'

'So what you're saying is: let's enjoy Paris at Christmas, and then even if all else goes to the dogs, we'll still have that?'

'Well, not exactly. Obviously, I want our stall at the Christmas markets to be a roaring success and I want us to be able to do many more of them, but...'

'But still, we'll always have Paris, just this once even if never again?'

Brooke gave a slight smile. 'Yes. We'll always have Paris, even if it's only this once.'

Felicity lifted her glass. It was a lot emptier than it had been only a few minutes before. Brooke noted that her own wasn't faring much better and was about to order another, but she raised it to touch Felicity's anyway.

'To Paris!' Felicity grinned.

'To Paris!'

CHAPTER THREE

Brooke moved the oil-fired radiator that heated her workshop closer to her chair.

Despite the cold, she had no real complaints about her workshop. Her mum had inherited the bungalow Brooke currently lived in from a maiden great-aunt and had sold it to Brooke for a price that couldn't possibly have been anywhere near market value, though Brooke wasn't about to complain and had snapped her hand off. She recognised a leg-up when she saw one, though her mum denied any such thing, and she was grateful for it. The house itself, though a little dated, was plenty big enough for her and, as it had both driveway and garage, meant that Brooke's sage green Hillman Imp could be parked on the drive, leaving the garage as a working space.

It had changed quite a bit from the garage of her great-aunt's day, where the main features had been the breeze-block walls and a rusting door. Brooke had plastered the walls and painted them burnt orange, then installed a practical but lovely vinyl floor which not only looked good but would easily clean in the event of spilt paint and dye, and the rusting door had been replaced by paned bi-fold doors to let in as much natural light as possible. By the time she'd done all that she'd run out of money for heating and, as it had been summer at the time, had drastically underestimated how difficult it would be to manage in winter. The upside was, if it got too cold and she needed a break, there was an interconnecting door to the house, so Brooke could pop in from time to time to get warm.

As for the house's dated decor, she hadn't minded that much – retro was her vibe and so it had taken only minimal tweaking to turn it into a home that might have others running for the IKEA catalogue but made Brooke perfectly comfortable. There were other perks too: the low mortgage meant she could quit the PR job she'd hated, and the money she'd been saving as a deposit on a more expensive house could instead be used to start up her own business. It had still been a risk, but it felt like a less scary one than it might have done with a huge mortgage hanging over her. Most of her sales were online, much like Felicity, but sometimes they both went out to sell too. Felicity's jewellery business had been going for a couple of years longer than Brooke's textile one and she was well established by the time they'd started sharing a stand at craft fairs and markets. It meant another cushion for Brooke in a way, because Felicity could show her the ropes and save her making all the disastrous mistakes she was sure she would have done without her friend's guidance.

Brooke's home-crafted items for sale had started with knitted and crocheted goods like bags, toys, collectables and household textiles. Clothes, she'd decided, were too fiddly and she'd have to produce many versions of the same thing in different sizes when there was no guarantee there would even be a buyer for that size, rendering all that effort useless.

At first she made a modest profit, barely enough to stay afloat. Then she'd branched out into screen printing and invested in a second-hand sewing machine, allowing her to create unique designs and artwork. Overnight, her range had grown to three or four times the size it had been when she'd started out four years previously. She'd always been good at art at school and had loved fiddling and making, but it had never seemed like a viable way of making a living. It had been a dream for others to pursue while sensible people like Brooke took sensible jobs and got on with them. Sometimes she had to pinch herself, unable to believe that she was now one of those people living the dream and doing a creative job she loved.

She was currently working on a range of tote bags and tea towels with colourful scenes inspired by early twentieth-century travel posters. There were views of her home city, Ely, and of the Broads, and of nearby coastal towns such as Cromer and Yarmouth. She was planning to add more festive designs for the Christmas market. In many ways she'd amazed herself – an artist with no formal training, she was proud of what she'd managed to produce, and her confidence grew with every admiring comment and online review. She never imagined for a moment she was in the same league as Felicity, but perhaps with a lot of work she might get there one day.

Business was going well. If only the same could be said for her love life.

She tried not to dwell on all that as she added a bright blue dye to the reservoir of the printing frame and moved it slowly across the screen with the squeegee, watching the colour spread. They had a golden opportunity coming up at the Paris Christmas markets, the biggest and most exciting opportunity since Brooke had gone into business, one that she ought to be focusing on. Brooke had set up stalls at smaller markets before and had even done one or two in bigger cities, but she'd been dipping her toe in rather than going all out to make maximum profits and expand the business. Felicity wanted more stalls at more places and maybe even a shop on Ely's high street and employees, and the money they hoped to make from one of

Europe's biggest Christmas markets might just help them on their way to that goal.

Thankfully, Felicity was managing to be enthusiastic enough for both of them. She'd single-handedly taken care of all the legal stuff, securing the appropriate licences and visas, the deposit on their stall, arranging transport for them and their goods. She'd done all this without fuss, recognising that although Brooke wanted to be useful, she was still struggling to pull herself out of her post-Johnny funk. For the last month she'd been trying to get Brooke into the spirit by sending her photos of Paris and the markets, but as Brooke kept telling her, it wasn't like she'd asked to be a sad sack who couldn't see past a split that her ex had long forgotten – it was just the way things had to be right now.

Brooke was shaken from her musings by a knock at the glass doors, and looked up to see the postwoman holding a parcel and smiling at her. *Talk about good timing.* Distractions that stopped Brooke from falling into maudlin thoughts were always welcome.

Wiping the dye from her hands on a rag, she went to open up.

'More equipment?' the postwoman asked cheerfully as she handed the box over.

'Hi, Lois. A replacement bobbin casing, I hope. I've been after one for ages. That's the trouble with second-hand stuff – you can't just go into a shop and buy the parts, you have to find someone who sells them, and then you've got to wait.'

'Ah... sign here would you, love?' Lois held out her portable tracking device and stylus. 'How are you these days? I saw you on Saturday, you know. In town. I waved but you didn't see me. You were watching the wedding at the cathedral... at least I thought you were. You were looking that way at any rate. I'd have said hello, but I had my mum with me and she's got no patience for standing around while I chat these days. It's her legs...'

'Are you sure it was me?' Brooke asked cagily. 'I don't think it was. What time would it have been?'

She knew full well it had been her but embarrassment at being caught out wouldn't let her admit it. Weird, stalkerish, a bit desperate... describe it how you would, it wasn't normal behaviour and even Brooke herself, the perpetrator, could see that.

'Oooh, about two. I'm sure it was you, my love.'

'Maybe... Was I coming out of the bakery?'

'Well, you were outside it.'

'That'll be it then,' Brooke said. 'I wasn't watching the wedding. I'd nipped in to buy some cakes and got distracted by it. Pretty dress, you know... I'm a sucker for a nice dress.'

'I can imagine,' Lois said. 'Aren't we all? Not that I get much chance to dress up these days. The bride did look absolutely stunning. I don't mind telling you, that's one lucky husband right there.'

'Indeed,' Brooke said, fighting to keep the grimace from her face and thankful now that Lois had only been on this round for the past six months, which meant that she'd never seen Johnny there when she'd called with the post and couldn't join the dots right now.

'Better get on anyway,' Lois said cheerfully. 'Directives at work: got to get round quicker, no time for chit-chat. They'll be asking us to time travel soon if they want the post delivered any faster. It's wrong, you know – people like to stop and chat. Postman used to be part of the community, a friendly face for the old folk and such... not anymore. Now it's all about how much you can carry in your bag in one go and whizzing around as fast as possible. I asked the boss for roller skates the other day and he laughed, but I wasn't joking...'

Lois was still talking even as she was leaving.

'I'd better crack on too,' Brooke said, shutting the door. 'I mean, nice to talk to you, even if it is only a few minutes.'

'A few seconds is all you'll get soon...' Lois's voice drifted away. 'See you tomorrow, if they allow us to stop... be throwing the parcels at you soon from bikes like American paperboys...'

Brooke turned the key in the lock and let out a sigh. Lois was lovely and a great postwoman because she always looked out for the customers on her walk, but she couldn't half talk. It must have been torture having her bosses tell her to speed up when she loved to stop and chat so much.

Brooke took the parcel to a spare counter and opened it, pleased to find her replacement bobbin casing. There'd been a growing pile of unfinished bags waiting for her sewing machine to be operational again, so she'd be able to get on with all that in the afternoon. It was a small victory but she'd take them where she could these days.

As she was fixing the machine, her mind replayed the conversation with Lois. Going over old ground seemed to be a feature of the day and not a welcome one. Had Lois believed her excuse about the bakery? Possibly not. At least she didn't know Johnny and she didn't seem to know Erin either – which was no mean feat in Ely. But it meant she wouldn't have realised that they had any connection to Brooke, because if she had, that would have been utterly mortifying. The only person who knew was Felicity, and she'd been too kind to say it outright, but Brooke now realised that spying on her ex as he got married to someone else was a pretty pathetic thing to do. It was unfair to the bride and groom too; aside from the weirdness of it, how would it have made them feel if they'd known she was there? Or if they'd seen her? It would have put such a damper on things. How would Brooke herself have felt had the shoe been on the other foot?

She shook her head as she closed the drawer on the machine and checked to see if it worked. This had to stop, and it had to stop now. She wouldn't dream of bothering Johnny, not now that he was married, but she had to stop thinking about him because that was almost as bad. It wasn't good for her either, and it certainly wasn't a healthy state of mind. She had to put this thing to bed once and for all and move on.

In a snap decision, Brooke went to the locker where she kept her belongings safe while she worked, removed her phone and started tapping out a text:

Hey, it's Brooke. Not sure if you still have my number stored, so in case you don't... anyway, I just wanted to say congratulations on your wedding. I genuinely wish you all the happiness in the world. I'm sure you'll have a great life.

Did the last sentence sound ever so slightly sarcastic? A bit passive-aggressive? Deciding it didn't really matter, she pressed send anyway. What he'd make of her message she had no idea, but perhaps that didn't matter. What mattered, in the end, was that Brooke had sent it – more for herself than for him – and that she desperately wanted to mean the sentiments expressed within. What was the point, now, in wishing him and Erin ill? It wouldn't change anything for her. Why not let them be happy? It was pointless all three of them being miserable.

It should have been expected, really, the way she and Johnny had ended, considering the way they had begun. They'd met at a house party, exchanging numbers while they were blind drunk. Now that Brooke thought about it, a penchant for getting very drunk together might well have been one of the few things they had in common. It certainly featured strongly in their first year – all they seemed to do was drink and have sex. It had been fun, but perhaps Brooke should have realised that they were going to need more than that to sustain a future together. They never shared anything concrete about their hopes and dreams and ambitions, and by the time they'd got bored of the drinking and the sex had become a bit too routine, it began to feel as if they were already in too deep.

Brooke had always been fascinated by other cultures and desperate to travel; Johnny was content to sit on a beach in Spain with easy access to British-themed pubs that served a decent pint and a greasy fry-up. Brooke was creative and Johnny was analytical. She was industrious and he just wanted to chill. She longed to go on long walks in the countryside on a Sunday and he wanted to watch the sports channels. They'd settled into a routine that was some kind of compromise, but clearly it hadn't been enough to save their relationship.

The split had proved to be messy too. They'd kept out of each other's way, but while together they'd become integrated into each other's social circles and so there had been a lot to untangle after they'd broken up. In a bid to keep things simple, Brooke had simply stopped going out with those people and it had effectively put an end to her partying days.

Maybe that was the next thing she needed to rectify if she was going to move on. Maybe it was time to get her social life back on track.

Her next text was to Felicity:

Fancy a night out?

Felicity's reply was immediate:

Don't you have bags to sew?

Yes, but even I can't sew day and night.

Why not?

Slave driver!

You'll thank me when we've made our first million in Paris.

> *Ha ha, if only. A few bags won't make that much difference.*

Where do you want to go?

Brooke pondered the question for a moment. Definitely not anywhere local – the risk of running into Johnny and Erin or any mutual acquaintance from her own days with him was too high.

> *Cambridge.*

Why Cambridge?

> *Loads of students after a bit of fun. What more do you need?*

So nothing to do with the fact that Johnny might be out in Ely?

> *Maybe. I'm a wuss, right?*

Actually, I have a better idea.

> *What?*

How about Paris?

> *Lol, we're going to Paris next week, or have you forgotten?*

*How about we go early and wring every scrap of fun out
of it before we're forced to work on the stall twelve hours
a day?*

Brooke thought about it for a moment. It seemed crazy, spontaneous, completely impractical, and yet she was tempted. Glancing around her workshop, she asked herself what was stopping them. Certainly no family or social commitments... she still had stock to produce, but perhaps if she put extra hours in over the next couple of days she could manage that and they'd have a few days to spare before the market at the Jardin des Tuileries opened for business.

*I'm not sure if I'll be ready to go early but I'll do my best.
It would be good to have extra time to see some sights in
Paris.*

I'd love that, I'll come over to help.

I'd feel bad.

*But you'd be done a lot faster. I was thinking of offering
anyway. I'm pretty much done, and I felt bad about
nagging you to work faster. I should have realised you
were still hurting about Johnny and your mind might not
be on sewing.*

*No, you were totally right to shout at me and I'm glad
you did – it was the shake I needed. Feel free to come
over and sew if you have time and you're all done – it
will definitely speed things along here!*

*The sooner you're done, the sooner we can organise an
earlier ferry and go. I'll get Fabien to ask if we can have*

*the accommodation earlier too, save us swapping from a
hotel if we could move straight into the apartment.*

You think of everything.

Ha ha, I know, I'm good, aren't I?

The best! x

CHAPTER FOUR

There hadn't been many occasions for Brooke to use a cross-Channel ferry service, and as she settled on a seat in the lounge with Felicity – having left their van filled with the belongings and stock they'd need for the next month – her gaze went out to a choppy sea and she felt that maybe she'd missed out.

Someone had done their best to make the space Christmassy and cheery for the passengers, but the tinsel and garlands that hung around the seating area were faded and listless and had only succeeded in making it look a bit tragic. The windows were vast, and on a good day the view would have been glorious. Today it was foggy and everything was grey, the horizon barely distinct from the plateau of tick-tocking waves, but it still looked strangely spectacular. There was something about the sea, deep and vast and unknowable, that stirred a soul no matter how unimpressed they pretended to be.

It was early morning, and they both had surprisingly decent coffees in front of them, having driven through the early hours to get to the terminal in time to board and both deciding it was still too early to eat breakfast. The lounge was quiet – a few of the sofas were occupied, mostly the ones next to the windows, but conversations were subdued or non-existent. Everyone was probably as exhausted as they were, Brooke thought, especially if they'd had to drive for hours to get to the ferry in the first place. Some had hot drinks, some had breakfast sandwiches, and some sat with nothing, resting their eyes as they settled into their seats.

'I feel like a kid again,' Felicity said as she gazed out of the window too. 'I've used the Eurostar for the last few years, haven't crossed on the ferry since I was about twelve – Mum always said it was too slow and she couldn't stand it when the sea got rough. I hated the Eurostar back then – you couldn't run up to the rear deck and watch the wash behind the boat or go to the gift shop and buy a load of plastic crap or watch the film at the little onboard cinema. The train was so boring; you just had to sit there and not make a noise. Until I got older of course, and then I kind of got where Mum was coming from. But I'm glad we decided on the ferry today; it feels like a really chilled way to get our trip started.'

'I mean, we could totally go outside and stand at the back to watch the sea get churned up by the engines today if you like,' Brooke said. 'I'd be game. I can't even remember the last time I went on a passenger ferry... unless you count the little rowboat from Southwold to Walberswick that you pay a quid to go on.'

'God yes!' Felicity reached for her coffee and blew gently to cool it. 'I mean, when we've finished these we've probably got, like, two hours to kill so I'd be up for that.'

Brooke sipped her drink. 'I'm so glad we decided to come early; I can't wait to see a bit of Paris before the markets open. We definitely wouldn't have had time once the stall got going.'

'I'm glad too, but I think we could have made some time even if we hadn't extended the trip. It would have been miserable to be there and not be able to see any of it.'

Brooke shook her head slightly. 'Think about it – if we're going to make this trip worthwhile, we might have to keep our stall open into the evening, maybe even until the markets close for the night, which is going to be pretty late. I don't think we would have done. Us packing up at five and swanning off to the nearest bistro might not be on the agenda once the market is in full swing.'

'Not even once? Not even to make the most of Paris with your best friend?'

Brooke grinned. 'OK, maybe once or twice... I suppose even my willpower isn't that good.'

'Or three or four times...?'

'We'll see. I hate to be the party pooper, but you said yourself we have to remember why we're going. You said friendship was one thing and business another. This is business.'

'Did I?' Felicity asked vaguely. 'What an arse.'

'Well, maybe, but you said it.'

'I bet we can manage a couple of early closes. We can't spend all those weeks in Paris and not see any of it – that doesn't seem right at all.'

'We've got these extra days; we'll just have to cram everything in.'

'We'll never do it, especially as all the Christmas stuff will be starting. If there wasn't more than enough to do in Paris as it is, there'll be insane amounts going on that we won't want to miss.'

'You're telling me. I still can't believe this is happening. Your cousin Fabien is a legend, you know. We'll have to find a proper way to thank him for doing so much for us – permits and cheap accommodation and all the other little things he's helped to sort for us to get a spot on the market.'

'And not just any old market – the best one; the Tuileries Gardens.'

'I'll bet it is,' Brooke agreed. 'It certainly looks like one of the biggest; that's got to be a good thing, right?'

'I hope so. By all accounts it gets mental busy there.'

Brooke settled back in her seat. 'I still can't believe you've never been. I mean, you're half French – how have you never been to Paris at Christmas?'

'Well, I've only been to Paris a handful of times. As a kid, I always got carted off to the Atlantic coast where all the relatives live, and most of them hate Paris so nobody wanted to take me. They were all like, "We've got a lovely seaside here, why do you want to go to filthy Paris?" Lovely seaside, yes, but boring when you've been there every summer for your whole life. And once you realise you're gay, even more boring because there are zero other gays to flirt with – or if there were any other girls like me, they weren't showing themselves.'

'Must have been tough,' Brooke said with a sympathetic grimace. 'I forget sometimes how hard you've had it.'

'Oh, I didn't have it that bad,' Felicity said cheerfully. 'Mum and Dad were pretty cool about me coming out, so there's that.'

'Not your other relatives, though.'

'The old dinosaurs struggled, but most everyone else is fine. I know people who had it way worse. Anyway, I've had action since, so it's not all bad.'

'They weren't all good either,' Brooke reminded her, recalling now that as many times as she'd cried on Felicity's shoulder over Johnny, she'd lent her shoulder to Felicity over the years for some girl or another who'd broken her heart.

'Yeah, but it doesn't do to dwell on that, does it? It only reminds me what terrible taste I have. How's your French coming along?'

Brooke put her coffee down. 'Hmm. So well that I have to keep going back to the first episode of the podcast to learn how to say "Hello, where's the train station?" because by the time I get to "Is it going to rain today?" I've forgotten what I learnt at the start.'

'Ah, going great then?' Felicity peered over the top of her cup at Brooke with a mischievous look.

'Oh yes.' Brooke smirked. 'Swimmingly. Languages just aren't my thing. I'm hoping there are going to be a lot of English speakers around. I'm wondering if we ought to have gone to Norwich Christmas market like we did last year. I mean, we were there separately and we could have gone together this time of course – I don't wish for a minute to be there without you.'

'Seriously? After all the trouble we went to in order to land this gig, you wish we'd stayed in England!'

'Oh, I didn't mean that!' Brooke said. 'God, no, I only meant I'm going to be absolutely useless and you'll end up having to translate for me all the time.'

'You worry way too much.' Felicity tucked her legs up onto the long seat. There was no one else on it and so no harm in taking advantage of the space. Brooke felt stiff as a board this morning after sitting in their van with its dodgy heating for hours on end. 'It'll be fine. In all honesty we were never going to look a gift horse in the mouth, were we? It's not often my cousin does me favours – swinging a stall on Jardin des Tuileries for us? Hell yes! No chance I'm passing that one up!'

'I know it's cool and I should be grateful, but I don't feel ready. I mean, I don't even speak decent French and I don't know the first thing about Paris – not really.'

'Neither does half of Paris at Christmas. How many French people are you expecting? I bet most of our customers will be from elsewhere.' Felicity took a gulp of her drink. 'And there's no need to feel like we're not ready. You got your stock done in the end, all the permits are sorted and the accommodation is booked... everything is in place. And if there is something we haven't thought of, we'll cross that bridge when we come to it. There's usually a fix if you look hard enough. And anyway, if language is your number one worry, then I wouldn't bother. There's really only one phrase you need to know. Well, maybe two...'

Brooke gave a slow smile. 'I think I might know what one of

these essential phrases is going to be, and it's definitely not covered on my podcast lessons.'

'The first one is: I don't understand, which is *je ne comprends pas*, and the second, far more important, is the old *voulez-vous coucher avec moi, ce soir?*'

'Hmm, I thought so.' Brooke raised her eyebrows. 'Even I know what that one means. Honestly, after the year I've had, the last thing I want to do is hop into bed with some random French bloke.'

'After the year you've had, it's the very least you deserve. You've paid your dues, Boo – time to have some fun again. Forget that knob Johnny. Let him have his boring wife. You're made of far more entertaining stuff. You know what I think?'

'What do you think?'

'I never wanted to say so before, but I think even if he hadn't met this woman, you'd have got bored eventually.'

'He got bored, that's *why* he went off with someone else.'

'No, I mean *you*. He was never smart or funny or nice enough for you, but for some reason that I just can't fathom, you can't see that you deserve better. I hope one day you will, but for the record, I think you actually had a lucky escape.'

'It doesn't feel lucky.'

'Not now, granted, but one day you'll see I'm right.'

Brooke reached for her coffee. It had cooled now and she took a gulp. She was enjoying the coffee and the view and the quiet time with Felicity – or she had been until Johnny had popped into her head again. He was like a case of shingles that she couldn't shake, and even when she thought she was over him, the memories and regrets were all lying dormant, ready to flare up again.

'Maybe, but right now I don't want to think about him,' she said. 'In fact, you'd be proud of me. I messaged him to say congrats on his wedding. That makes me the bigger person, right?'

'Did you also say good riddance?'

Brooke laughed. 'No. But maybe if I'd had *her* number I'd have texted her to tell her she was welcome to him and to wish her luck because she was going to need it.'

'Yes!' Felicity grinned. 'You want some lotion for that burn?'

Brooke took a little bow. 'Why, thank you. Maybe not my most eloquent comeback but it might be my finest.'

Felicity finished her drink and put the cup down, leaning back on the seat again and closing her eyes. 'I feel like I'm finally getting my old Boo back,' she said approvingly.

Brooke finished her coffee too and placed her empty cup next to Felicity's. 'So how about that blow-dry up on deck?'

Felicity opened her eyes and grinned. 'See – the old Boo! That's more like it! I'll race you there!'

Brooke pushed open an external door and almost immediately it pushed back to close again. She gave it another shove and was greeted by a fierce, biting wind. She turned to Felicity, who was behind her.

'I changed my mind! I think I want to be boring again – it's too cold to be fun!'

'No chance!' Felicity shoved her out onto the deck and tumbled out after, the door slamming shut as soon as they'd gone through it.

Brooke's hair was scraped into a ponytail, but the wind tugged clumps free and sent it whipping around her face so she could barely see where she was going as they made their way along the deck. Dawn hadn't long broken, and the light was grey and strange, made heavy by low clouds and fog. They were the only souls on a dangerously slippery deck, and this made the situation oddly spooky but all the more exciting for it.

'Do you feel like a kid yet?' she yelled at Felicity.

'I feel like someone who's about to get blown clean off the ferry!'

'Want to go back inside?'

'Hell no!'

Brooke laughed as they pushed on, folding her arms tight across her chest to try – vainly – to keep some body heat in. She was wearing a huge padded coat, scarf, big knitted gloves and a hat, and yet she was still absolutely freezing. But then, a stiff wind on a boat in the middle of the sea at dawn and in the depths of winter would probably do that to you.

'Fancy recreating the scene from *Titanic*?' Felicity shouted.

'No, but I bet the sea's about the right temperature if you fall in!'

They couldn't get right to the bow, but they went as far along the deck as they could and peered out towards the horizon, clinging to the rails as they did so.

'That way lies France' – Felicity pointed – 'and our new adventure. What do you reckon? It's going to be a Christmas to remember, right?'

Brooke grinned. 'One way or another, I have a feeling it will be. If you have anything to do with it, that is.'

'Oh, I'm going to make sure this is the most amazing month ever. Boo, Paris is going to change our lives!'

CHAPTER FIVE

'Watch out!'

'I am watching out!' Felicity yelled. 'It's that dick who's not watching out!'

Brooke gripped the door handle as the van left the round-about, narrowly missing a weaving Audi with a seemingly blind-folded driver – at least he was driving like someone who couldn't see where he was going. The fact that it had started to snow wasn't helping. On another day, Brooke might have marvelled at how pretty it was and how it just took the magic of being in Paris at Christmas to a whole new level, but today she was far too stressed. Maybe in fear of her life was a more accurate description of her current state. Either way, the snow could go to hell as far as she was concerned.

'Traffic in Paris is mental!' she gasped. 'Don't the French have to pass a driving test?'

'It's a big-city thing,' Felicity said sagely.

'Is it? Then remind me never to live in a big city.'

'You'd last five minutes anyway.' Felicity glanced across at her.

'I'm not that bad.'

'Yes you are – you hate London.'

'I don't.'

'Last time you were there you wanted to find a way to sabotage the Thames Barrier so it would be lost under the sea like Atlantis.'

'Oh, yeah... well it was *really* expensive coffee that made me say that. I don't like being ripped off.'

'It's what you expect in London. Like you expect bad driving.'

'Even there the driving didn't seem this scary. I suppose being on the other side of the road isn't helping.'

'It's definitely more confusing,' Felicity agreed.

The electronic voice of the satnav interrupted them.

In three hundred yards, turn right.

'What's that?' Felicity asked. 'Totally missed it talking to you.'

'She says next right.'

Turn right.

Felicity yanked the steering wheel at breakneck speed, sending the boxes stacked in the back of their van sliding across the floor. If all their stock arrived in one piece it would be a Christmas miracle, but Brooke knew better than to say so. Felicity was far more confident behind the wheel than her and was used to driving on the continent, and so Brooke was happy to let her friend do the driving – however badly – at least for the first few days until she got used to Paris and felt brave enough to give it a go. If she thought Felicity was being slightly erratic (and erratic was pretty much her default setting anyway) then she'd have to grin and bear it or she might find Felicity's chauffeuring services withdrawn.

'What the hell is going on with this road now?'

Felicity frowned and Brooke's grip tightened on the door handle. There was traffic coming towards them seemingly from all directions, like they were fugitives in a movie car chase and had finally been cornered.

'I think... I think we're on the wrong side of the road,' Brooke whimpered.

'Well what was Google Map lady doing sending us this way then?'

'Maybe we didn't take the right street after all.'

'Maybe Google Map lady is just a little bit thick. Hang on.'

Felicity swung the van around to do a full 180 and Brooke wondered whether this was the appropriate time to get religious. It seemed rude to meet her maker otherwise, and she was in serious fear that she might be about to.

'Ah, see...' Felicity said, glancing at the phone on her lap. 'She's rerouting us. Stupid cow.'

'Don't say that – she might hear you,' Brooke said. 'She won't direct us if she's pissed off.'

Turn right.

Felicity turned into another side street, almost taking three cars with her and causing a cacophony of furious car horns.

'Alright, alright...' Felicity grimaced. 'God, someone needs their coffee.'

Brooke wanted to shout that maybe Felicity had drunk too much coffee, because she seemed wired, but she held on to it.

'I bet you wish you'd driven,' Felicity said to her.

'No, but I am wondering if we should have just swallowed the cost and hired someone else to bring our stock over. A lovely sedate Eurostar journey seems very appealing right now.'

'You'd still have to get from the station to our flat somehow, and it probably would have involved a car journey, so you wouldn't have been any better off.'

I might have been with a less terrifying driver, Brooke thought, impressed with her self-restraint for not saying it out loud.

She paused, formulating a more positive reply, while her gaze went to the window. 'Is that...'

Brooke shuffled closer to the glass and peered up at a strangely familiar landmark. They hadn't seen it on the way here, had they? No, she didn't think they had, so why did she know it.

'Oh!' She turned to Felicity. 'I've just seen the Arc de Triomphe!'

'Cool!' Felicity said cheerfully.

'No, not cool! It means we're in central Paris! We're not supposed to be in central Paris – our accommodation is nowhere near here!'

Felicity frowned. 'But Google Map lady...'

She grabbed her phone to look, and Brooke snatched it from her. Seriously?

'I'll check,' she said. 'You drive.'

'I don't know where I'm supposed to be driving to now though, do I?'

Brooke ignored the jibe and stared at the phone. Then she unlocked her own and checked her emails before looking up with a groan.

'It's the wrong address!'

'What is? You mean they sent the wrong address?'

'No we put the wrong code in...'

By which, Brooke meant Felicity had put the wrong code in, though she knew better than to pin it on her friend. At best it would cause an argument, and at worst Felicity would slam the brakes on and storm off, no matter what road they were on and how illegal it might be to stop there.

'Oh, lol. I had thought these roads were rather busy,' Felicity said.

God help us.

Brooke programmed the map with the correct postal code and put Felicity's phone in her own lap. She shook her head as Felicity followed the new instructions of the Google Map lady and headed towards the nearest place where they could turn around.

We definitely should have stuck to Norwich this Christmas.

An hour later they'd arrived at a damp underground garage-cum-warehouse, close to the apartment block they'd booked for their stay, where they planned to keep their stock. Although it was expensive to do things this way, a fact that vaguely alarmed Brooke, it was still the cheapest and most practical way they'd been able to think of. Because of the budget (and despite being more than they'd wanted to pay), the neighbourhood they found themselves in was less than glamorous. They'd wound down grotty roads flanked by wire fencing and piles of rubbish, seen graffiti-covered walls where gangs of sullen youths glowered at them as they passed, and Brooke prayed that each miserable-looking building wasn't going to be their destination. It was a world away from the affluent grace and romance of the city's most famous boulevards.

Eventually they'd found their building, which had been surprisingly well kept, and then they'd gone to locate the nearby lock-up on foot – which Felicity had insisted would be easier. Brooke hadn't liked the idea but she couldn't argue with the logic, considering the drive they'd had to get here. They'd found it a few minutes later, and as Brooke clapped eyes on the rusting doors, she just knew they'd find a freezer inside containing the body of some disposed-of gangster.

The fact that it looked as if it might double up as a crack den didn't seem to bother Felicity.

'I can't believe we're actually here!' she cooed as they unlocked the doors with the keys they'd picked up from their landlord. 'And look at us – like natives, doing our thing as if we lived here!'

'I wouldn't go that far,' Brooke said cagily. She desperately wanted to catch some of Felicity's enthusiasm, but her nerves wouldn't let her.

'Oh, you'll have the hang of all this in no time.' Felicity threw up the rolling doors to reveal a dark space beyond. She began to feel along the wall. 'The light switch is somewhere here apparently...'

A second later the switch was located and clicked on to reveal concrete walls and floor and a collection of sickly strip lights on a flaking ceiling.

'OK!' Felicity clapped her hands once and turned to Brooke. 'Want to wait here while I bring the van round?'

'You're sure you can find your way back and then get here again?'

'Of course! It wasn't that complicated. I'll only be a couple of minutes... unless you want us to lock up again and you walk back with me?'

'I think that might be best,' Brooke said, eyeing the space warily. She didn't fancy Felicity walking back alone, and she didn't fancy waiting here by herself either.

'No worries...'

Felicity turned off the light and reached for the doors, yanking them down again.

'*Quoi de neuf?*'

Brooke and Felicity turned as one to see a woman speaking to them. She was maybe late twenties, early thirties. She was about the coolest-looking woman Brooke had ever seen – cobalt hair, piercings all over the place, paint-splattered jeans and army boots, the kind of precision eyeliner that Brooke could only dream of achieving.

'*Bonjour!*' Felicity said.

'You're English,' the woman responded. But when she said it, she wasn't looking at Felicity but Brooke. As Felicity was half French and her grasp of the language (and therefore accent) was pretty decent, Brooke had to assume that the reason the woman had guessed their nationality so easily was that everything about her right now screamed *totally out of her depth Englishwoman.*

'This is my brother's garage,' the woman said.

'Oh, right...' Brooke smiled in what she hoped was an encouraging way. 'Yes... we're renting it.'

'I'm Felicity.' Felicity stepped forward. 'This is my friend, Brooke. We're here for the Christmas markets.'

'You are hoping to buy a lot?' the woman said, eyeing the garage meaningfully.

'Oh, no!' Felicity laughed. 'We're hoping to sell a lot! At least we've brought a lot with us to sell – we've got a stall at the Jardin des Tuileries.'

'Ah...' The woman looked at Felicity with new interest. 'So you will be here for a long time?'

'Well, until the New Year when the market closes down...'

'You are staying nearby?'

'Yes, we have an apartment on Rue Serge. You know it?'

'I live there. We have only one apartment block on Rue Serge, so you must be staying there?'

'I expect we are then!' Felicity said. 'Sorry, I didn't catch your name.'

'I didn't offer it,' the woman said.

'Any chance you might feel like sharing it?' Felicity asked. 'I mean, as we're probably going to bump into each other quite a bit over the next few weeks, it would be nice to have a name for you.'

The woman grinned, and then Felicity grinned, and Brooke sighed. She'd seen that look on her friend's face before.

'I am Manon,' the woman said.

'It's very nice to meet you, Manon,' Felicity said.

'Yes,' Brooke agreed. 'Pleased to meet you. Sorry we had you worried about your brother's garage.'

Manon gave a short nod, and then glanced between the two of them as if trying to work something out.

'You are good friends?' she asked after a moment.

'And business partners,' Felicity said.

'I see...' Manon seemed satisfied with this information and gave them another brief nod.

'We're about to walk back to our apartment to fetch our van. If you're going that way, perhaps we could walk with you?' Felicity asked.

'I'm not,' Manon said. 'I have someone to see right now.'

'Oh, right. But perhaps we'll see you around...'

'Perhaps,' Manon said carelessly.

With the most ridiculous confidence, Manon gave them the vaguest wave and then turned to go on her way.

'Go on,' Brooke said to Felicity in a low voice as they watched her go. 'Say it.'

'Oh, I definitely would,' Felicity whispered back. 'And I think she would too.'

'How can you tell?'

'I just can. And I hope I'm not wrong.'

'Do you want to find out if you're right?' Brooke asked. 'Considering everything else we have going on right now? We're going to be pretty busy over the next few weeks...'

Felicity turned to her. 'Did you *see* her? Who wouldn't?'

Brooke recalled now the instant impact Manon had made on her. She was stunning, stylish in an edgy and very cool kind of way that Brooke herself had never been – in a way that most people could never achieve no matter how they tried. The style seemed effortless, as though she simply oozed cool, as though she'd emerged from the womb smoking a cigarette and listening to a punk band. Brooke thought about her own rumpled track-suit bottoms and baggy sweater – she'd dressed for comfort, not style, and largely in the dark of the early hours, and then sat in a van for hours, followed by a chilly ferry – and felt suddenly very inadequate. Felicity looked better than she did, but even Felicity's outfit was suffering some travel fatigue right now.

'Well,' she said with a brisk nod, 'I'm forced to agree on that point. I'm not into women and even I could see the attraction.'

Felicity laughed. 'Exactly! And I'm only human after all.'

Brooke shot her a sideways glance. 'Hadn't we better go and get that stock?'

'You know what? I'm gasping for a drink. Could we go and get one first?'

'I'm not sure how long we can leave the van where it's parked without getting a fine or something. I think we ought to do that first.'

'I didn't see any parking notices.'

Brooke shook her head. 'Once we stop I won't want to start again. Besides, if we're going to do any exploring today we need to get a wriggle on or we'll run out of time. It's getting dark already. Get this done, then we know it's sorted and we can relax. There's plenty of time to go and get drinks.'

'I just hope we sell it all,' Felicity said as they started to walk back. 'There's loads, and I don't fancy putting it all back on the van and taking it home again in a few weeks.'

'Amen to that!' Brooke agreed. 'Me neither!'

'Right...' Felicity pulled the garage doors shut and then looked up at the street sign. 'Let's get cracking before it gets dark.'

'Hmm, because that doesn't sound ominous at all.'

'For someone who has always wanted to experience new

ways of life and culture, you don't seem to be enjoying this much.'

'Well this wasn't exactly the new ways of life and culture I had in mind. I like my culture less scary.'

'It's not that bad. Honestly, you should see the neighbourhoods some of my family live in.'

'Remind me never to visit them then.'

As she started walking, Brooke falling into step alongside her, Felicity laughed. 'You'll be alright once we're sorted and you've had a good night's sleep.'

A few minutes later they were outside the building they would be staying in for the next few weeks. There were period features such as brickwork and windows that suggested the building had been built in the early twentieth century, but it was far from grand. Nobody loved a period building more than Brooke, and as she gazed up while Felicity checked her emails for the exact number of their rental, she tried to love it, but the state of disrepair made it very hard. Still, it was cheap – even cheaper once Felicity's cousin Fabien had knocked the owner down on the price – and it wasn't going to be their forever home, so she supposed she could stick it for as long as they were there.

Felicity looked up from her phone and was about to speak when a sleek black car with tinted windows pulled up alongside them. One of the back windows was lowered to reveal a man looking out at them and showing a mouthful of very white teeth in what was probably meant to be a smile, though David Attenborough would have had a lot to say in one of his nature documentaries about it. Brooke waited for some sort of announcement from him to at least explain why he'd pulled up, but he got out of the car and held out his arms for Felicity. She let out a squeal and launched herself at him.

'Fab! Why didn't you tell me you were coming over? It's about bloody time!'

'*Salut, ma crotte.*'

Felicity laughed. 'You know that means something very different in England, right? And yet you've been calling me a poo for thirty years.'

'I will always call you *ma crotte*,' he said with that toothy smile. 'You are not in England now.'

'Honestly...' She gave him a fond look. 'Oh, this is my bestie, Boo... I mean Brooke. Her name is Brooke. And, Boo, this is my cousin Fabien.'

'Boo?' He smiled, turning to Brooke. 'I like Boo – it is *très charmante.*'

'Oh, only Felicity calls me that,' Brooke replied, flushing. 'It's lovely to meet you.'

'The feeling is mutual.'

Was Brooke supposed to do the kiss thing? They were sort of connected through Felicity, but this was the first time they'd ever met. What was the etiquette? Brooke could never remember this stuff, and usually she didn't have to because Felicity would be there to help her out. But as she wondered, she noted that he made no attempt to do it either and so she simply stood smiling at him, feeling slightly awkward and hoping she wasn't offending him by not initiating anything.

'I ought to say thank you,' she said. 'For all your help in getting us the pitch at Jardin des Tuileries.'

He waved away the thanks. 'It was nothing.'

'Not to us. It's a fantastic opportunity!'

Fabien wasn't at all what Brooke had expected. He was far better dressed and looked respectable in a tweed coat and shiny shoes, a shirt and tie peeking out from beneath his scarf. A bit on the short side, she supposed, but somehow he still cut an imposing figure.

Felicity had said on many occasions that even she didn't

know what Fabien did for a living, but he was constantly calling in favours from all sorts of people from city councillors to butchers and bakers, both in Paris and beyond. She said he had photos of himself with at least three previous presidents on the walls of his flat, which she thought was suspect, even if nobody else in the family did.

He was clean-shaven and his skin strangely flawless, as if he had regular facials, his hair was neatly parted and there was a keen look in his eyes. She could see how some might find him attractive, though he wasn't her type, and she knew that he was recently divorced because Felicity had told her all the gory details. As far as she recalled, he was ten years older than his English cousin, which would make him forty. He carried forty very well, Brooke decided. She also decided to keep very firmly in mind Felicity's warning that he might be a bit less than law-abiding and that he had a real eye for the ladies.

'Have you come to see us for any particular reason or just to say welcome to the neighbourhood?' Felicity asked him. 'Not that I mind either way.'

'I came to ensure all is in order.'

'Well, we picked up the keys OK, but we haven't been in to look around yet. I'm sure it's fine though.'

'I trust that it will be,' Fabien said. 'Now I must go. I have a meeting shortly. But I would be honoured to have your company tonight. I have tickets for *Carmen*.'

'Opera?' Felicity groaned. 'Fab, we would, but I think we're both going to be knackered later.'

'But I have the tickets,' he said, clearly offended.

'I know, but—'

'But *Carmen*!' he insisted. 'At the Palais Garnier! Do you know how difficult it is to obtain those tickets? It is so rare to see an opera there these days!'

'I'd love to go,' Brooke said, throwing Felicity a subtle

warning glance – at least she hoped it would be subtle. 'I've
never been to an opera – it'll be exciting.'

'It won't, trust me,' Felicity grumbled. She turned to her
cousin. 'I wish you'd checked with me first.'

'Why would I do that?' he asked, looking genuinely mysti-
fied. 'So that is settled. Shall I send my driver?'

Felicity scowled. 'No,' she said, 'we might go out and about
first, so we'll meet you there. Which theatre is it again?'

'Palais Garnier,' Fabien said with slight impatience. 'I will
wait inside for you – do not be late please.'

'We won't,' Felicity said.

'*Bon.*' He nodded and started to walk back to his car. 'Seven
thirty p.m., if you please. Dress appropriately. Goodbye,
Brooke. I look forward to seeing you later.'

'Got it,' Felicity called.

Brooke paled at the mention of a dress code.

'I don't have anything to wear!' she said in a low voice as
Felicity waved him off.

'Serves you right for agreeing to go,' Felicity replied.

'I had to! I didn't want to offend him!'

'Well then, now you've got us into it we'll just have to deal
with it.'

'What sort of thing do you wear to the opera?' Brooke asked
as the car disappeared around a corner, snow in her hair as it
started to fall again.

Felicity shrugged. 'I don't know, never been either. Let's go
as we are – with a bit of luck they'll kick us out for not meeting
the dress standards and we won't have to sit through the damn
thing.'

Brooke flopped onto the sofa of their apartment, a cloud of dust
erupting from it as she landed, and grimaced. The room itself
wasn't too bad... if you squinted hard you could imagine that the

faded elegance was deliberate shabby chic, but she did think someone could have cleaned a little before their arrival. It was one more job she would have to fit in at some point, and they'd already have enough to do once the markets opened.

It was a shame that the apartment had been allowed to get so run-down. There were some beautiful period features, including high ceilings and long windows with intricate iron-work balconies. But the cornicing was chipped and crumbling, the chandelier caked in so much grime that it almost looked like a rock formation in a cave, the parquet flooring needed a good re-sand and varnish, and the furniture was so threadbare that some chairs were practically just frames. Still, the heating worked, along with the fridge and the shower, so at least they had all the basics. And it was only for a month, Felicity reminded her, and there was something a little romantic about slumming it in Paris, like they were a pair of literary heroines. Brooke couldn't deny she rather liked that idea, and perhaps she'd look back on this period of time with fondness, once she was back in her comfortable house in Ely and didn't have to look at the huge cracks in the plaster and listen to the way the glass rattled in the frames of the windows with the slightest gust of wind.

They hadn't ended up going to explore any of the tourist sites. By the time they'd unloaded the van and familiarised themselves with the amenities in the immediate vicinity of their apartment, an early dusk had claimed the city. And while they had a date at the opera with Fabien – which Brooke was sort of looking forward to even if Felicity wasn't – she was so tired now she was tempted to stay home, cook a modest dinner and fall into bed. They'd been up since the very early hours in order to make the Channel crossing, drive to Paris and then get their stock sorted, and Brooke wasn't sure how much longer she could stay awake, even if she wanted to.

Not only that, she didn't have a clue what she was going to

wear. She hadn't packed expecting a night out like this. Though she'd banked on the odd hour in a bar or restaurant, a visit to an ice rink or maybe even a trip up the Eiffel Tower or a stroll around the Louvre, she'd assumed those activities would require only the barest nod to formality, and the items she'd packed were meant to keep her warm. The style was smart casual at best, not full-on opera house formality. And not just any old opera house, as Felicity informed her once Fabien had left them, but the most famous opera house in Paris, the opera house that had been the inspiration for the actual *Phantom of the Opera*.

Brooke closed her eyes, head resting against the upholstery, the notion that it might be full of dust or fleas or something even worse not enough to stop her from wanting to snooze right there.

'Don't you dare nod off,' Felicity said, coming in from the kitchen with a coffee. They'd stopped off at the nearest store to buy it. The store hadn't had a huge selection of goods and it was overpriced (according to Felicity), but it had the basics they needed to keep them going until they had the energy to shop properly. 'We've got an evening at the opera to get ready for.'

'Don't I know it,' Brooke said wearily.

'Well, you told him we'd go.'

Brooke opened her eyes. 'I know, but only to be polite!'

'Nobody's polite to Fabien – gets you into trouble.'

'He's your cousin; I was doing it for you. And because he's done so much for us – you have to admit he's gone above and beyond. The least we owe him is a night out, even if he has bought the tickets.'

Felicity sat on the opposite seat with her coffee. 'You do realise he's only asking us because he fancies you?'

'Don't be daft.'

'He never asks me to go anywhere swanky.'

'Maybe because he knows you'll say no.'

'Exactly, so what's the difference this time? You, that's

what.'

'He's never met me before today – how could he fancy me?'

'Social media – duh! Your photos are all over my feed.'

'That means nothing – he still hadn't met me before today. For all he knew, I could have been the world's most irritating woman.'

'You are,' Felicity said with a grin. 'Not that it would stop Fabien. You're female and you've got a pulse – as far as he's concerned, you'll do.'

Brooke stretched and yawned widely. 'Well, I'm sure when I fall asleep in my seat tonight and start drooling, he'll change his mind.'

'I doubt it; he's not easily put off. If he asks us to go for drinks after the opera, for the love of God let me answer.'

'Again, I feel I ought to point out how much he's done to help us get this spot at the market. It's going to be hard to say no because I feel as if we owe him.'

'That's why I'm going to say no for us.'

'But—'

'He'll get over it. I'll tell him we've been on the road since stupid o'clock this morning – which is true – and that we're knackered – also true. He can hardly argue with that without sounding like a total arse. Fabien might have an inflated ego but he's not totally unreasonable. We'll do this yawnfest and head back to the flat to get some sleep, and we'll see him another day to make it up to him.' She put down her coffee. 'We probably ought to think about getting ready to go.'

'God, yes...' Brooke held out a hand. 'Help me up – I don't think I have the energy to stand up alone.'

Felicity stood and yanked Brooke to her feet.

'God knows what I'm going to wear,' Brooke continued. 'Probably should have made the effort to go shopping after all.'

'I told you to borrow my black dress.'

'I know but... well, it's not really me, is it? And I'm not sure it's appropriate for the opera; it's a bit... short.'

'Beggars can't be choosers, right? Anyway, you'll look amazing.'

'And what are you going to wear if I borrow that?' Brooke added, not at all convinced by Felicity's reassurance.

'I expect I'll be able to find something.'

'I suppose I should have realised we might do something posh,' Brooke said ruefully. 'We are in Paris after all.'

'I wouldn't worry – this is probably the first and last time. Just wear my dress.'

'What if the venue doesn't think it's suitable and they don't let me in?'

'Are you saying my dresses are tasteless?'

'I'm saying they're very sexy – and that's the problem. Aren't we supposed to wear a ballgown or something?'

Felicity laughed loudly. 'I think we'll be OK. Fabien will come to the rescue if there's any danger of us not being let in.'

Palais Garnier was about the grandest, most ornate building Brooke had ever seen. It was so beautiful, so majestic she could scarcely believe it was real. They'd got off the metro a stop earlier and had walked the rest of the way, just to soak up the atmosphere of Paris at night and to calm Brooke, who was strangely jittery about the upcoming evening with Fabien. The nearest thing to a cultured musical experience she'd had so far was a Take That comeback concert, so a night at the grandest opera house in Paris – possibly the world – was a whole world away from anything she'd done before. What was the right way to look, the right way to behave? Did it matter that she wasn't going to understand a word they were singing? Would everyone be staring because of how painfully obvious it was going to be that Brooke was totally clueless?

As they approached, Felicity took a few photos. She was

clearly more at ease with the situation, chatting and snapping and pointing out each new detail she spotted with a squeak of excitement.

The building was exactly like a palace, but then that was sort of implied in the name – even Brooke's limited French told her that. The facade stretched for what seemed like miles in either direction, a mass of golden stone, pillars and columns, and vast windows adorned with intricate stonework and uplit all along its length to turn it into a beacon of grandeur that could be seen from all around. But Paris was the city of light, and like every other grand building, Palais Garnier had to fight to get noticed – and boy, was it putting up a fight, because there was no way anyone could fail to notice it.

As Felicity led them to the doors, Brooke took in the very well-dressed crowds and felt like turning around and running for home. There was no way they would be admitted – the guardians of this particular treasure would take one look at Brooke and know for sure she was not the sort of person who belonged inside.

At the entrance, Felicity spoke to a member of the door staff to explain they were meeting someone who had their tickets and that he was waiting inside. But the man on the doors seemed reluctant to allow them in.

Felicity huffed and pulled out her phone. 'We have to show our tickets before we can go in,' she said, taking Brooke to one side to allow others access to the doors.

'But Fabien has them.'

'Duh, I know that; I never thought about it though. Fabien's such an idiot at times.'

'I don't suppose he thought of it either.'

'More like he didn't want to stand outside getting cold. I'll phone – he'll come and get us.'

As Felicity dialled and held the phone to her ear, the doorman who had previously denied them entrance looked across and beckoned them to come back. Felicity ended the call with a vague frown and they went over. He spoke to Felicity for a moment, and then waved them both in.

Just inside the doorway, Fabien stood waiting. He was wearing full evening dress, including white bow tie and shirt, a tailed jacket, and the shiniest shoes Brooke had ever seen. If she was being perfectly honest, he looked faintly ridiculous because, while other men were wearing formal dress, they didn't look like side characters out of a Jeeves and Wooster novel. He looked like Brooke felt – out of place, like someone who didn't know the rules either, and something about that instantly relaxed her. She might have been wearing the wrong clothes, but from what she could tell, so was Fabien.

'It is good to see you,' he said, kissing Felicity and Brooke in greeting. 'I am glad you could come.'

'Us too,' Brooke said, though her gaze had drifted from him to her surroundings, mesmerised by the cavernous space she now found herself in. Everything was gleaming marble and more golden stone, floors inlaid with intricate designs and vast sweeping staircases leading up to other levels, while dazzling chandeliers hung from impossibly high vaulted frescoed ceilings. Women in sumptuous gowns and men in classic suits paraded up and down, almost as if they were a part of the decor themselves. It was as if Brooke had suddenly stepped into a movie.

'It is beautiful,' Fabien said with a knowing smile as her gaze returned to him.

'I've never seen anything like it!' Brooke replied warmly. 'It's... I don't even have any words!'

'Come, follow,' Fabien said. 'I have champagne waiting for us.'

'Oooh, champers!' Felicity said. 'I don't need telling twice to follow anyone who's leading me to champagne!'

They walked along a corridor with more high ceilings, more

marble and more chandeliers and into an oak-panelled bar area where the walls were painted with more classical scenes and an even bigger chandelier than the ones they'd previously seen lit the space. Brooke stared up at it and wondered how the hell it stayed in the ceiling; it must have weighed a ton. In the bar was the only nod to the impending festive season that Brooke had spotted so far – a gigantic real spruce tree, ceiling high and decorated with parchment-coloured candles, that filled the space with the most incredible scent. There would be no inflatable reindeer or sprigs of mistletoe hanging around in this place; everything was tasteful to the point that, if not for the tree, a casual visitor would be forgiven for missing the fact that Christmas was just around the corner.

Fabien handed a bartender some cash and then an ice bucket was produced that had clearly been waiting, along with three glasses. The bartender popped the cork on the bottle with the ease of someone who popped champagne corks day and night, and then poured for them, leaving the bottle in the bucket and going to serve someone else.

'Cheers, as you English say.' Fabien handed them both a glass and then picked up his own.

'Thank you,' Brooke said, 'and cheers.' She took a sip. 'God, this is incredible! I've had champagne before but never like this!'

Fabien looked visibly pleased at her praise and tapped the side of his nose. 'You must know about these things if you are going to buy the best.'

At this, Felicity snorted, but when Fabien turned to her, the pride quickly wiped off his face, she straightened her own into an expression of innocence.

'Sorry... bubbles went up my nose,' she excused. 'It's very nice, Fab – well done you for picking such a good one. So what's this opera about?' Felicity continued. 'Is everyone going to die at the end?'

'I am not going to tell you because I do not want to spoil it for Brooke,' he said. 'I thought you would already know.'

'Me?' Felicity drank some more of her champagne. 'Why would I know?'

'Because it is French and you are French.'

'Half French,' Felicity reminded him. 'And the half of me that's English has the best music taste I'm afraid – never seen an opera before in my life.'

'Me neither,' Brooke put in. 'I'm a bit worried I won't understand what's going on but very interested to see it.'

'We'll google it at half-time and see what's happened,' Felicity said. 'Then we'll google it again at the end to see if we figured it out right.'

Fabien looked faintly appalled at the idea of them googling the story as they went along, but he didn't say so. Instead he turned to Brooke, clearly eager to talk to her as the person he was able to impress, because Felicity was having none of it.

'Do not worry. I will explain if you are confused – just ask me.' He put his empty glass down. 'Would you like to have your coats taken to the cloakroom?'

'We'll keep hold of them,' Felicity said.

Brooke wasn't about to argue. She felt underdressed as it was – at least if she kept her coat on until they got to their seats, the fact might go unnoticed.

'As you wish.' Fabien topped up their glasses before refilling his own.

Brooke had another sip. It was very bubbly, and she could feel it almost instantly going straight to her head in the most delightful way. But then she noticed Fabien throw a hungry look in her direction and suddenly wondered whether she needed to keep her wits about her.

An announcement was made over the speakers, and Fabien drank down the rest of his glass.

'Nearly time to take our seats,' Felicity said to Brooke. 'You want to knock that one back so we can finish the bottle before we go in?'

'We can't take it with us?'

'A bit awkward to carry the bucket and everything... I expect Fab can order us some more when we get to the box.'

Brooke stared at her. *'The box?* Like... *a box?'*

Felicity grinned. 'If I know my cousin, it'll be a box – right, Fab?'

He grinned back at her. *'Naturellement...'*

The auditorium was every bit as opulent as the rooms and corridors leading to it, only instead of the colour palette of more neutral creams and biscuits of the marble walls and floors, here it was vibrant scarlet and gold. Row upon row of seats faced out towards the stage, every level bedecked in ornate gold and plush red velvet.

As the performance began, Fabien reached for a set of binoculars stowed in a pocket of the seat and put them to his eyes, nodding seriously as he listened to the singers, and every so often Brooke would glance at Felicity and catch her watching him rather than the stage, wearing a smirk.

An hour later, as the show went on, Brooke felt her eyes glazing over. She'd finished gazing in wonder at the auditorium and the other patrons and the sets and the amazing costumes and the fact that the women could sing so loudly and with such a pitch that the chandeliers rattled, and now all she could think about was how she didn't know what was going on and how every song blended into the next and she couldn't tell where one ended and the next one began. She wanted to ask Fabien, but he seemed engrossed, with his binoculars pressed to his face, and then she thought about getting more champagne but she didn't want to ask him about that either, and so she sat in her seat in the unbelievably posh box in full view of the entire audience, desperately fighting sleep. It had been a long day, after all, and though she'd imagined the excitement of the occasion would keep her awake, she hadn't banked on the dullness of the show counteracting that. Opera was very definitely not her thing, and at least she could say that now with absolute certainty.

With no idea how it had happened and how long she'd been out, a prod in her ribs woke her. Felicity was grinning. Brooke struggled up in her seat, groggy, realising after a moment that Felicity had reached behind Fabien's seat to poke her back to the land of the living and that, thankfully, Fabien was so engrossed with watching the show (or doing a very good job of pretending to watch) that he hadn't noticed. Brooke was thankful for small mercies – she would have been mortified if he had. She wanted to ask how much longer she had to go but was afraid it would be very rude, but she also desperately wanted to know when she could expect to be in bed, which was really the only place she wanted to be now.

Then Fabien dropped the binoculars to look at her. 'You understand so far?' he whispered.

Brooke nodded. She wasn't about to say anything to the contrary, having been asleep; she didn't want to give him any kind of clue that she hadn't been watching at all. These tickets had to have been expensive, though Felicity had told her he would have made some dodgy deal to get them and she oughtn't to worry about the cost, but Brooke didn't want him to think she didn't appreciate his efforts, even if secretly she longed to go back to her apartment. If the main chandelier had come crashing down at that moment, just like it did in *Phantom of the Opera*, causing the theatre to be evacuated, nothing would have made Brooke happier.

.   .   .

At the interval they had more champagne, which certainly helped alleviate the boredom during the second act, though even half-cut Brooke was praying for the final act to come to an end before she lost the will to live. There was one bright spot where she actually knew one of the pieces of music and got ridiculously excited by that fact, but it didn't last long. By the time Carmen died (she wasn't sure if that was what was happening but it seemed to be the case judging by the very depressing song and the fact that she'd been stabbed), Brooke realised that they must be close to the end and was ready to punch the air.

As the bows were taken the audience stood to applaud, and no one louder than Brooke, who was overjoyed it was finally over, but even the bows seemed to last forever. Eventually, everyone started to file out.

Fabien turned to Brooke and Felicity. 'Would you like to meet the cast? I can arrange for us to go backstage.'

'Nah, you're alright,' Felicity said, much to Brooke's relief.

'Hmmm.' Fabien gave Brooke one of those looks again, one that lasted too long and was a little too interested, and if she'd been more sober she'd have been a bit unnerved. 'Then perhaps you'd join me for a nightcap?'

'Much as we'd love to,' Felicity replied, 'we've been up for a very long time now, like almost twenty-four hours, and we're knackered. Mind if we save that for another time?'

Felicity glanced at Brooke, who gave a nod of agreement. 'I'm quite tired too, though we've had a lovely evening. Thank you for bringing us to see such a wonderful show.'

'I'm glad you enjoyed it!' Fabien beamed. 'Perhaps you'd like to see another? I think *Madame Butterfly* is being performed at—'

'Oh,' Felicity cut in, 'we'll be way too busy to do another one. Market gets going in another couple of days, doesn't it?'

'*Bien sûr.*' Fabien nodded as they all began to make their

way out of the auditorium. 'But you must make time to meet with me again before you leave Paris.'

'Oh, we will!' Felicity said. 'I only meant that we wouldn't be able to do a full-blown three hours of opera. But a quick drink or a bit of lunch – we could definitely do that.'

'I would like that very much,' he said. 'I will message you to arrange it.'

'Give us a couple of days first,' Felicity replied. 'We have some stuff to do and, you know, we need time to settle in and get sorted at the apartment.'

'*Mais oui, ma crotte.*'

Outside, Fabien insisted on his driver taking them home. And when Felicity refused, he insisted on putting them in a cab.

'Why didn't we go home with the driver?' Brooke asked as they got into the taxi. 'Wouldn't it have cost him less as he's already paying the driver?'

'If I know Fab, he'd have been in the car with us and he would have wormed his way into that nightcap at our apartment, and I don't know about you, but I'm way too tired.'

'I can't argue with that,' Brooke said. 'But won't he be offended?'

'See – and that's how he would have got in,' Felicity said. 'He knows you're a soft touch who doesn't want to offend him. I'd have said no and you'd have said yes. You need to be tougher with him – borderline offending him is the only language he understands, otherwise he won't take no for an answer.'

Brooke thought back to the reasons they'd ended up at the opera in the first place when Felicity hadn't wanted to go and had to admit her friend had a point. It was Brooke who'd been guilt-tripped into saying yes.

'We'll do lunch with him in a couple of days,' Felicity added. 'That should keep him happy for a while.'

'If you say so,' Brooke agreed doubtfully.

'Seriously, you'll thank me. If we're not careful we'll end up being his own private entertainment for the next few weeks.'

'He must have loads of other friends.'

'Oh, he does, but he fancies you and when he fancies someone...' Felicity shrugged.

'Surely not?'

'Come on, you can't have missed those looks. And trust me, that's somewhere you don't want to go – he's been married three times, don't forget. I think we can safely say it never ends well.'

'He's not my type at all,' Brooke said. 'No danger of that.'

'Yes, but he's charming and persuasive. He probably wasn't their type, but they still ended up marrying him.'

'He doesn't look a bit like Del Boy either.'

Felicity laughed. 'Random change of subject there.'

'I know, but you said he looked like Del Boy.'

'I said he *was like* Del Boy.'

'Oh. Well, I just didn't expect him to look so... like a proper businessman.'

'He is a proper businessman... sort of. I've no idea whether the business is legitimate or not, but it's definitely business of some description.'

The lights and scenery of Paris flashed by as the taxi whizzed them to their apartment, and though Brooke was vaguely aware of it, she was too tired to take it in as it deserved. 'What shall we do tomorrow then?'

'I don't know. What do you want to do? We should probably get some groceries.'

'That won't take long. I'd like to explore.'

'Right then.' Felicity closed her eyes and leant back in her seat. 'If we can get up before noon, then exploring it is.'

CHAPTER SIX

Despite what Felicity had said about lying in, something woke Brooke early and she went from her bedroom to the kitchen to find her friend already firing up the stove for coffee.

'Couldn't stay in bed either?' she asked, yawning.

Felicity grabbed a second cup from a cupboard. 'I didn't close the blinds properly and the daylight got me up. What about you?'

Brooke gave a slight shrug. 'I think it's being in a strange room, and maybe a little bit of anticipation for our first full day in Paris. As soon as I woke a bit my brain was like, ding! Time to do stuff! And then I was too wired to go back to sleep.'

'At least it's giving us a full day. We did intend to see as much of Paris as we could before the stall opens for business.'

'So what do you want to do?' Brooke asked.

Felicity turned to her with a grin. 'How about we be shamelessly touristy?'

'What do you have in mind?'

'Oh, something that the French side of my family would be absolutely appalled by!'

. . .

Sapphire-blue skies stretched across the city, the low cloud and grumblings of snow of the previous day a distant memory. It might have been bright and sunny, but all the colder for it. Both Brooke and Felicity shivered at the bus stop, despite their many layers of clothing.

'I had no idea Paris could be so cold,' Brooke said. 'I mean, I know people told us it gets cold in the winter, but I didn't think it would be like arctic cold.'

'To be honest, neither did I.' Felicity pulled her scarf further up her neck. 'I'm sure it will be toasty warm on the bus.'

Brooke shot her a sideways glance. 'On the top deck of an open-top bus? Are you sure about that?'

'But they'll have heaters by our feet – right?'

'Oh, of course, silly me. So our feet will be warm, even if our fingers are at risk of dropping off with frostbite.'

'Well, we don't *have* to do the bus tour.'

'Are you joking? Your face when you suggested it tells me otherwise! I think if I backed out now you'd burst into tears. You might even roll around on the pavement having a tantrum. It would certainly be the end of our friendship!'

'That's possibly true,' Felicity said with a laugh.

'I'm sure it'll be fun. So long as I try not to think about how cold I am.'

'You'll have so much fun you'll forget how cold it is,' Felicity said.

There were about thirty people ahead of them in the queue, every one of them stamping their feet as they stood in line on the Champs-Élysées, in the impressive shadow of the Arc de Triomphe, which was way bigger in real life than it looked in photos.

A ripple of excited anticipation ran the length of the queue as the scarlet bus arrived to pick them up. Felicity paid the driver and refused to tell Brooke how much it had cost (so Brooke assumed it was a lot) and said that it was her Christmas gift and not to worry about it. Brooke knew better than to argue – she wouldn't win because she never did.

Their first stop was Grand Palais. They got off the bus and marvelled at yet more golden-stoned, classical architecture, made stunning by towering feature arches, colonnades and statues, and finished by a truly incredible glass-domed ceiling. The same opulence they'd seen at Palais Garnier the previous evening was in evidence here. They weren't allowed in because of renovation work, but simply to see it from the outside was a treat they couldn't miss.

They got back on the bus and went past the Trocadéro, which was basically a huge park, but didn't get off as it was so vast they decided they'd need a lot of time to enjoy it, time they didn't have today, and there were sights they were more interested in.

Then came the Eiffel Tower. As the bus pulled up nearby, Brooke leant over the side and noted the heaving crowds of visitors.

'Bloody hell, this looks insane,' she said.

Felicity shifted to get a better view and nodded. 'It'd take us all day to get close. You want to get off the bus here? I mean, we could, but we could always stay on and see the other things and then catch this when the bus comes back round if it's less busy.'

'That sounds like a good idea,' Brooke said, though she took some photos just in case. Then the bus started on its way again, taking them down the Champ de Mars, which was basically another huge park, along past Palais Garnier, which looked every bit as impressive in the daylight as it had done the previous evening, and then along to the Louvre, unmistakable with its glass pyramid. Brooke was particularly interested in visiting the gallery because she'd recently seen it on a Netflix show, but by this point it was already lunchtime.

'We could nip into the Louvre, skate round and get something to eat afterwards,' Felicity said.

'I'd want to see it properly if I'm going in,' Brooke replied doubtfully. 'Not just run around and then out for chips.'

'That's the problem with trips like this. Great for seeing a bit of everything but not so good if you want to stay somewhere for a while. What time does the bus stop running?'

'I'm not sure. I suppose it will keep going into the evening? Let's get off anyway, maybe take a look around the outside and grab some lunch. I can make time another day to go inside and look at the art.'

'So that's the Eiffel Tower and the Louvre we need to make more time for.'

'Maybe we'll get to the Eiffel Tower later.'

'OK. And don't forget there's another museum on the route today, not to mention Notre-Dame.'

Brooke scurried down the stairs to the lower deck of the bus, Felicity following, so they could get off before it started up again.

'*Merci!*' she called to the driver.

On the pavement she turned to Felicity. 'We're never going to get round all of it today, even on the bus. I really wanted to look at Notre-Dame and have a good poke round at the Musée d'Orsay too.'

'Why don't we just chill in that case? No point in racing round if we're not going to do it anyway. We still have tomorrow – we could do some sightseeing then, and our bus tickets are good for two days. I vote we have lunch, nosey around here, and then see what time it is. If we have time, we'll fit in a couple more things.'

'OK.' Brooke turned towards the Louvre, the glass panes of its pyramid glinting in the sun, wishing she had time to wander its halls and corridors but sensible enough to know that she was better saving that pleasure for a day where there was more time. 'That sounds like a plan.'

.   .   .

After lunch at an outrageously expensive café, the lure of going inside the Louvre had been too strong to resist, and by the time they'd pored over the artworks contained within and marvelled at the architecture of the building itself, darkness had fallen over the city and the afternoon had been used up.

'You know what we should do now?' Felicity said as they emerged onto a square that definitely felt colder than it had done earlier, leaving Brooke wondering how that was even possible.

'What?'

'Moulin Rouge!'

'But the bus...'

'In reality, how much more are we going to get to see at this time of the day? We'd do whistle-stop at best and everything would be in the dark. I know the city looks nice lit up at night, but you still can't see things properly. I say let's save the rest of the sights, go home, get changed and go to the Moulin Rouge.'

'If I walk back into that apartment, all I'll want to do is go to bed,' Brooke said. 'I'm only awake now because I'm too bloody cold to be sleepy.'

'Come on! It's the Moulin Rouge! We did say we'd go, and I think we'd be sorry if we miss it because it will be amazing.'

Brooke was thoughtful for a moment. 'I'm sure you're right, but we didn't get tickets before we came. I bet you'd have to book those tickets years in advance.'

'I reckon Fabien could get us a last-minute admission,' Felicity said. 'He's sure to know who to ask.'

'I'll bet. He probably knows every shady dealer in Paris.' Brooke saw Felicity's expression darken and immediately regretted her statement. It was nothing Felicity hadn't said herself, but she supposed family got to comment on things that were off-limits to outsiders.

'He got us the permit to be here...' Felicity said tartly.

'God, yes, I'm sorry, I know... that was out of order. I'm just tired, that's all.'

'And I know he can be shady,' Felicity said, the moment passing quickly, 'but that's what makes him so useful. Come on, Boo. If we can get tickets, why wouldn't we go to the most famous cabaret club in the world...? And you bloody love that film.'

Brooke couldn't help a tired smile. 'I suppose I do, but I doubt it's like that in real life. I bet it's all seedy and full of perverts.'

'Nah, it'll be full of tourists I expect. Anyway, there's only one way to find out, isn't there?'

'I still say we won't get tickets at this short notice.'

'But I can try? And if I get some, we can go?'

Brooke let out a sigh. 'Sure, why not?'

Felicity let out a little squeal as she pulled her phone from a pocket. Brooke didn't react. In fact, she felt safe agreeing to the plan, convinced that there was no way they'd be able to get tickets no matter how *resourceful* Felicity's cousin was. Besides, Felicity had asked him for a lot of favours over the past few months, including the highly sought after and coveted permit to trade at the Christmas markets, which would probably piss off plenty of French traders, and there had to be a limit to what he was willing to do no matter how fond he might be of her.

'Fab, *coucou! Ça va?*'

Brooke could hear Fabien's tinny reply at the other end, and she was certain she detected a sigh of resignation. Clearly he'd already guessed that Felicity was going to ask him for another favour.

She listened now to the back and forth, unable to make out much of what was being said because Felicity was speaking to her cousin in his native language and the traffic of central Paris was so loud. After a few minutes of wheedling and joking, she finished the call and put her phone away.

'He says he can't make promises but he does know one or two people to ask.'

'That's good of him,' Brooke said. 'I hope he doesn't put himself out too much, though. He's already done so much for us, and I don't want to think we're taking advantage of him.'

'Oh, I'm totally taking advantage of him and he knows it!' Felicity laughed. 'He'd be shocked at anything else. And let's face it, he knows he can ask me for stuff, only it just so happens that he doesn't need to because he knows how to get everything he needs himself. But if he did... then I'd have his back.'

'You're pretty good at having people's backs too – I can't think of a person I'd trust more with having mine.'

Felicity gave Brooke a fond smile. 'You've got mine too – that's what friends are for, right?'

'Always,' Brooke replied. 'Whatever else happens, lets always have each other's backs.'

CHAPTER SEVEN

For the second night in a row, Brooke found herself feeling desperately underdressed. She'd decided against the dress Felicity had lent her as it didn't feel quite right but, then again, nothing she'd packed seemed right either. Fabien had worked his magic and got their tickets, and Brooke was faintly relieved that he had a prior engagement and wouldn't be able to join them.

One thing was for sure: the maddest, most exotic, most extreme fever dream of a nightclub hadn't featured on her list of things to pack for. At short notice and with no time to shop for anything else, she'd pulled on a pair of printed bell-bottoms and a purple satin shirt. It was very *Brooke*, though she couldn't help but feel it wasn't very Moulin Rouge, and even though Felicity had told her more than once that she looked amazing and not to worry, she still felt as if she stuck out like a sore thumb as they walked from the metro station to the scarlet-lit entrance of the club.

Felicity had gone for her usual black and slinky. It was understated, but she didn't need to make an effort to look good. She never did. It was being half French that did it, she often joked, but Brooke had thought on many occasions that she was probably more right about that than she realised.

'Oh my God!' Felicity gasped as they looked up at the huge lit windmill sails of the signage. 'It's so cool! We need a photo!' She took her phone out, clicked a few and then grabbed Brooke's arm. 'Selfie time! Come on – get in!'

Brooke put her head close to Felicity's and they took a selfie, but when they inspected it, they were both disappointed to see the background was hardly visible behind their heads.

'We could be at Blackpool Illuminations as far as anyone could tell from this,' Felicity said. She looked up at the crowds hurrying this way and that. Some were heading for the club, while others were fighting the tide to get away from it, on their way elsewhere. 'I'll ask someone to...'

Her sentence trailed off as she disappeared into the crowds, like a swimmer jumping into the waves of a choppy sea. No sooner had she gone in than she'd disappeared, leaving Brooke only able to catch a glimpse of her head every now and again.

A moment later she returned, grinning, with a man in tow. He was tall, with a head of dark hair that curled at his neck, and the most intense green eyes, wearing a stylish woollen trench coat. He looked vaguely startled to have been singled out. Brooke could see why that might be – the poor guy had been going about his business trying to get through the crowds on the pavement outside, probably late for his tea or something, and two mad Englishwomen grab him to do a photo shoot for them. He probably thought they were sad for wanting photos of the Moulin Rouge at all. Still, he was being very courteous about it, regardless of what he thought.

'*Merci, monsieur,*' Felicity said, handing the phone to him and grabbing Brooke by the shoulder to pose while he took the photo.

'One more?' he asked in English but with the most delicious French accent.

Why was it, Brooke wondered, that everyone suddenly started to speak English as soon as they saw her. It had to be her, because she was quite certain Felicity would have spoken to him in French until they'd got here. 'To be certain it's good?'

'That would be amazing!' she said. 'You're a gent!'

'A gent?' he asked as he took another picture.

'A gentleman,' she clarified as he returned her phone. 'An absolute legend. Thank you! Are you going in to see the show?'

'In there?' he asked, looking confused.

'Yes,' Felicity said cheerfully. 'We are. I'm so excited; I've wanted to come for ages.'

'And now you are here,' he said with a faint smile. 'Sadly, I am only on my way to the metro station for a dull meeting.'

'Oh!' Brooke said. 'It's late for a meeting... I hope us stopping you hasn't made you late!'

'Not at all,' he said smoothly.

He gave them both a good-natured nod. '*De rien*. Enjoy your evening.'

'Thank you,' Brooke said. 'Enjoy your evening too.'

With a brief smile he turned and strode back to the road.

'Hey,' Felicity said, 'when I go out to get a volunteer, don't I just know how to pick them?'

'What do you mean?'

'How fit was he?'

Brooke gave a small laugh. 'How do you know? He's absolutely not your type.'

'Yes, but I bet he's yours. You should have got his number while he was here.'

'How was I supposed to do that? You dragged him over to take a photo and then immediately sent him on his way again! Even I can't work that fast!'

'Well, if you snooze you lose.' Felicity grinned. 'But I expect there are plenty of other *poisson dans la mer*... But don't be so dopey next time or you'll never hook one.'

'I've told you, I don't want to hook one. In fact, if it needs hooking then it's bound to want to wriggle free eventually. You can never keep what you need to trap in the first place.'

Felicity waggled her eyebrows. 'Who said anything about keeping?'

'OK, OK... well, that one's gone now, so let's go in and find our seats.'

Going inside was like travelling through a portal to another world. The icy streets and traffic noise of Paris was gone in an instant, replaced by a foyer decorated in sumptuous scarlet wallpaper and velvet curtains, noisy with excited chatter and laughter, heat radiating from the crowd as they filed in. If not for the modern clothes of their fellow guests, Brooke could easily have been persuaded that they'd travelled back in time to when the Moulin Rouge had first opened its doors, and that she might well see a famous artist or two amongst the patrons. She hadn't really been that bothered about coming, and was almost resentful that Fabien had come good with their tickets, but now she was here, she was so glad.

'It's amazing!' she breathed. 'Oh my God, it's gorgeous!'

An usher opened a set of double doors for them, and they walked through to find an auditorium furnished with row upon row of tables, each with a scarlet cloth and a gold-fringed lamp. The ceiling was decked with billowing gold cloth too, and the stage was painted a glossy black, so smooth it was like a mirror.

'I think this is ours,' Felicity said, pointing to one.

'This is an amazing view!' Brooke said. 'Are you sure?'

'Yeah, I think so. I guess dodgy Fabien is dodgier than we thought because he must have blackmailed someone pretty high up to get this spot.'

'I don't care!' Brooke said, laughing as they made their way to sit. 'My morals have completely gone out of the window now because I'm so excited to be here.'

They sat, smiling at people on surrounding tables who were also getting comfortable.

'I know I said I didn't want to come but now I can't believe I was willing to miss it,' Brooke continued. 'It's a once-in-a-life-time thing, isn't it? It's like... it's like someone distilled sex and made it into a club.'

Felicity burst out laughing. 'And you haven't even started drinking yet!'

'I know, I'm giddy on all the excitement. Isn't it an amazing atmosphere? Isn't it just the most incredible place you've ever set foot in? I mean, just look at it! I keep expecting Nicole Kidman to come out from behind the stage curtain in her costume.'

'It would certainly make my night if she did,' Felicity said. 'As long as Ewan McGregor made an appearance for you so it was fair.'

'God, I wish!' Brooke grinned. 'I'd jump on that man before he could even open his cute little singing mouth! I know I keep saying it but this... it just doesn't feel real to be here.'

The auditorium steadily filled while Brooke and Felicity marvelled at every tiny thing, and then the waiters started to appear to take food orders. One arrived at their table with an ice bucket containing a bottle.

'*Mademoiselles...* your champagne.'

'But we didn't order any champagne,' Brooke began, but then Felicity shushed her and waved him to put it down.

'Fabien,' she said, smiling at Brooke. 'I bet he's ordered it for us. God I love that cousin of mine! *Merci*,' she added to the waiter. 'We can take it from here.'

'Oh! Well, I hope so because we can't afford it!' Brooke said as Felicity put a glass down in front of her and poured some out.

'Stop worrying. You're here now, you're never going to do it again, so enjoy it.'

'You're right – I'm being ridiculous. I mean, this sort of thing is what I always wanted to do all the time I was with Johnny, but he never would have done. Now I'm not with him and I can do what I like and I'm still not doing any of the stuff I dreamt of.' She knocked back the glass of champagne and held it out. 'That's not half bad; I'll take another please.'

'No problem, *mademoiselle*,' Felicity said, refilling it and then holding up her own. 'Cheers, Fab!'

'Cheers, Fabien,' Brooke said, 'and here's to hoping this champagne is actually from you, because I'm not sure my credit card will take it if we have to pay!'

Dinner was accompanied by a fairly tame cabaret singer who had a beautiful voice, but it was all rather middle-of-the-road and a bit disappointing. But as the last course was cleared away, that's when things really livened up. Felicity had ordered a second bottle of champagne, and by that point Brooke was too tipsy to care about the cost. Then the big acts began, the huge glitzy numbers featuring a stage full of dancing girls that the Moulin Rouge was famous for. Most of it was sung in French so Brooke didn't have a clue what any of the songs were about, but it didn't matter. What mattered was the spectacle, and in that regard it was impossible for anyone to be disappointed.

There was a number where the stage must have contained at least a hundred performers in white sequinned nautical-themed outfits, and then another one where the women wore massive feathered headdresses and tiny little silver bras, one where they had sort of belly-dancing costumes on, and, of course, the most famous act, the one where the women wore skirts with layer after layer of petticoat, which they wafted up to show not only their knickers but the red, white and blue of the French flag woven into the fabric.

Brooke and Felicity jumped up and danced around in the aisles and, come the final act, decided to join in. As they were both wearing trousers, they could only mime the action of waving their skirts as they kicked their legs.

'Am I getting up as high as them?' Felicity asked with a giggle.

'Um, yeah, totally!' Brooke replied with a huge grin. 'Am I?'

'Absolutely!' Felicity laughed. 'We could do this job – shall we join up?'

Brooke was sweating and her hair had flattened to her face with the heat, and it was possible she'd never looked less glamorous, and she definitely wasn't kicking her legs anywhere near as high as the dancers on stage, but that was all part of the fun.

With a drunken roar, she and Felicity joined in, singing the famous tune almost loud enough to compete with the orchestra, every so often breaking off with a breathless giggle. Some of their fellow guests did the same, and Brooke grinned madly at them.

'Are you having fun?' she yelled, and whether they spoke English or not they seemed to understand, grinning back at her. Once or twice she'd catch someone glowering at her and presumed they didn't approve of the coarseness of their behaviour.

'Get that miserable old trout,' she said, inclining her head at one woman in a way that she thought was discreet but really wasn't at all.

Felicity turned to look. 'Ha ha, poor thing. We ought to start an appeal for people who've never had fun in their lives – must be an awful affliction!'

The woman glared at them – she must have known they were talking about her, but by this point Brooke was having too much fun to care. She kicked her legs higher, trying to ignore the very real risk of actually pulling a muscle, and sang louder than ever.

'Look at us in Paris!' she cried.

'Yeah! Stick it to that guy who said you were no fun... what was his name again?'

Brooke laughed. 'I've forgotten it already! Jim, Joe... something very boring beginning with J.'

Felicity dragged her into a huge hug. 'I bloody love you!'

'I bloody love you too! I'm so glad you talked me into this!'

'I told you it would be amazing here.'

'Not just this, I mean Paris. I'm so glad you persuaded me to come.'

Felicity hugged her again before turning back to the stage to whoop her approval.

Brooke gave her a fond smile before turning to the stage to join in. She was so glad she'd come, and she had a feeling that, one way or another, this Christmas in Paris was going to be one that she'd remember for the rest of her life.

At the end of the night, it had been so cold outside the club it had taken them both by surprise. Brooke had suggested a cab instead of the metro, and a tipsy Felicity had agreed.

'I think we've had too much champagne,' Felicity said as they tumbled out of the cab half an hour later outside their apartment block.

'I *know* we've had too much,' Brooke agreed as she followed. 'I don't think all that other stuff in between helped either. What was it now, brandy...?'

Felicity giggled. 'You had absinthe, you mentalist! You said you wanted to try it because... I don't know, something about Kylie Minogue popping out of the bottle if you did.'

Brooke laughed. 'Oh yeah. I forgot about that.'

'I mean, if she'd popped out of the bottle, I'd have fought you for her number.'

'I'd have got her number for you.' Brooke put an arm around Felicity's shoulder. 'Anything for my bestie.'

Brooke paid the driver, and with no word of acknowledgement he sped off into the night. 'Oh, a pleasure doing business with you too!' she called after him. Then she opened her bag. 'Keys...'

There was an electronic keypad and code for the front entrance of the building, and then for all the doors beyond that it was good old-fashioned keys. Brooke couldn't remember the code and she was relying, once again, on the fact that Felicity would have it memorised.

'We're so going to regret this tomorrow,' Felicity said.

'Yes,' Brooke replied. 'And we're going to regret how much money we've spent on the booze that caused our hangovers. We're going to have to step up our sales game to make it back.'

'Yeah, but it was worth it, right?'

'God yes!' Brooke said. 'Although I still say you're far too much of a bad influence to be a good business partner.'

'But I'll do as a friend?'

'Oh, you make a pretty decent friend,' Brooke said with a fond smile. 'Ah!'

She shook her keys as they made their way to the gates that led to the courtyard of their building.

'I'm so glad you persuaded me to go,' she continued. 'Tonight was one of the most amazing experiences of my life. Seems all the cool things that I've done have been thanks to you.'

'Oh, I wouldn't go that far...'

Felicity stopped and stared at the keypad.

'Oh no,' Brooke said. 'No, don't even play me. Please say you haven't forgotten the code too.'

'I do know... I mean, I will – just give me a minute to think—'

'Oh, wait!' Brooke interrupted. 'I might have it on my phone somewhere—'

'Urrrgggg!'

Both of them spun round to see a toothless old man gesticulating madly in their direction.

'*Je... voudrais... je suis...*'

He continued to waft his hands at them in a fashion that could only be described as disturbing.

'*Monsieur?*' Felicity asked sharply. '*Qu'est-ce qui ne va pas? Qu'est-ce que tu veux?*'

'What's up with him?' Brooke lowered her voice as she asked Felicity the question, even though he apparently couldn't understand.

'That's what I'm trying to find out,' Felicity said.

He shouted something else at them.

'Even I don't know what the hell he's saying,' she added with a frown. 'I'm guessing it's French, but it doesn't sound like any sort of French I know. I'll tell you one thing though – he's certainly not welcoming us to the neighbourhood.'

'Actually, I think he might be,' Brooke replied as the man reached for his crotch. 'And I don't think it's the sort of welcome we'd like.'

'I doubt he'd manage what he'd like to,' Felicity said with a look of faint disgust. 'He's totally out of it.'

'He might be, but I still think we'd better get out of his way because I sense trouble here.'

Felicity turned to her with a withering look. 'Ya think? You might want to get that code right about now so we can get inside.'

He slurred something again and Felicity held a hand up to silence him. '*Monsieur! S'il te plaît arrête!*'

But he didn't stop, as Felicity had asked – instead he started to inch forward, one hand cupped around an area Brooke tried not to look at as she unlocked her phone and frantically scrolled through her notes app.

'Come on, Boo...' Felicity growled. 'A bit faster if you don't mind. I don't want to have to punch this guy's lights out.'

Then the man lunged at Felicity, forcing her into Brooke, who lost her footing and her phone. With a strangled cry she reached across the tarmac to retrieve it. As she knelt down to inspect the damage and saw, to her relief, only a faint crack across the screen, another voice joined the fray. She looked up to see Manon, who had presumably just turned into the alleyway on her way home and would have witnessed the fracas immediately, step in between the man and Felicity.

'*Sors d'ici!*'

He mumbled something but Manon was having none of it. '*Va!*'

The man shot a surly look at all three of them before evidently deciding that Manon was too scary to tackle and finally skulking away, muttering to himself the whole time.

She turned to Brooke and Felicity. 'Are you OK?'

'Thanks to you,' Brooke said, getting to her feet. 'I don't know what we would have done if you hadn't shown up.'

Manon gave a vague shrug. 'I see him all the time. He looks scary, but he's not that bad.'

'Not that bad?' Brooke squeaked. 'You mean we might encounter worse than that?'

'I mean' – Manon held up her finger and flicked the air – 'he would fall over easily.'

'I don't know what his problem was,' Felicity said. 'We didn't do anything wrong.'

'Some people have a problem when nothing is wrong,' Manon replied. 'It's life, right?'

'Well,' Felicity replied, the colour returning to her face now, 'thanks. You're our knight in shining armour.'

Manon frowned.

'She means thank you for rescuing us,' Brooke said. While Felicity looked as if she was already recovering, doubtless due to Manon's appearance, Brooke's own heart was still racing, and she was definitely still shaking.

Manon waved a purple-nailed hand. 'It was nothing. It is very late. Perhaps it is too late in this neighbourhood for you to be walking.'

'You're out,' Felicity said.

'Ah yes, but I know how things are here.'

Felicity laughed a bit more than necessary and Brooke resisted the urge to roll her eyes. Instead, she touched her arm to get her attention.

'We should probably go in. We've got an early start tomorrow, don't forget.'

Felicity nodded. 'You're right.'

'What is tomorrow?' Manon asked.

Brooke turned to her. 'The first day of the markets.'

'So soon?' Manon raised her eyebrows.

Felicity laughed. 'I know, that's kind of how we feel. Do you visit? We'd love you to come and see us at the stall? You could choose something, whatever you like... if you see something you like, of course... as a thank you for tonight.'

'Hmm...' Manon dug her hands into her pockets and eyed them both keenly before her gaze settled on Felicity once more. 'I am sure I will see something I like if I come.'

'We'd better get inside,' Brooke said to Felicity again. 'I'm actually pretty cold now; not sure if my fingers can even work my phone.'

'Manon will know the code, won't you, Manon?' Felicity asked.

'For the door? Sure. Don't you have it?'

'Somewhere,' Felicity said. 'It was in my brain but has fallen out, and Brooke was trying to find it on her phone when that man started on us.'

'Ah...'

Manon breezed past them both, punched the code into the keypad and the gate clicked open. She held it and gestured for them both to go in before following.

'You're making a habit of saving us,' Felicity said as they filed past her. 'I could get used to this.'

'I hope we don't need to,' Brooke put in darkly. 'I'd rather we didn't make so many cock-ups in the first place.'

'Goodnight,' Manon said, heading for a door across the courtyard from the one they needed.

'Sweet dreams!' Felicity called before turning to Brooke with a grin.

'Honestly,' Brooke said wearily. 'You're a right piece of work sometimes, you know that?'

'I know,' Felicity chirped, clearly already over her ordeal. 'But you wouldn't have me any other way!'

CHAPTER EIGHT

There had been a thick frost on the ground as Brooke and Felicity arrived to set up their stall for the opening day of the markets and their first day of trading in Paris. It was now midday, but the temperature was still bitterly cold and the skies still heavy with cloud, ice clinging stubbornly to lamp posts and paving stones. At least their stall, encased in the traditional wooden chalet of most Christmas markets they'd worked before, had a roof and three walls to keep out the worst of the elements and, more importantly, a portable heater. Thankful as they were for all that, Brooke was still unutterably grateful for her thermal underwear and arctic-grade coat and hat she'd purchased from a climbing surplus store before they'd left Ely, not to mention the steady supply of coffee from a nearby crêpe van.

They'd discussed often how lucky they'd been to score a pitch at the Jardin des Tuileries, arguably the best-known and biggest Christmas market in Paris. It was perfectly placed for passing tourist trade as well as for locals, located a stone's throw from famous sites such as Place de la Concorde, the Louvre, the Champs-Élysées and the Eiffel Tower. The market was like a mad Christmas fever dream, but in the very best way, with lights and tinsel everywhere, not to mention the huge Christmas-themed figures such as nutcracker soldiers, fairies, elves and reindeer at every turn. Once or twice, Brooke had turned a corner only to start as she was confronted by a particularly big reindeer looming at her when she hadn't been expecting it.

Once they'd got the bulk of their displays sorted, they took it in turns to nip off and explore the rest of the market, but it was huge and they had too little time to even scratch the surface. Brooke wasn't all that fussed about buying. She was more interested to see what sort of competition they had, and was relieved and pleased to find that very few of the other stalls she saw were selling anything like them.

There was food... *a lot* of food: the usual snack vendors selling sausages, burgers, waffles, crêpes, doughnuts, Belgian fries, mulled wine and mulled cider; and then there were the stands selling gift foods – fine cheeses and wines, sweets, chocolate boxes, cakes and spirits. Then there were stalls selling housewares, but most of these weren't like the goods Brooke had created. There were crystal ornaments, paper lanterns, bronze and iron candleholders, wooden spoons and spoon rests, chopping boards made of marble and slate, vases and pots, and even a stall that sold Viking-style drinking horns made of real horn.

There were some that had knitted clothing and felt toys and a stand with textiles, and more than one with jewellery, but none of it was quite like what Brooke and Felicity had. In fact, as Brooke returned from one of her wanderings, she noted that Felicity's unique brand of jewellery made from recycled plastic was causing quite a stir among the small crowd who had gathered around the stall. Some were full of praise, some didn't seem to like it, though they were intrigued despite this, and some appeared confused by the concept. Brooke kind of got their confusion. It wasn't every day you saw bottle tops and old toys melted down to make earrings and necklaces after all. Brooke's own creations, though far less radical, had generated a steady flow of interest too. They'd sold a bit – hardly enough to retire on, but it was a good start, and there was still a month for trade to hot up. With luck, the closer they got to the holiday season, the busier they'd be.

With so much going on and so many people around, it was also reassuring to see pairs of gendarmes patrolling the walkways. Brooke aimed the odd tentative smile as one or another caught her eye but didn't get much of a reaction. She supposed they were too focused on their duties for niceties. But Brooke's lack of success in any kind of interaction wasn't about to stop Felicity from having a go.

'*Bonjour!*' She waved at a pair of male officers who passed by. '*Il fait froid, non?*'

Neither replied, but both gave a nod of recognition before marching on their way.

Brooke turned to her. 'What was that about?'

'Just being friendly,' Felicity said.

Brooke raised her eyebrows and Felicity grinned. 'And I was testing the water, seeing how friendly they could be persuaded to be.'

'Since when do you care how friendly they might be?' Brooke asked, getting the gist of what Felicity was up to immediately.

'Since I decided to make you my pet project.'

'Right... and should I be worrying about what the nature of this project might be? What is it?'

'It's project let's get Boo laid by a hot French guy. So what do you think? Were they a good start?'

'I hardly think they've got the time and certainly not the inclination to come over here and flirt with me. And even if they did, there's a city full of hot French women I'm sure they'd prefer.'

'You don't know that.'

'What, that there are no women? I'm pretty sure there are a few around here somewhere.'

'No, daft! I mean you don't know they'd prefer any of them to you.'

'Well...' Brooke stamped her feet, which had gone numb from standing in one spot for too long, 'as they've gone on their way, I don't suppose we'll ever find out.'

'They might come back this way...' Felicity winked. 'Especially if they want to get a closer look at what we have to offer...'

Brooke gave her a playful nudge. 'You're a nightmare!'

'I know...' Felicity gave an exaggerated shiver. 'Blimey, that crept up on me – I'm suddenly freezing; might be time for another hot chocolate. Want one?'

'Yes, but you might want to hold that thought for a minute...' Brooke nodded discreetly in the direction of an approaching figure.

'Oh, well that certainly has warmed me up,' Felicity said quietly, and then continued more loudly: 'Manon! Good to see you!'

'I have come to see your goods,' Manon said, her gaze taking in the stall. 'I nearly gave up; I couldn't find you.'

'It's huge, isn't it?' Felicity agreed. 'The market, I mean. I've never seen anything this big.'

Manon took a pair of earrings from a stand to inspect them. 'Usually I don't care for it, but this year I am a little more interested.'

'Do you like those?' Felicity asked.

Manon held them up to the light for a closer look. 'How much?'

'To you, free,' Felicity said. 'I did tell you last night to come and choose something.'

'I did not know if you meant it.'

'Of course we did!'

As Manon caught her eye, Brooke smiled and nodded agreement. 'Absolutely. I don't know what we would have done if you hadn't turned up and saved our skins.'

'Hmmm...' Manon put the earrings back and took a different pair from the stand. She barely gave Brooke's textiles a second look, but that wasn't surprising. Manon's style was completely wrong for what Brooke made; her fitted black leather biker jacket, sharply cut cobalt hair and piercings gave off edgy, post-punk vibes that were a million miles away from Brooke's homespun vintage/hippy creations.

While Manon continued to peruse Felicity's jewellery, Brooke got distracted by an old lady asking about her tote bags. The lady wasn't French, Brooke was sure about that, but she spoke to Brooke in French anyway. Brooke was doing her best to reply when Manon tapped the woman gently on the arm to get her attention. They had a brief conversation and then Manon pointed to a bag.

'She likes that one but wants to know if the designs will come off in the rain.'

'Oh, no,' Brooke said, glancing between Manon and the customer. 'Not at all. I've made them totally washproof.'

Manon nodded and then relayed the information to the woman, who smiled and then indicated that she'd like to buy the bag by getting her purse out.

'Right...' Brooke gave her a brisk smile and wrapped up the bag before handing it over. The lady paid and Brooke gave the change. '*Merci!*'

As the lady went on her way with her purchase, Brooke turned to Manon. 'Thanks so much. You don't want a job on here, do you? My French is nowhere near as good as Felicity's, so when she's distracted it's a nightmare.'

'You must have more confidence in what you are saying,' Manon told her with a shrug. 'I'm sure it will get better the longer you are in Paris.'

'It'll have to,' Brooke said. 'Thank you all the same.'

Manon waved away Brooke's gratitude. '*Pas de problème.*' She turned back to Felicity. 'I think... Those...' She pointed to a pair of orange triangle-shaped earrings with a white swirl running through them.

'Perfect,' Felicity said. 'If you'd asked me to choose for you, I'd have chosen these exact ones.'

As Felicity wrapped them, Manon reached over the counter to a little stack of their business cards and took one. Brooke noted it, and also that the business cards were kept close to their cash box. If Manon had been able to reach that easily, then they really ought to keep it somewhere else.

As Brooke tried, discretely, to put it out of sight, Manon slipped their card into her pocket. When Brooke looked again, Manon was taking a second card.

'Do you have a pen?' she asked.

'Um... hang on...' Brooke went through her handbag. A pen was a thing she always carried, though finding it wasn't always so simple. Somehow they always slipped to the bottom of her bag and refused to show themselves when they were needed. 'Here we go,' she added after a few moments.

Manon took the pen from her, wrote on the second card and handed it to Felicity. 'There is a bar near our apartment block. Perhaps you'd both like to join me for a drink.'

She said *both* but gave the card to Felicity, along with a lingering look that had Brooke convinced it was only one of them she was interested in.

'We'd love to.' Felicity took the card before handing Manon the wrapped earrings.

'Thank you for my gift,' Manon said.

'Thank you for the invite,' Felicity replied. '*A bientôt!*'

'For sure,' Manon said, and then, with a last look of acknowledgement at Brooke, disappeared back into the crowds.

Felicity inspected the card for a moment and then grinned at Brooke.

'Well played,' Brooke said in a wry tone. 'Little Miss Determined has manifested another win.'

Felicity laughed. 'Hey, this one's on her! I think I played it pretty cool, all things considered.'

'Sure you did,' Brooke said, refolding some tea towels that had got crumpled up as a customer had looked through them. 'So cool we could have fried eggs on you.'

Dusk fell early, as it did in the darkest depths of winter, and as the sky turned lilac and orange, a day that had struggled to shake the early morning frost now became bitterly cold. Despite this, Brooke was happy. Their first day of trading had gone well, and, as Manon had promised, the more she practised her French, the more confident Brooke became. It was far from perfect, but she was beginning to feel that if she kept things simple and didn't ask for any life stories, she'd be able to get by.

Daytime was busy but fairly low-key, but it was night-time when the market really came alive. The Christmas-themed pop-up bars pumped out music – pop and rock and more traditional seasonal tunes – while the crowds swelled with revellers as well as shoppers, out to enjoy the atmosphere and the food and drink on offer. Couples strolled hand in hand and sometimes lips to lips, while families passed by with skipping children between them or taking extra care with elderly relatives, and all joked and laughed and marvelled at the lights and decorations. The air was filled with scents – both sweet and salty and potently alcoholic, frosty lungfuls bringing a different smell each time, while the lights of the carousels and Ferris wheel and skating rink and all manner of other amusements filled the space with colour.

Brooke had attended many Christmas markets in her time –

her home city hosted one every year and it was such a pretty affair that visitors from all over the local area and beyond came to see, but she'd never experienced anything like this one. It was as if the whole world had been covered with lights and colour, not an inch left untouched. With all the music and laughter and the smells of the food and drink and the magical scenery all around, it was impossible to feel anything but festive, and that was true even for the people who were there to work. Though being here certainly didn't feel like work – not for Brooke at any rate, especially when Felicity wandered off for a quick break and returned with two cups of piping hot *vin chaud* for them.

'To keep our spirits up and our cockles warmed,' she'd said as Brooke raised a questioning eyebrow. It had certainly done that and was so strong it had made Brooke – who usually had no problem holding her drink – a little tipsy into the bargain.

They worked late, taking advantage of the crowds gathering to get food and entertainment, curious to see how it would affect trade for them. They were there anyway, enjoying the atmosphere, so it was no hardship to keep the stall open at the same time. Some of their fellow traders had packed up for the day by the early evening, but many had remained open like Brooke and Felicity.

They left as the crowds began to thin and the bars, food stands and amusements had started to pack up too. Although the crowds had thinned out, there were still enough people for Brooke and Felicity to feel safe. They walked some of the way to their apartment, through the most famous streets and boulevards, soaking up a little more of the addictive atmosphere, and then hailed a cab. Brooke would have been happy to go back on the metro, but Felicity was tired and they weren't yet familiar with their stops, and they decided that just this once – it was too expensive to be a regular thing – they'd make life easy for themselves.

At the apartment, as Felicity paid the driver, Brooke

happened to glance up at the block to see a face at a first-floor window. She could have sworn it was Manon, watching them, but a moment later whoever it was disappeared behind closed curtains, and with one thing and another, Brooke completely forgot to tell Felicity about it.

CHAPTER NINE

Now that the stall was set up and ready to go, all that was required at the start of each trading day was to unlock the log chalet that housed it, open the shutters and welcome the customers. Well, not quite of course – there was still a daily float to organise, payment machines to connect and stock to replenish, but as the market as a whole didn't open until 11 a.m., Brooke and Felicity had time to sleep in for an hour or so in the morning.

On the second day, there had been no lie-in for Brooke, however. As they had only bought a few groceries to tide them over on their arrival, she took advantage of waking early to go out and find a supermarket, leaving Felicity still drinking coffee in the apartment in her pyjamas. The one nearby seemed expensive, and so they'd decided to check out one or two others to see if they were better, if only because they didn't want to spend all of the money they made here on food.

She found one, thanks to the map function on her phone, a couple of blocks away. It was small, with a faded sign and shabby window displays, and chaotic shelves inside where everything seemed to be stacked on top of each other and the presentation made absolutely no sense, but it had the basics they needed and a certain hectic charm. It was certainly authentic, and because of its less than gleaming facade and downmarket location, the prices weren't too bad either.

It hadn't taken Brooke long to figure out that Paris was going to be even more expensive than she'd anticipated, so it was a relief to find a local shop that was a bit more affordable. And like all French supermarkets, even though some of the goods on offer weren't exactly top-notch or healthy, they had a fresh produce section that looked wonderful and an in-store bakery where she could get fresh warm pastries and bread.

Brooke's gaze ran along the baskets of the bakery. Everything was so tempting, and she was so hungry she wanted to buy it all.

When she finally got to the till, her basket contained apples and pears and boxes of mixed nuts to nibble on, some cheese with holes in and bread and cooked meats that she wasn't sure about but looked like some kind of mortadella or something else ham-like, and enough baked goods to last them for a month – though she was fairly sure they'd be gone by the end of the day.

'*Bonjour*.'

Brooke loaded her shopping onto a conveyor belt that was almost hidden behind shelves crammed with everything from chewing gum to haemorrhoid cream, their contents spilling over and completely obscuring the back of the cash register. The shop assistant looked to be about a hundred, peering at her over thick spectacles, with nicotine-stained fingers and a cough that backed up the suggestion that she was no stranger to a pack of full-tar cigarettes. This was the real Paris, Brooke thought as she handed over her money and packed her own bag – raw and unfiltered, and it was thrilling to feel a part of it, of the proper lives of ordinary Parisians instead of just being another tourist. This was what she'd come for. Four weeks of this would have the old Brooke back, only better, more travelled, more exciting.

Who's stuck in a rut now, Johnny? she thought as she left the shop.

Striding down the road, she felt like the main character from a movie. That was, until her purse slid out of her jeans pocket where she'd shoved it in a hurry to make way for the queue at the till behind her, and it burst open, sending coins and notes across the pavement. As she hurried to pick them up, a young man stopped to help her.

'*Merci, merci...*' she said, taking the notes from him. '*Merci beaucoup!*'

He said something about being careful as he walked away – at least that's what it sounded like.

OK, Brooke thought, *perhaps not quite so cosmopolitan yet. Baby steps after all.*

But still, it felt like starting again, and that could only be a good thing.

After breakfast, they arrived at the stall so full of pastry and coffee that even the already sweet scents of the nearby crêpe van as it opened couldn't persuade Brooke to feel hungry. The way she felt now, she wouldn't be hungry again until March. There had been a vague panic that they needed to open up in good time, and as the metro had been very busy they'd eventually arrived at the market with only minutes to spare. They needn't have worried though. There were shutters that remained down around them, and customers were still thin on the ground, even half an hour after opening. The lights were all switched on, but daylight – even the grey dishrag of a morning they had today – diluted them so that they barely made an impact. It was a far cry from the whirl of colour and excitement of the night before. Brooke had to conclude that perhaps it really was after dark that all the magic happened.

Today, as things got underway, Brooke already hitting her

stride and more relaxed for it, she was able to take more notice of people as well as surroundings. She was mildly surprised to pick out so many foreign voices as they passed by: British of course, as well as Irish, American, Canadian, German and Italian, Japanese, Chinese, Korean... and so many others that she could only guess at. In fact, it seemed to Brooke that native French speakers were in the minority judging by what she could hear today.

Trade was steady, as it had been the day before. They had a lot of interested browsing but not all of it turned into sales. Brooke's printed tote bags were her bestselling item – some people were buying them because they liked them, but some were buying them just to carry things they'd bought at other stalls. Not that Brooke was going to complain – a sale was a sale after all – but it did seem a little sad that her hard work on the designs wasn't being noticed by those people.

As the bags continued to sell, she began to panic that she hadn't made enough of them and was going to sell out long before the markets were over in the New Year. There was still almost a month to go before the big day, and the thought made Brooke seriously consider outsourcing the job of making more to some local company – there wouldn't be much point in being there if she had nothing to sell.

It was 9.30 p.m. when Brooke was taken by surprise by a huge yawn.

'Sorry!' she said. 'That came out of nowhere!'

Felicity looked out at the crowds filling the walkways. 'It still looks busy, but I don't think they're here to buy stuff,' she said. 'Not this late. Maybe we should pack up.'

Brooke shook her head. 'I'm fine. It's my fault for getting up so early. One thing's for sure, I won't have any problems staying in bed tomorrow morning.'

'I'll believe that when I see it. You've never been good at staying in bed.'

'True. I'll have a bloody good go, though.'

'I'm a bit tired too, and I really don't think it's going to be worth staying much longer. Why don't you start totting up the cash and I'll deal with the card machine? Then we can think about packing up if we haven't had a customer in that time.'

'Go on then.'

Brooke wasn't too worried about counting out cash on the stall. They were inside a little log cabin with three solid walls and a counter she could hide the money beneath, and there was so much going on beyond their pitch that nobody was likely to notice what she was doing anyway. Still, for some reason, something spooked her.

'You know what,' she said pensively, 'I might just bag all this up and count it back at the apartment. We can go to the bank deposit place first thing in the morning.'

'Do you think that's a good idea? Taking it all the way back to our place and keeping it there overnight? I could take it to the bank now.'

'Not alone you couldn't. And it's further away than you think.'

Felicity sounded unconvinced but nodded. 'Whatever you want.'

As Brooke stuffed notes and coins into a cloth bag she heard Felicity's professional tone change into something more familiar as she greeted someone and looked up to see Manon at the counter. She was wearing full leathers and, most notably, had her short hair tucked behind her ears to show off the earrings Felicity had given to her.

'Oh, hi, Manon,' Brooke said.

'I thought we might visit that bar tonight,' Manon said, though Brooke, once again, got the impression that Manon meant just her and Felicity. It was obvious in the way she looked at her and barely gave Brooke a second glance.

'I'm pretty tired,' she said. 'But I don't mind at all if you two want to go without me.'

'Awww, Boo...' Felicity began, 'we couldn't—'

'Honestly,' Brooke replied. 'It's fine. I'd be rubbish company tonight anyway; we've just had a conversation about how shattered I am.'

Felicity looked doubtful. 'Are you sure you'll be OK?'

'Perfectly. Listen, why don't I finish packing here and you go with Manon now? Are you going via the apartment?'

Felicity looked at Manon. 'Could we? I could do with getting changed if we're going to a bar.'

'Sure. I have my motorbike – it would not take us long to go there first.'

'Then could you take the thing we just mentioned?' Brooke asked Felicity. 'It makes sense, especially now you're with Manon on the bike.'

'OK. But will you be alright packing up?'

'Yes!' Brooke smiled at her and, as discreetly as she could, Brooke handed the now full cash bag to Felicity, who zipped it into her jacket.

'It's going to be alright in there?' she asked.

'Safe as houses,' Felicity said with a firm nod.

'Right, clear off then. I'll see you in the morning. Have fun, won't you?'

'Take a cab home,' Felicity called back as they walked away. 'No walking alone.'

'I won't! Now bugger off!'

Half an hour later, Brooke pocketed the keys to the shutter padlock and turned for home – or what counted for home for the next few weeks. She'd told Felicity she'd get a cab but now, with plenty of people still out on the streets, she didn't feel that she wanted or needed one. She'd start out on foot, make the most of the atmosphere around the Jardin des Tuileries, and if she felt unsafe once she left the crowds she'd either head for the nearest metro station or find a taxi to take her the rest of the way.

As she passed the crêpe van she noticed a lull in trade and decided to take advantage of that by grabbing a snack. Once again, not particularly healthy, but it did smell divine and would save her the bother of cooking when she got back to the apartment. She ordered one filled with hot apple and cinnamon from a good-looking man whose nimble fingers wrapped it so quickly he could probably wrap crêpes in his sleep before sitting on a nearby seat to eat it.

Lost in the sights and sounds of the market, Brooke was content. Felicity had been right about one thing: being here had begun to feel like a fresh start, and she'd barely given Johnny or her broken heart a second thought.

Two men sat on the bench along from hers, dressed in dark colours with hoods pulled up. She didn't pay them much attention, except to remark inwardly that she hadn't expected to find the sort of lads here that she'd usually cross the road to avoid back home. But as they talked amongst themselves, heads low, they were quickly forgotten. Perhaps she ought to have been more nervous, but she was too weary and full of sugar for that. Besides, the markets were still swarming and she felt safe here. As she finished her crêpe and screwed up the packaging, she noticed them get up and move away.

Shortly afterwards, Brooke got up too. After finding a bin to dispose of her wrapper she went on her way. Though she was quickly getting used to the area immediately around the market, she still had to pay close attention to street signs and handily placed tourist maps. And though she wasn't too worried, she knew better than to get her phone out and walk around with it in her hand while she used the map function. As a last resort, if she got very lost, she'd have to, of course, but if she could leave it in her bag, that seemed like a much safer idea.

Once she'd got past Place de la Concorde, the crowds started to thin, but there were still plenty of people strolling down pristine avenues and boulevards strung with lights and decorations, their marble pavements gleaming.

Stopping to look at another city map pinned to the side of a bus shelter, Brooke frowned. She was heading out of the main tourist haunts now and a little confused about the next section of her route. Maybe it was time to hail that cab after all, or, as she was already at a bus stop, if she could work out whether the one she needed ran from here, she could hop on a bus instead.

As she walked round to see if there was a timetable on the inside of the shelter, she was suddenly yanked violently backwards. She somehow managed to keep her feet, but realised someone was trying to pull her bag from her shoulder and clapped a hand to it. They pulled harder and this time she wasn't strong enough to stay upright. She lost her footing but stubbornly clung to the bag. Everything she needed was in there and she wasn't giving it up without a fight.

A dark figure bent down and grabbed at the strap. Brooke held it tighter, and it was then she saw the second one and recognised the two youths who had been sitting close to her on the bench as she'd eaten her crêpe. Had they been scoping her out, gauging how much of an easy target she might be? Had they followed her all this way until they'd reached more deserted streets? Just how much danger was she in right now?

There was no time to ponder any of this. The one who was trying to pull her bag from her growled something she didn't catch, though there was no mistaking the menace in it, and the other one advanced on her now.

'Get off!' she screamed as the second tried to pull her across the pavement by her hair. Luckily it was tied in a bun so he couldn't get a decent hold, but that didn't stop him from trying again, grabbing for her while his accomplice tried once more to loosen her grip from her bag. 'Help! Someone please help! *Aidez moi!*'

It was no good – Brooke could feel the bag slipping from her grasp and was now too frightened by what the second man might do to her to worry about what the first was going to do with her handbag. Was this worth getting beaten up – or worse – for?

But then she heard another voice and looked up just in time to see a stranger punch the man who was trying to grab her. A seriously impressive left hook sent him skidding backwards. It also distracted the man who was trying to get her bag so that he let go long enough for Brooke to back out of range.

Despite the blow, the one who'd been punched scrambled to his feet. He swung at Brooke's would-be rescuer, but the stranger ducked and hit the mark with a second blow. Whoever this guy was, he knew how to fight, and from what Brooke could see, he was far bigger and stronger than the two youths who were trying to mug her. The mugger got his balance back and paused, eyeing the stranger keenly, seeming to weigh up his odds for a moment. He must have decided he didn't fancy them, because instead of retaliating again, he ran, leaving his accomplice alone.

The other youth wasn't so easily spooked. He gestured arrogantly at the stranger, willing him to attack. The man moved in, but this guy was quicker than his accomplice and swerved, aiming a retaliatory blow that failed to land on target but did succeed in shoving Brooke's Good Samaritan with such force he staggered backwards into the steel tubing of the bus shelter and slid down it.

Brooke got to her feet and aimed a kick at the remaining mugger, missing the groin she'd been going for but managing to connect with his thigh and knocking him off balance. She went for another go and he backed off, feeling at his pockets. Something glinted in the lamplight, something steely and sharp in his hand.

He's got a knife! Brooke suddenly thought, and cold dread washed over her. But then there were more voices, and he looked up at the same time as Brooke to see people who'd begun to take notice of the fracas coming towards them. Seeing this, the second attacker did the same as his partner in crime: he turned and ran off into the night.

Perhaps half a dozen people crowded round her, asking if she was OK.

'*Oui, merci... merci beaucoup...*'

It was then that she noticed a couple of people kneeling down at the bus shelter. Then she saw why – the man who'd come to her aid at the beginning was still crumpled at the foot of the bus shelter, his eyes closed and his head lolling to one side.

'*Monsieur!*'

Brooke ran to him.

'Hey... please... *monsieur*, wake up!' She turned to the others. 'Someone call an ambulance! He's hurt!'

While a young woman who seemed to know what she was doing checked his pulse, someone else was already dialling for help. Brooke turned back to the unconscious man.

'This is all my fault! I'm so sorry!'

Not that he could hear a word of it, but still, she felt an overwhelming need to apologise and keep apologising until her throat was so hoarse nothing new would come out.

'Miss...'

A soft voice and an accent... American perhaps? She looked up to see an older man address her. 'Help is coming – please don't get so distressed.'

'Thank you,' she said but turned back to the man on the ground and willed him desperately to wake.

'Is he your friend?' the American asked.

She shook her head. 'I don't know him at all. He literally

just stepped in to save me from being mugged. There were two of them, you see...'

'Wow, good job!' the American said. 'A shame he got knocked down. You should be careful walking the city alone at night, though, miss.'

Well, thanks for the sage advice...

She turned to the man on the ground and watched intently, desperate for some sign that he was coming back to consciousness, but although he let out the odd groan and seemed as if he was trying to move, he didn't.

The group of people who had come to her aid started to drift away, probably assuming that the woman who was checking the injured man, the American who'd called for the ambulance and Brooke herself had it all in hand.

'Do you think he'll be alright?' Brooke asked the American, but the woman kneeling next to her answered.

'I think so,' she said. Her accent didn't sound French, and definitely not English or American. Brooke was so tired and so confused and shaken it was hard to tell – she was only relieved that she'd chanced upon so many English speakers in her time of need.

'Are you a doctor?' she asked her.

'Oh no.' The woman smiled. 'Not at all. I have a little knowledge of sports injuries, but there are plenty of concussions on the sports field, so I know what to do.'

'He's concussed then?'

'Most likely.'

'Is that bad? Will he be brain damaged or anything?'

'I don't think so.'

Brooke twisted nervous fingers together as she stared at the man again. Why hadn't she just let the stupid handbag go? A well-meaning stranger was badly injured because of her. He looked about forty. He probably had a wife and kids and people who needed him – he probably ought to be somewhere right now and someone would be worrying about why he wasn't there.

The sound of distant sirens reached them. It wasn't an unusual sound in central Paris – Brooke had gathered that much in the short time she'd been there – but it held a new and horrible significance for her now.

As the sound grew louder as if drawing closer, Brooke hoped they were on their way here – as far as she was concerned, the professional help couldn't come quickly enough. By now she was feeling desperate and wretched and almost wished she could swap places and be lying on the pavement concussed instead of this poor man who'd done nothing except try to help a stupid stranger who wouldn't let go of a stupid, worthless handbag. What was a phone and a few euros worth now? She didn't even have the stall's takings with her – Felicity, in an unwitting stroke of genius, had taken those out of harm's way. There really hadn't been anything in her bag that couldn't have been replaced.

He let out another faint groan and she turned back to him. But then she peered closer and something clicked.

'Wait a minute... I *know* him! Where do I know him from?' She looked at the woman. 'Do you know him? Is he famous? Bloody hell! Have I concussed someone famous?'

'I don't think so,' the woman said. 'I don't recognise him.'

'I do! I know I know him from somewhere, I just can't work out where!'

'Miss,' the American cut in, 'you seem a little distressed again. There's a bar over there – would you like me to get you a glass of water?'

'I *know* him!' Brooke insisted, looking intently at the man on the floor. 'How?'

'The cavalry is here!' the American said as an ambulance stopped nearby, lights flashing but sirens now turned off. Two paramedics rushed over and the American began to explain to them what had happened. With a brief nod of understanding, they started to tend to him, asking the sports injury woman and Brooke to move out of the way so they could work.

She stood and watched, fingers still knotted together, listening hard to try and catch what they were saying. And then the injured man started to come round. Brooke heaved a sigh of relief as he opened his eyes, though he was barely focusing on anything. Then a phone on the pavement next to him began to ring. It wasn't hers, so Brooke realised it must have fallen from the man's pocket during the altercation with the muggers. He confirmed it by staring at the phone as it rang, though he looked confused and made no effort to answer it. One of the medics reached for it instead, swiped to answer and had a brief conversation with someone, presumably someone who said they knew the patient, before ending the call and putting the phone on the ground again.

'Maybe I should keep that safe,' Brooke began, worried that it would get left behind when they put the patient in the ambulance. 'Just until you're done.'

Nobody replied, and instead, the man on the ground groped around until his fingers closed over it and then he slipped it back into his pocket. He didn't look to see who'd been trying to contact him and he didn't ask what they'd said to the medic.

Strange, Brooke thought, but, then again, she supposed he was concussed and probably not thinking straight.

There followed some mild disagreement. While they'd been with him, the injured man did seem to improve. He could focus more now and was sitting straighter and talking a little. It seemed that the medics still wanted him to get in the ambulance, but he didn't appear to think that was necessary. To prove his point, he tried to stand up, only to stumble against the bus shelter and slide back down it to sit again.

A moment later, a shrieking voice echoed around the boulevard and a woman came running out of the darkness towards them. Her long coat was flapping around her, hair flying behind like she was some kind of goddess – though her voice was more siren or harpy than anything more ethereal. To Brooke's surprise, she sounded very pissed off.

'Armand!'

The man on the ground looked up and groaned at her approach. If she was his nearest and dearest, he didn't seem very pleased to see her.

'*Que s'est-il passé?*' she asked sharply.

He shook his head but didn't speak. But he could, right? Hadn't Brooke just heard him argue with the medics? Maybe the speech came and went. Maybe he simply didn't know how to start explaining it. She turned to one of the medics.

'*Que s'est-il passé?*' she repeated.

He didn't seem very interested in her demands either, only pointed vaguely at Brooke and her two helpers as he put away one of those finger-clamp things that Brooke had seen on hospital programmes that she thought monitored someone's blood pressure, though she'd never been too sure.

The woman got up and marched towards them, firing questions before she'd even got halfway. Brooke raised her hands in a gesture of surrender – in this situation literally because she felt as if she was under attack all over again and she'd had enough of that tonight.

'I'm so sorry,' she began, but then checked herself. '*Je suis désolé. Je ne comprends pas; je suis anglais.*'

The woman rolled her eyes as if to say she might have known some soppy tourist would have had something to do with all this but then smoothed her expression.

'The driver reports that you can tell me about the incident,' she said in heavily accented English.

Brooke nodded. 'I'm sorry but I think it might have been my fault. In fact, it was definitely my fault... I was almost mugged, you see... robbed, I mean – some men tried to steal my bag and...' She nodded towards the injured man. 'He was helping me and hit his head. I mean, the robbers pushed him... you see?'

'Tsk! *Idiot!*'

Brooke wondered whether she was calling her an idiot or the man, or perhaps both of them. She chanced a closer look at her interrogator. She was tall, close to five ten, Brooke would have said – certainly taller than Brooke's five four. She was well dressed in the same way the man was, with long, sleek hair that might have been dark blonde or brown, though it was hard to tell in the street lamps. Both dressed in tailored coats, both good-looking, both around the same age... they looked like they ought to be a couple and Brooke quickly decided that they probably were.

'Will he be alright?' she asked, glancing to her side and noting that sports-injury woman had already gone. She probably hadn't fancied the same scrutiny that Brooke had been subjected to, and Brooke could hardly blame her for that.

'How should I know?' the possible-girlfriend snapped.

Brooke clamped her mouth shut to prevent a less than courteous reply from slipping out. It was her fault, granted, and the woman had every right to blame her entirely for the situation, but it wasn't like she'd got mugged on purpose, and she'd hardly asked him to wade in. Well, she'd put out a general SOS, but he'd elected to answer it of his own free will. She'd felt bad about it until now, but under this new onslaught she had started to feel distinctly aggrieved. Her rescuer was injured, but she wasn't exactly having a picnic here either.

'Who are you?' the woman asked, dragging Brooke's gaze back from the man on the ground, where it had wandered as she tried to figure out for herself whether he was any better than the last time she'd looked.

'I'm nobody,' Brooke said.

'Why were you with him?'

'I wasn't. As I explained, he was passing by and he helped me. I've never met him before...'

The last bit was a tiny white lie, because Brooke was still convinced she had met him somewhere, though she couldn't think where. It wasn't a detail she was about to give this woman, though.

'Actually,' she added as an afterthought, though she had no idea how it might go down, 'I don't suppose I can have your telephone number?'

The woman stared at her. 'My number?' she asked incredulously.

'Yes. Just so I can call later to see if everything is alright. I'd only call once and then I'd delete it.'

The woman gave her head a vigorous shake. 'No. Give your number to me. I will call you.'

'Oh, OK...' Brooke got her phone out. 'Sure... I suppose that's a much better idea, from your perspective, at least.' She found the page and showed it to the woman, who copied the digits into her own phone.

The woman put her phone into a clutch bag. 'You are on vacation?' she asked, not unkindly this time.

'Actually I'm working,' Brooke said, hoping the change in tone meant she was getting somewhere with her. 'I'm here for the month – I have a stall at the Jardin des Tuileries. You should come... I mean, if you need anything at all or if there's anything I can do, you know, in light of what's happened, you can come and see me there and you can choose whatever you'd like for free?'

'Hmm...' the woman said. 'You may go. There's no point you hanging around.'

It was Brooke's turn to stare in disbelief. She'd just offered an olive branch and she was being *dismissed*? Surely this woman could understand that Brooke had a vested interest in the man's well-being... actually, it was much more than that.

He'd risked his life to save her – she *had* to know that he was going to be alright, and she didn't want to leave until she could be sure.

'They are taking Armand to the hospital,' she added.

Brooke glanced over. He was allowing them to put him on a stretcher but he didn't look any happier about it than he had when he'd been arguing with them earlier.

Brooke turned back to the woman in front of her. If this had been her partner, she'd have done what she was told too.

'Don't forget to phone me,' Brooke reminded her. 'Just so I know. I'll worry for weeks otherwise.'

'Why?'

'Because... I just will.'

'But Armand is not your concern.'

'I know but... well, I sort of feel as if he is.'

'He is not your boyfriend.'

Brooke held in a frustrated sigh. 'I feel responsible for the accident, that's all.'

'You are,' she said tartly.

'And I'm trying to say I'm sorry.'

'Will your sorry make Armand well again?'

'Well, no, but...'

The woman turned away at the sound of the ambulance doors being closed and strode towards the vehicle. After a brief word with the driver, she began to walk away, down the boulevard in the opposite direction, leaving the ambulance to drive off. Brooke stared after her. If she was this guy's partner, it was a strange thing to do, leaving him to go to hospital alone. All that fuss and she didn't even get in with him?

'Miss... are you OK?'

Brooke looked at the American. His voice was so very nice and soothing...

It was then she realised the reason for his concern – she could feel herself shivering violently.

It was cold and she'd been standing in place for a long time, but it was more than that. It was only now, in the aftermath of events, adrenalin subsiding, that the full force of what had happened hit her. She'd been attacked. She'd been vulnerable and helpless and very much in danger in a city she didn't know and where everyone spoke a language she barely spoke, and if not for the timely intervention of a stranger who'd happened to be passing at the right moment and had the inclination to help, God only knew where she might be right now. In an alleyway bleeding out? At the bottom of the Seine?

Suddenly the street began to spin, bile rising in her throat, her legs weak.

'Miss...?'

'I'm OK,' she said in a tiny voice that she could barely hear coming from herself.

'Miss, you don't look fine, if you don't mind me saying so.'

'Maybe I'm a little bit not fine,' she said, doubling over and trying to steady herself.

'Do you have someone you can call to come and get you?'

'Um... yes, I suppose...'

She dragged in a breath and tried to straighten up. With shaking hands she got out her phone and dialled Felicity's number.

'Hey, Boo!' Felicity said. 'Guess where we are!'

'Oh, thank God!' Brooke said in a weak voice, and it was as much as she could do not to sob with relief at the sound of her friend's voice. 'I'm sorry, but could you—'

'What's wrong?' Felicity cut in sharply.

'I... well, I'm kind of... oh, could you come and get me?'

'Get you? Where from? Aren't you at the apartment yet?'

'No, I'm at the...' Brooke looked vacantly around. It was getting harder to take anything in. 'I'm on a street. Sorry...'

'Hang on,' Felicity said. 'I'll put Manon on the phone. Describe where you are – she'll know it.'

'No, I...'

Much as she wanted Felicity's reassuring presence, she didn't want to talk to Manon. With one thing and another, she was beginning to feel as if she was giving Manon plenty of reasons to think her silly and a bit pathetic and useless. Certainly, she was developing a habit of being rescued by their new friend – in fact, she was developing a habit of needing to be rescued, full stop, and it wasn't one she liked.

Another wave of nausea washed over her. 'I just want... I'll walk. Don't worry – I'll be back soon.'

'Don't be stupid – I'm coming to get you.'

'No... don't ruin your evening for me... I'll be...'

Brooke ended the call. Felicity had still been talking, but she couldn't listen because of the buzzing in her head, and because she was afraid that if she didn't put her phone away she was going to drop it, given how her fingers were numb and the pavement wouldn't stay still.

'Miss...'

'I don't feel so...'

Brooke dropped onto a bench, unaware of how she'd even found it, and buried her head in her hands.

'Shall I call you a cab?'

Brooke wanted to tell him it wasn't necessary but it probably was. And then she started to cry.

'Oh my Lord!' the man said. 'Miss, what can I do?'

Pull yourself together...

Brooke's breath caught in her throat as she tried to get a grip on her sobs. She sucked in as hard as she could, but there was no plugging the breach now it had opened.

A gentle hand on her arm caused her to look up. A waiter, perhaps from the restaurant the American man had mentioned earlier (at least he was dressed like a waiter) stood in front of her with a glass in his hand. He held it out.

'Brandy, *mademoiselle*,' he said.

Touched by the simple gesture of kindness, Brooke started to cry again.

'*Mademoiselle*,' he said. 'Please drink. It will help.'

Brooke sniffed hard and took the glass, taking a sip.

'You must drink it all.'

Brooke sipped again and again, until the glass was empty. Almost instantly, its heat spread through her, returning life to her numb fingers and helping her to finally calm down.

'Thank you,' she said, handing back the glass with a small, grateful smile.

'Officers...'

The American man was now talking to a pair of gendarmes who had just arrived.

'When I saw the trouble I called the police,' the waiter explained, seeing her confusion. 'They have taken too long to come – everything is almost over.'

Brooke nodded. She supposed it was to be expected that the police would be involved at some point, and if it helped to catch her attackers, then she ought to make a statement. Besides that, the call had been made and now they were here they wouldn't allow their journey to be a wasted one. But she was exhausted now, emotionally spent, and all she wanted was to head back to the apartment and see Felicity.

Perhaps they'd take her home, she thought vaguely as the waiter went to talk to them. Driven back to her lodgings by French police... now that would be a story to tell when she got home.

CHAPTER TEN

Somehow, when Brooke woke the next morning she was still exhausted. She'd slept heavily – going to bed almost as soon as she'd got in and managed to impart the barest details to satisfy Felicity, who'd hurried home after their call – despite the events of the evening playing on her mind. She might have replayed some of it again while she dreamt, but thankfully she couldn't remember that now. Whatever her subconscious had been doing during the night, she only knew that when the alarm woke her, she wasn't ready at all.

The first thing she'd done on waking was reach for her phone, but there were no messages from the woman she'd asked to keep her informed on Armand's welfare. Brooke couldn't decide whether this was a good thing or not.

A watchful Felicity made breakfast and questioned her carefully while they ate. Was she alright to work? Was she sure she wasn't still traumatised? Ought they to seek medical attention just to be sure?

Brooke tried her best to reassure her and tried to turn the conversation to Felicity's evening with Manon. She didn't want to talk about hers because that would involve having to think about it again. It was far too soon for that. But Felicity gave very little away, preferring to concentrate on Brooke's well-being, and only said that they'd both enjoyed the bar and that Brooke would have to go and try it for herself when she was up to it.

The metro ride into the centre of the city was quiet – at least Brooke and Felicity were uncharacteristically subdued, though the train itself was busy. Brooke was almost relieved to see the market appear in front of her. Here, at last, was something she could get on with to take her mind off the horrible events of the previous evening.

But that was not to be. They'd barely opened up when Brooke gave an involuntary gasp. Felicity followed her gaze to see a man walking towards them. He was tall with dark hair that curled at the neck, green eyes that demanded attention and was wearing an expensive-looking tailored coat.

'Isn't that the guy who took our photo outside the Moulin Rouge?' she asked.

Suddenly, the answer Brooke had been searching for was clear. Of course! How had she failed to make the connection? No wonder she'd been convinced she knew him! Felicity had casually and unwittingly dropped the answer into her lap. The man who'd taken a battering for her the night before and the man who'd taken a photo for them was, in fact, one and the same!

He smiled as he approached, and for anyone who didn't know, it would have been hard to believe that only hours before he'd been concussed and hospitalised. He looked well now, positively rested, as if he'd taken a fortnight off and sat on a beach somewhere, which was more than could be said for Brooke herself. Not only did he look rested, but despite vague thoughts about how good-looking he was, for the first time Brooke noticed that he was more than good-looking; he was incredibly handsome, the sort of handsome that you only saw in movies.

'*Bonjour.*'

'How are you?' Brooke asked anxiously. She didn't even wait to find out if he spoke English, such was her hurry to talk to find out. 'I'm... *je suis désolé*... I'm sorry... about what happened to you. *Je suis...*'

He stopped her. 'I'm quite well,' he said in perfect English.

'That's good,' she said. 'I'm so sorry about what happened. What did the doctors say? Did you have to stay in hospital all night? Did they let you out today? I was so worried about you! I would have come to the hospital with you, but the ambulance had already gone and I thought your...' She flushed. 'The lady who came to you last night, I thought...'

'Lisette,' he said. 'No, she did not come. I did not need her.'

'She seemed very upset,' Brooke said. 'She was upset with me, but I think she seemed upset with you too. I mean... I asked her to let me know, but...'

She flushed again. Had she said too much? Was there something going on here that she ought to keep her nose out of?

He gave a shrug. 'She was. She says trouble follows me.' He felt at the back of his head with a rueful smile that suggested he might laugh at his own silliness. 'Last night, for once, she was right.'

It was at this point Brooke noticed Felicity following the exchange with interest. She'd probably got the gist of it, but Brooke decided she ought to fill her in anyway, out of courtesy if nothing else.

'Felicity, this is my knight in shining armour from yesterday.'

'Pleased to meet you,' Felicity smiled. 'Monsieur...'

'Call me Armand. I am pleased to meet you too.'

'You took our photo, you know,' Felicity said.

'Ah!' he exclaimed warmly, his eyes almost mischievous. 'Now I remember! Outside the...'

'Moulin Rouge!' Felicity prompted him.

'Yes, yes,' he replied. 'I am sorry I did not recognise you last night. Now that I see you, I wonder why I did not.'

'God, I wouldn't expect that!' Brooke said fervently. 'I think you might have been a bit busy fighting off muggers like some kind of superhero.'

'I have never been called a superhero before,' he said. 'I must not get used to it or I may start to believe it.'

'You should!' Felicity cut in. 'Brooke told me what happened. I wish I'd seen it – sounded like you were awesome.'

'Oh, I do not think it was anything special,' he said sheepishly, giving Brooke a smile that warmed her as if spring had suddenly arrived. 'Did you enjoy your evening at the Moulin Rouge?'

'God yes!' she replied. 'It was brilliant! Have you ever been? I expect you've been loads of times, haven't you?'

'Actually, no,' he said.

'Never? Not once?'

He gave a careless shrug. 'I live in Paris. When it is there all the time, it seems less appealing.'

'You take it for granted,' Felicity said. 'I get it. Like my great-aunt on the French side of my family who lived by the sea on the Côte Atlantique but never made time to go to the beach because she was like, "It's there all the time. If I don't go today, it will still be there tomorrow." You know what? She lived there all her life but for the last twenty years she never went once. And then she died. What a waste of a house by the beach, eh?'

'Indeed.' He smiled politely. 'So you are French?'

'Only on my mother's side,' Felicity said. 'My dad is from Norfolk originally.'

'Norfolk? Forgive me, where is...?'

'Oh, he's English,' Felicity said. 'Shame, but I suppose it's not his fault, and we can't all be perfect.'

Armand laughed lightly and then turned to Brooke. 'I hope you do not mind me coming to see you.'

'Of course not. It's very kind of you, but how did you...?'

'Actually, the police informed me you worked here. I came to see if you were OK.'

'God, I should be asking you that!' Brooke said breathlessly. 'You were the one who took the clobbering!'

'I did what any citizen would do. I am only sorry this horrible thing happened to you here. All you wanted was to work here and this... sometimes I am proud of this city, and sometimes not so much.'

'It could have happened anywhere – being in Paris makes no difference. I should have had my wits about me.'

'You shouldn't need to have your wits about you,' Felicity put in. 'You should be able to walk the streets at any time of the day in any city without fear of attack. That's the real crime here.'

'Very true,' Armand said. 'It is everyone's right to feel safe.'

'That's what I'm saying.' Felicity nodded vigorous agreement. 'That's exactly what I'm saying.'

'I never got a chance to thank you properly for what you did,' Brooke said to Armand. 'I feel as if there must be something more that I can offer than just thanks for everything. Is there anything we can do for you?'

'There is no need to thank me. Thank you for getting help when I was injured.'

'I wish I could say that was me' – Brooke looked embarrassed – 'but it was someone else. If I'm being truthful, I was a bit rubbish. After you went off in the ambulance, I sort of had... well I sort of freaked out. I wanted to go in the ambulance with you but I... I don't think I would have been much use in the end, even if they'd let me.'

'You stayed,' he said. 'I have seen people walk away from the stranger who has helped them when they in turn needed help.'

Brooke stared at him. 'Who would do that? I'd have never... How awful!'

But then she thought about it, how Lisette had walked away and left him to go to the hospital alone. Who was she to him? She had to be a girlfriend or fiancée or some significant other – that was the only thing that made sense in the context of what she'd seen. But the woman was cold as ice if she was able to do that. Was it her he'd been talking about or was he talking more generally?

'I'm not sure we have anything on the stall you'd be interested in,' she continued, unable to process the previous question without tying herself in knots, 'but please, to show my gratitude, if there's anything you'd like to take for anyone else who might like it... a gift of course. I wouldn't expect you to pay for it. I mean, maybe there's something on here your...' she paused. 'I mean, it's mostly girly stuff. Is there anything Lisette or any other woman in your life might like?'

He looked doubtful as he scanned their goods and, recalling Lisette, Brooke wasn't surprised. From what Brooke had seen of her, she looked like the sort of woman who'd favour chic designer shops rather than her retro, rustic offerings. It just seemed like the courteous thing to do, as they had with Manon, though, at the rate they were going, they'd have nothing left to sell as it would all get given away as thank-you gifts for their various saviours. And a little bit of her wanted him to refuse because perhaps that meant there was no significant woman in his life – not one he was related to at any rate.

Try as she might to deny it, she could barely tear her gaze from those green eyes. She felt like there was a connection too, even though good sense told her not to be so stupid. He was far too handsome and probably had queues of women chasing his affections – he was hardly going to be interested in her. Still, a girl could always have hope, and she couldn't deny she needed a bit of attention from a handsome man to help rebuild the self-esteem that had been so royally shattered by Johnny.

'That is not necessary,' he said after a pause. 'I'm only glad I was walking by at that time.'

'Me too!' Brooke replied, her tone utterly heartfelt. 'You'll never know how grateful I am! Please, you're sure there's nothing you'd like to take?'

'No, thank you. You have come to sell these things, not give them to me.'

'Then... how about we buy you a drink? Or join us for dinner? There must be something we can do for you.'

'Really, it is not necessary,' he repeated. 'I am happy to help.'

'We actually owe you twice now,' Felicity said, 'when you think about it. Once for the photo and again for Brooke's sorry arse. At least let us buy you a crêpe or a coffee from the van over there.'

'Ah...' He gave a small smile as he followed her gaze. 'That belongs to my friend, Jean-Luc. I can have coffee from him whenever I like. But the truth is' – he lowered his voice to a stage whisper – 'his coffee is terrible.'

'Wow, it certainly is a small world,' Brooke said. 'We've been buying coffee and chocolate from over there since the first day of the market.'

'Paris is a big city but a small town,' Felicity said.

Brooke gave her a sideways look.

'Manon says it,' Felicity explained. 'And I guess that demonstrates how true it is. Look how many times we've bumped into Armand already without even trying, and then we find we've been buying coffee from his friend.'

'Exactly,' Armand agreed.

'Well,' Felicity continued, 'I know you said you didn't want anything, but I agree with Brooke – we do owe you. So if there's anything we can do, anything you want, anything we can help with, no matter what it is, drop by. The stall's not moving any time soon.'

'You are only here for the markets?' he asked.

'Yes,' Brooke said. 'We'll be going home after that.'

'To England?'

'Yes.'

'A very nice bit of England,' Felicity said. 'If you're ever in Ely, you should look us up.'

Brooke shot her another sideways glance but Felicity didn't flinch. She was the picture of innocence, as always, even though Brooke recognised scheming. She'd said at their first meeting how good-looking Armand was, how she thought Brooke might enjoy a little fling, but had she forgotten the very inconvenient possibility of Lisette being his girlfriend as she plotted? They might not know exactly what the deal was, but still, there was as much of a chance that Lisette was his significant other as there was of him being single.

'I'm sure you are busy,' he said.

'Not yet, but we will be,' Felicity said cheerfully. 'At least we hope so.'

'Then I will leave you to work. I'm glad to see you looking well, Brooke,' he said, his smile so warm and his gaze so attentive that it was like seeing her well had made him the happiest man in the world.

'Thank you for coming,' she replied, the idea of throwing herself at him for a kiss ever more tempting. 'It was kind of you. If you're passing please come and say hello – we'd love to see you. We don't know too many people in Paris yet, so every friendly face is most welcome.'

'I will,' he said. 'Goodbye.'

'*Au revoir*!' Brooke replied.

Felicity left it a whole twenty seconds before she spoke. 'Interesting...' she said in a voice full of mischief.

Brooke glanced at her. 'I know what you're thinking, and don't. There's no chance, not in a million years!'

'Why not?'

'Look at him – he's like a god! He's not going to be interested in me.'

'Come off it. He was totally interested.'

'Well...' Brooke watched him disappear into the crowd. 'It's probably not a good idea, even if I was interested, which I might be, but we don't have time to get involved in a romance even if I was and he was.'

'You say that but... you can always make time for romance. You said as much when I met Manon – I'd totally have your back if you started something with Armand. Who's this Lisette woman again? The person who was supposed to text you how he was?'

'Yes, but it looks as if she couldn't be bothered.'

'Or maybe she doesn't know,' Felicity said, her tone very deliberate.

Brooke gave her a puzzled sideways glance. 'What do you mean?'

'You're assuming they're a couple, but perhaps they're not. He certainly wasn't saying so, and if she didn't go to the hospital with him and they're not a couple, maybe she doesn't yet know that he's been discharged and that he's alright.'

'Surely she'd have made an effort to find out? She gave him enough grief last night when it first happened.'

Felicity shrugged. 'I suppose she was shocked – someone she was meant to meet for whatever reason got beaten up. People act in weird ways when they're in shock. I mean, it's a big deal, no matter who they are to you. Unless it was Johnny, of course, and in that case...'

Brooke grinned. 'Don't even go there. So you don't think they're together? Armand and Lisette, I mean.'

'How should I know? But he never said she was his girl-

friend and you gave him plenty of prompting. And... he definitely liked what he saw when he looked at you.'

'No he didn't!' Brooke said with a self-conscious laugh. 'And
if Lisette isn't his girlfriend, what is she to him?'

'Sister, friend, colleague, client...? Honestly, could be any
number of things. You said you got her number; why not ask
her?'

'I couldn't do that. Besides, I don't have her number – she
has mine, and as she hasn't contacted me...'

'Ah, yeah, I see...' Felicity dug her hands deep into the
pockets of her coat. 'What about the crêpe guy? If he's such a
good friend, he'd be able to tell you the situation.'

'I couldn't just go up and ask him that – it'd be weird.'

Felicity raised her eyebrows. 'Would it?'

'And desperate.'

'Maybe it would be, but do you care? In a month you'll be
leaving Paris so what would it matter in the grand scheme of
things if you looked a bit desperate for five minutes with a
stranger you'll never see again?'

Brooke shook her head. 'I don't think I know either of them
well enough to be asking that sort of thing. Anyway, we won't
have time.'

'I'm sure we could work things out between us if we wanted
the odd hour off to do our own thing. We did say we shouldn't
be joined at the hip.'

'True, but we do need to focus on the stall when all is said
and done.'

'Hmm...' Felicity sighed, going to tidy her display cases in a
clear signal that she was now bored of the conversation. 'In that
case, you'll just have to be content with never knowing.'

An hour later, Brooke was wrapping a stack of tea cloths for a
customer when she noticed a girl with a tray of takeout drinks

coming to the stall. The girl gave the tray to Felicity and after a brief, pleasant exchange, walked away again. Felicity put them to one side, and once Brooke's customer had gone, she went over to investigate.

'Got a delivery service set up now, have you?' Brooke lifted the lid on a cup and sniffed. 'Coffee... God, do I need this – I can barely keep my eyes open today.'

'Actually, they're compliments of the crêpe guy.'

'What's his name again... Jean-Luc, was it?'

'Uh huh. At the request of his very good friend, Armand,' Felicity replied in a voice that was a bit too smug.

'That's very nice of him, isn't it,' Brooke replied in a purposely neutral tone.

Felicity was silent for a moment as she drank her coffee. But then, not to be bested, she began again.

'And you still don't think he fancies you?'

'Maybe, but I reckon it's probably more trouble than it's worth.'

'Oh, OK, so you don't fancy him? That's fine then, just so I know. Better not mention him again.'

'Of course I do! That's not the issue. Remember when Johnny dumped me for a woman he'd only met that week? Remember what a mess I was? That's why I'm not going near this with a long stick. Lisette was an absolute nightmare, a cold, stuck-up, rude, arrogant cow, but if there's any chance they're a couple... I could never do that to another woman, not even her.'

'It's not unknown for an attached person to be attracted to a different person to the one they're attached to. It happens. It wouldn't be your fault if so, and, actually, you'd be doing the other poor cow a favour because if it wasn't you now, it would be someone else turning his head further down the line. If your house is built on sand, sooner or later it's going to collapse, however much you ignore the cracks in the walls. And you still don't actually know if Lisette is his girlfriend.'

Brooke sighed. 'Look, it's been a weird couple of days. I just want to settle in and make some money without all this drama – is that too much to ask?'

'And enjoy the change of scenery in the process... I know.'

'And being here is enough, I don't need complications.'

Felicity was thoughtful for a moment. 'Like Manon?' she asked finally.

'God no!' Brooke put the lid back on her coffee and set it down. 'Not at all! Your situation is totally different. Of course I don't think you making friends with Manon is a problem.'

'What about more than friends?'

'You know whatever you have with her is fine by me! If she's a distraction, a bit of fun I'm happy for you, you deserve it! I mean... are you actually...? Has anything happened yet?'

'Not yet, but I think it might,' Felicity said, suddenly radiant. 'She's kind of amazing, isn't she? We haven't discussed the actual details yet, and I don't know if she's bi and likes guys too, but I know she's into girls, so that's a good sign, right? At least I have an outside chance, which is more than I usually get.'

'I'd say you have more than that,' Brooke said, shaking any doubts she might have about Manon. She certainly wasn't about to air them to Felicity, who seemed to have none at all and was clearly besotted, and she couldn't even say exactly what those doubts were about, only that she had a vague sense of misgiving when she thought about their new friend. Manon was far too mysterious, far too secretive – she'd appear and disappear, and she wouldn't say where she'd been or who she'd been with, and she gave off the kind of vibes that didn't invite you to ask, and something about all that didn't sit well with Brooke. But Felicity would say Brooke was being overcautious, like she was being with Armand, and that her trust issues stemmed from her stinging at Johnny's hand, and she'd probably be right.

'I don't plan to leave you alone every night,' Felicity broke into her thoughts. 'Just so you know.'

Brooke gave her a vague smile. 'Don't worry, I didn't think that for a minute.'

'And we'll probably want you to come out with us most of the time.'

'I'll be happy to come. Honestly, I don't have any problem with you and Manon.'

Felicity smiled. 'Thanks, Boo. I really like her.'

'I know. You're not the only one with eyes, you know. I can see she likes you too.'

'You think so?'

'I'm certain of it. Haven't you even broached that subject with her yet? It's not like you to be so slow.'

Felicity's smile turned into a grin. 'It's not, is it? But she's so out of my league and—'

'No she's not – you're every bit as gorgeous as she is.'

'Why thank you, but I know you're only saying that as my best friend.'

'I'm saying it because it's true. So, back to Manon... what are you waiting for?'

Felicity was about to reply when her attention was caught by someone at the stall.

'*Bonjour. Puis-je vous aider?*'

Brooke watched as they fell into easy conversation. Felicity showed her the mirror and told her she could try on anything except for earrings. She loved how open Felicity was, how unafraid to speak her mind, to call things exactly how she saw them. Wouldn't it be lovely to be even a little bit like that? Perhaps then she'd be able to follow Felicity's lead and simply enjoy pursuing or being pursued or whatever might be happening with Armand, the same way Felicity was enjoying the game with Manon. Whatever happened in the end, at least Felicity would have had the courage to try.

Obviously Brooke was attracted to Armand – most women would be, but in her mind it wasn't a good thing. It was a very

bad thing that needed to be nipped in the bud. And she was no
naive teenager either – she knew how these things often
worked. He'd come to her rescue, yes, and so he must be a good
man, but things were never quite as simple as that. He might
have seemed sweet and kind and charming and earnest, with
the sort of eyes that could remove knickers at twenty paces, but
that was only a first impression. For all she knew, he saw a challenge in her, someone he could seduce without consequences
because he knew she wouldn't be around long enough for there
to be any. The theory didn't fit what she knew of him, but that
wasn't very much at all. It was unlikely, but that didn't mean
she ought to disregard it entirely.

Her gaze travelled to the shoppers filling the walkways
between the stalls, some with food, some loaded with bags and
boxes, huddled in coats and scarves and hats, braced against a
freezing Paris day. Of all the people in this place, how was it
that Armand was the one who kept crossing her path? First
outside the Moulin Rouge, then the mugging, and then the reve-
lation that his friend owned the van where they'd been buying
most of their drinks as they'd worked over the last couple of
days. Why? Was there some significance? Or was it a set of
coincidences – however unlikely – that she was reading too
much into? What if it meant nothing at all?

Armand had been right about one thing, she recalled with a
faint smile as she retrieved her coffee and took another sip –
Jean-Luc's coffee might have been hot and strong and welcome
on a cold day, but while she wouldn't go as far as saying it was
terrible, it wasn't exactly great either. Then again, who was she
to look a gift horse in the mouth?

'Thanks, Armand,' she murmured, then smiled hopefully at
someone who'd wandered over to check out her textiles.
'Bonjour, monsieur.'

He looked up, barely acknowledged her, and then walked
away.

Well, you can't win 'em all, I suppose.

Brooke and Felicity took it in turns to have lunch, so one could take a break from the stall and maybe explore a little while the other minded the shop – so to speak. Felicity went first and duly returned after the allotted hour.

'Right, your turn,' she told Brooke.

'Great! I'm so ready for a break.'

'Oh, and I thought we ought to try this Lebanese restaurant I heard about near Montmartre.'

'Sounds good,' Brooke said vaguely, rooting in her bag for her purse. 'When?'

'Tonight, after we pack up here.'

'It'll be late,' Brooke replied doubtfully. Her concerns weren't only about the fact they'd be eating very late, but the ordeal of the previous night was still very fresh in her mind, and she wasn't sure she wanted to risk another late-night encounter with bad people.

'It doesn't have to be too late – we could head straight there on the metro.'

'Maybe. Let's see how things pan out. Where did you hear about it anyway?'

'Manon mentioned it,' Felicity said carelessly.

'Hmm... and would Manon be joining us?'

'I'm not sure...' Felicity repositioned a necklace on a board that hadn't needed repositioning. 'She said she might have something on tonight but if it falls through she could come and find us.'

Brooke smiled. 'I've never eaten Lebanese food so I suppose it would be nice to try it.'

'Yeah, we can't live on crêpes and hot dogs for the next month, no matter how good they are. So don't eat too much lunch – we don't want your appetite spoiled for later.'

'God, have you even met me? There's never any danger of spoiling my appetite no matter how much I eat for lunch! I'll see you shortly!'

Brooke let herself out of the little side door of the chalet and joined the crowds of the market, instantly going from player to spectator. It was a nice break, not having to be ultra polite and attentive constantly. She could let the current of bodies take her with no particular place to be other than to, at some point, get some food. She didn't care what that was either – she was happy to wander and stop if something took her fancy. And it was certainly never going to be dull, not in the most romantic city in the world.

As she walked she was more attuned than ever to the soul of Paris. There was romance, not only in the sense of love, but romance of culture, of history and spirit. It was in every stone of every grand building, in every lamp post and fountain and statue, in every iconic view. Paris was a work of art in itself, bigger and more beautiful than anything its galleries housed. Today she was filled with the sense that it was more than a place – it was a feeling, a way of life.

Brooke's wanderings took her out of the market and towards the river. Not just any old river, of course, but the Seine, possibly the most famous river in the world. Despite the cold, the sky spitting flurries of powdery snow every now and again, and clouds on the air with every breath, the walkways of the riverbanks were packed with people eating, drinking, laughing or taking photos, or simply meditating on the views. She sniffed, detecting toffee on the air. The smell was incredible and when she spotted the source – a vendor selling caramelised nuts from a steaming vat – she knew she had to get some.

They were sweet and warm as she munched on them from a paper cone and walked along.

A little further on a crowd was gathered to listen to a choir. Brooke stopped to listen too. She had no clue what they were singing about, only that there was an ethereal sort of quality to the crystal-clear voices as they rose into the air. A group of children came round with tins to collect for whatever charity the performance was in aid of. Brooke dropped all the euros she had spare in her pockets into one of them.

'*Merci beaucoup*,' the young girl said. She was so adorable that Brooke was sorely tempted to sweep her up and give her the biggest cuddle.

She stayed to listen to two more songs, and then it seemed as if the choir was packing away. She decided to walk some more, but then realised she hadn't been keeping track of the time at all. Pulling her phone out to check, she noted the missed call from Felicity and a text.

Don't tell me you've got into more trouble!

It was sent in jest, but Brooke had a feeling Felicity was genuinely worried, and she supposed she could see why. Brooke had a pretty terrible track record so far, and she hadn't even been in Paris a week yet. She typed a reply:

*Sorry! I got carried away exploring. On my way back –
I'll make it up to you!*

She put her phone away, ate the last of her nuts and pulled her scarf up high around her chin to keep warm. Now, she found herself pushing against the current of people that she'd found so pleasing earlier, and trying to go in the opposite direction from where it seemed everyone else wanted to go was far more frustrating. Searching for a clear path, perhaps at the edge of the promenade that ran this section of the river, her eyes locked onto a face in the crowd. But then the woman put her head down and hurried away.

Had that been Lisette? Brooke had met her only briefly, at

night and in very trying circumstances, so she couldn't be a hundred per cent certain, but she thought it was. She supposed it wasn't such a stretch to presume that if the woman lived and worked in Paris, she'd be out and about and maybe she'd end up in the same spot at the same time as Brooke. It wasn't so much that fact which had unnerved her – it was the way she'd been staring in Brooke's direction like someone had glued half a lemon into her mouth that was unsettling. And when she was spotted, instead of acknowledging Brooke, as would be far more normal, she'd hurried away, as if she had something to hide.

Now *that* was weird.

CHAPTER ELEVEN

When Brooke got back to work Jean-Luc from the crêpe van was talking to Felicity. The market was noisy now and they spoke in rapid French, and Brooke struggled to catch a single word, but she nodded and smiled at him.

'*Bonjour*, Jean-Luc.'

'*Bonjour*,' he said.

Felicity turned to her. 'Jean-Luc popped over to introduce himself properly. He says he's heard a lot about us from Armand.'

'Oh?' Brooke glanced at him quizzically.

'Well, I think what he means is he's heard a lot about the mugging and Armand's heroic rescue,' Felicity said with a light laugh.

Jean-Luc said something else to Felicity but looked at Brooke as he did.

'Armand did ask him to look out for us,' Felicity told Brooke. 'And he says he told Armand he would, and he'd do it for any of the traders who'd had trouble. We're like family while we're here and family takes care of each other. Which I think is nice, isn't it? Feels like we're a proper part of the gang even though we're not one of the regular traders.'

'Well, I suppose I see what he means, though I disagree that we need looking out for, and the family bit is quite nice. Before we came I was worried that they'd see us as outsiders, but maybe I needn't have.'

Felicity relayed Brooke's response to Jean-Luc, who replied.

'He says at the first sign of trouble we're to go and get him,' Felicity translated.

Brooke smiled at Jean-Luc. '*Merci beaucoup.*' Then she turned to Felicity. 'But I don't think those guys would try again, would they? Certainly not around here, now that I've given the police a description – they'd be worried about getting caught, wouldn't they?'

'Probably,' Felicity agreed before telling Jean-Luc what Brooke had said.

He replied shortly and seemed, from what Brooke said, to agree. Then he nodded at them both, bade them good afternoon, and walked back in the direction of his van.

'That was nice of him, wasn't it?' Felicity said, her gaze still trained on his retreating figure.

Brooke went to the side door of the chalet and let herself back in before locking it again. 'It was. Nice to know we're not viewed as outsiders here.' Brooke paused. 'The more I think about it, the more I'm certain those muggers won't dare show their faces round here again,' she added.

'I doubt it – they'd be too scared of your handbag kung fu.'

Brooke grabbed the nearest tea towel and Felicity ducked out of range as she flicked it at her. 'You're soooo funny!'

'I know – that's why you love me.'

'I *tolerate* you,' Brooke said with a grin. 'Don't get carried away there.'

'Well you've been tolerating me for a very long time so you must like me a bit.'

'I have, haven't I? I must need my head looking at.' Brooke refolded the towel.

'What did you get for lunch?' Felicity asked.

'Nuts.'

Felicity blinked. 'So you *did* see Armand on your travels?'

'You're not getting any funnier, you know.'

'Sorry...' Felicity grinned. 'You had actual nuts for lunch?'

'I saw somewhere selling those toffee ones you get hot and I couldn't resist... and then I sort of forgot to buy anything else. So I guess it's nuts for lunch.'

'You'll be starving in a bit.'

'Now that you mention it, I'm starving already.'

'That'll teach you to take an hour off for lunch and only eat nuts. I doubt we'll have time to eat anything this afternoon if the crowds are anything to go by.'

'You might be right,' Brooke said ruefully, and was spared any elaboration by the approach of a group of women keen to check out Felicity's creations. Brooke watched them and her stomach growled to remind her just how right her friend was. She tried to ignore it, but then it got louder. Digging in her bag, she pulled out a stick of gum, hoping to fool her stomach for a while and keep the pangs at bay. That was about the best she was going to get for a good few hours yet.

The afternoon had been as busy as Felicity had predicted. Brooke wasn't about to complain – they'd come to make money, after all, and it took her mind off other questions that hovered at the edge of her thoughts like irritating flies she couldn't bat away. Like had she really seen Lisette staring through her soul like a baddie from a cheap horror movie? And why was Armand so invested in two women he'd only just met? One of whom had almost got his head caved in for him. Were her instincts right? Was he interested romantically in her? And if he was, what was she meant to do about it? Already she was beginning to realise he was a man she could fall for. She was only in Paris for a few weeks – did she really want to get into something she wouldn't be able to finish, something that might leave her a heartbroken mess all over again?

Dusk came early and with it an even sharper temperature drop. Even with thick socks and sturdy boots she could feel the ice of the pavements numbing her toes. Standing in one spot for hours on end didn't help either, and she was stiffening up to the point where she wondered if she'd ever be able to move properly again.

'I'll get some *vin chaud*,' Felicity said during the briefest of lulls. 'That'll sort us.'

'Good idea. I could definitely use something to warm me up and something stronger than Jean-Luc's coffee.'

While Felicity was gone, a few people mooched at the stall but nobody bought anything. The lights began to brighten against a sky that rapidly darkened and music from the pop-up bars and rides got louder.

Brooke was tired and wondered whether it would be worth their while keeping the stall open into the later part of the evening. They'd noticed some winding down earlier than them the night before and though Brooke had been initially reluctant to do that and lose potential trade, she could see why others might be tempted. Once the bars and skating rink and rides were in full swing, those things were mostly why anyone was coming to the markets. They might get the odd drunken crocheted teddy purchase, but trade would definitely lessen later on. And they'd agreed to try out the Lebanese restaurant, and boy, was she ready to eat already! Her stomach hadn't stopped growling since she'd got back from her lunch break, and if someone put a pie in front of her now she'd happily bury her face in it.

When Felicity returned, she had two cups of mulled wine and a paper parcel.

'I got you a slice of pizza from that stone oven place.' Felicity handed it to her. 'I thought it might just see you through until dinner later.'

'*You* are a mind reader!' Brooke opened the bag to reveal a cheese-smothered delight. 'What's on it... oh! Goat's cheese and red onion! You really are a mind reader!'

Felicity put the coffees on the counter and went round to let herself in at the side door of the chalet. 'Honestly, I just couldn't hear myself think over the sound of your stomach. And the owners of the disco bar were complaining that you were drowning out their PA system.'

Brooke grinned broadly as she bit into her pizza. 'Oh wow! This is soooo good!'

'It does look good,' Felicity agreed. 'I think I'll get some tomorrow for my lunch.'

Brooke moaned as she bit off another mouthful. 'Oh my God!'

Felicity laughed. 'Steady on. We're not doing a budget remake of *When Harry Met Sally*.'

'You've got no idea how good this actually is!' Brooke held it out to her. 'Taste it!'

Felicity pulled off a corner and chewed on it. 'OK, now you mention it, that is pretty orgasmic. Maybe I'll go and get one now.'

'I would. And get me another one while you're there.'

'You'll have no room for the restaurant later.'

'Want a bet on that?'

As Felicity started to leave she was stopped by a customer asking about a choker on her display. While they talked, Brooke tried to be discreet with her slice of very greasy and very messy but delicious pizza, taking it to the corner of the chalet to finish off. She might have waited, but she was far too hungry and to let it go cold would be a crime against food.

Finishing the slice, she wiped her hands on a paper napkin and was wondering whether she ought to go and get the second helpings herself while Felicity was busy, but was thwarted by a customer asking about her crocheted toys.

Customer after customer followed, and by the time they had another gap an hour had passed. Brooke collected their wine cups ready for the bin and was about to go and get rid of them, having agreed with Felicity that there was probably no point in going to get more pizza now, when Jean-Luc's assistant from the crêpe van came over. She handed two cups to Felicity and explained he'd sent them thinking they hadn't been over to get a drink all afternoon. Flushing with guilt, Brooke hid their empties behind her back until the girl had gone.

'On the house again, I suppose,' Brooke said wearily.

'Just accept it and get over it,' Felicity said. 'They've been made and they're here now – might as well drink them.'

'I feel so bad. He must not be able to afford to keep doing this. Does he do it for anyone else?'

'God knows. I wouldn't get too worried – I'm sure it won't last. Like you say, he can't afford to do it indefinitely.'

'I'm glad she didn't see the other cups I was binning.'

'She wouldn't have cared. She works for him, probably minimum wage and probably be laid off after the season ends. I'm sure it won't worry her if she sees you with someone else's cups.'

'OK, you're right, as always.' Brooke peeled back the lid of her cup and detected the scent of coffee that was even stronger than the one they'd had from Jean-Luc earlier that day. 'I think he might be trying to tell us we look knackered. There has to be half a jar of coffee in here.'

'It *is* a bit like rocket fuel,' Felicity agreed. 'I might be tripping by the end of tonight if I drink all of this.'

'We're going to have to say something.'

'I wouldn't bother.'

'No, I mean, we'll have to ask for different drinks if he insists on bringing them over!'

Felicity laughed. 'You might have a point there.'

Brooke sipped her drink anyway. At least it was hot and that was always welcome on nights as cold as this. 'I was wondering if we ought to pack up soon. We'd be able to get to the restaurant to eat earlier.'

'I don't think closing is an issue here,' Felicity said mildly.

'No, but I'm getting tired as well. I might be asleep before the first course arrives.'

'I suppose you did have an eventful one last night. Well, let's see how it goes over the next hour or so, and if it dies off we could sneak away. I wouldn't complain – I'd be glad to get out of the cold. I've seen some people with those patio heaters in their chalets. We could have done with one of those.'

Brooke grinned. 'They didn't give us one because we're English.'

'Probably. Or because my dodgy cousin got the pitch for us.'

'Oh, that's definitely it.'

Brooke was about to reply when a figure emerged from behind a family wearing Santa hats caught her attention.

'Armand?'

He made his way over.

'Hi,' Brooke said. 'What brings you here...? Is everything OK? Your head – there's nothing—'

'There is no problem,' he said. 'I came because I have been thinking about you... I mean to say, I have been thinking about if you are alright after so much stress.'

'Oh, I'm honestly not all that stressed.'

'Are you certain? And you feel safe to go home tonight?'

'Yes. Felicity and I will go together, and there's safety in numbers, isn't there? And we'll probably take a cab or something, to be sure.'

Felicity nodded. 'Manon is meeting us too, so actually there will be three of us going back together.'

Brooke turned to her. 'She is? I thought she was maybe meeting us at the restaurant if her other thing fell through.'

'She was – there's been a change of plan.'

Brooke narrowed her eyes slightly. 'I hope this change of plan wasn't to do with mollycoddling me. I told you I don't need it.'

'No, but it does make sense.'

Ah,' Armand cut in. 'Then I think you will be quite safe.'

'Absolutely. Especially with Felicity's friend around – anyone would think twice before messing with her.'

'That's what's so cool about her,' Felicity said with a hint of pride.

'We're going to a Lebanese restaurant in Montmartre later,' she added. 'You should come with us – it's the least we can do for helping Boo last night.'

It was all Brooke could do not to let her mouth fall open. They definitely hadn't discussed this, and though the idea gave Brooke an excited little flutter in the pit of her stomach, she was completely unprepared for the invite.

'Perhaps not...' he said, glancing a little warily at Brooke, as if weighing up what she wanted him to say. Undoubtedly he'd seen the expression on her face and taken that to mean she didn't approve of the invite, even though nothing could be further from the truth.

'I don't mind,' she put in, trying her best to sound cool and unfazed but not doing a very good job. 'It's just a friendly invite... bring someone if you like... you know... maybe your friend, Lisette...?'

He winced at the name and suddenly Brooke's excitement fizzled out. Had she said something very wrong?

'Or come on your own...' she added lamely. 'Whatever you'd like. We're only saying we'd love to see you there if you could make it. But we totally understand if you can't. I suppose it is rather last minute and—'

'I think I would very much like to come,' he said, giving her another of his magnetic smiles. 'I've never tried that restaurant, but I've often thought I might.'

'And it's our treat,' Brooke added. 'We pay for you.'

'No! That is—'

'We pay or nobody goes – that's the deal,' she cut in.

His smile spread. His smiles had the power to steal Brooke's breath. They transformed his whole face, so that the intensity of his gaze softened and warmed, and his cheeks showed faint dimples beneath his stubble. 'What time should I be there?'

'Nine?' Felicity asked. 'Is that too late for you? It's just that we have to pack up here first.'

'Nine is perfect. I will meet you inside. I have some business to attend to first so if I am late please don't wait to order.'

'Nah, we wouldn't do that,' Felicity said. 'We'll wait. We can drink while we do. So you know the place?'

'Behind the Sacré-Cœur?'

'Yes, I think that's it.'

'I will be there.'

'We're counting on it!' Felicity said. 'Later!'

With a last farewell, he left them. Felicity turned to Brooke.

'Not a word!' Brooke said.

'And did you clock him when you mentioned that Lisette woman? If you were worrying that they're an item, I'm pretty sure they're not. And if they ever were, she must have really pissed him off.'

'You think so?'

'Take it from me, that's it. Something happened between them and it wasn't good. And he's coming tonight so he definitely wants to be distracted from that. So you know what that means?'

'What?'

'You're the distraction!'

Brooke let out a sigh of resignation. 'You're not giving up on this, are you?'

'I'm calling it how I see it, that's all. Even you must be able to see it.'

'Maybe...' Brooke said slowly. 'Maybe see how it goes later, eh?'

CHAPTER TWELVE

Manon had come to meet them as they arrived home. At the apartment, Manon had made herself a drink while Brooke and Felicity had hurried to freshen up and get changed before heading back out to the restaurant. Brooke had been strangely stressed about her outfit choice. She was beginning to wish she'd packed more dressy clothes rather than the mountain of knitwear and thermals she'd brought with her. For goat-herding in the Alps she'd have been fine – but if there were going to be a lot more evenings out like this, she might have to go shopping. Armand was so well dressed, so confident and put-together that she couldn't help but imagine that being seen out with her nerdy, retro-loving self would somehow be an embarrassment to him.

But the fact remained that there was little she could do about it now. She'd brought nothing terribly feminine with her, nothing more formal than a tailored blouse with a funky collar, and there was no time to go out and shop before dinner. Felicity's style was very different to hers too, so she could borrow but she'd never really feel like herself. Felicity was far more punk-meets-Primark – about as far from Brooke's seventies-inspired vintage looks as you could get.

Reluctantly, she'd settled on the same blouse and flares she'd worn at the Moulin Rouge, though she was far from happy with her choice. Even as she decided what she was going to do with her hair, she found herself dashing through to Felicity's bedroom for a second opinion.

'What do you think?'

Brooke stood at the door with her arms outstretched.

'About what?' Felicity asked vaguely as she returned to the mirror to apply a second layer of mascara.

'The outfit! Do you think it's OK?'

'Of course I think it's OK – it's a great outfit; I said that last time you wore it.'

'Yes, but that's the problem – I've worn it before.'

'Isn't that what we do with most items of clothing? I don't know about you, but I can't afford to have something new every day.'

'You know what I mean – I've worn it recently and in front of Armand.'

'I'm almost certain he won't remember, and even if by some miracle he did, I'm sure he wouldn't care.'

'I know, but...'

Felicity fastened the top onto her mascara and turned around with an impish grin. 'You're very bothered about this... anyone would think you were hoping for something to happen tonight.'

'I'm not, I just... I just want to look good. That's not a crime, is it?'

'No,' Felicity said, smirking as she turned back to her make-up bag.

'OK, I know I said I don't have time for romantic shenanigans, but that doesn't mean I don't like the idea that he might fancy me,' Brooke admitted.

Felicity was still smiling as she caught sight of her in the reflection of her vanity mirror and Brooke offered a sheepish one of her own in return. 'I'm pathetic, right?'

'No, after the year you've had with Johnny shitting on you, I'm surprised you didn't do any of this sooner. You deserve to let your hair down a little and you deserve to be worshipped – or better still lusted after – by someone. And as someones go, Armand's not a bad place to start.'

'He's not, is he?' Brooke agreed, her gaze wandering to a spot in the distance as those green eyes and that delicious accent and those dimples when he smiled and the feeling they gave her crept into her thoughts. 'So the outfit is alright?'

Felicity laughed. 'Of course it is! Stop stressing!'

'I'm not stressed.'

'Of course you're not...'

'You look good, by the way,' Brooke added.

'Thanks.'

'I'm sure...' Brooke lowered her voice, casting a glance towards the living area, but Manon wasn't there. Brooke could only assume she'd gone to the kitchen to top up her drink, the sound of the fridge opening immediately confirming that. 'I'm sure *someone* will think so.'

'That's the idea,' Felicity said as she fastened an earring – one of her own creations. 'Hoping to make a breakthrough tonight, if I'm honest. If nothing else I'm going to clear up whether there's any point in me making the effort...'

Having spent next to no time trying on outfits, she had more time to attend to her hair and make-up. Brooke pinned up her chestnut waves and retouched her eye make-up to create a more smoky, night-time look, then examined herself in the full-length mirror in her room.

It wasn't perfect, but it would have to do.

Felicity was already dressed and sharing a drink with
Manon on the sofa when Brooke emerged once again from her
room, now ready. They were sitting close to one another,
laughing easily at some joke or another.

As Brooke walked in, they both turned to her.

Felicity whistled. 'Looking good, Boo!'

'I wish.' Brooke grimaced. 'But thank you.'

'Felicity is right,' Manon agreed, with a cute little accent on
the way she pronounced Felicity's name that made her sound
more French than if she was actually speaking French. 'You
look good – be proud!'

'Thanks, Manon,' Brooke said, and though she appreciated
the sentiment, she couldn't help but feel they both looked way
cooler and sexier than she did. Manon was in her trademark
black, this time sporting leather trousers and spike-heeled boots
with a bra top, while Felicity had gone for a charcoal bodycon
dress, so fitted it could have been sprayed on.

'Has anyone made a reservation for this place?' Brooke
asked as she dropped a lipstick and a fresh packet of gum into
her handbag.

'No,' Felicity said. 'Manon says they always have tables so
there's no need. Besides, we weren't sure what time we'd be
ready. Let's just get there when we get there, no need to stress
about it.'

'Yes, but don't forget we told Armand to meet us there at
nine.'

'He said he'd probably be late,' Felicity replied.

'He said he *might* be late.'

'We will be there,' Manon cut in. 'Who is this man? Felicity
tells me he rescued you.'

'Yes, he did.'

Manon raised her perfectly groomed eyebrows, sat back on
the sofa and took a long drink but said no more. Instead of
feeling evasive, Brooke was now faintly irritated by the smug-

ness of the gesture. Felicity was smitten by Manon – that much was clear – but Brooke, though she was in awe of the woman, still wasn't exactly sure she liked her all that much.

'Do you think we ought to go?' Brooke asked. 'How long will it take to get to the restaurant?'

'We have time for another drink,' Manon said. 'Relax – you are too tense. Come and sit with us.'

'What are you drinking?' Brooke asked as she joined them. Though reluctant, she didn't want to seem like an uptight party pooper so said no more about leaving.

Manon's made this thing with brandy,' Felicity said. 'I hate brandy but this is amazing.'

'So you do not hate brandy,' Manon said glibly.

'Well,' Felicity countered, 'I thought I hated brandy because nobody had managed to change my mind until now.'

'I bet we'd change our minds about most things we don't think we like if they're presented to us in the right way.'

'Yeah, like you thought you didn't like aubergine until I made you that curry.'

'Oh yeah.' Brooke sat on the sofa, rearranging herself so that her blouse wouldn't crease. 'I'd forgotten about that – it was pretty good. I'm sure I still don't like aubergine, but I'd definitely eat that again. I'm not sure I like brandy either, but I'll give one of those drinks a go if it's managed to convert you.'

'You make no sense to me,' Manon said carelessly. 'Your conversations are silly.'

Brooke stared at the comment, but Felicity simply laughed and looked at her like an adoring puppy. 'That's what we aim for,' she said. 'What's the point in being serious all the time?'

Manon gave her a lazy smile. 'You think I am serious?'

'I think you're intense,' Felicity said. 'But intense is good – not the same as serious at all.'

'Good,' Manon said. 'Intense is sexy, no?'

'Very,' Felicity said.

Brooke pulled out her phone and stared intently at it. She'd never felt more like a gooseberry in her life, but one thing was for sure: she didn't think Felicity was going to need much of a conversation about whether Manon was up for a fling – that much was perfectly obvious to anyone who spent a second in their company.

They were practically running to the restaurant – or rather, Brooke was. Manon and Felicity didn't seem to care that they were going to be late to meet Armand if they didn't get a move on. As far as Brooke was concerned, that was not an option. They'd invited him and it would be very rude to let him down, especially when he'd practically put his life on the line for her and this was meant to be a thank you.

Despite her vague sense of panic, Brooke was still bowled over by the sight of Montmartre. While there was grandeur in the white-domed Sacré-Cœur standing proudly on its grassy hill, the quaint cobbled streets and tiny pastel, wooden-shuttered cafés made it look as though someone had lifted a sleepy village from central France and dropped it into the centre of the capital. The pavements were lined by artists working at easels and street vendors, and above the top of the low buildings stood the outlines of the last remaining windmills that had once been plentiful in the district. They'd passed through before when they'd gone to the Moulin Rouge but hadn't seen it properly; tonight was a chance to get a real sense of the place. It was a welcome change of scenery, and while it was still buzzing as the cafés and nightclubs it was famous for came to life, it felt like a refreshing change of pace too. It was far more relaxed here than in the stuffier, grander districts. Brooke imagined they might spend a lot more time here after today, if they could get away from the stall now and again.

As the restaurant finally came into view, Brooke wondered

if they'd find Armand waiting on the pavement outside, but there was nobody there. Perhaps he'd already got them a table.

'I'll ask when we get in,' Felicity said.

She pushed open the door to enter, Manon and Brooke following.

'Oh, isn't this gorgeous!' Felicity gazed around. The walls were bare, aged brick, vaulted ceilings of stone and plaster and frescos hanging around the room of medieval coast and village scenes.

'It's lovely,' Brooke agreed. 'It looks quite full, though.'

Manon spoke to the greeter at the door. Then she turned to them. 'Your friend is not here yet. There will be a wait for a table too – about an hour, I think.'

'It's never actually an hour,' Felicity said. 'That's exactly what I used to say to customers that summer I worked at the pizza parlour. They tell you an hour but they mean about forty minutes – they're only covering themselves so you don't start complaining if their timings are out.'

'Well, I suppose Armand isn't here yet anyway,' Brooke said, checking the room again, even though Manon had said he wasn't there. Not because she didn't believe her, but she harboured a vain hope that the greeter had been mistaken and that he might be sitting at a reserved table right now waiting for them.

'So if he's late that's not a bad thing,' Felicity said. 'At least we won't have started without him if we're not even at a table yet.'

'We are allowed to sit in the waiting area, and they will serve us drinks and appetisers,' Manon nodded towards a collection of sofas by the window.

If they hadn't been expecting Armand to meet them, Brooke might have been tempted to suggest they look for somewhere else to eat so they wouldn't have to wait. She was a little tipsy now as the drinks they'd had in the apartment on a relatively empty stomach had gone to her head. But they couldn't because they had no way to let him know about the change of plans. In hindsight, it had been silly not to get his phone number, but at the time it had seemed presumptuous and forward to ask, especially as he hadn't offered it. There was an outside chance, Brooke supposed, that Armand might have her number, courtesy of Lisette, who'd taken it on the night of the mugging, but considering Lisette had never actually called or messaged Brooke as she'd promised, and as Armand had said nothing about it, Brooke could only assume that Lisette had, in fact, deleted the number from her phone immediately and had never intended to update her on Armand's condition. Why was a mystery she might never get the answer to, but she couldn't help but wonder.

Once they'd settled on the sofas a waiter brought them drinks and a tray of nibbles. They had garlic labneh and something called muhammara, which was roasted pepper dip, and hummus, all accompanied by soft warm pitta bread, along with little spiced meatballs called kibbeh. Brooke was ravenous by now and she fell on it with some enthusiasm, making Manon laugh.

'Be careful not to eat your fingers,' she said.

Brooke shook her head. 'I'm so hungry now my fingers would probably taste good.'

Manon arched a perfect brow. 'Now I am worried for you.'

Brooke couldn't imagine super-cool Manon being actually worried about anyone for real, but the notion suddenly filled her with doubt.

'Do you mind me asking,' she said as she reached for some more dip from the bowl, 'have you always lived in Paris?'

Manon shook her head. 'Not always.'

Brooke waited, but nothing more was offered about where Manon had come from or how long she'd lived in the capital, which was usually how those sorts of conversations went.

'Oh,' she said. 'What made you come here?'

'I came to find excitement.'

'And did you find it?'

'*Mais oui.* This is Paris.'

'There's no way you wouldn't find excitement here I suppose,' Brooke agreed. 'And that's it? You just stayed here? What about friends and family back home? Do you miss them?'

'No,' Manon said shortly. 'I have all the friends I want here. My family do not like the way I live and I will not change for them. I will not change for anyone.'

'The people who matter wouldn't want you to change,' Felicity cut in, clearly a bit sozzled and gazing at Manon as if she was an ancient Roman watching a statue of Venus come to life. 'My family were a bit shocked when I came out, but they were cool about it.'

'You have never been with a man?' Manon asked, licking some hummus from her finger.

Felicity shook her head. 'At school I sort of pretended to be into boys, but that was early on. By the time I was fifteen I'd given up pretending because I felt like nobody was being fooled anyway. All I was doing was making sure that if there was another girl like me who maybe liked me, she'd never say a word because she'd think I was into boys and she'd be wasting her time.'

'And did the girl find you?' Manon asked.

'No,' Felicity said. 'After school I started to date, but there was never anyone who meant anything. I got messed around a bit by someone who thought she might be gay, but I suspect she was only playing at it to seem edgy. And then there was another girl who might have been *the one,* only she decided to run off to Canada before we had the chance to find out. After that there were a lot of casual things, but...'

Brooke sipped at her drink. Felicity wasn't afraid of speaking her truths, but this was open, even for her. Perhaps it was the drink talking, or perhaps this was her way of baring her soul for Manon. Either way, Manon's subsequent silence as she mulled it over, nodding solemnly as she munched on a square of pitta bread told Brooke that she wasn't about to be as generous with her own history. But she did look at Felicity with a new sort of interest and the closest thing to compassion Brooke had ever seen on her face. Maybe Brooke had got her all wrong after all – maybe she could be a good thing for Felicity.

With the drinks and the snacks, a bit of decent conversation and some covert people-watching, the time flew until, as Felicity had predicted, forty minutes later someone came to show them to a table.

There was still no sign of Armand. They'd commented on it briefly as they'd been in the waiting area but agreed there was little they could do about it if they had no way to contact him. Now, at the table, Brooke had to admit to a growing sense of annoyance and disappointment.

'He's not coming, is he?' she asked no one in particular.

'Well,' Felicity replied, 'he did say he might be late and that we should start without him.'

'Yes, but *this* late?'

Felicity filled Brooke's glass for her. 'Is it such a big deal if he doesn't turn up? You're the one who keeps saying you ought to keep a distance from him.'

'I never said that.'

'I'm pretty sure you did even if not in so many words.' Felicity filled Manon's glass – she was scrolling through her messages on her phone – and then put the jug down.

'Maybe I did then,' Brooke said into the brief silence. 'But only because I didn't know what to think.'

'So if he doesn't come tonight then there's nothing to worry about. There'll be no danger of him seducing you over a plate of

Lebanese purse bread and then leaving you broken-hearted, will there?'

'OK, so now I know I sound like an idiot. You're right – what does it matter if he comes or not? We invited him but it's no big deal either way. Forget it; let's enjoy our meal. If he turns up, great; if not, we'll still have a good night.'

'Exactly.' Felicity grabbed the menu and scanned it. 'I vote we order one of everything and we don't stop until it's all gone!'

Brooke would have complained about her hangover but the evening had been worth every thump of her head the following morning. Her disappointment at Armand's eventual no-show had faded with each glass of potent arak they downed and, despite her hesitation around Manon, Brooke had to admit the woman knew how to have a good time.

They ate a whole heap of meze that seemed to keep on coming, though that was probably because Felicity ordered more and more the drunker she got, giggling helplessly at the jokes of the waiters, who were clearly used to dealing with parties of drunken women. There was live, traditional music, and Manon decided to order shisha, which the waiters only brought out once all the guests had finished their food. They called it something entirely different, that Brooke now couldn't remember, and it had made Brooke cough like mad, which they all found hilarious.

Afterwards, Manon had taken them to a very exclusive backstreet club where the ceilings were low and the air sweaty, and the music had been too loud to talk over, so the only thing they could do was dance. It was a bit too techno for Brooke's taste but she threw herself into it anyway, and if anyone tried to pick her up she finally found her very poor French a distinct advantage, because they soon got tired of trying to communicate with her and wandered off, which was exactly the result she'd hoped for. How much easier it was to brush off unwanted attention when you didn't have to make any excuse other than you couldn't understand a word the other person said.

At the end of the night they'd walked back to the apartment block together, the drink and the company making them brave, and Brooke wondered if Manon would spend the night with Felicity. But at their building she simply bade them goodnight and went to her own apartment alone. Though Brooke could see the obvious disappointment in Felicity's face, she said nothing about it for fear of making it worse. It seemed, though they'd had a great night, it hadn't exactly gone the way either of them had envisaged.

This morning it was Brooke's turn to get the croissants and bread from the bakery. They'd given up on the supermarket for fresh goods, having been given better recommendations by Manon, and Brooke was at one of them now, yawning widely as she stood in the queue. The bakery was small with brown floor tiles and baskets along the walls full of various breads. The pastries and more delicate items were on shelves behind the counter – no supermarket-style self-service in here. The smell coming through the doorway before Brooke even walked in made the visit worthwhile, even if the bread hadn't lived up to it.

'Be careful,' a voice said from nearby. 'You will swallow us all.'

Brooke turned to see Manon, a faint look of wry amusement on her face. As always, she looked like perfection on legs, even after their rowdy night. Brooke was fairly sure the same couldn't be said of her.

'Sorry,' she replied sheepishly. 'I'm so tired I could sleep right here.'

'You had a good time?' Manon asked.

'A bit too good. I'm sure we'll regret it once we start work today. At least we didn't have to get up at the crack of dawn – I suppose that's something. Will we see you later?' Brooke added, but what she was really asking was if Manon had made any arrangements with Felicity.

'Perhaps,' Manon said. Brooke waited for her to elaborate but she didn't.

A sharp voice caused Brooke to turn back to the front of the bakery, and then she realised that the queue had shuffled forward without her and it was now her turn to order.

She got her croissants and bread and then waited at the door of the shop for Manon to get hers, thinking they'd walk back to their building together. But then Manon got her pastries too and walked right past Brooke, only offering her a brief nod before going outside and crossing the road to go in the opposite direction. Taken by mild surprise, Brooke watched for a moment, and a little further down the road saw a young woman join her and fall into step alongside. Manon handed her a bag of pastries and they went on their way.

'Where do you go?' Brooke murmured as she watched them. 'What's your game?'

When they'd turned a corner and disappeared from view, Brooke walked slowly back to the apartment block by herself. Should she tell Felicity what she'd seen? Was there even anything to tell? So far Manon and Felicity had spent time together, but as far as Brooke could tell there'd been nothing romantic, despite plenty of flirting on both sides. What did Manon want from this? It was obvious what Felicity wanted, but Manon was much harder to read. And her walking off with a woman this morning might well have meant nothing at all.

In the end, Brooke decided to see how the land lay. If she needed to tell Felicity anything, she would, but maybe it wasn't worth making a fuss over.

CHAPTER THIRTEEN

Less than an hour after opening the stall, Jean-Luc's assistant brought coffee over for them. Felicity took them and thanked her, but then raised her eyebrows meaningfully at Brooke when she'd gone.

'I don't know what to make of it either,' Brooke said. 'Armand doesn't bother turning up to dinner but is still asking his friend to bring coffees over the next day.'

'Unless Jean-Luc hasn't got the memo yet.'

'What memo would that be?'

'The one that says Armand is bored of babysitting us now and that he can stop with all the taking care of us.'

Brooke took a coffee from her. 'What do you think happened last night? I hope it wasn't something bad. Here we are slagging him off – what if it turns out to be some emergency that kept him away? I'd feel pretty bad about that.'

'Who knows?' Felicity sniffed at her coffee. 'Well, at least Jean-Luc's rocket fuel will clear the last of our hangovers.'

'Do you think he just changed his mind about eating with us? Like he didn't fancy it after all?'

'Maybe it's got something to do with that Lisette woman.'

Brooke took the lid from her coffee to allow it to cool a little. 'Like he had to meet her or someone else? Maybe he forgot he'd arranged it when he'd agreed to meet us? I kind of hope it's that simple. I hope he's alright.'

Felicity's phone pinged the arrival of a text. 'Hold that thought...' She unlocked it to check and then broke into a smile. 'Manon says she had a good night last night. Wants to know if we want to do it again.'

'Surely not tonight?' Brooke said. 'She can't possibly be ready to go again that quick!'

As Felicity typed out a reply, Brooke smiled at a couple who had come over to look at her tote bags.

'*Bonjour!*'

Then there was another ping and Felicity grinned. 'She's up for tonight if we are!'

'I don't know about that. We'd have to close the stall early again.'

'It wasn't that early yesterday in the end, and I don't think we lost out all that much, from what I can gather talking to some of the other traders. Maybe we don't need to be open the whole time the market is? Most people seem to have done gift shopping by six or seven and are more interested in the leisure stuff.'

'Are you just saying that because you want to go out and play again?'

Felicity pouted but Brooke could tell she didn't mean it.

'Listen,' she added, 'why don't you go with Manon? I can keep things ticking over here for the last couple of hours.'

'Oh yeah,' Felicity said, her voice heavy with sarcasm. 'Remember how well that went last time?'

'You'd taken the cash at least,' Brooke replied evenly. 'If Manon would pick you up on her bike again, you could take the cash with you again and deposit it before you go back to the apartment to get changed. I'll get a taxi, so I won't be walking alone. I'll be fine.'

Felicity was thoughtful for a moment as she stared at her phone. The couple who'd been examining Brooke's bags moved on.

'This thing with Manon...' Brooke said into the silence. 'Is it a thing?'

Felicity looked up. 'Honestly? I have no idea. Nothing has happened yet and I don't know that it will. I just... well, she's fun, isn't she?'

'She is,' Brooke agreed. 'Only... well, I saw her this morning at the bakery,' she added, deciding to come clean. 'She bought some stuff and then went off with a woman.'

'What's that got to do with anything?' Felicity's tone was deliberately careless, but Brooke wasn't fooled.

'Nothing probably, but I felt like I ought to tell you.'

Now that she'd said it she felt a bit silly. She'd no doubt blown whatever it was she'd seen out of all proportion.

Felicity nodded. 'You know she has a younger sister, right?'

'No. I didn't know that. I thought she had a brother.'

'Can't she have both?'

'But they don't live in Paris. She told us she moved here from somewhere else and she didn't like her family.'

'People say that as a very general thing. It doesn't mean they don't love their family or want to see them, does it? She might still want them to visit even if they don't always see eye to eye or even if she doesn't want to live at home with them any longer.'

'Yeah, you're right...'

'And obviously she's going to have friends other than us?'

'Obviously... I expect it was one of those people I saw her with... that would be it.'

Brooke waited for some comment about how she saw betrayal everywhere because of Johnny, but any further discussion was halted by a group of teenage girls perusing Felicity's stock. Brooke, in all honesty, was relieved. Wasn't it just like her to make a drama out of nothing? If Felicity had said that, she would have made a valid point. Brooke's experience with Johnny was in the past, but she had to wonder if it had entirely finished with her, because she *did* still see betrayal where there was none. Just because Johnny had behaved that way, it didn't mean everyone was at it. But still, it was hard to trust, and Brooke couldn't do much about that. The wound would heal when it healed, she supposed.

'Santa!'

Brooke heard the bells and the music before she saw the sleigh. It was being pulled slowly down the walkways by a motorised cart while Santa, flanked by elves, sat on a huge red seat waving like royalty. Everyone stopped to look, and even the faces of the oldest shoppers lit up.

'Boo!' Felicity pointed. 'It's Santa!'

'Yes,' Brooke said in an indulgent voice, 'I can see that. Looks pretty authentic too.'

'That's because he's got to be the real one!' Felicity grinned. 'You don't think the mayor of Paris would let an impostor visit the markets, do you?' She dug out her phone. 'I'm going to see if I can get a selfie with him! Want to come?'

'I'm good, thanks. You go – I'll keep an eye on things here.'

By this point the procession had come to a halt and families had begun to gather around the sleigh. There was a Rotary Club Santa who went round Ely every year to collect for charity, and although she couldn't see anyone nearby with collection tins now, she wondered if this was something similar. If so, she was sure Felicity would donate for the both of them.

Brooke watched as Felicity waited with everyone else for a chance to get close to Santa. Quite rightly, he was prioritising the children, so Felicity was probably going to have something of a wait.

'Ah... Père Noël!'

Brooke looked to see who had spoken, and saw Fabien at the stall.

'Hey! Hello, Fabien!'

'Hello, Brooke.' He angled his head in the direction of Santa. 'In France we call him Père Noël, or sometimes Saint Nicholas,' Fabien said. 'In a moment or two, Felicity will try to jump the line to meet him.'

'You know her so well.'

'*Naturellement...*'

His gaze ran over their stall. 'You are happy with your place? It is going well?'

'Brilliantly!' Brooke beamed. 'Honestly, we can't thank you enough!'

'Good,' he said, letting his gaze roam over their goods for a moment.

'Is there anything I can do for you or did you just drop by to see Felicity?' she asked.

'I came to see you both. And I see you're looking very charming today; Paris must suit you.'

Brooke flushed. Not knowing how to respond to such an outright compliment, she bustled about tidying her stock while he chuckled.

'I have embarrassed you,' he said. 'I must apologise.'

'No, it's not that—'

Brooke was saved further awkwardness by the return of Felicity.

'Hey, Fab!' She kissed him on both cheeks. 'What brings you here? No high-level meetings or deals to make today?'

'I cannot visit my cousin when she is in Paris?'

'Yeah, of course you can. I just didn't expect it to be in the middle of the day. You want to grab some lunch?' Felicity asked.

'If you like – I have time.'

'We can't both go,' Brooke reminded her. 'But if you want to catch up with your cousin, I can hold the fort here for an hour or two.'

'Perhaps, instead of leaving you alone here, we could all go out to dinner one evening?' Fabien said. 'Then I can have the pleasure of your company also.'

'We'd have to take her anyway,' Felicity said. 'If you leave Boo on her own she gets into all sorts of trouble.'

Brooke gave a self-conscious laugh. 'I'm not that bad! It was only the once!'

'I would never leave Boo out,' Fabien said, giving her a lingering look that she wasn't sure what to do with.

It was strange and overfamiliar to hear someone else use Felicity's nickname for her, especially a man she hardly knew. Brooke was thrown momentarily, but then she gave a courteous smile. 'That sounds lovely. I'm sure we can arrange something for one night after we close up.'

'Do you have plans for tonight?' he asked.

Brooke glanced at Felicity. She wasn't desperate for another late night but guessed that Fabien's idea of a night out might be a lot more civilised than Manon's, and, considering all the strings he'd pulled to get them here, and then the tickets to the opera and to the Moulin Rouge and all the champagne, dinner was the least they owed him. In all fairness they ought to pay, but Brooke was fairly sure that his idea of a decent restaurant would be pushing the top of their affordability range.

Felicity looked at her phone and paused as she checked something. But then she looked up and gave Fabien a bright smile. 'Well, seems my other plans are cancelled, so tonight is perfect.'

'I will send a driver for you.'

'Oh, there's no need for that,' Felicity began, but he stopped her.

'I insist. We cannot have your Boo getting into trouble, can we? What time shall I instruct the driver to collect you?'

'Um...' Felicity looked at Brooke.

'Well nine worked OK last night,' Brooke said.

'Nine then.' Felicity turned back to her cousin. 'Is that too late for you?'

'Not at all. I will look forward to it.'

As Felicity said an affectionate goodbye, Brooke watched. Her vintage flares and blouse weren't going to cut it this time and she didn't want to keep turning up everywhere in the same stuff or to keep borrowing Felicity's clothes. When he'd gone, she said as much to her friend.

'Don't be daft,' Felicity replied. 'He won't care what you wear.'

'But what if he takes us somewhere posh? He will, won't he? Tell me if it's likely because I don't want to embarrass him. What about the bill? Will we have to pay some of it? Because I don't think we can spare—'

'He'll pay,' Felicity cut in. 'Chill. He always does. Money's nothing to him: he gets it, he loses it, he gets it again; it's all the same.'

'Right... but you think we'll be going somewhere a bit upmarket tonight? Somewhere respectable?'

'I guess so – I really couldn't say. I'm sure there's a swanky restaurant owner somewhere who owes him a favour so I suppose he'll take us there. Honestly, he won't care what you wear. Stop worrying.'

'OK,' Brooke said. 'Anyway, how was Santa?'

'Oh, I didn't get near him in the end. Stupid kids, always getting in there first.'

Brooke laughed. 'Never mind, I'm sure he'll come round again before the markets are over.'

Despite their discussion, Brooke couldn't stop thinking about how much she wanted to get something new to wear for their dinner with Fabien. She mentioned it so often over the course of the afternoon that eventually Felicity ordered her to go and search for something in the nearby boutiques.

'If you get busy, phone and I'll run back,' Brooke said.

'If we get busy while you're gone I'll kill you when you get back,' Felicity replied.

Brooke went, promising to be as quick as she could.

Her first stop was the rue Saint-Honoré, which was lined with exclusive-looking boutiques. The window displays were breath-taking, each one a wonder she could have stared at for hours, but there were very few prices on show, and that in itself meant Brooke probably couldn't afford them. In those sorts of shops, the only clients they wanted were the ones who didn't need to ask the price before they purchased. It was a shame because there were some lovely pieces – if a bit contemporary for Brooke's usual taste – but she didn't even dare go in to take a closer look.

Next was the underground mall at the Carrousel du Louvre. It was dazzling and magical, and she could have happily spent hours trawling the shops, but most of them were geared up for the gifting season so, unable to find what she needed there, she forced herself to move on.

Back in the open air she wanted desperately to wander the famous Champs-Élysées, but knowing it would be full of designer stores that she definitely couldn't afford forced her to focus. While it might be fun, she'd have to save that pleasure for another day.

Clean out of inspiration, Brooke sat on a bench and googled vintage shops. It was a long shot in this capital of high fashion and designer luxury, but vintage stores were where she felt truly comfortable. It was far more likely that she'd find some-thing that was a bit more in her budget and a bit more 'her'.

Really, she ought to have done that in the first place, because there were a few nearby and it would have saved her a lot of time to go straight to them.

From the information on her phone she could see there was one that sold second-hand haute couture and so was probably still quite expensive, and one on the Rue de Rivoli that she'd, annoyingly, probably passed without realising on her way out of the Jardin des Tuileries.

'Right!'

Brooke got up and began to follow the map. She'd find an outfit in this shop if it killed her.

An older woman with cheekbones that belonged on a high-fashion model was behind the counter when Brooke walked in. She looked up with a brisk greeting. '*Bonjour! Puis-je vous aider?*'

'*Bonjour! Je peux regarder?*'

'*Oui, bien sûr.*'

Brooke thanked her and headed for the nearest aisle. There was a faint musty odour, but she didn't mind that. The old wooden floor had been stripped and sanded before being polished to a diamond-hard shine, and the walls were stippled plaster, adorned with shelves of stock and old advertisements for long-gone brands of cigarettes or toothpaste. In one corner there was a leaflet stand like the sort you saw in tourist information offices, but this one was filled with old knitting and sewing patterns. A revolving stand close by was stuffed with vinyl records. There was a display case full of costume jewellery and one that housed elaborate hats. There was no sense to the layout or, indeed, the stock, which seemed to swing from era to era. Anything and everything was there, from the turn of the century right up to the noughties. It might have been frustrating to some – to Brooke, however, this was heaven.

Passing rails of tailored jackets of all colours and prints, and trousers, pencil skirts and blouses, and sumptuous coats that she was desperate to get stuck into, Brooke made her way to the rear of the store. There she found a long rail of dresses. There were short cocktail dresses, tailored work ones, long romantic summer gowns and evening gowns for the opera or some ball or other. There were some that were so outlandish they could never be worn on the streets in daylight, and some that Brooke would have worn quite happily every day for the rest of her life. But she had to ignore those, because she had to focus on her mission, which was to find the perfect dress for her dinner later. She had no clue where Fabien was planning to take them, but even Felicity had agreed it wouldn't be anywhere near as relaxed as the Lebanese restaurant they'd been to with Manon. Brooke wanted to look the part and, more importantly, she didn't want to embarrass Fabien – or Felicity, for that matter – by looking scruffy.

And then she found it. Flirty, knee-length bronzed crushed velvet, flared sleeves and a deep V-neck. Brooke pulled it from the rail with a smile, running her hand over the decadent fabric. It looked about her size.

Please let it fit!

'You would like to try?' the assistant asked as she took it to the desk. What was it about Brooke that screamed English to everyone?

'Yes please.'

The woman pointed to a door. 'In there.'

Brooke took it in and ripped off her layers. She could scarcely wait to put the dress on. She shimmied it up over her hips and then over her shoulders. The zip was a little tricky on her own, but she got it as far as it would go and then stood back to inspect her reflection.

She'd need the right shoes, and jewellery that would complement it, but that could all be sorted. As for the dress...

It could have been made for her, it fit so perfectly. She swished the skirt back and forth. It was the most divine piece of fabric that she'd ever put on her body.

She snapped a photo and sent it to Felicity. A moment later there was a reply.

Get it!

After a final admiring look at herself, Brooke wriggled to get it undone again, slipped it off and got dressed before checking the label.

Her sharp intake of breath had been completely involuntary. It had been love at first sight and so she'd never even thought to check how much it cost. If she had, perhaps she wouldn't have tried it on. But she had, and she was besotted, and she had to have it.

CHAPTER FOURTEEN

'I'd have had to disown you if you'd left that in the shop – it's gorgeous!'

Felicity gave a nod of approval as Brooke emerged from her bedroom, hair done, make-up finished and wearing her new dress. She'd found the perfect necklace to go with it on the way back to the Jardin des Tuileries, which had really made her day. It wasn't often she felt good about herself these days – Johnny had seen to that – but today she was owning it. She looked good and wasn't afraid to think so.

'Isn't it? That shop's amazing; I'll have to go back in before we leave Paris.'

'Absolutely,' Felicity agreed. 'You'll have earned a few treats by then. We could go together – I wouldn't mind a snoop around too. What are you doing for shoes?' She glanced at Brooke's bare feet.

'I didn't want to spend more time shopping for a pair... I was hoping I could borrow your knee-high boots; I think they could work. I don't have anything in my stuff.'

'Knock yourself out. What's mine is yours.'

'Thanks. Are they in your room?'

'In the bottom of the wardrobe...' Felicity waved a vague hand before turning back to her phone. She'd been ready for a good half hour and had been sitting at the dining table during that time. Brooke had heard her phone pinging like mad from her bedroom as she'd got changed. She didn't know who was messaging but would hazard a guess that it was Manon, who, in the end, had suggested going out at the very last minute. Felicity had told her that they'd made plans in the interim to go to dinner with Fabien, and now Manon was sulking. As she relayed this information to Brooke, she said that, cousin or not, Fabien wasn't the sort of man you stood up, which sounded a tad ominous to Brooke and did nothing to settle her vague misgivings about him.

In Felicity's bedroom, Brooke found the boots. As she was pulling them on, the intercom buzzed.

'Car's here!' Felicity yelled.

They grabbed their coats and bags and rushed out.

A black Range Rover with tinted windows waited for them outside the building.

'*Bonsoir...*'

The driver opened the doors to let them in before climbing into the driver's seat.

'This is mad!' Brooke said as they did up their seat belts. 'I feel like a VIP!'

Felicity laughed. 'He must like you. Fab would never send a car like this for me.'

Brooke smiled. 'I bet he would. He must be fond of you, all the stuff he does.'

'He's probably trying to make up for all the times he bullied me on my visits to his house when I was a kid. He still calls me his little poo now – that's got to be child abuse, right?'

Brooke laughed. 'It might be, if you were still a child. I bet you gave as good as you got.'

'When I was big enough, yeah, but I still owe him years of torment.'

The car whizzed them smoothly through the streets of Paris. Going through their neighbourhood it drew a few curious stares, but once they reached the more prosperous centre nobody gave it a second glance. The streets and boulevards were illuminated by thousands of lights. They were everywhere: wrapped around lampposts and woven into trees, garlanded around buildings and balconies and rooftop gardens.

'I bet you can see Paris from space,' Brooke said. 'You must be able to. It must look like a giant bauble from up there.'

'I bet you can,' Felicity agreed.

'I was a bit nervous about this,' Brooke said. 'But now I can't wait to see where we're going.'

Felicity's phone pinged.

'This is Fab now with instructions for when we get there. I don't think you'll have to wait much longer.'

'Instructions? That sounds a bit... complicated.'

'Apparently the restaurant is in a penthouse, so he's telling us how to get up there. Hang on...'

Felicity tapped something into her phone and then turned the screen to Brooke. 'I just googled it. What do you reckon? Not too shabby?'

Brooke's mouth dropped open. The website showed ornate gold chandeliers hanging from gold-painted ceilings, deep crimson carpets and chairs dressed in crisp white. There were photos that showed the views from the windows that reached far across Paris, the most prominent landmarks clearly visible.

'*That's* where we're going?'

'Yep. That must be one hell of a favour Fab's calling in! He must really like you because he's definitely never taken me anywhere this good!'

'Oh God... I hope he's not expecting us to pay for any of this!'

'Don't worry, I cleared it with him. He'd never suggest somewhere like this and expect everyone else to be able to afford it – he's not that out of touch. And he knows I've always been the poor relation.'

Fabien was already at their table when they arrived. They'd had to go through extensive security checks before they'd been directed to the appropriate lift, and Brooke felt flustered as he greeted them.

'Brooke... Felicity.'

This time they did the kissing thing, but in the end it wasn't nearly as stressful as dealing with the security on the door down below. One waiter took their coats and hurried them away, while another waiter rushed to pull out her chair so Brooke could sit.

'You look enchanting,' Fabien said to Brooke.

'Um... thank you.'

'What about me?' Felicity asked.

'You, not so much.'

Felicity grinned. 'Pig!'

'You are my cousin – what else am I to say?'

'Yeah? Well I hate your suit, so there.'

'Thank you,' he said.

Fabien had ditched the tie in favour of an open collar. It seemed to be a rebellious thing to do in here, because almost all the other men, as far as Brooke could tell, wore some sort of formal neckwear. It was one more sign that Fabien was a man who did what he wanted and usually got away with it. Perhaps that was her imagination running wild, of course, but she wasn't planning on crossing him, just in case.

He looked up, and another pair of waiters appeared out of

nowhere, as if they'd spent their whole lives in that restaurant waiting for him to summon them. He gave instructions and they left again.

'I've ordered some champagne,' he said. 'I hope that's OK.'

Brooke glanced at Felicity, who gave her a reassuring smile. She hoped her friend was right about the bill, because they'd have to take out a mortgage to pay for anything in here.

'Sounds good,' Felicity said.

'It's lovely,' Brooke said. 'Thanks so much for inviting us.'

'There's a waiting list,' he replied. 'That is always the sign of a good restaurant.'

'So you booked well in advance?'

'Oh no, I called today. They were only too happy to accommodate us.'

Brooke took that to mean that Fabien had influence, but that much she already knew from Felicity.

'Wow,' she said.

'Nobody's falling for that old line,' Felicity said. 'Honestly, you don't change, Fab.'

Fabien grinned. 'It is not too bad for a boy from Nantes who sold cigarettes at school, is it?'

'Not bad at all,' Felicity said.

'Will your space on the market make you large profits?' he asked.

Felicity laughed. 'I doubt it – not the sort of money you'd take seriously anyway.'

'It's been worth the trip, though,' Brooke said. 'Business is good so far and we still have three weeks to go.'

The champagne arrived and the waiters poured for them.

'I am glad to hear it,' Fabien said. 'Perhaps you will come again next year if it is a success.'

'We'd love to! If we could get the permit again, obviously.'

'I'm sure you will.' He sipped at his champagne and picked up the menu. 'Menu one looks very good.'

Brooke picked up hers and saw that the choices were split into courses that went together – presumably that was how the diners were meant to order. She didn't know what most of menu one was. Then again, she didn't know what most of menus two, three or four were either.

'I like the look of the fishy one,' Felicity said. 'Haven't had a good sea snail for years.'

'Is there such a thing as a good sea snail?' Brooke said in a low voice.

Felicity laughed softly as Brooke turned back to the list. She searched for one that mentioned poulet. As far as she was concerned, you couldn't go far wrong with a nice bit of chicken.

Fabien looked up and another waiter teleported over to appear at his side. He wrote quickly on a little pad as Fabien gave his order, followed by Felicity's.

Fabien looked at Brooke expectantly.

'Oh... you're waiting for me...' she said. 'I haven't chosen yet.'

Fabien reached for his glass of champagne, watching her as he did, and Brooke said the first number that came into her head.

'I'll take number three please.'

The waiter dutifully added it to his list and then left them again.

'So, Brooke.' Fabien folded his hands over one another on the table. 'Tell me about your life.'

'Oh, I'm not that interesting,' Brooke said.

'Your dress would suggest otherwise,' Fabien said.

Brooke gave him a sharper look than she'd meant to.

'I only mean that it is obviously a one-off and quite unusual. Someone who wears such a unique style must be a unique person.'

'Thank you.'

'Come,' he said, 'there must be something of interest in your background.'

'I expect Felicity has told you everything worth knowing. I went to a normal school, did a boring job for a while and then left to start the business I run now. That doesn't make me huge amounts of money but I'm happy.'

'What about your family?'

'The usual – Mum, Dad, an older half-brother from Dad's first marriage...'

'And you have a husband?' Fabien's gaze went to her left hand.

'No, never married.'

'Wise,' he said with a wry smile. 'But you are promised, surely?'

'Actually, I—'

'She has a fiancé – Johnny,' Felicity cut in. 'Don't you, Boo? Lovely guy. They're due to be married next year... yes, I know, no engagement ring. Boo left it at home, because it's so valuable. Johnny's looking after it, so...'

She shrugged and grabbed her glass while Brooke tried not to stare at her. What the hell was going on? There had to be a reason for her friend's uncomfortable lie, though she couldn't for the life of her work out what it was.

'I see,' Fabien said. 'So you are in love?' he asked Brooke, though she barely had time to open her mouth for a reply before Felicity jumped in again.

'God, she never shuts up about him!' she said. 'Morning, noon and night, Johnny this, Johnny that, isn't he the greatest? Honestly, I could kill her just to shut her up sometimes!'

Fabien looked at Brooke with some amusement. 'Is that so? How wonderful. I don't think any of my wives ever felt that way about me.'

'Hmm,' Brooke said carefully. 'I'm sorry to hear that. Was it terrible when—'

'Boo!' Felicity turned to her. 'I couldn't just borrow you for a minute? In the bathroom? You know, that going-to-the-toilet-in-pairs thing?'

'What... oh, sure.' Brooke got the hint, and it seemed like an opportune moment to figure out what was going on.

'Excuse me,' she said to Fabien and got up to follow Felicity to the bathroom.

'What was that about?' she asked as soon as they entered the ladies, trying not to be distracted by the fact that it was like being inside a Ferrero Rocher wrapper.

'He wants to take you out.'

'He is taking me out – what do you think is happening tonight? He's taking us both out.'

Felicity rapped her knuckles on Brooke's forehead.

'Ow!'

'You're not that dim surely? You know what I mean.'

'Maybe, but I can't refuse him flat out, can I? I thought if we skirted around it a bit he wouldn't ask. And maybe I could go somewhere with him, just for a friendly thing like we're doing now.'

'Oh, grow up, Boo. He'll want sex.'

'Oh, well that's definitely more than a friendly drink.'

'Look, he's my cousin and I love him, but I also know enough about him that I don't want him anywhere near you. The man's a total nightmare when it comes to women. Why do you think he's already had three wives by the age of forty? Not to mention all the nearly wives and mistresses. He makes Henry VIII look celibate. Anyone else I'd say fill your boots, but trust me, even a friendly drink with Fabien is a bad idea.'

'I suppose I ought to say thanks for digging me out of the hole then.'

'Well, I can't guarantee your fictitious fiancé will put him off. He obviously fancies the arse off you.'

'I'll do my best to dodge the bullets when they come my way then. You could have warned me this might happen.'

'I didn't think it would be an issue. No offence, but when you've got your fifteen jumpers on during the day on the stall, nobody is fancying you. It's not my fault you went out and bought a sexy dress and gave him ideas. He'd already been giving you the eye but now they're on stalks!'

'Thanks for that! And did you *have* to use Johnny in this charade?'

'First name I thought of. Don't they say the most convincing lies are the ones that are almost true?'

'Maybe, but there was no danger of me ever marrying him, so I'm not sure how convincing that lie is.'

'Not for want of trying. Anyway, that was ages ago. You keep telling me he doesn't bother you anymore.'

'I suppose—'

They were interrupted by a woman coming into the bathroom. A flawless, exotic beauty, with perfect skin, an obviously designer gown, a figure that seemed impossible for any mortal woman to achieve.

'*Bonsoir,*' she said before setting her clutch bag on the marble counter and searching inside. She rummaged for a moment, and then seemed perturbed.

'*Puis-je vous aider?*' Felicity asked her.

The woman's answering smile was guarded. 'You are English? I'm sorry, I heard you talking...'

'Yes.'

'Ah. Do you have... woman's things? I have none.'

Felicity looked in her own bag and then handed the woman a small package.

'Ah, you are so kind! Thank you!'

'No worries.'

The woman went into a cubicle.

'Gotta have a sister's back, right?' Felicity said to Brooke.

'Always,' Brooke said. 'And you are the best in the business when it comes to having someone's back.'

'Right. We'd better head back to the table before Fabien gets suspicious.'

'Don't you think he's maybe already worked out we're telling porkies? I mean, it was hardly subtle.'

'Probably, but he can't very well come out and say that without sounding like a prize knob, can he? And he'd never have that.'

'I suppose not.'

'It's a good thing he's so vain.'

Brooke checked herself in the mirror. Perhaps the dress had been a mistake after all. But she'd felt so good in it, and she didn't want that tainted now. Then again, Fabien's interest, although unwelcome, wasn't completely unflattering. For a long time after Johnny had dumped her she'd felt staid and unattractive. He'd practically told her she was boring after all. But this amazing dress and being noticed in Paris was doing wonders for her shattered confidence.

'OK,' she said finally as she tidied her hair. 'Ready.'

As they were leaving, the woman Felicity had helped came out of the cubicle.

'Thank you once again,' she said to Felicity as she washed her hands, then she smiled at Brooke. 'That is a beautiful dress. Most unique.'

Brooke beamed. 'Wow, thanks.' This perfect creature was wearing a gown that probably cost more than Brooke and Felicity earned in a year, and yet she was admiring Brooke's dress.

Then Felicity paused and looked keenly at the woman. 'Have we met before?'

'Oh…' The woman dried her hands on a thick towel before

dropping it into a linen basket. 'I don't think so. I never forget a face.'

'Me neither,' Felicity replied. 'And you really do look familiar.'

'I cannot imagine where we have met.'

'Ah, well... I'll think of it. If not, it was nice meeting you anyway.'

'You too.' She followed them out of the bathrooms. 'Enjoy your evening,' she added as she crossed the restaurant floor back to her table.

'Nice woman,' Felicity said as they made their way to their own.

Fabien was watching them closely.

'What?' Felicity asked him.

'Do you know who that was?' he asked keenly as they sat down.

'I did think I recognised her, but no.'

'That is Pascal!'

'Pascal who?' Brooke asked vaguely.

'Oh my God!' Felicity spun in her seat to search out the table the woman had gone to. 'I bloody knew I knew her!'

'Who is she?' Brooke twisted to try and find her too.

'Only one of the most famous actresses in France!' Felicity squeaked. 'No wonder she looked so perfect!'

'And she was so nice too,' Brooke said, recalling the gracious compliment on her dress.

'I must meet her,' Fabien said.

Felicity grinned at him. 'Fab... are you actually starstruck? That's not like you!'

'She is so beautiful,' he said. 'Who would not be?'

Felicity topped up her champagne. 'I suppose I can't argue with that. Alright, go and meet her, but don't you dare try to pick her up. I have to draw the line at that. It'd be mortifying.'

'I give you my word I will just speak to her,' he said. 'One moment...'

'Now?' Felicity asked. 'Won't our food be here soon?'

'I must go now...' He got up from his chair. 'She may leave before I have the opportunity.'

Felicity rolled her eyes and let out an impatient sigh. He searched the room for a moment, until he spotted the table he was looking for and strode over.

'I told you he was a nightmare with women,' she said as she watched him.

'So where is she...?' Brooke asked, trying to see where he'd gone. 'What the...?' Brooke's quizzing frown turned into shock. 'What's he doing here?'

'Huh?' Felicity looked again, and then her eyes widened too. 'Oh my God! What's he doing with Pascal?'

With the utmost grace and courtesy, Pascal greeted Fabien and listened politely, but it wasn't their exchange Brooke and Felicity were interested in now. Sitting at the table with the star was Armand.

'Why is he having dinner with her?'

'How should I know?' Felicity rolled her eyes. 'Why don't you go and ask him?'

'Don't be daft! Do you think he's going out with her? Like they're together? I thought it might be Lisette, but maybe it's her.'

'I doubt it. If he was dating Pascal, it would be all over the French press and social media, but we've seen nothing.'

'We haven't read any French press,' Brooke said, wanting to be convinced that Felicity was right but finding it hard. Pascal was clearly more in his league than she herself was. 'And as for social media, they might be really good at keeping it under the radar.'

Felicity shook her head, unconvinced. 'Under the radar is

easier said than done. And they're not exactly dining in secret right now, are they?'

'Hmmm. Though I have to admit, I'm a bit offended that he stood us up yesterday and now he's here with a film star. Feels as if we weren't important enough or something.'

'I hate to say it, but I think that sentence just summarised why that happened.' Felicity mimicked a set of scales with her hands. 'Hmmm, dinner with some rando British women in a dowdy backstreet café or dinner with Pascal the film star in the poshest restaurant in Paris...'

'He could have done both,' Brooke said, her tone tinged with reproach that wasn't meant to be directed at her friend. Felicity's reasoning hadn't helped her to feel better at all, though. In fact, it had made her feel worse and slightly vexed with Armand.

'I'm sure something cropped up at the last minute and he couldn't make it. I think you're reading too much into the situation, and it's not like he's our best friend or anything, so he hardly owes us. *And,*' Felicity continued airily, 'we did tell him we'd be going anyway, regardless of whether he joined us or not, so he probably didn't think it was a big deal if he didn't come because we'd still go. I thought you weren't bothered about it in the end either.'

'But it's so rude, isn't it?'

'Maybe he couldn't help it. You said yourself that was probably it.'

When she looked again, Armand had joined in the conversation. Sitting at an angle, he would have had to turn right round to see Felicity and Brooke, as they were doing to see him, and so he hadn't noticed them yet. Brooke wondered whether they ought to go and speak to him but felt as if it wouldn't be welcome, considering he was there with Pascal. And the fact that he'd stood them up the previous evening had her wrong-footed in a way she hadn't expected.

'Pascal looks charmed,' Felicity said as they watched. 'Bugger. I bet Fab's loving this. I bet he tries to get her number.'

'Seriously?'

'Yeah, seriously. You think I have no filter when it comes to asking people for things – Fab takes that to a whole new level. Where do you suppose I learnt it from?'

Brooke's gaze went back to the other table. She could see now that Fabien was handing Pascal a card. They bade each other farewell, and Brooke suddenly spun away as Armand looked across.

'Shit! Do you think he saw us? If he did, that makes it weird, right? Like do we go and talk to him or not?'

'Um, yeah, maybe. He doesn't seem too concerned with doing anything about it though.'

Before Brooke could think of a reply, Fabien returned to the table.

'Seriously, Fab?' Felicity chided. 'After what I just said?'

'Relax! She has my card, that is all. I have invited her to my gallery opening.'

Felicity narrowed her eyes. 'You don't have a gallery.'

'True...' Fabien lifted his glass. 'So tomorrow I will have to buy one. I will have a grand opening – you will be invited naturally.'

'You're an absolute nightmare,' Felicity groaned.

'Did you invite them both?' Brooke asked.

'*Mais oui*,' Fabien replied. 'It would have been rude to leave the gentleman out.'

'So they're going together...?'

'Perhaps.'

'So that's Pascal's partner...? Like boyfriend?'

Fabien gave her a shrewd look. 'You are very interested.'

'Well, it's...' Brooke blushed under his sudden scrutiny.

'We met him a couple of times,' Felicity cut in. 'That trouble Brooke got herself into... he got her out of it, that's all. So there's a connection.'

'Why didn't you say before?' Fabien asked. 'I would have asked them to join us at the table.'

'No!' Brooke said. 'I mean, I wouldn't have wanted to disturb their evening. We hardly know him at all, not even his full name. It's a strange coincidence, though, isn't it? That's what we meant. Him being here with Pascal and us being here with you and then meeting Pascal in the bathrooms and we didn't even know they were connected.'

'Ah.' Fabien sipped at his champagne. 'I can give you some information that might help if you want to know more.'

'Yes!' Brooke leant in a bit too eagerly and, as soon as she realised it, checked herself. 'I mean, that would be useful.'

'Then...'

Fabien paused and looked beyond her. A second later, waiters were at their table, one for each of them. Brooke waited with some impatience as the ceremony around presenting their first course was completed. Honestly, did there have to be so much fuss? Sweeping the tablecloth? Repositioning their tableware? Announcing each individual dish with a complete description and history of the ingredients? Why couldn't they simply put the stuff down like they did in every other restaurant in Paris? It would taste just as good and probably be a lot hotter by the time she ate it.

Finally they cleared off. Brooke was about to remind Fabien of the information he'd promised when Armand himself approached the table with Pascal.

'Hello again!' Felicity greeted the pair, glancing from one to the other with obvious interest.

'Hello,' Pascal replied. 'You are enjoying your meal?'

'Oh, well, we haven't actually tried anything yet,' Felicity said. 'It looks good though. How about you? Was yours nice?'

'Delicious,' Pascal said. 'Wasn't it, Armand?'

Armand nodded, looking faintly awkward as he caught Brooke's eye.

Probably feeling terrible for standing us up yesterday. Good.

But there was something else going on too. His gaze lingered, long enough for Brooke to register but not long enough for anyone else to notice. And it was as if she saw something click in him, some understanding or enlightenment in his eyes, like he'd finally worked out a puzzle that had vexed him. It was a strange moment, and one that Brooke wanted to understand herself, but there was too much going on to process it.

Pascal motioned to a waiter who was stationed at a desk. The waiters here were like robots programmed to know without words what was required of them, because he dashed off and a few seconds later returned with a pair of coats.

Armand finally spoke. 'I must apologise for yesterday evening,' he said to Brooke and Felicity, though Brooke couldn't help but notice it was mostly to her. 'I was... *detained*...'

'It doesn't matter,' Brooke said airily. 'You did warn us you might be late so we didn't wait for you. We assumed you'd arrive at some point and then we forgot about you.'

She could feel Felicity's slightly incredulous stare but ignored it.

'Still,' Armand said, 'it was unforgivable. I did not know how to contact you—'

'But you did know how to contact the restaurant,' Brooke replied triumphantly.

'Yes...' He gave a sheepish smile that was rather winning for its awkwardness, and even though Brooke was trying her best to be careless and aloof, she couldn't help the flutter in her tummy at the sight of it. 'Then my apology grows.'

'Forget it,' Brooke said, still trying to be cool but definitely feeling her resolve slip. 'It doesn't matter.'

'Thank you for your understanding,' he said, that smile still playing about his lips, and Brooke couldn't tell if he was being sarcastic or not.

Pascal's coat was slipped over her shoulders by a waiter, while Armand held his arms out for another to do the same. Brooke could almost hear what Felicity would have said:

They make a fit couple.

They did. A very handsome couple. Whatever fantasy Brooke had secretly harboured about Armand, despite many denials, was obviously just that. There was no way a man like him was going to look twice at a woman like her. And if he did, there was certainly no future in it.

'I really do love your dress,' Pascal said to Brooke. 'Isn't it beautiful, Armand?'

'Enchanting,' he said, and there was that strange look again, like he'd finally found the answer to a puzzle that had been troubling him.

'You must tell me who your designer is; I do not recognise the style,' Pascal continued.

'Oh, this is vintage,' Brooke replied.

'*Charmante.*' Pascal smiled. 'That is why it looks so unique. I hope you all enjoy the rest of your evening.'

She laid her hand on Armand's offered arm, and they left the restaurant together, Armand throwing a last unreadable look at their table before escorting Pascal out.

'Well, that was interesting,' Felicity said as she picked up her cutlery.

Fabien's answering look was shrewder than Brooke would have liked. 'How did you say you know him?'

'When I was attacked on the street a few nights ago he chased them away,' Brooke said.

'Attacked?' Fabien shook his head, tutting loudly. 'Terrible! It was lucky he passed by.'

'We said we'd buy him dinner,' Felicity continued. 'Just to

thank him, but he didn't show. Not that it was a big deal. We couldn't afford it anyway – we were only being nice.'

'So you were going to tell us what you know,' Brooke prompted Fabien.

'Ah, I was yes...' He cut into what looked like a tiny roasted sparrow. Surely it wasn't roasted sparrow? 'That is Armand Heroux.'

Brooke looked blankly at him.

'That name is not familiar to you?'

'Should it be?' Brooke asked. 'Sorry for being a bit thick, but I didn't even know who Pascal was so...'

'*La Lune est Rouge?*'

Brooke shook her head.

'Winner of the Palme D'or two years ago. Oscar nominated...'

'It's a film?' Brooke asked. 'Was he in it? Is he an actor too?'

'He wrote it. He is a successful screenwriter here in France.'

'Oh...' Brooke looked down at her plate. She still had no idea what she'd ordered and it was making no more sense to her now than it had on the menu.

A famous screenwriter? No wonder he was dating an actress. Or was he? And where did Lisette fit in? Was he seeing them both? Had he gone from one to the other? That would explain his expression every time Lisette's name was mentioned. How many other women were going to pop up? Was a woman the reason he'd stood them up at the Lebanese restaurant?

Brooke picked up her knife and fork and prodded at the pinkish lump on her plate. What did it matter? No doubt tonight was the last they'd ever see of Armand Heroux so he was welcome to his glitzy life and posh girlfriends. Brooke wasn't going to waste another minute of hers trying to figure him out.

CHAPTER FIFTEEN

So much for that being the last they'd see of Armand Heroux.

It had been an unexpectedly mild day and quieter than usual on the stall. Felicity was humming to herself as she stared out onto the market. The scents of doughnuts and sweet crêpes hung in the air while white clouds tumbled across a washed-out sky. The myriad lights that were strung across every stall front were on but barely made an impact in the daylight, though lush reams of tinsel compensated to remind everyone that Christmas was just around the corner.

'Funny how trade goes up and down like this,' she said, breaking off mid-tune.

'Maybe there's some event going on elsewhere that's got people's attention for now,' Brooke said. 'It might pick up later.'

'I can't say I'm not glad of the breather, but I hope you're right. It makes me uneasy when we're not making money.' She paused and stared at the crowds.

'Isn't that...?' She squinted. 'Yep. That's Armand.'

'What?' Brooke followed her gaze, her previous lethargy now replaced by keen interest. 'Where?'

'Over by the crêpe van. Looks like he's having a chat with his mate Jean-Luc.'

Brooke took off her woolly hat and fluffed and straightened her hair as best she could. Felicity shot her a wry look. It was too far away to hear any of the conversation, too far even to glean much from facial expressions, but both men looked relaxed as they chatted. Armand's gaze travelled to Brooke and Felicity's stall, and Brooke turned quickly to mess with her stock, face burning as she was caught in the act of spying on him. When she dared to look up again, Armand gave his friend a hug and bade him farewell before heading their way.

'Look lively,' Felicity quipped. 'Your destiny's coming over.'

'Stop it!' Brooke nudged her sharply and tried not to laugh.

'Good morning,' he said warmly. 'Are you well today?'

'Very, thank you,' Brooke said, her expression unreadable.

'I hope you enjoyed your dinner,' he added. 'You have eaten there before?'

'Not likely!' Felicity scoffed. 'We only went because my cousin insisted – we'd have gone somewhere far less stuck-up.'

'If I am honest,' he said in a conspiratorial tone, 'I must agree with you. It is rather snobby, but I was obliged to dine there because my guest was—'

'Pascal, we know,' Felicity said. 'Which is very cool. Is she nice? She seems lovely, from what we could tell.'

'She is very nice,' he said neutrally.

Maybe there wasn't anything going on between them, Brooke thought. A neutral *very nice* didn't suggest lustful fireworks; it didn't even suggest a deep friendship. It looked as if it was merely a working thing, as Fabien had suggested it might be.

'Please, about that... I must apologise once again,' he said.

'For what?' Brooke asked.

'For standing you up—'

'If this is about the Lebanese restaurant there's really no

need. And you didn't really stand us up; we didn't have concrete plans and we did our own thing anyway.'

'But at the restaurant last night... there was no time to explain.'

'Please, Armand, it's fine – we completely understand. There were no firm arrangements and we didn't really expect you to come anyway. There's no harm done.'

'I feel there is. How can I make amends?'

'You honestly don't need to. Did you enjoy your meal with Pascal?' Brooke asked, deciding she'd had enough of going over and over their failed meet-up and wanting to change the subject.

'It was successful,' he said. 'We came to many agreements.'

That was a strange word to use. Successful? OK, so now she was curious, and perfect unreadable courtesy went out of the window.

'Agreements?' she asked.

'Yes. Pascal and I were meeting to discuss a film.'

'That sounds exciting! One you wrote?'

He raised an eyebrow. 'You know?'

'Well, we didn't until last night,' Felicity cut in now, having sent her customer away happy. 'My cousin filled us in. So what's this about Pascal? Are you two an item? Is it a big showbiz secret?'

'An item?' It was Armand's turn to look confused.

'You know,' Felicity said, 'a couple? Are we not supposed to know yet?'

'Oh!' He smiled broadly, his expression coming to life finally. 'You think...? No, we are not a couple. I am trying to persuade her to read my new script. Her agent is not so keen, but I have written the part of Agnes just for her and I must have her.'

Felicity laughed. 'Now it makes sense! And did the charm offensive work? Has the expensive dinner changed her mind?'

'She has agreed to read it, but she will not take it if her agent cannot be persuaded. But I hope if she reads it, she will fall in love, and if she is passionate about it she will use all her powers to change his mind.'

'Hmm, well, good luck with that,' Felicity said.

'I have not come to talk about that, however,' he continued. 'I am very sorry I did not join you for dinner. I had some personal business. Perhaps we can try again?'

'Sure,' Brooke said vaguely. 'At some point before we leave Paris we should do something.'

'I would like that,' he said. 'But do we have to wait so long?'

'I don't know...' Brooke began uncertainly.

'Of course we don't,' Felicity said cheerfully. 'Actually...' She shot Brooke a sideways glance that seemed loaded with mischief. 'I think you were about to go off for your lunch, weren't you?'

'Well, yes, but...'

'And I'm sure Armand wants to know how you've been doing since the mugging, and I'm sure you want to know how he's been doing since he got bonked on the head by a bus stop, and so, you know, you've got an hour right now to catch up.'

'What about the stall?' Brooke asked.

Felicity laughed. 'That's what I'm here for, cretin! Don't worry, you can cover for me when you get back and I'll take an hour too.'

'I have an hour to spare,' Armand said to Brooke. 'I would very much like to have lunch with you.'

Brooke hesitated, and then wondered why she was hesitating, so she nodded. 'That sounds nice,' she said. 'I'm ready to go right now if you are.'

Their steps took them out of the Jardin des Tuileries and towards the river. Armand made a real effort with small talk, which centred mostly around what she'd seen of Paris so far.

'So you have not yet been to the Pont des Arts?' he asked.

'It was on the route of the tourist bus, but we never got time to go,' Brooke said. 'I'd like to. Then again, there are loads of things I want to see before we leave and I probably won't get time.'

'We are not far from the bridge,' he said. 'This is why I asked. We could see it now if you like.'

'Are you sure?'

'Of course,' he said with a bemused smile. 'That is why I made the offer.'

Brooke nodded eagerly. 'I'd love to see it!'

They made their way past the Louvre and out towards the river, until the bridge was in sight. It was an elegant construction of symmetrical arches and ironwork, and the instant Brooke saw it she realised she'd already seen it in endless photos, films and TV programmes. It was so familiar, it was as if she knew every girder and every inch of concrete, but that didn't detract from the impact at all.

'It's lovely,' she said as they stopped to look. 'Can we walk across?'

'Absolutely,' he said with a chuckle, 'it is a bridge after all.'

Brooke laughed lightly. 'No! I meant, do you have time for us to walk across or do you need to get back to work?'

'Ah! I have a wonderful boss called Armand who tells me I can work when I please and walk across bridges with a beautiful woman when I please too.'

Brooke blushed. Coming from anyone else the compliment might have sounded corny or even seedy, but coming from him, strangely, she didn't mind. When Armand said it, there was no seediness – there was only a sense of old-fashioned chivalry that was very appealing.

'Come,' he said, offering her his arm.

Brooke wrapped her hand around it and they began to cross the bridge. At the centre, where the Seine snaked into the distance in either direction, vast and silvery in the afternoon light, they paused to look out. In the distance the Eiffel Tower stood proud. The bridge was lined with artists, and almost all of them faced that direction, faithfully rendering the scene with paints or charcoals or pencils in their own unique way.

'It must be so old,' Brooke said, gazing out across the river.

'The Tower Eiffel?'

'No – I mean, that too, but the bridge. The bridge must be old, right?'

'Actually,' Armand replied, 'it is not. There has been a bridge here for many years, but not this one. The first bridge collapsed in 1979.'

Brooke stared up at him. 'Really?'

He nodded. 'It was rebuilt in exactly the same design. This one has only been open since 1984. And it nearly collapsed again.'

'God.' Brooke looked at the pavement beneath her feet. 'It's not still in danger of collapsing, is it?'

He laughed. 'No. It is safe. It did not collapse completely the second time, but there were so many lovelocks on it that sections were damaged so that they gave way.'

'Lovelocks?'

'Yes, tourists would come to fasten on locks with a promise to their loved ones, and then throw the key into the Seine so that the lock – and their love – would never be undone.'

'That's very romantic. I bet it looked lovely.'

'I would not say that to a Parisian,' he replied, leaning in to lower his voice, making her turn to look, so close to those green eyes and those lips that she didn't quite know what to do with herself.

'Why not?' she asked in a whisper.

'Parisians hated them; there were too many – thousands and thousands – and they were weighing down the bridge. People thought they looked ugly. They demanded the authorities cut them all down. Eventually all the locks were removed and it was forbidden to attach new ones.'

'Oh. I suppose I understand why if it was wrecking the bridge, but it seems sad. I feel like they should have thought of a new way to do it. All those declarations of love just taken away and dumped. What happened to all the locks they took down?'

'I agree,' he said. 'It is sad. I do not know what became of the locks.' He paused, studying her for a moment. 'You have a romantic soul, like a writer. Do you write?'

'God no!' Brooke said, blushing again. 'I wouldn't know where to start! As for my romantic soul, that just gets me into trouble.'

'It does?' He raised his eyebrows.

'You don't want to hear about all that now,' she excused. 'Tell me more about the bridge.'

'What else do you want to know?'

'What have you got? Hit me with all your knowledge!'

To her surprise, he straightened up and laughed loudly. Brooke watched and wondered what was so funny.

'Ah!' he said, still trying to stop his laughter. 'Well, it was the first metal bridge in Paris.'

'OK, quite cool but not as interesting as the lock thing. Why is it supposed to be so romantic?'

'I cannot say,' he mused. 'I have never heard why, only that people think so.'

'But that's the thing, it's in Paris and pretty much everything here is romantic to tourists. Is it the same to you when you live here?'

'I suppose there is a certain magic,' he said, smiling down at her.

'Magic?'

'Yes. Magical things happen here.'

'Is that why you came here to write?'

'A little, I suppose. But as well as magical things, business things happen too.'

'Well, that's a lot more boring.'

His smile grew wide again. 'I like talking to you,' he said.

'I like talking to you.'

'I believe you do, and I like that also. I like that you want to know about this bridge and romance, and not how many films I have written or which stars have been in them or how much money I have.'

Brooke shrugged. 'I didn't think any of that was relevant to today's activity.'

'Exactly!' he said. 'And I am glad not to think of it for a while.'

They walked to the far end of the bridge. There Armand pointed out the Institut de France, though he couldn't say much about what went on there and was very apologetic about that. And then they turned right round to walk the bridge back in the direction of the Louvre, though this time they stopped every so often to admire someone's painting or sketch and – if the artist was willing and friendly – to ask questions about the work.

'Thank you for my tour,' Brooke said as they arrived back at the outskirts of the market, too soon for her liking, though she reminded herself that she needed to get back so that Felicity could eat. Brooke herself had completely forgotten that she was supposed to buy lunch and had been enjoying her walk so much that she didn't let it worry her. It had obviously slipped Armand's mind too, because he didn't say a thing about it.

'Brooke, I would like very much to—'

Whatever he'd been about to say was cut short by a loud

ringing from his pocket. He looked faintly irritated but he didn't reach for it, just listened to it ring for a moment.

'You want to get that?' Brooke asked. 'Might be some hot-shot producer.'

'Perhaps,' he said, though he still didn't look as if he wanted to take the call. But then he pulled out his mobile and looked at it, and his expression darkened like a sudden summer thunder-storm as he read the caller ID.

'Forgive me, I must take this,' he said.

'Oh, right...'

Brooke was about to say something else, but he'd already swiped to take the call and moved a little out of earshot. Was she supposed to wait for him to finish to say goodbye properly, or to hear what he'd been about to tell her? Whoever was on that call, it was very obviously pissing him off, because he wore a deep frown and his speech, though Brooke couldn't make out any of it, was agitated to the point where she felt he might throw his phone into the Seine.

Just as she was about to give up and return to the stall, he ended the call and came back over. He was no longer the smiling and relaxed company she'd enjoyed for the last hour but a man who was fighting to keep it together.

'I am sorry – I must go.'

'Oh, OK. Will I see you again? Before we leave... We were going to go out...'

Brooke paused. Armand didn't even seem to be listening, his gaze searching the crowds as if he expected to be ambushed at any moment.

'It's fine,' she said. 'You need to get on, I understand. You know where we are if you want to meet up, right?'

'Yes, of course,' he said, but again, she got the impression that he wasn't fully engaged in the conversation and his atten-tion was still on the faces of every passer-by.

'So I'll see you around?'

'Yes. Goodbye, Brooke.'

He turned and strode back towards the bridge, and Brooke watched him, unable to keep the frown from her forehead.

She had to wonder if her instincts had been right and if she should have listened to them. What had she got herself into now?

Felicity had gone for lunch straight after Brooke's return, and so Brooke had been gifted an unwelcome hour alone to muse on Armand's strange behaviour. She'd always valued Felicity's input into almost everything, but when Felicity returned and Brooke told her all about it, her usually insightful friend was as stumped as Brooke was. So they'd spent the next hour or so talking it through and getting precisely nowhere. Felicity guessed that it might be something to do with his job, but Brooke didn't think so. The way he'd been scanning the crowds – it was like he'd been expecting trouble at any moment. More than anything, Brooke hoped that it wasn't trouble he couldn't handle. She'd seen him fight off a pair of attackers and do a pretty impressive job of it, but trouble didn't always come in a form you could fight off.

They'd no sooner given the topic up and turned their attention to a Facebook update on the market's page when a voice made them look up from Felicity's iPad.

'So now you are living in the clouds?'

Manon leant on the counter of the stall and grinned up at them.

'Oh hey, Manon. How's your day been?'

'Boring. But you have not answered my question.'

'What? Do I live in the clouds? You've lost me I'm afraid,' Felicity replied.

'Me too,' Brooke said as she folded a stack of tea cloths that had been thrown about by a particularly zealous customer searching through them.

'I saw you get out of the car with your driver and sexy clothes. Tell me, Felicity, are you a secret millionaire playing games with me?'

Felicity laughed. 'Not me, but my cousin isn't short of cash. It was his car and driver – we met him for dinner last night. That's why we couldn't see you.'

'Your cousin is a millionaire?' Manon asked. 'So you are worth knowing?'

'He's definitely got enough, though nobody knows the details. So I'm more interesting now?'

'Perhaps,' Manon said with a coquettish tilt of her head.

Brooke listened to them in silence. They were having fun, but something didn't sit right with her. She couldn't get the morning she'd seen Manon with another woman out of her head. Not only that, but she was so secretive and unwilling to part with any personal information that it only set the alarm bells ringing louder still. As protective of Brooke as Felicity was, Brooke felt the same about her. She hated the idea that Manon might be stringing Felicity along. Felicity had told her there was nothing to worry about, that it was probably Manon's sister or a friend, but still, Brooke couldn't shake her doubts and she didn't know why. Perhaps it was something in the body language she'd seen, perhaps it was an overactive imagination or perhaps, as Felicity often told her, her experience with Johnny had ruined her trust forever.

'So I am bored!' Manon announced. 'Come to the Louvre with me!'

Felicity laughed. 'Now?'

'Why not?'

'I can't go now! You see me working, right?'

Manon turned to Brooke. 'You can look after the customers?

Place de la Concorde is not far away if you need us to come back.'

'Later!' Felicity replied for Brooke. 'It'll be busy this afternoon and we'll both need to be here. You should have come this morning when there was nothing going on.'

'How do you know it will be busy?' Manon pouted. 'Can you see the future?'

'Go if you like,' Brooke said. 'I'm sure I'll manage.'

'See!' Manon gave Felicity a look of triumph. 'Brooke agrees with me.'

'Although I'm sure you have lots of other friends to go with,' Brooke added pointedly.

'They have all seen it a hundred times,' Manon said.

'I saw it a couple of days ago,' Felicity replied.

'Yes,' Manon said, 'perhaps. But not with me.'

'I know, and I'd love to,' Felicity said, 'but just not right now.'

'Later it will close,' Manon whined.

'If it's closed we can go somewhere else, can't we?'

'Later is no good – I am bored now.'

'Sorry,' Felicity said shortly and was spared any further debate by a family with two teenage girls coming over to look at her stock.

Brooke turned to Manon. 'We've found that trade is much slower after about seven. Come by then and I'm sure I can take over here so Felicity can do something with you.'

'I will have died of boredom by then.' Manon rolled her eyes dramatically.

Like I will by the end of this conversation, Brooke thought. She held in a sigh.

'In that case we'll make it quarter to.'

'She will not leave you again.'

'I'll be fine. I'll be certain to get on the metro instead of walking.' Brooke turned to Felicity. 'That'll be alright with you, won't it?'

Felicity nodded, though she didn't look entirely convinced.

Manon waved an irritated hand at them and then sloped off without committing either way.

Brooke let out the sigh she'd been holding in. Was nobody what they'd first seemed around here? How had she and Felicity managed to attract the most frustrating, changeable, least reliable new friends since their arrival in Paris? Was it too much to ask to meet some nice, normal, perfectly predicable people? People who were where they'd said they'd be when you arranged to meet them and weren't constantly shrouded in mystery and riddles?

She let her gaze idly wander the crowds for a moment as Felicity dealt with her customers. It had been sparse when they'd opened up but things were getting steadily busier. Then she stopped and stared. She could have sworn... surely not?

It couldn't have been Lisette, staring right at her again, just like she'd been down by the river during the choir performance, could it? But the woman – if it was Lisette – was now walking away with her head low, to merge and disappear almost instantly into the crowds.

Nice normal people, Brooke thought. *Whatever happened to those?*

CHAPTER SIXTEEN

Manon didn't come back, and when Felicity called her at 6.45 p.m. to see where she was for their Louvre date, she said she'd changed her mind and found other things to do. And so Felicity had stayed on until the end of the trading day, and now they had two subjects to mull over – Armand's weird exit and Manon's impetuous and impatient nature, and neither of them knew what to make of either dilemma.

After the first quiet evening they'd spent in the apartment together since their arrival in Paris, Brooke and Felicity took the metro back into the city the following morning to start work again. A folk band playing a free Christmas concert nearby had brought lots of people into the city and so the stall had been a lot busier than the previous morning, meaning Brooke and Felicity barely had time to think of anything except their jobs. Brooke didn't mind that at all, and she had a feeling Felicity didn't either. They were so busy they skipped lunch and so were very glad indeed to see Jean-Luc passing by. Felicity grabbed him and explained that they hadn't been able to get away and could he bring them crêpes over if they gave him the money. He immediately went off to fetch them and refused to take a penny in return.

The grind continued. By 5 p.m., night had cloaked the markets, the darkness of the inky skies broken only by a blaze of whizzing and blinking lights from the stalls and rides. As they'd come to expect, with the evening came the freezing temperatures, and while it had been cold all day, now it became a challenge not to turn into a block of ice.

Brooke stamped her feet to test if she could still feel them.

'I'm going to get some hot drinks,' she announced. 'What do you want?'

'I'd kill for one of those Swiss hot chocolates,' Felicity said.

'That sounds pretty good to me too.'

'Although, you might want to hold that thought...' Felicity nodded at an approaching figure.

While the sight of Armand walking towards the stall with a warm smile gave her that little kick of excitement that she was beginning to associate with his appearance, she couldn't forget the odd way they'd parted the day before when they'd been to the Pont des Arts together.

'Hi!' Brooke wasn't sure what to say next. Did she ask about what had troubled him yesterday? Would he want or expect her to? Or would he want her to keep her nose out?

'I am sorry about rushing away like that,' he said, tackling the question for her. 'Something... there was something I had to attend to.'

'Nothing serious, I hope.'

He shook his head. 'It is done now.'

'Oh, good,' Brooke replied, though his expression didn't entirely convince her that was true.

'Boo,' Felicity cut in. 'As you're chatting here, want me to run and get those drinks?'

Brooke shook her head. 'I'm going in a minute.'

'You need refreshment?' Armand asked. 'Jean-Luc is not—'

'He's been more than generous,' Brooke said. 'In fact he's just fed us because we couldn't get away from the stall, but we can't keep tapping him every time we want a hot drink; we'd rather buy our own from now on.'

'Would you allow me to walk with you?'

Despite the fact that he still confused the hell out of her, she couldn't help but notice that when he was around, Paris suddenly felt warmer and friendlier.

'That would be nice,' she said. 'I'd like it.'

She turned to Felicity. 'Will you be OK here?'

Felicity laughed. 'For God's sake, will you just go already! The market will be closing by the time you get anywhere!'

Brooke grabbed her purse and let herself out of the side door of the chalet to join Armand.

They walked to a stall of his recommendation. The crowds jostled and bumped into them, and they were almost shouting to make themselves heard above the noise. The sheer weight of bodies all around forced them close, so close she could smell the soap he'd washed with. Despite the competition, once she'd detected the scent, it was the only one she could focus on.

Being near him like this unlocked something that took her completely by surprise. She'd felt undeniable attraction the day before on the bridge, but this was different, altogether scarier and far less predictable. It was so sudden, so lightning fast she hardly knew how to recognise it. But though it was hard to process, she knew it was something significant, something she hadn't felt for a long time, not since the early days with Johnny, but she tried not to think of that.

Unlike those early days with Johnny, where a feeling like this had been welcomed, this was a very different, far more complicated and definitely more temporary situation. Brooke could not allow the feeling to take root because it could only end badly, at least for her. Besides, Armand was surrounded by famous actors and glamour at every turn – why would he even notice someone like her? If they hadn't met under such dramatic circumstances, if perhaps they'd just passed on the street, or even if the photo outside the Moulin Rouge was their only encounter, she was certain he would never have given her a second thought.

'This is the best chocolate in Jardin des Tuileries,' he announced, stopping at a brightly lit cart.

'How do you know? Have you tried them all?'

'*Bien sûr*,' he said with a smile.

'Well, it had better be good because we've given up our usual Swiss chocolate for this. If it doesn't make the grade, I'll never believe a word you say again.'

'I thought, perhaps, that had already happened...'

Brooke looked up at him. 'We're not still talking about that dinner, are we? Forget it.'

'So I am forgiven?'

'I was never mad.'

He raised his eyebrows at her.

'OK,' she said, 'maybe a bit. Not mad exactly, more irked.'

'Irked?'

'You know, brassed off... needled... feeling slightly inconvenienced. It's fine now, I really don't want to talk about it anymore.' She nodded towards the cart. 'So are you having one with us?'

'I would like that.'

He reached for his wallet but Brooke frowned. 'Don't you dare. I'm not so poor I can't buy you a drink.'

'But—'

'No!' she warned.

He relaxed into a warm smile and put his wallet away. 'Thank you.'

Brooke ordered three drinks and then shoved her hands in her pockets while they waited. Her fingers were numb and she was wearing fingerless gloves – good for working on the stall where she needed to use her hands, but not so good to keep warm.

'What are you doing tonight?' he asked.

'Working, I expect.'

'After that? I know you don't always stay open as long as the market does.'

'Sometimes we do – it depends on how we think trade is going.'

'Tonight? Is it going well tonight?'

'Pretty well.'

'So you would not be able to come to dinner with me tonight?'

'Not really. Felicity has plans for a start.'

'But you do not.'

Brooke stared up at him. 'I can't leave her out.'

'She is leaving you out? She has plans, you say. But you did not say you had plans with her.'

'That's different.'

'Why?'

'It just is.'

'So you must do everything with her?'

'Since I got mugged, she kind of likes it that way.'

'Tonight she does not. Brooke, I would like to make amends for missing... I know, you do not want to talk about it. Then I would like to take you to dinner, just one dinner. Would it be so bad to have one dinner with me?'

'If I'm honest, I've had enough posh dinners this week to last me a lifetime. It's been sort of exhausting. You know what I mean? Sometimes all you want is to relax and spill soup down your chin and not have to worry that you've broken about a million etiquette rules.'

'I see,' Armand said with a chuckle. 'Yes, I do know how that feels.'

Brooke took the drinks and paid the vendor. They began to walk back, Armand carrying his and Felicity's, and Brooke's hands cupped around her own, relishing the warmth and the comforting sweetness on the air.

'But you must eat tonight, surely?' he continued.

'Obviously, but I'll probably grab a box of noodles or make some toast at the apartment.'

'That sounds boring.'

'I *am* boring.'

'I do not think so. You design, you create, you have great flair, you show a business mind by coming to Paris with your goods...'

'OK I'm beginning to enjoy the flattery – keep going.'

'You look like nobody else.'

'Now I'm not so sure. Have we wandered into insult territory here? Have you finished with your list of positives and started on the negatives? Because you might have warned me first.'

'Brooke,' he said, suddenly serious, 'when I saw you at the restaurant I could barely think of my meeting with Pascal. I only wanted to look at you.'

'Me? But you hardly knew I was there!'

'But once I did...'

'That's silly.'

'It is not. You did not see everyone looking? To me, you were the most beautiful woman in the room.'

Brooke had never been someone who placed particular value on physical appearance. She enjoyed a compliment as much as anyone else, but to her, more practical attributes, like intelligence and capability and goodness were far more important. The streak of feminist pride that ran through her would argue that beauty was the last thing a woman ought to be measured by, and yet hearing those words from Armand now banished those principles clean out of her head. She wanted to hear it again, those words whispered in his rich voice, with that accent, his lips brushing her ear while his skin was so close, the smell of that soap...

'I have offended you?' he asked into her silence. 'I do not mean to make your beauty superficial. I think you are beautiful because you are also fascinating and you speak to my mind as well as my eyes.'

'Wow...' Brooke said quietly, still taking his praise in and trying to make sense of why it meant so much to her.

They were silent again as they walked, until he broke it once more.

'I *have* offended you, yes? I have been too forward?'

'No, no. I just... I don't know what to say.'

'You don't believe me? You think I am reading a line from one of my scripts?'

Brooke looked up at him. His breath curled into the air from perfect lips.

'Are you?'

'No. I write lies. All writers write lies. They are made-up feelings that made-up people feel, even the ones that are supposed to be true. But when I speak to you like this, I am real, and my feelings are real.'

'This is...' Brooke searched for their stall but she couldn't tell where she was. 'This is... I didn't see this coming, I'll admit.'

'You wish me to stop speaking of it?'

'Kind of... It's so unexpected and I don't know what to think.'

'Then I will not say another word unless you allow it.'

'Thank you. It's not that I don't appreciate the sentiment, but...'

'I understand.'

Brooke wasn't sure he did. She didn't understand it herself, so how could he? She wanted to hear words like that whispered to her from those perfect lips of his, but it was too confusing.

She wanted him and yet didn't all at the same time. She wanted to trust that he meant it, but there were doubts that wouldn't let her be and things he still hadn't explained that might make all the difference to the way she felt.

'You have not given me your answer yet,' he added. 'You have not told me if you will meet me tonight.'

As she pondered his request, their stall finally came into view. Manon was already hanging around, which meant Felicity would be itching to knock off soon. Brooke could stay on and she'd intended to, but would they really lose such a huge chunk of trade if she packed up shortly afterwards? She'd come to Paris to work, but hadn't she also come to see and experience the city itself? To lose herself in the history and culture and a completely different way of life?

'It would be just food and nothing else?' she asked.

'It would be anything you like.'

'Maybe I could spare an hour then. I can't come now, but if you're happy to drop by later...'

'I will see Jean-Luc and come back afterwards.'

'Good idea.' Brooke took Felicity's cup from him. 'While you're there, let him know he doesn't have to keep bringing free stuff. I feel so guilty about that I can hardly enjoy it. We'd happily take things, but we have to pay for them.'

'He will be offended.'

'I'm sure you can find a nice way to put it so he won't be. I mean, you could start by *not* saying his coffee is terrible.'

He leant in with a conspiratorial smile. 'But it is, no?'

'It's very strong, I'll give you that. So I'll see you later. Maybe around half eight or nine?'

'I will be here.'

Inside the chalet, Felicity took her drink. 'What was all that about?'

'What?'

'You giving Armand the gooey eyes? Is all forgiven now?'

'I wasn't giving gooey eyes!'

'Could have fooled me.'

'Hey, Manon,' Brooke said, turning to her. 'I'm sorry I didn't get you a drink – I didn't know you'd be here.'

'*Pas de problème*,' Manon swatted the apology away. 'You are going home with that man?' she asked.

'Not home, exactly,' Brooke said, almost choking on her chocolate. She glanced at Felicity, wondering what had been said about Armand in her absence, but Felicity was the picture of innocence. 'Have you two got plans then? I mean, I know you were meant to be meeting up, but are you going anywhere in particular?'

'We don't have to go anywhere if you need me here,' Felicity said.

'You don't have to worry about me,' Brooke replied. 'If Manon is waiting for you, take off and do whatever it is you were planning to do. I'll be able to manage for the next couple of hours.'

'What about the takings? I can't leave you to get those back alone.'

'If Manon is with you, perhaps cash up what we have so far and take it to the deposit box with her? There won't be much more after you go – I'd be alright taking that much by myself.'

'I don't know...'

'And I wouldn't be on my own when I leave anyway.'

Felicity's frown turned into a slow smile. 'You sly hen!'

'Well, Armand kept on asking, and it was the only way to put him out of his misery.'

'Right! I want details as soon as you're back at the apartment!'

'Who says you'll be there when I get back?' Brooke glanced at Manon, who was reading something on her phone.

'Never mind that – Operation Get Boo Laid is back on!'

'No it is not! Don't get any ideas!' Brooke jabbed a finger at her.

Just then, Manon straightened up and waved at someone in the crowd. Without a word to either of them, she took off and threw her arms around a young woman. Brooke couldn't say for sure, but it didn't look like the same one she'd seen outside the bakery.

Manon and the woman walked away. 'She'll probably forget to come back later,' Felicity said quietly as she watched. 'It'll be me on my Jack Jones tonight, not you.'

'She'll be back,' Brooke said in a voice that held more conviction than she felt. 'She's been waiting all day to spend time with you.'

'I'm not sure that's true either. I'm sure she's been doing something, but I don't know that it was waiting for me.'

Brooke sipped her chocolate thoughtfully. It was smooth and sweet and velvety. Armand's promise was a good one; he'd said it was the best on Jardin des Tuileries, and she had to admit she'd yet to try a better one. 'What does she actually do?'

'She sculpts.'

Finally a concrete detail, though not much of one, Brooke thought. 'There can't be a lot of money in that. How can she afford to live? In Paris of all places? I know our block isn't swanky but it's not exactly cheap.'

'I think the bank of mum and dad makes regular donations.'

'Ah...' Brooke took another sip of her drink. This new information certainly explained a lot. Spoilt-rich kids pretending to be poor and edgy – she'd seen plenty of those over the years at home. 'Must be a nice life,' she said.

'Must be,' Felicity agreed.

They were interrupted by the arrival of a customer. If there were deep and meaningful conversations to be had, the stall was definitely not the place to have them – at least, they very rarely got finished there. While Felicity charmed her customer, who was trying on a scarlet choker, Brooke made a start on tidying up. And though she tried not to, she couldn't help a tingle of anticipation at the thought of Armand's return. Poor Felicity didn't know where she was with Manon, and Brooke was in pretty much the same position. Like Felicity, she harboured a secret hope that she didn't want to acknowledge, but it was there all the same. Perhaps tonight would provide some answers.

CHAPTER SEVENTEEN

Brooke pocketed the keys to the chalet and fell into step with Armand. 'Where are we going?'

'I do not know. Where would you like to go? I'm happy to let you decide.'

'I don't know either. I thought you might want to show me places you know.'

'But you do not want to eat?'

'I never said I didn't want to eat; I said I didn't want to go to dinner – there's a difference. Anyway, I'm hardly dressed for a restaurant.'

'Ah, so you do want to eat?'

'Not right now. I'd like to do stuff first. What would you recommend for someone like me who has never been to Paris before?'

'It depends on your tastes. What sort of things do you like? The carousel perhaps? A walk around Galeries Lafayette? The Eiffel Tower? Or the Champs-Élysées?'

Brooke's gaze travelled to the rink from where she could hear peals of laughter above the music of the rides. 'Can you ice skate?'

'I can. Is that what you'd like to do?'

'Actually, I've never done it but I've always meant to give it a go.'

'You have never skated? How is this possible?'

'I just haven't,' she said with a smile. 'I never got round to trying it out.'

'Then come,' he said, offering his arm in the same way he'd offered it to Pascal in the restaurant.

Armand paid and they were each given a pair of skates. When Brooke took her boots off to change into them, she was tempted to abort the mission because it was so cold without them. And walking the short stretch of matting that led from the changing area to the rink on a pair of blades was a feat in itself. Brooke allowed Armand to steady her with a gentle hand beneath her elbow until they got there. At the edge of the ice, she took a moment to get ready, while he glided on and turned elegantly to wait for her, his arms outstretched.

'Oh, of course you'd be bloody brilliant at this,' she said. 'Kept that quiet, didn't you?'

'You will soon be good too; I will help you.'

'I want to do it myself.'

'You will, but let me help you begin.'

Brooke rocked back and forth, wanting to go but hesitant. And then she launched herself onto the ice. Before she realised what was happening, she'd barrelled right into him, sending them both to the ground. Armand skidded across the ice with her draped over him like an extra coat and came to a stop around six feet away from where they'd started, him on his bottom and her now with her face between his legs. She'd definitely been in more dignified situations.

'Oh God, I'm so sorry!'

Armand just started to laugh. Brooke was taken by surprise.

Not by the laughter – it was a pretty funny situation now that she thought about it – but by the way he laughed. It was full of pure joy, like he hadn't laughed for a hundred years.

'Perhaps you *should* do it yourself!' he said between bursts.

Brooke struggled to her knees and began to laugh too – it was hard not to. 'My God, my jeans are soaked!'

Armand got to his feet and, with one hand anchoring him to the guard rail that ran the circumference of the rink, he offered the other to haul Brooke up, guiding her to grab the rail too.

'Now,' he said, trying, but failing, to stop laughing. 'Shall we try again?'

'OK! Now I know it's slippery, I'm ready this time!'

'So, you move your feet like this...' Indicating she should watch what his feet were doing, he swept his skates in a sort of outward, crescent shape, one after the other, always starting behind and moving forward. 'And to stop...' He turned and dug a blade into the ice. 'Understand?'

'That doesn't look too difficult, now that you've shown me.' Brooke glanced at the swiftly moving circle of people already doing circuits of the rink. Young or old, they all seemed to be coping perfectly well. 'Let's go for it before I lose my nerve.'

'*D'accord.* Would you like me to help?'

'No, I think I can do it. I'll stay near the rail to begin.'

Armand let himself drift backwards so he could watch out for her as she pushed off. Copying what she'd seen him do, for a moment she was thrilled to move under her own steam. It was a wobbly sort of progress, but she'd take progress however it came. But then she let go of the rail and pushed away to join him, overstretched and her skates got away from her control. She almost did involuntary splits as they took her feet in opposite directions.

'Oh!'

Once again she found herself flat out on the ice and looked

up to see Armand's outstretched hand waiting to pull her back onto her feet.

'I'm not as good at this as I thought I might be.'

'We have time,' he said. 'You will get better.'

'I'm not so sure about that, but, hey-ho, let's give it another try. You've paid for an hour after all, and I'm going to skate a yard inside that hour if it kills me.'

'OK.' He let go of her hand again.

'Honestly,' Brooke said as he moved backwards to give her room, arms ready to catch her if necessary, 'I feel like a baby learning to walk. In fact, a baby could skate better than me even before they learnt how to walk.'

'Come,' he said with a warm smile. 'Everyone has to learn.'

'This lot look like they were born skating.'

'I'm certain they all fell the first time. I did, much more than you.'

Brooke pushed off again and let herself glide towards him without trying to power her movement. This time he caught her, helped her to get steady, and then moved back again to catch her once more. All the while people skated past and sometimes got between them in a most unnerving way.

'I think we're causing an obstruction,' Brooke said warily. 'Maybe I should stay right at the edge by the rail, so I can get out of the way and I'll be able to grab it if I need to.'

'OK,' he said, leading her back.

She grabbed hold of the rail, braced herself and then pushed off again. Armand skated slowly alongside her this time to shield her from others flying past.

After another wobbly start, Brooke found a rhythm of sorts – not perfect but enough to stay on her feet. She glanced up at Armand and grinned, but the lapse in concentration had her overstretching again, and once more she found herself a crumpled heap of hair and coat on the ice.

'This is hopeless!' she huffed. 'I'm on my backside more

than on my feet! I just want to skate around like everyone else – is that too much to ask? I mean, even the little kids are doing better than me!'

Armand stifled a grin. Perhaps he'd realised this wasn't the time to laugh at her, but he looked as if he wanted to.

'They have help,' he said gallantly.

They did have help, Brooke acknowledged as she looked again. Some of them, anyway, had a stabilising aid in the form of a large, fibreglass penguin with skates for feet and handlebars sticking out of its head. Armand looked thoughtfully at the equipment booth as he helped her back up.

'One moment,' he said, before leaving her at the rail and skating off.

She watched him go, talk to an assistant, and a moment later he was returning with two of the penguins.

'Oh, come on...!' Brooke groaned. 'You're not serious?'

'Why not?'

'It's embarrassing! I'm a grown woman!'

'And I am a man, but I will use one too.'

'I'll look stupid.'

'Then we will look stupid together. At least you will be able to skate.'

'But...'

'Nobody will care. If they look, do *you* care? You do not know these people and they do not know you. You will never see them again.'

'That's what I thought about you outside the Moulin Rouge,' Brooke said, 'and look how that worked out.'

He pushed a penguin over to her. 'I have paid for them now so we should use them.'

'Oh, the old waste-of-money argument. How did you know that would get me in the end?'

'A lucky guess.' Grabbing the handlebars of his penguin, he grinned. 'Ready?'

'Oh, what the hell? You only live once, right?'

Feeling like a total idiot, Brooke took the handlebars of her own penguin and pushed off to follow him. At first she was embarrassed and was convinced everyone was looking and laughing, but as they whizzed round together, unimpeded by Brooke's terrible balance, she couldn't help but start to forget she was going round with what was essentially a children's scooter on skates and began to enjoy herself. It wasn't the glamorous, capable and accomplished image she'd perhaps envisaged she'd project to the rest of the people gliding round the rink, but at least Armand looked as stupid as she did.

The funny thing was, for a man who wrote scripts for the most famous actors in France, who won prizes at Cannes and Oscar nominations, he didn't seem to mind that he might look goofy and hopeless, and that made Brooke care a lot less about the way she looked too. And it was sweet, that he'd put himself on one too so that she wouldn't be embarrassed on her own, so that they'd take the stares together. She wondered if any of her previous boyfriends would have done this for her and had to conclude that she didn't think so, not even Johnny. Actually, especially not Johnny, who'd called her boring but was as straight-laced as it got.

Their allotted hour on the ice went by so fast in the end that Brooke could barely believe they hadn't somehow been cheated out of their time. With some reluctance, she pulled off her skates and laced up her boots, cheeks glowing and nose dripping in a less than sexy manner.

'Next time I come I'm going to make sure I can skate first,' she said. 'I'm going to practise at home all year and then next Christmas I'll be doing back flips and everything.'

'It was very busy,' he replied, doing up his own boots. 'It would be difficult for anyone to learn today.'

'You're only trying to make me feel less useless – and thank you, it's appreciated.'

'I was not, but you are welcome.'

'Can we eat now? I'm starving!'

'OK, let's find somewhere.'

'Shouldn't be too hard around here,' Brooke said.

'Somewhere good,' he elaborated. 'In fact, I know some good places just outside Jardin des Tuileries, if you can walk a little.'

'Once my legs have stopped thinking they ought to be skating, I should be able to.'

He chuckled.

'What?'

'You are funny.'

'Is that good?'

'Very,' he said.

'Anyway,' Brooke replied, not sure what to make of his statement, 'I'm happy to let you guide me. This is your city after all.'

'It wasn't always so. I'm not certain it could ever be called my city.'

'How come?'

'I came to live in Paris only three years ago. My agent said it would be good for my career. I can write anywhere, but the connections I needed to be successful were all here in Paris.'

'That makes sense I suppose. So where did you live before then?'

'My family, my friends, everyone is in Burgundy.'

'Is it nice there? I suppose you must miss it if your family are all there.'

He nodded and seemed a little affected by the question, and so Brooke wasn't sure she should ask more. Instead, they headed to the exit of the rink and began to walk away.

'So much,' he said after a moment, and Brooke wondered whether he'd spent all that time trying to collect himself so that he'd be able to answer her question. 'Half of my heart is always there.'

'What about the other half?'

He patted his chest and gave her a sideways smile. 'Something must continue to beat in here.'

'So no... well, what I actually meant was...' Brooke paused. How did she ask her next question without making it obvious that she was very attracted to him? Not just attracted, but the kind of attraction that grew with every minute they spent together, something that had her afraid that she might not be able to control it. Hadn't she promised herself that she wouldn't act on it? Was it even a promise she'd be able to keep? Why was she here? What had possessed her to agree to something that was bound to lead to her breaking it? And why did the answer he might give matter so much?

She shook her head. 'You know what, it doesn't matter.'

They walked in silence for a time. Brooke sensed his hand at the small of her back – not exactly touching her, but as more of a protective gesture guiding her safely through the crowds.

Towards the boundaries of the market the crowds thinned out somewhat, though even as they crossed Place de la Concorde it was still bustling. Brooke was knocked regularly by people coming the other way or those hurrying to get past.

'It's a bit mad, isn't it?' she said. 'Not that I expected anything else but... I suppose after a day of crowds my patience is wearing thin. I feel as if I need a quiet space to breathe, you know?'

'You would like to return to your apartment? If so, I—'

'No, it's fine, not yet. I'm happy to be out for a while longer and I'm too hungry now to go all the way back there without eating first. Like, don't stand still too long – I might try to eat you.'

He laughed softly. 'I would not complain.'

Realising what she'd said, Brooke blushed. 'That did *not* come out the way I meant it!'

'It was funny,' he said.

There it was again. Was she really that funny? Nobody had ever said so before.

'Ah...' He nodded at a lit kiosk. 'How do you feel about fondue?'

Outside the kiosk was perhaps half a dozen small tables with chairs, open to the elements, but the customers who were seated at a couple of them seemed perfectly content bundled up in outdoor clothes and huddled over a pot of steaming melted cheese.

'I've never had it,' she said. 'But I'm game if you are.'

He shrugged. 'It is cheese, I am French...'

'Way to reinforce that stereotype.'

He grinned. 'Come,' he said, leading to a vacant seat. 'I will order.'

'I have to be honest.' Brooke dipped another chunk of bread into the pot and swirled it round to coat it. 'I always imagined fondue would be kind of gross.'

'Then why did you agree to it?'

'Well, you seemed pretty keen and I thought, if you like it, maybe I ought to give it a chance. And actually, it's pretty good – better than I thought.'

'I'm glad it's not too disgusting for you,' he said with a wry smile.

'I wanted to ask you... your English... it's close to perfect. Where did you learn?'

'Most French children learn some at school. Then at university I spent a year studying in London. It's useful to practise; some of my contacts are from the UK and the United States. It's often easier to speak to them in English than them speaking in French, and it's quite a universal language, isn't it? Two people from, say, Korea and... Norway, for instance, will likely not speak each other's languages, but if they both know a little English, they will be able to communicate.'

'So you got good at it in London?'

'You have to learn fast in London, don't you? Some of the accents I encountered were difficult at first but I got used to them.'

'Cockney, I bet that was the worst. Even English people don't know what's going on there. Pony? Apples and pears? Ruby Murray... what's all that about? Anyway, I was going to say it's lucky your English is so good because my French is not. This conversation would be a lot harder if we had to do it in French.'

'It does not sound that bad to me. I hear you at the stall.'

'I get by with the basics, but anything more abstract...' She popped some more cheesy bread into her mouth and chewed with a look of contentment. 'I tell you what, this stuff doesn't half make you thirsty, though.'

'Another beer?' he asked, indicating her empty glass.

She laughed. 'Oh, God, I wasn't hinting! It was only an observation!'

'I know,' he said, but got up to order more beer anyway.

Brooke watched him. What was strange to her now, as she thought about it, was not only how ridiculously attractive she found him, but how quickly she'd begun to feel comfortable in his company. Perhaps because she'd decided this wasn't a date and that it wasn't going anywhere, there was no pressure to make any kind of impression at all. There were none of those horrible first-date jitters, stilted conversations and crushing realisations that this person she'd fancied like mad beforehand was, in fact, turning out to be a dick. And she'd have never eaten runny, dribbling, totally unsexy cheese on a first date before. Probably not even on date ten or twenty. She already felt as if she'd known Armand for years despite it being days and yet, simultaneously, that it was all new too, but in the best kind of way. She just hoped that there'd be no weird running off after mysterious phone calls tonight.

He came back to the table with two fresh beers that paired so well with their food it was like it had been made only to be enjoyed in tandem with that dish. Brooke took a long drink.

'I like to see you enjoy things,' he said.

'What does that mean?'

'You are not ashamed to show that you like something. Some of the people I meet here... they would die rather than someone see them enjoying a bowl of fries. They pretend to be better or different than they are.'

Brooke put down her beer, her forehead creased. 'Does that include Lisette?'

He winced again, as if she'd taken Lisette's name and slapped him across the face with it.

'Can we talk about something else?'

'But you were together? Once? I'm only guessing but the night I first met you she was there... well, the second time. And she acted like she was your girlfriend.'

'She has not been my girlfriend for a long time.'

'What does that mean? A long time – is that like two weeks or two years?'

'We were together in Burgundy.'

Brooke's eyes widened. 'So she came from Burgundy with you?'

'Not exactly like that.'

'What happened?'

He caught a droplet from the side of his glass and studied it as it sat on his glove for a moment before soaking into the fabric.

'You do not need to worry about her,' he said finally.

'You say that, but...'

Brooke wondered whether to tell him that she felt as if she saw Lisette everywhere she went but then decided it sounded quite mad and maybe even a little bit arrogant, like Lisette would think her so important she'd spend her valuable time following her around and staring at her from afar. It had probably never been Lisette at all – Brooke had only met the woman once so it was possible she could be mistaken, and loads of women in Paris looked similar.

'Did she leave Burgundy because you came here?'

'Yes.'

'Why hasn't she gone back if you're not together?'

'I don't know.'

'Is it because she still loves you?'

'I do not love her.'

'But if she loves you then—'

'It does not matter if one loves the other if it is not both. There can be no future when only one is in love.'

'Hmm, that's kind of what my ex said to me, but it's easy to see it that way when you're the one doing the dumping. When that happens, sometimes, the other person believes that if she tries hard enough she can bring the love back for him too, and it's hard to convince her otherwise. I have to feel sorry for Lisette if that happened to you two. I hope you were kind to her when you finished it. I'm going to assume from what you've told me that you were.'

'Yes. I hope I was kind. I tried... And you are right, she believed I was mistaken and that we could stay together. She refused to let go.'

'And now? Has she let go now?'

'She is... finding things difficult. I am helping as much as I can.'

So he was still in contact with her? It seemed like a safe assumption from what he was saying. Was that the reason she was close by the night of the attack? Was he helping her then? Had they arranged to meet to clear something up to do with the end of their relationship? That would also explain why she didn't accompany him to the hospital – if they weren't together and he didn't want her in his life, she'd have known he wouldn't have wanted her in the ambulance with him either.

Some of it made sense, but there was still so much more that didn't, though Brooke found her doubts hard to latch on to and turn into questions for him right now.

'Was there someone else? Is that why you ended things with Lisette?'

'You mean Pascal?' he asked with a shrewd look.

'Oh, did I make it that obvious?' she asked with a sheepish smile.

'No, I am not interested in Pascal. I am interested in someone else.'

'This someone else... did you fall for her while you were still with Lisette?'

'Hmm, now you are reinforcing the French stereotype. We all have mistresses waiting for us in an apartment somewhere. No, I did not, and I am not sure she even wants me so...'

Brooke blushed again. 'Sorry. It's just... well, my ex dumped me in the morning and was with the woman he ended up marrying by the afternoon of the same day. He met her getting his morning coffee and... that was the end of me.'

'That is...' His gaze dropped to his beer again.

Had she said too much? Was she now that woman who went on and on about her ex to every new man she met? Was stupid Johnny about to ruin something else for her? Perhaps she'd made herself sound like Lisette? Was Armand wondering what was wrong with her that a man would dump her and immediately get with someone else?

'I'm sorry... I shouldn't have started this conversation. You didn't want to talk about Lisette, but I did it anyway and now it's led to all this.'

'No, *I* am sorry,' he said finally. 'I was not thinking of that. I was thinking how hard it must have been for you to endure the end of your relationship. I was not sure how to say it. Did you love him?'

'I guess I must have done. If I did, it's hard to imagine why when I look back on it all. I'm better now. It's partly why I came to Paris. I decided to focus on my business, see a new place, maybe have an adventure or two.'

'Have you done all those things?'

'I think so. At least, I'm getting through the list.' She smiled. 'In fact, I'm having a great time and it's getting better by the day.'

He regarded her carefully as he reached for his beer.

'Is there someone now in your life?' he asked. 'Someone important?'

'Not really. Unless you count Felicity, who looks after me like a wife, which is funny because I'm about the only woman in England that she doesn't actually fancy.'

He broke into a broad smile. 'I'm glad you have her. I have seen how she takes care of you. You're lucky to have such a friend.'

'Is there no one who does that for you?'

'Not in Paris. Perhaps Jean-Luc is about the closest.'

'But back home?'

'My family call me often.'

'That's good.'

A chill wind suddenly lifted Brooke's hair and she shivered. 'Blimey, I hadn't realised how cold I'd got sitting here. I think I might be frozen to the chair.'

He checked his watch. 'It's late. Would you like to walk?'

'Maybe I ought to finish this beer and go back to the apartment,' she said. 'It's been a long day.'

'I will come with you, to see you are safe.'

'There's no need—'

'I have to insist. I will only see you to your door.'

Looking at him now, Brooke half wished he wanted to do

more than just leave her at the door. Her guard was dropping – she could feel it, the promise she'd made to herself to resist becoming a memory. He'd told her there was nothing with Lisette and there was nobody else – or rather, he'd said he wasn't currently in a relationship...

'It's putting you out to go all that way across town for me,' she said finally. 'It's so late, and you must want to get home too. I mean, you have work tomorrow like I do? Or is your work not scheduled like that?'

'I work when I like. I stay up late tonight, I work late tomorrow. It doesn't matter. It's not so far to your neighbourhood.'

'How do you know? You don't know where my apartment is.'

'I'm sure it will not be too far for me,' he replied with a smile.

'OK,' she said. 'I suppose it would be nice to have company on the metro.'

Brooke closed the door of the apartment behind her and flopped onto the sofa with a deep sigh. She was tired, and yet she felt strangely younger and lighter and happier than she had in a long time. But she also felt perplexed and uncertain and unsure of anything that had been discussed that night with Armand. He'd been a perfect gentleman and hadn't tried anything and yet there had been an undoubted connection.

Was this the start of something? They'd clicked – at least their personalities had. She'd enjoyed her evening in a very different way to all the other nights out she'd had in Paris so far. This had been quiet and informal, almost humble. It had been pure, uncomplicated fun, and yet she hadn't been bored for a second. She'd loved listening to Armand, watching the way he looked at this or that, the way he walked, the way he thought about things, even down to the silliest, most inconsequential details, like the way he searched through his wallet for the right change to pay for something. They'd drunk beer and eaten cheese and made asses of themselves at the skating rink and it had been just about the most perfect evening she could remember.

The apartment was in darkness, apart from a lamp left on in the corner of the living room, and for a moment Brooke assumed Felicity had left it on by accident. She was probably still out with Manon – though it was late for most, it was early for Manon. But then the bedroom door opened and Felicity shuffled out in her pyjamas.

'What time do you call this?' she asked with a bleary grin. 'Dirty stop-out.'

'I know – it's usually you.'

Felicity joined her on the sofa and pulled a nearby throw over her knees. 'Come on then, how did it go? Are you now the future Madame Heroux?'

'Nothing like that happened. I'm pretty sure it wasn't a date – not as far as he was concerned anyway.'

'But you'd have liked it to have been – and don't lie! I can tell by your face.'

'I don't know...' Brooke paused, mulling things over. 'I mean, you know I fancy him. It's tempting... but I'm not after a cheap fling. I'm not sure my fragile confidence could take it for a start, and my heart definitely couldn't take it if I ended up falling properly for him and then he either ditched me because he was done, or worse, he ended up liking me too and I had to leave him behind because the market was finished and we were going home.'

'Who says it has to end there?'

'Realistically, it would. Stringing it out, trying to do long distance would only make things messier in the end.'

'It doesn't always happen.'

'More often than not.'

'Oh...' Felicity stretched and yawned. 'A one-night stand then. You need to get something out of it.'

'Tempting, I'll admit. I think I like him too much for one night to be enough. I think it sort of has to be all or nothing.'

'Then what's the answer? Are you going to see him again?'

'I don't know. I suppose we're likely to see him around.'

'But you're not going to go on another night out, just you and him?'

'I don't know if I ought to. I think common sense is telling me not to.'

'Common sense is overrated if you ask me.'

Brooke kicked off her boots, lifted her legs onto the sofa and pulled a spare corner of Felicity's throw over her feet. 'So how was your night?'

'Weird,' Felicity said.

'Weird how?'

'Manon wanted to show me the catacombs.'

Brooke frowned. 'Catacombs?'

'You know, underground... where all the bones are because they couldn't find space to bury people in the old days...'

'Yes, I know what they are but I didn't think you'd be up for that.'

'Manon kind of insisted.'

'Of course she did,' Brooke said wryly. 'So you went?'

'I kind of wanted to see them too. I mean, it wouldn't have been top of my list, but you've got to be a bit curious, right?'

'No, but go on. What were they like?'

'Closed – we'd missed the last entry. But she knew a bit where you could get down there, like an unofficial entrance... we sort of broke in, I suppose.'

Brooke clapped a hand over her mouth.

'I know,' Felicity said. 'I don't know what came over me.'

'I think I might.'

'Anyway, we had a quick look but... it was creepy. Way

creepier than I thought, especially at night and on our own. I got spooked. I kept thinking about the way we got in and how if we got stuck nobody would know we were there, and so I told her I wanted to go back up top. She wanted to go further on first.'

'And did you?'

'A bit, but honestly, there's not that much to see. I'm sure if you have a proper guide who tells you stuff about it, it's fascinating, but all I saw were rows and rows of bones. Let me tell you, once you've seen one mucky skull you've seen them all. So in the end I made her take me back out. She said I was boring and then I came home.'

Brooke prodded her big toe into Felicity's leg with a grimace of sympathy. 'I'm sorry. That's too bad.'

'Yeah, that's the way it goes sometimes. So what did you do with Armand?'

'Ice skating. And then we got fondue.'

'Cool. Your night sounds very different from mine.'

'You can say that again.'

Felicity broke into another yawn and Brooke followed immediately afterwards.

'We should probably turn in.'

'We should,' Brooke agreed. 'Don't worry if you hear weird noises coming from my room – it'll be cheese dreams from the massive vat of fondue we ate between us.'

'Thanks for the warning. I'll be sure not to rush in to rescue you then. See you bright and early.'

Felicity got up and padded to her room, leaving Brooke to yawn again on the sofa. It was so tempting to settle down where she was and sleep in her clothes, and she was certain that getting up to do her bedtime routine would make her wide awake again and fill her head with thoughts of Armand that wouldn't let her sleep at all.

CHAPTER EIGHTEEN

Brooke didn't see Armand the following day, nor the one after that. He didn't try to contact her and he didn't turn up at the market to see her.

It was frustrating, perplexing and, frankly, annoying. They'd hit it off, had this great connection, been open and vulnerable with each other, and now, for her pains, she'd got radio silence. She wasn't asking for a great commitment – even popping his head in at the stall to see how she was doing or to express his enjoyment of the evening would have done. But to simply ghost her? Actually, it wasn't even that because that would have required them to have had phone contact at some point and she, stupidly, hadn't even asked for his number. It was as if their evening together had never happened, as if he'd valued it about as much as a tasty sandwich – enjoyed in the moment but forgotten by the next meal.

'Ask Jean-Luc about it,' Felicity said, hands in her pockets, her gaze trained on a spot beyond the stall that seemed to be somewhere miles in the distance. 'It's not that complicated.'

'That would make it look as if I care where he is.'

'You do care where he is. That's why you can't shut up about it.'

'Yes, but I'm not going to tell him that. Anyway, I care against my will. And why should I? He obviously doesn't. I wish I didn't care.'

Felicity rolled her eyes. '*Ask* him. Why torture yourself? There might be a perfectly good explanation.'

'We said that when he stood us up at the Lebanese. He's probably a man who stands people up.'

'Did you ask him why he did that when you went skating with him?'

'No, because he told us it was personal and I didn't want to pry. I wish I had now. At least I'd know what's going on.'

'If you wanted to see him again you should have arranged something last time you saw him. Why didn't you get his number?'

'I sort of forgot. And I don't suppose he thought he needed mine. I mean, it's not like he doesn't know where to find me every day from 11 a.m. to 11 p.m.'

'Maybe he doesn't realise you expected him to call to see you straight away?'

'It's a given, though, isn't it? I shouldn't have to explain it.'

'In *your* head, yes. But everyone else doesn't always share your logic.'

'I'd have thought that much was logical to everyone.'

'Right!' Felicity went for the chalet door. 'I'm going to ask Jean-Luc!'

'No!' Brooke lunged to stop her, but Felicity was too fast. Before she could do anything about it, Brooke's friend was marching towards the crêpe van.

Brooke sighed as she watched her go. What was the point in trying to shout her back? She'd only go anyway. And in the end, perhaps this was more about the fact that Felicity hadn't seen Manon since the last time Brooke had seen Armand than anything else. Although Felicity knew the reasons for that, maybe the opportunity to fix Brooke's situation was a vicarious balm to soothe her own disappointment.

Felicity didn't want to see Manon again, or so she'd said. Manon was spoilt, childish, insensitive and incapable of empathy. Manon wanted people to dance to her tune or none at all. And once she was bored with someone she'd discard them like a toddler discarded an old toy.

'That Jessie doll in *Toy Story*,' Felicity had said savagely. 'Stick a red wig on me – I'm her!'

Felicity had been attracted to Manon from the start, but that attraction was gone now. Brooke wondered how true that was, but knew better than to say so.

Half an hour later, during which Brooke had been too busy to give the matter much more thought, Felicity returned.

'OK, so Jean-Luc doesn't actually know much because Armand hasn't been in touch with him either but he doesn't seem too worried. He says Armand does this sometimes when he's working on a script. Like, the muse will strike and he'll work all day and night and nobody will hear from him. Sounds like a total nightmare to be honest, all that tortured genius stuff.'

'Oh...' The wind had well and truly gone out of Brooke's sails. Was that it? As excuses went it was oddly disappointing. 'Well, I suppose if that's all it is. I mean, it's weird but it's an explanation of sorts.'

Felicity gave her a slip of paper.

'What's this?' Brooke asked, unfolding it.

'What do you think? Armand's number so you can text him, call him, breathe heavily down the line... whatever you want to do with it.'

Brooke refolded it. 'I'm not texting him.'

'Why the hell not?'

'If he wanted texts from me, he'd have given me this himself.'

'He probably forgot. You know, back to the tortured genius thing. Maybe he doesn't do technology, just quills and ink.'

'Whatever, I'm not using this.'

Felicity folded her arms. 'That's stupid.'

'He'll think I'm desperate.'

'You are!'

Brooke shook her head. 'I made a fool of myself with Johnny and I won't do it again.'

'For God's sake. Johnny's totally different!'

'Not to me.'

Felicity locked the chalet door. 'Suit yourself. Suffer if you want to. But if you did decide to call or text, all you'd have to say is Jean-Luc gave you the number because you wanted to thank him for a lovely night and ask how he's keeping. I don't think there's anything dangerous in a message like that. It's not going to compromise you in any way.'

Brooke put the slip into her pocket. 'I'll think about it.'

Felicity started to tidy her stands with a huff. 'God you're hard work!'

In the end, Brooke had the dilemma of whether to text Armand taken away from her. Against every instinct and all common sense, her heart leapt at the sight of him in his tailored coat as he made his way towards the stall. As if there had been no gap, as if he'd only left her minutes before, his green eyes were bright with a hidden mischief and good humour that the formality of his dress couldn't hide.

'Hello,' he said with a warm smile.

'Oh, hi,' Felicity said wearily. She shot Brooke a significant glance. 'Don't mind me,' she added. 'I'm just off to see if I can get some change from any of the other vendors – we're running a bit short.'

Armand turned to Brooke. 'I enjoyed our evening together,' he said. 'I have thought of it a lot since.'

'Have you been very busy? I suppose you must have had a lot of work as I haven't seen you at all.'

'Quite a lot. But in truth... I didn't know whether I would be welcome here so soon after.'

Brooke frowned. 'Why not?'

'I thought perhaps... how do you say it? I might be coming on too strong.'

Brooke smiled. 'No, you wouldn't have been! I didn't want to bother you for the same reasons! Silly, eh?'

'So does that mean we could do it again?'

'I'd like that!' Brooke replied breathlessly.

'I know you are busy right now. Name the day and I will be here.'

'I should probably ask Felicity. She's got to—'

'What's that?' Felicity asked as she arrived back. 'Ask me what?'

'And of course,' Armand said uncertainly, 'you are more than welcome to come, Felicity.'

'God no!' Felicity snorted. 'If this is what I think it is then I don't fancy being anyone's gooseberry!'

Brooke looked at Armand. What was it exactly? She knew what she hoped it was, but did either of them really know? And did they both want the same thing? Were either of them brave enough to say what they wanted it to be?

'Go tonight for me,' Felicity said, dropping her coins into the cashbox. 'I can manage here.'

It was Armand's turn to aim a silent question at Brooke. This time was as spontaneous as the last. It always seemed to be the way with him. Perhaps in life he was the same as he was in his writing – having to be struck suddenly by the muse before throwing himself, heart and soul, into it. Maybe that wasn't such a bad thing. If he'd said tomorrow or next week, perhaps that would have given Brooke too much time to overthink it and chicken out. Maybe he felt that too.

'Yes,' she said, drawing a breath. 'If we keep things low-key again, I suppose we could go straight from the market and I wouldn't have to waste time going back to the apartment to get changed. If you don't mind having me in my hat and boots.'

'Shall we say eight?' he asked.

'Maybe nine? If that's not too late for you. I don't want to leave Felicity on her own for too long.'

'What am I, five?' Felicity scoffed. 'I'm right here, you know – just ask me what time I can manage from.'

Armand chuckled softly. 'Felicity, what time would you be able to spare your partner?'

'Now,' she said. She turned to Brooke. 'Bugger off – you're driving me mad!'

'But it's not yet—'

'Don't care. You're so useless today I'm sure I'll hardly notice you've gone.'

'What about the takings?' Brooke reminded her. 'It's too early to cash up and I can't leave all that money here with you – it's too risky.'

'Do you think I'll spend it all on mulled wine?'

Brooke frowned. 'You know what I mean.'

'Jean-Luc has a safe,' Armand said.

They both looked at him.

'That's information we'd have found handy far earlier than this,' Felicity said.

'I'm afraid I only now thought of it. It's not far from here – you could go with him at the end of the night to store your cash there until you are ready to take it to your bank.'

'So that's sorted,' Felicity said.

'It's too busy now,' Brooke said stubbornly. 'Far too early to be knocking off... sorry, Armand, but you'll have to come back.'

'No you don't, Armand. It dies down over the next couple of hours,' Felicity said. 'You know it always does, Boo. Go! You can return the favour another day when I get invited somewhere.'

Brooke gave her a look of sympathy. It wasn't hard to guess what Felicity meant by that.

'Thank you,' she said, with a small smile that told Felicity she understood.

She turned to Armand. 'I suppose that means I have time to go and get changed after all. Depends what you want to do, of course. I mean, if you want to go to dinner at a proper restaurant or something. Though I guess if you wanted to go to the ice rink again, I'm good to go as I am.'

He pushed his hands deep into his pockets and smiled at her. 'What would you like to do?'

'I can choose anything?'

'Yes, whatever you like.'

'Well, I suppose it might be kind of boring to you, but I haven't seen that much of Paris yet. I mean, we did the bus trip and you took me to the bridge, but there's still so much we haven't seen. So I'd quite like to do the sad tourist thing. Does that make you wish you hadn't asked?'

'Not at all. Don't you know there is no greater pleasure than sharing a place you love with one who has yet to discover it? Come! Paris awaits!'

'I don't know whether to feel sad, happy, hopeful or... I don't know what to feel when I look at it.'

'Even half destroyed it is still beautiful, no?'

Brooke and Armand stood side by side, staring up at the shadowed hulk of Notre-Dame. Where the lights of the building site now surrounding it touched, evidence of the construction was plain to see, as were the scorch marks, rivers of melted and then reformed lead and fire-blackened buttresses and walls and the skeleton of what had once been a magnificent, historic building. Armand had promised that seeing it, even though it was badly damaged, would bring a feeling of courage and optimism and awe for the skills of the armies of people fighting to save it after the great fire that had almost wiped it from existence. Brooke wasn't sure she felt any of those things. She appreciated his sentiments, but she only felt a deep sense of melancholy and a sense of the loss she'd feel if the same fate had befallen her own beloved cathedral back in Ely.

'Would you like to walk around it?' he asked. 'I can show you the places where everything used to be. Perhaps you will be able to imagine what it will look like once it is rebuilt.'

'Sure – why not?'

She followed where Armand led. The building, for obvious reasons, was out of bounds, and a very distinct perimeter stopped anyone from getting too close. The white barriers, plastered with safety notices and work lamps, were jarring seen against the ancient stonework, an odd, uncomfortable clash of function and beauty, old and new.

As they inspected what they could see of the building from a distance, stopping to review it from each new angle, Brooke supposed there was a sort of tragic beauty to it, but still, all those centuries of history, of toil, of humanity, all gone up in smoke. Notre-Dame had survived war and plague and revolution, only to be caught unawares by some random fire in the twenty-first century that had almost done what all the other dangers had not been able to.

'It gives me inspiration,' Armand said. 'Sometimes I come to look at it and then I am struck.'

'Seems like a funny sort of inspiration to me,' Brooke

replied. 'I wish I could say the same, but all I can think of is what a terrible waste it is.'

'I am sorry. My intention was not to make you sad.'

'I'm not sad. I suppose I must not be in the right frame of mind to appreciate it right now in the same way as you. Maybe if I came back another day I'd feel differently.'

'Then we will go somewhere else for now.'

'I think I'd like that.'

'Where to?'

Brooke thought for a moment. 'Is it too late to go up the Eiffel Tower?'

'I do not think so,' Armand said. 'It is usually open until late, and at night the view is spectacular.'

'Then I'd like to do that.'

'Are you hungry? Perhaps we could eat on the way?'

'I am actually. But no more fondue please. I mean, it was good, but I don't think my arteries could take that much cheese in one week.'

He smiled. 'I have something very different in mind. We have a little walk first.'

'To where?'

'That is a surprise.'

'Come on – tell me where we're going.'

'You do not like surprises?'

'It depends what they are,' Brooke said darkly, and he laughed.

'You must be patient or you will spoil it.'

'Ah, well I've got no patience, so...'

'I'm sure that is not true. After all, you waited for me.'

'What do you mean...? Oh! I suppose Jean-Luc told you that Felicity was asking where you'd got to.'

'Yes, and I am flattered that I was in your thoughts often enough for you to wonder. I'm sorry I did not let you know sooner, but now you have my telephone number, you can ask me whenever you like.'

'Hmm. I suppose that means you ought to have my number too.'

'I think it only fair.'

'When we get where we're going, I'll let you have it.'

'I very much look forward to getting it from you.'

Brooke giggled. 'My number! I'm talking about my number!'

'As was I,' he said in an impish tone.

'You really did spend too long in London, you know!'

'I have no idea what you are talking about.'

His profile was lit warmly by the orange lamps that lined the banks of the river. It was almost too perfect.

'You're secretly a massive tease, aren't you?' she said. 'You pretend to be all serious and intellectual but you're actually a wind-up merchant.'

He frowned slightly. 'What is a wind-up merchant?'

'You are! Don't tell me you never heard that phrase in London, because I would have imagined people saying it to you all the time.'

He shook his head slowly. 'Explain to me.'

'A wind-up merchant is someone who likes to tease and make fun, or make someone look a bit silly.'

'I would never do that to you,' he said, suddenly serious. 'I would never make fun of you – I like you too much.'

'I mean, it's not as bad as I made it sound. Not always anyway. So where are we going?'

'You will find out very soon now.'

'You seem to have something very definite in mind.'

'I do.'

'And you were adamant that we had to go to Notre-Dame first.'

'I thought you wanted to see it too.'

'Yes, but it was a strange order to do things – map wise. And this place we're going now is close to Notre-Dame?'

'It is not too far away.'

'So this is something you planned?'

'Perhaps.'

'So you knew I'd say yes to coming out tonight?'

'I had hoped so.'

'And this thing we're doing... is it, like, a booked thing?'

'Yes.'

'Booked for what time?'

'You are Sherlock Holmes now?'

Brooke grinned. 'So this thing that's booked... we're here in the right place at the apparent right time... but how did you know I'd say yes to food right now? I might not have been hungry yet.'

'There was some guesswork involved.'

'Hmm...' Brooke paused. 'I don't know whether to be impressed or scared.'

'Impressed is more flattering for me,' he said with a smile. 'But it wasn't as difficult as you may suppose. I simply took out my telephone' – he waved his mobile at her – 'opened a page and booked as we walked from Notre-Dame.'

'See, now you're winding me up again. Nothing is going to be available that short notice in Paris, surely.'

'If you know where to look, it can be.'

They followed the riverbank for another fifteen minutes, all the while Armand pointing out sites of interest on both sides of the river, until they reached a set of stone steps leading down to a jetty. A river cruiser, the roof entirely of glass, was moored up while a queue of people waited to board.

Brooke looked up at him. 'A river trip?'

'A river cruise with dinner. All the tourists do it. You wanted to be a tourist today, didn't you?'

'But I'm not dressed for dinner.'

'Do not worry about it,' he said. 'You look lovely.'

His words warmed her. 'I suppose no one is going to care... why would anyone be looking at me?'

'I will be,' he said, causing her to blush violently.

'This is amazing!' she said. 'Thank you.'

'I hoped you would say that.'

'You knew I would, I think. You just seem to get me; I don't know how. How is it that you get me the way you do, even though we've only just met?'

He smiled but didn't give her an answer. Instead, he got out his phone to display the tickets for their reservation.

There it was again, that niggling doubt. Could it be that simple? Was it really as it seemed? Or was this Armand, doing what he did with many women, an elaborate con that flattered them into thinking this special treatment was reserved for only them.

She checked herself, the notion threatening to ruin what was turning out to be an amazing night. Perhaps she oughtn't to care so much. So what if this didn't last? So what if it was only a fling? At least for tonight, perhaps she ought to focus on enjoying their evening. And so she promised herself she would, that she'd savour every delicious moment, and if he took a thousand women on the same trip after she'd gone back to England then it wouldn't matter because tonight was all hers and the others would never be able to take that from her.

Half an hour later the boat was gliding on the water so smoothly Brooke could hardly believe they were on a boat at all. But outside the vast windows was all the proof she needed: the lights of Paris reflected like stars on the blackness of the water as they cleaved a path, the gentle hum of a finely tuned engine, and rows and rows of elegantly lit buildings at either side as they moved through the city.

Inside, the dining tables were dressed in white damask cloths, silver cutlery and Tiffany lamps, and waiters moved between them in formal suits delivering the first course.

'This is like being on the Orient Express!' Brooke whispered across the table. 'I mean, like the Orient Express but on a boat, not a train. Like if the Orient Express was a boat it would look like this... do you think there is a boat Orient Express already? I bet there is – I bet it's amazing!'

'So you like it here?'

Brooke reached for her wine. 'Are you kidding me? It's amazing – I love it!'

'I am glad.'

She took a sip of her crisp Chablis and regarded him in the lamplight. His features were softened by the glow but so much more handsome for it. Instead of being impressively chiselled, somehow he seemed more approachable and human, and she liked that. He seemed like the sort of man who would hold you as you went to sleep, who would take you in his arms and listen to your troubles, in doing so making them fade to nothing. It felt suddenly so natural to be here in his company and right that she should want to kiss him, as she did so badly. She had to remind herself that she wasn't going to allow it.

But what even was this? Was this still an evening with a new friend? Or had this suddenly, stealthily slid into date territory? Was he expecting to be kissed? Had this been his plan all along? After all, this dinner was a touristy thing, to be sure, but it was also a pretty romantic thing to do.

'How is your wine?' he asked.

'Lovely. How's yours?'

'The same as yours...' He shook the bottle and she giggled.

This place, the atmosphere, the excitement of the new was

making her far giddier than the alcohol. The space was filled with chat and laughter, and that was infectious too.

Armand had chosen one of the set menus for them, and as the first course arrived and the plate was set in front of her, she glanced up at the waiter.

'Your brie tartlet, mademoiselle.' He placed an identical plate in front of Armand. '*Bon appétit.*'

As he walked away, Brooke grinned at Armand. 'More cheese? How come spending time with you always involves cheese?'

'Because I am cheesy?' he asked, sending her into another giggling fit.

'I'm glad you said it!'

'I thought I would save you the job.'

'You're not cheesy,' she said, her laughter subsiding. She looked around. 'Actually, maybe this boat thing is a bit – Felicity will definitely think so – but I don't care; I love it. Sometimes a bit of cheese in your life is a good thing, right?'

She cut into her tartlet and put a chunk into her mouth. 'Oooh, that's good. I wasn't sure it would be, but I could eat another twenty of those.'

'Why not?'

'Well, because this is for the tourists, isn't it? I thought maybe the locals kept all the good food for themselves and gave the undiscerning foreigners all the muck. I mean, it's not like most of us could tell the difference.'

Armand chuckled softly as he cut into his own tartlet. 'Did you think I would take you to a place with terrible food? After all, I have to eat it too. Have you forgotten I am French?'

A waiter appeared to pick up their wine bottle and fill their glasses.

'Bit presumptuous,' Brooke said, grinning as he left them again. 'I might not have wanted my glass filling.'

'But then he may have removed you from the boat for being crazy.'

Brooke laughed as she picked up her glass. 'True. So you know your really famous film?'

'It's not really my film.'

'But you wrote it. What's it called again...?'

'*La Lune est Rouge.*'

'That one, yes. What's it about? I mean, sorry, but I haven't seen it. *Obviously* I'm going to watch it now, I mean, as soon as I have time...'

'Hmm... would you like a simple or a complicated version?'

'Keep it simple. If we get through all this wine tonight, I may have to ask you again tomorrow anyway.'

'Love,' he said.

'Oh...' Brooke put down her glass. 'That old chestnut. I'm sure it's great, but just once I wish something wouldn't be about love. No offence.'

'Isn't everything about love, in the end?'

'I don't know about that, but I know it causes trouble wherever it goes.'

'That I must agree with,' he said. He raised his glass. 'To troublesome love.'

'To troublesome love.' Brooke laughed before putting the glass to her lips.

A few minutes later there were only crumbs on the plate where Brooke's tartlet had been.

'You enjoyed it?' Armand asked.

'You mean to say I ate it very quickly?'

'A little,' he replied with a grin.

'In my defence, it's been a long day in the cold and I was getting very hungry, and that tart was very tasty. I'm only human.'

'If you were hungry you should have told me earlier.'

'And totally cock up your lovely surprise? No, I'm glad I

didn't. But… they'd better get their skates on in that kitchen because I'm ready for that next course!'

'It is lucky you are not wearing the skates because it would have taken a long time to arrive.'

'Cheeky bugger!' Brooke squeaked. 'I wasn't that bad! Well, not once I got my penguin.'

'Ah, yes, I forgot about the penguin. So they must have a penguin for you in the kitchen?'

'They'd have to fit some contraption to the front to hold the plates for me. I couldn't very well balance them *and* myself. Maybe fit a tray between the handlebars.'

'I would very much like to see that restaurant.'

'Maybe I should pitch it on *Dragon's Den*?'

'What is *Dragon's Den*?'

'Oh, it's a TV show in England. I suppose you never saw it – nowhere near intellectual enough for you I bet. Come to think of it, maybe it wasn't even on air when you were in London… what year did you say you studied there?'

'It was 2002–2003.'

'Hmm, so you're…' Brooke counted on her fingers. 'How old are you?'

'Forty-one.'

'Oh, that's good. I mean, I'm thirty-five so we're practical-ly… not that far apart… I mean, I'm trying to say we're the same age because…'

She knocked back the rest of her wine.

'Oh, what the hell? Armand, this might sound presump-tuous and, God, I hope I don't make the night suddenly weird, and maybe it's a bit dim of me not to know, but… are we on a date?'

A slow smile spread across his face. 'Would you like it to be a date?'

'At first I wasn't sure, but now… maybe.'

'Then it can be whatever you want it to be. You tell me.'

He reached for the bottle and filled her glass. Brooke watched him, his features soft and approachable in the lamplight, and oh so sexy.

The sound of violins suddenly filled the air, followed by deeper tones, and Brooke twisted in her seat to see a string quartet had begun to play in the corner of the room.

'Oh my God! This is the best thing ever!' She turned to Armand. 'Nobody has ever done anything like this for me before!'

'No?'

'Not once! Nothing this lovely and thoughtful.'

'Then that makes me sad.'

'Why? I didn't mean it to be sad – it was meant to be a compliment.'

He shrugged. 'This is not even difficult. A few clicks on my telephone, a short walk... it is done. But you say nobody has ever done that much for you? Nobody should have to say they were not even worth a few clicks and a short walk to someone else.'

'But I didn't mean it that way...'

'Perhaps you must think more about what you have said and what it means. You say it does not matter, but then you are agreeing that you are not worth that much, and I have to tell you that it is not true.'

Brooke was thoughtful for a moment. 'I suppose I just met the wrong men.'

'I think *that* must be true.'

'Well...' Brooke glanced appreciatively at the quartet and then back at Armand. 'I won't be doing that again. If they're not taking me to dinner on a boat with a string quartet for our first date then I'm not interested.'

Armand readjusted his cutlery with a smile. And then he looked up.

'Our next course has arrived, and look... not a penguin in sight.'

· · ·

As the evening wore on Brooke found herself opening up to
Armand – perhaps more than she would have liked. But it was
difficult to resist his silky tones and thoughtful words, the attentive looks and soft lighting, the band playing sweetly, the delicious food and bewitching ambience, and perhaps the wine
played a part too.

The wine definitely played a part. All winter chill had been
banished by the first glass, and by the third Brooke had forgotten, or ceased to care, that she was woefully underdressed for an
occasion like this, sitting there in her jeans and jumper, a beautiful dress that would have been perfect hanging up in her
apartment.

As the meal concluded, to more hilarity at the appearance
of the cheese course, Armand smiled across the table at Brooke,
and her insides turned into a cloud of madly fluttering wings.

'What would you like to do now?' he asked.

She had some ideas, but it probably wasn't a good idea to
tell him those ones.

'Do we still have time to go to the Eiffel Tower?'

He checked his wristwatch. It looked old, like it might be an
antique or an heirloom. Brooke found it quaint that he had one
– Johnny had always said it was pointless when you had a
phone to tell you the time.

'I think we could make it. The tower closes at 11 p.m. Do
you have your penguin to hand? I ask because we would need to
get our skates on.'

Brooke giggled. 'I've started something, haven't I?'

'A terrible joke?'

'Yes, and it's not going away any time soon.'

· · ·

After they'd put on their coats and disembarked, Armand offered his arm. 'Your skates are ready?'

'Willing and able.' Brooke smiled, looping her arm through his. It wasn't weird or forward at all; it all felt perfectly natural, more so in light of the fact that this was now officially a date – of sorts. And as it was, perhaps there was no reason to deny herself the closeness she was itching for.

What was all that nonsense about not letting her guard down?

They made it just in time for the last trip up the tower. The lift was full and they were forced to stand close. His coat smelt of cold and of the soap he used, and there was a faint whiff of something more expensive, like a good cologne. It was late, and although it was usually possible to walk the steps that led to the viewing platforms, the guide had not recommended it in the dark and at a time when it might be difficult to make it before the tower closed for the night. And so they were now in a strangely industrial-looking elevator that was more like a service lift, and not nearly as opulent as Brooke had imagined. If anything, the trip to the top was long and disappointing, and if not for Armand being with her, she'd have felt a little like she'd wasted her money.

But then the lift doors opened and they stepped out and all her negative thoughts disappeared. The passengers all filed out to find the lights of Paris spread out below them.

Brooke gasped.

'It's beautiful?' he asked.

'Incredible!' Brooke went to the edge and looked out. The view was obscured somewhat by safety measures, but if she pressed her face close to the grille she could see it more clearly.

Armand drew close. 'It is cold.'

'It's freezing,' she said. 'But for this view, I'll suffer it.'

He looped an arm around her. It wasn't sleazy or overfamiliar, just protective and comforting. 'Does that help?'

'It's lovely, thank you. So what can I see from here?'

'So...' He pointed to a glittering, wandering line. 'The Seine obviously. And there is an iron bridge...' He moved his finger a little. 'Pont de Bir-Hakeim. Have you seen the movie *Inception*?'

'Yes,' Brooke said, trying not to think of sitting through an excruciating three hours with Johnny on his sofa.

'The bridge was in that movie. And there...' He moved his finger again. 'Jardins du Trocadéro. Have you been there yet?'

'No. Are they worth a visit?'

'They are beautiful – I will take you. And there...' He moved his finger again. 'That is—'

'Can I be honest?' Brooke cut in. 'I'm kind of pretending I can tell where you're pointing, but I really can't. You could be showing me anything... Maybe we can just enjoy the view after all. I don't suppose it matters what's down there, only that it all looks so pretty from up here.'

'You are not too cold?'

'No, I can manage.'

He stepped back and opened his coat. 'Step in,' he said. 'It will warm you a little.'

Brooke snuggled in and let him wrap the coat around her. She turned her gaze back to the city, her head resting on his chest, the soft wool of his sweater against her cheek. There was that scent again, the distinctive concoction of all the things that made him more potent than any wine.

'Better?' he asked, his voice reverberating through his chest as it reached her.

'Lovely,' she said.

There was a brief silence. Around them, other visitors gasped and pointed and snapped photos, but Brooke hardly noticed them.

'So if this is a date,' she said after a completely comfortable pause, 'and we're at the top of the Eiffel Tower, which is kind of romantic, this would be the part where kissing would occur, wouldn't it?'

She twisted to look up at him.

'Would you like me to kiss you?'

'Yes, I think I would.'

With the lights of Paris below and the icy wind whipping around their bundled, entwined figures, they did just that.

CHAPTER NINETEEN

As Brooke emerged from her bedroom the following morning, Felicity was letting herself into the apartment.

'I went to get breakfast,' she said, holding up a bag. 'As you weren't up yet I thought I might as well.'

Brooke peered closely at her. 'Have you... did you even come back last night? Because you look as if you didn't.'

Wearing a full face of dramatic make-up (and she never did any make-up at all until they'd had breakfast), and almost certainly still wearing her nightclub-type clothes, Felicity definitely had the look of someone who'd been out all night, and Brooke would have been very surprised to hear her deny it.

'I stayed at Manon's place,' she said airily. 'That's alright, isn't it?'

Brooke's eyes widened. 'You're back on? When the hell did this happen?'

'Last night. She texted me and we went out to this live lounge place to hear some music. One thing led to another and...' She shrugged.

'Well, I hope you know what you're doing.'

'What's that supposed to mean?'

'Nothing. I didn't mean anything bad; I only meant you said yourself that Manon can be high maintenance. She's not exactly the most easy-going, reliable person in the world, is she?'

'True. I know none of that is going to change either. But, you know, I'm going to take things as they come.'

'Well, as long as you're happy.'

'Oh, I'm happy,' Felicity said with a smirk. 'So how was your night? Did you manage to resist his charms?'

At that moment, the door to Brooke's room opened and Felicity's mouth fell open too.

'*Bonjour,* Felicity.'

Armand's dark hair was dishevelled and his feet were bare. He wore the trousers he'd taken Brooke out in the previous night and just the T-shirt that had been under his sweater.

'Shall I make some coffee?' he asked, a faint look of amusement on his face as Felicity continued to stare.

'Sounds great,' Brooke said. 'Give me a second and I'll come show you where everything—'

'I'm sure I will find it. I remember from last night, your kitchen is very small – it cannot be hard to find your coffee.'

As he went through, Felicity turned to Brooke. 'You dirty dog!' she whispered. 'Why didn't you warn me he was here?'

'I was getting round to it, but, if you recall, you had some dirty secrets of your own to divulge and I was busy getting through those first.'

Felicity gave a manic grin. 'My God! Get us!'

'We're hopeless, aren't we?' Brooke said. 'Like teenagers!'

Felicity giggled and Brooke couldn't help but join in. In the cold light of day she was faintly mortified by what she'd done and the way Felicity had discovered it, but she also felt more alive, more attractive and desired, more a whole woman than she had since Johnny left her. Maybe even before that, because Johnny had never shown her the sort of passion Armand had. A gentleman during the day, he was satisfyingly less so during the night, but Brooke had no complaints on that score.

Felicity yanked her over to the sofa. 'I need to know everything!'

'He's right there in the kitchen!' Brooke protested, but Felicity shook her head.

'Don't care. Talk quietly. Need to know!'

Brooke tried to frown, but this morning anything other than a soppy smile was going to prove beyond her.

'Later. We'll have time when he's gone.'

'We'll have to man the stall in an hour and we haven't even had breakfast yet!'

'There will be lulls in trade – there always is,' Brooke said patiently. 'There'll be plenty of time to gossip. You're always bored by about four, so it'll give us something to do.'

'I'm not waiting until four! That's ages!'

'OK, the first quiet minute we get, I promise I'll tell you everything.'

'Fine.' Felicity folded her arms. 'But don't think I'll forget.'

'I'd never think that – I know you too well.'

'I'll tell you one thing, though – Fabien will be annoyed.'

'Fabien? But we told him I was with someone anyway.'

'He didn't buy that for a minute. He's still asking about you.'

'You never said.'

'And I wasn't going to. But now you're all loved up with someone else I suppose it doesn't matter. There's no likelihood of you accidentally ending up with my dodgy cousin now, so there's that.'

'I was never going to end up with him.'

Felicity pointed at the kitchen door. 'Didn't you also say you were never going to sleep with him?'

'Coffee!' Armand said brightly, coming through the door Felicity had just indicated. If he'd heard any of their conversation, he didn't show it. On a tray he was carrying a pot and some cups.

'Perfect!' Felicity said. 'We've got croissants.' She went to the dining table and ripped open the bag. Armand put the tray down, looked at the croissants and then back at Felicity expectantly.

'We're not all monsters,' Brooke said with a faint smile, getting up from the sofa. 'I'll get the plates and jam, and if Felicity wants to eat hers straight out of the bag like a feral child, she can.'

It had been a strange but not unpleasant breakfast. Even stranger to have Armand use the shower before her and then accompany them both to Jardin des Tuileries on the metro. They were all in good spirits as he walked them to their stall and then turned to Brooke as Felicity unlocked it.

'When can I see you again?'

'Hmm, what's the norm here? If I say tonight is that making me look too keen?'

'I was hoping you'd say tonight. I will meet you here; tell me what time.'

'I'd better talk to Felicity first, see what her plans are. I'll let you know later. I have your number now after all, so there's no rush to sort it now, is there?'

'I will look for your message.' He leant closer, as if to kiss her, but then they both turned sharply at the sound of his name being shouted. Jean-Luc was hurrying towards them.

'Salut!' Armand said, but Jean-Luc simply waved away the greeting, pulled Armand to one side and began to speak in a low tone in French so rapid Brooke didn't catch a single word. He seemed agitated about something and kept glancing at Brooke, which was hardly reassuring her. Then, to her dismay, Armand's expression darkened too.

'I am sorry,' he said, turning finally back to her. 'I must... I have something to discuss with Jean-Luc... in private.'

'Oh, that's OK,' Brooke said. What else could she say? She tried not to let him see that his mood change had rattled her – whatever the problem was, she had no wish to add to it. 'I need to get on anyway... you know, this stall won't open itself. I'll see you later?'

'Yes.'

Armand strode off with his friend, their heads low in earnest conversation as they went. Brooke frowned as she watched them go.

Later, maybe Armand would tell her what it was all about, but she had a feeling he wouldn't, even though it appeared to involve her somehow.

Suddenly, she wasn't quite so sure of Armand all over again.

The morning had been too busy to worry about it and too busy for Brooke to tell Felicity much about her date with Armand. It was snowing, and between serving customers and trying to keep the snow off their stock, they hardly had time to breathe, let alone anything else.

As Brooke's thoughts turned to lunch and their first drink of the working day, her phone announced the arrival of a text message.

Have you decided? What time shall I come to you?

Brooke typed her reply, and then smiled as his arrived almost immediately. It was a relief to hear from him, because the way he'd gone off with Jean-Luc that morning had thrown her. But all seemed well again now – at least, his text message gave no clue of anything to worry about.

'I think we're going out tonight, about nine,' she said to

CHAPTER TWENTY

As they walked the grounds of Jardins du Trocadéro, Armand giving her the guided tour, Brooke could appreciate that the marble statues and fountains and endless lights were beautiful, but she couldn't concentrate on them. She couldn't concentrate on anything. All she wanted to do was push Armand up against a wall and kiss him. But while they explored the gardens, he seemed reserved – far more than he had been at the top of the Eiffel Tower. Brooke wondered if that was because this place felt more public and he was being gentlemanly. Their fingers entwined as they walked side by side, but that was as close as they got.

Armand wasn't exactly famous, per se, but he seemed to be well known in Paris and so, perhaps, he didn't want to be seen doing anything that might get gossiped about. The vague thought crossed her mind that he might not want to be seen with her, but she pushed it out. He'd been out and about with her more than once now, and there had never been a problem before.

They had eaten at a very Parisian bistro that looked like something from *Lady and the Tramp*, with checked tablecloths and candles and flowers. The food had been rustic but amazing, and Brooke had enjoyed it far more than anything she'd eaten at the posh places she'd been to since she arrived in Paris. And afterwards, as he escorted her back to her apartment, came the anticipation, fizzing up inside her. The tension crackled in the air as they sat next to each other on the metro, and as she punched the code into the gates of her building, she thought she might explode from her lust.

'Felicity?' Brooke called out as they switched the lights of the apartment on, but there was no answer.

'I suppose she's out with Manon still,' Brooke said. 'Would you like a drink of something?'

'A coffee would be good,' he said.

'Right... although, I think you proved this morning that you make way better coffee than I do. Perhaps you ought to do it.'

'Of course.'

She followed him to the kitchen and leant on the door frame, watching him move about the space with the confidence of someone who'd been there many times and not just the once. It was strange that he'd only been there that morning. The day had seemed short and yet simultaneously seemed to stretch out endlessly as she'd waited to see him.

His phone buzzed, and as the kettle warmed on the stove he took it out to read a notification.

'Ah,' he said, looking pleased. 'Pascal's agent wishes to meet. This is very good!'

Brooke beamed at him. 'That's amazing! So you think you might get this deal through?'

'He is due to fly to New York for a week the day after tomorrow, so he would like to meet as soon as possible. Would you be upset if I arrange to meet for dinner tomorrow night with them? I am sorry, I realise that we—'

'God no!' Brooke said. 'I don't expect you to abandon the rest of your life to take me around Paris! Of course you must go!'

'Thank you,' he said, typing a message.

'Just remember when you make your Oscar speech who it was that let you go,' she added with a smirk.

He laughed. 'The film must be made first. You like to move fast.'

'Don't I?' Brooke said. She sidled over and slipped her hands around his waist. He was still typing, but he paused and closed his eyes as her hands travelled his back.

'Brooke... I must...'

'Must what?' she asked, nibbling at his lip.

'This message... please, you are making it very difficult.'

'You mean I'm distracting you? Good, that was the idea.'

'I must send this and then you can have me.'

'Hurry then,' she whispered in his ear. 'Hurry, and then maybe you can have me...'

She waited as he finished the message, impatient for him to be done so that she could have him to herself again. She didn't want him to abandon the rest of his life for her, but perhaps the next hour or two wouldn't go amiss.

As he typed the kettle began to whistle and she turned it off. They weren't going to be having coffee any time soon.

'It is done,' he said.

Brooke took the phone from his hand and switched it off. 'No interruptions,' she said, handing it back. 'For now, you're mine.'

When she and Armand emerged from her room for breakfast the following morning, Felicity was already sitting at the table with a coffee. She looked up from buttering her croissant with a smirk.

'Good night?' she asked wryly.

'Yes,' Brooke said, knowing perfectly well what Felicity was getting at and refusing to acknowledge it. 'Lovely, thanks. How about you?'

'Not as good as yours I'll bet,' Felicity said.

'What time did you get in last night?' Brooke asked. 'I never heard you come in.'

'Well, you wouldn't have, would you? If you must know, I got back just in time to see your bedroom door close. I thought about knocking to say goodnight, but... well, something else was already knocking... think it must have been the headboard on your bed or something.' Felicity's knowing grin grew wider. 'Can't imagine why that would be. I mean it got rather noisy after I went to bed; I had to use my noise-cancelling head-phones to drown it out so I could go to sleep.'

Brooke glared, her face burning. 'We weren't that noisy!'

'You weren't on the other side of the door trying not to listen,' Felicity said with a snigger.

'I must apologise!' Armand said fervently. 'I had no idea... I am sorry!'

'Don't listen to her,' Brooke told him. 'She's being a wind-up merchant. There's no way we were that bad.'

'Let's just say' – Felicity reached for another croissant from the bag in front of her – 'if I'd thought to make a recording, I could have made a fair bit of cash on the black market for it.'

'Oh... jog on!' Brooke exclaimed, which only made Felicity laugh. 'We'll eat our breakfast somewhere else if you're going to take the piss.'

'Well don't do it in your bedroom, will you? God knows what would happen if you went back in there.'

Brooke stuck her middle finger up and Felicity laughed even harder.

Armand stood up. 'Perhaps I will make fresh coffee,' he announced, clearly mortified.

Later, Brooke would have to explain to him that Felicity

didn't care at all about what they'd got up to, but she did love making Brooke squirm, given the opportunity.

After breakfast they all travelled back to Jardin des Tuileries together, as they had the day before, but this time Armand had clasped Brooke's hand the whole time they were on the metro. Felicity had stopped her ribbing and seemed pleased to see them display such obvious affection. But then she'd always championed Armand and Brooke getting together. It looked as if she'd been right to – Brooke couldn't remember when she'd been so excited about a new relationship. There were so many variables, so many uncertainties, and it seemed like the most difficult one she'd ever embarked on in so many ways, and yet Armand made her deliriously happy whenever he was close by.

'I am sorry I cannot see you later,' he said as they arrived at the stall.

'Don't worry about it; I'm just happy you got your meeting. I want to hear all about it when I see you next, and I want to hear you sealed the deal. Employ that charm of yours – after all, when you do, you can get anything you want.'

'Anything?' he asked, pulling her into his arms.

'Anything.' She smiled up at him. 'I should know; I've fallen under your spell more than once, and, ask Felicity, I was determined not to.'

'You were?' He raised his eyebrows. 'You thought the idea so terrible?'

'I hardly knew you,' Brooke said. 'I'm a respectable woman.'

'But you know me now...'

'Oh, boy, do I know you now...' she said, her thoughts turning to the things they'd done the night before.

He grinned. For a moment she thought he would leave without kissing her, as he'd done the day before, but as she gazed up at him, already in his arms, he moved closer and placed his lips tenderly over hers.

'As soon as the meeting is over I will call you,' he said.

'You'd better.'

They stayed that way until Felicity cleared her throat loudly to remind them that they weren't alone. Reluctantly, Brooke let go.

'Good luck for later,' she said.

'Thank you.'

He kept looking over his shoulder as he walked away, and Brooke stood and watched until he was out of sight.

She'd once told Johnny that love at first sight was a stupid thing and couldn't possibly exist in the real world.

This morning she wasn't quite so sure.

'Some woman's been staring at you.' Felicity nodded at a spot in the crowd. 'She's gone now – clocked that I was watching her and went.'

'How do you know she was staring at me?' Brooke asked, a vague unease bubbling up. She hadn't seen Lisette for a few days – or rather, the person she thought was Lisette – and she'd almost forgotten how scary the thought of being stalked by her was.

'She just seemed to be.'

'Could have been looking at the stall.'

'She'd have come over to look at the stall. But she stayed over there and stared in this direction.'

'Well then she could have been staring at you. Perhaps she knows Manon.'

Felicity snorted. 'She definitely didn't look like the sort of person who'd know Manon. Normal colour hair and not a piercing in sight. She looked like the sort of person Manon would point at and laugh.'

'Can you see her now?'

'No,' Felicity said. 'I don't know where she went – she sort of scuttled off. Are you thinking it might be that Lisette woman?'

'I don't... well, I thought I saw her a few times, but I haven't seen her since before I started to go out with Armand. And he told me it's definitely over with her and that she knows it is. So...'

'Crazy stalker type... could be.'

'God, I hope not. Armand would have told me if she was anything to worry about, surely?'

'Maybe he doesn't realise how crazy she is. She's not about to advertise to him that she's of a mind to terrorise his new girl-friend, is she?'

'Hmm.' Brooke was silent for a moment. But then she smiled. 'Do you think I am his girlfriend?'

'I should bloody hope so, the amount of time he spends in your bedroom lately.'

'Yes, but that doesn't mean anything really, does it?'

'Come on – you must see it when he looks at you. He's so into you it's sickening.'

'Oh, you can talk, you and Manon.'

Felicity picked some lint from her scarf. 'Manon isn't into me. She finds me entertaining sometimes, but I don't think for a minute she'll miss me when I go home. But Armand... he won't know what to do with himself.'

'He'll be busy soon if he gets this deal, too busy to think about me. I hope it goes well for him later.'

'It will – he's got charm by the bucket.'

'That's what I said. Imagine if this explodes and he gets super famous. I can say I was dating him.'

'You might still be dating him.'

'Nah. I'm the same as you – once we go home, I suppose that will be it. We come from different worlds, don't we? This is amazing, don't get me wrong, but I don't suppose it's built to last. For a start where would we even live? Paris? I couldn't afford that, and he wouldn't last ten minutes in Ely – it wouldn't be exciting or glam enough for him.'

'Well, for the right person, we're all willing to make sacrifices, aren't we? Isn't that what love is – sacrifice?'

'That sounds a bit intense.'

'But it's true. You both give up bits of yourself, change how you are and what you do, switch your lives around to accommodate the other, and someone always gets what they want at the other's expense. It might be you or it might be him, but it's going to happen time and again, with every decision you make together.'

'I never thought of it like that.'

'I have – that's why I'm never falling in love. I like who I am too much to change for anyone.'

Brooke smiled as a customer approached the stall. *'Bonjour. Puis-je vous aider?'*

'Je peux jeter un coup d'œil?'

'Oui, bien sûr.'

Felicity nudged her with a grin. 'Is he giving you French lessons as well as French kissing lessons? Because I've never heard you sound so confident on the stall.'

'Well, we have been here for almost two weeks now. I had to start getting better at it eventually. So long as you don't ask me to translate the works of Shakespeare, I think maybe I'll get by just fine.'

Brooke checked her phone for the fourth or maybe fifth time that hour. She and Felicity had finished late on the stall, with neither of them having any plans and thus seeing no point in rushing to pack up, and they'd arrived at the apartment just over an hour before to eat a simple supper and spend a bit of time together, something they hadn't really done, other than at work, since they'd first arrived in Paris.

The idea that Lisette had been watching her on the stall had nagged at Brooke all day. She hadn't seen for herself, and Felicity didn't actually know what Lisette looked like, so it might not have been her at all. Still, Brooke hoped not – something told her that would be a bad thing. She didn't tell Felicity this. She didn't want to cause her worry. Felicity was very good at pretending she didn't care about anything, but Brooke knew that wasn't true at all. Felicity worried about everything and everyone, and the reason she pretended not to care was to protect herself from caring too much. If she could sell her careless persona to everyone else, maybe, eventually, she might swallow the lie too.

'I'm going to have a bath,' she announced.

Brooke picked up the remote for the TV and flicked through the offerings. There were only French channels, but she could now get the gist of what was going on without too much difficulty. Earlier that evening they'd watched a murder mystery. Brooke had told Felicity not to explain what was going on and tried to work it out for herself, and was gratified, and a bit smug, when she guessed the killer without a single clue from her French-speaking friend.

'OK,' she said. 'I think I'll check out the news and then I'm going to head to bed.'

'We've become boring, haven't we?' Felicity said as she got off the sofa. 'Here we are in Paris and we're in the apartment watching telly and having baths.'

Brooke laughed. 'We have to be boring sometimes. Even you can't be constantly on the go – you'd have a meltdown eventually.'

'I'd last a long time, though, before I conked.'

'I reckon you probably would,' Brooke agreed. 'Longer than me. I might be in bed when you finish in the bath,' she called after Felicity, who was already on her way out of the room.

'And on your own for once!' Felicity said, laughing as she closed the door to the bathroom. 'It's a Christmas miracle!'

Brooke giggled as she turned back to the TV. She flicked past a cooking show, a live broadcast of a rock concert featuring a band she'd never heard of but presumed were big in France, and then she happened across a film starring Pascal.

Brooke put the remote down. She'd caught it when it was over halfway through but was soon mesmerised by Pascal's performance. Even sobbing her heart out in a rainstorm she looked utterly enchanting – no wonder she was so in demand in France.

Brooke's thoughts went back to Armand. She wondered how his meeting was going. She'd sent him a text to ask but didn't expect to hear back – at least not until the morning.

Twenty minutes later the titles went up. Brooke hadn't understood much of what had gone on in the section she'd watched, but the film had looked beautiful and Pascal had been amazing. She felt lucky to have met her now. Had Fabien got his gallery yet for that totally bogus opening he was supposed to invite Pascal and Armand to? Brooke made a note to ask Felicity about it when she got out of the bath – if she was still up by then.

Grabbing the remote again, she was struck by a thought. Did they have a movie channel here? She clicked onto the channel listings. Maybe she'd be able to find Armand's movie.

Her search was distracted by her phone pinging a message.

I am downstairs!

Then the buzzer sounded for the main door of the building. Brooke ran to press the button to release the catch. 'Come up!'

She barely had time to brush her hair and chew on a mint before there was a knock on the door. She ran to open it. Armand was on the landing, beaming, a bottle of champagne under his arm. He pulled her into a long kiss.

'She said yes!' he cried, kissing her again. 'Pascal will be my Agnes!'

'That's amazing!' Brooke ushered him in. 'Tell me about it!'

'I will,' he said. 'First we must open this!'

He took the champagne to the kitchen, opened it and then searched for some glasses, while Brooke tried to tidy herself and hoped that her pyjamas weren't too off-putting. Then he handed her a glass before taking one himself and knocking the whole lot back.

'I feel like a king!' he said, pouring some more. 'I can do anything!'

'I'm so happy for you,' Brooke said. 'I knew you could do it.'

'You did. You are amazing, Brooke!'

She laughed. 'I didn't do anything.'

'You came to Paris! You changed everything!'

Brooke sipped her champagne as he gazed at her. And then he stepped forward, took the glass from her hand and lifted her into his arms. As he carried her into the bedroom, she uttered a silent apology to Felicity, who was still in the bath, and then thought no more about it.

CHAPTER TWENTY-ONE

'I'm not going to say one word about it,' Felicity said as she munched on an almond and apricot pastry. 'I can't even leave you alone for one minute without Armand turning up to ravage you. Do you send out some kind of pheromone or something? Like a Bat Signal across Paris? *Come and get me!*'

Brooke grinned. 'I thought you weren't going to say one word about it. I lost count there but that was loads.'

'*Bonjour,*' Armand said wearily as he came out of the bedroom and went directly to the bathroom.

'And you've finally broken him!' Felicity added. 'He looks knackered!'

'Well, it was late by the time he got here, so...'

Felicity shoved the rest of the pastry into her mouth and chewed lazily. 'Boo getting more action than me... there is something wrong with this picture.'

As Armand came back out of the bathroom and joined them at the table, Felicity got up.

'Nothing personal, A, but I've got to get ready for work.'

'Of course,' Armand said.

'A?' Brooke said to him once Felicity had gone. 'She's already got a nickname for you – it means she likes you.'

'I'm glad to hear it.' He reached for the coffee pot. 'I wondered if she might be angry because I came last night without invitation.'

'Well, she doesn't seem to be. She tends to be chilled about stuff like that.'

'Good. I hope you are not angry either.'

'Why would I be angry?'

He picked up his black coffee. 'It may seem that I only come when it is convenient for me. My work is not always easy for others to understand.'

'Well, I definitely understood last night – the meeting was a big deal. I'm happy it worked out for you.'

'And you were happy to see me?'

'You bet I was! Didn't you get that by what we did after you arrived?'

He gave a tired smile. 'I am glad. I like you, Brooke.'

'I like you too,' she said, but wondered whether there was a part of her, against her judgement, who was wishing he'd use the word love instead of like. It wasn't a language thing because his English was faultless. His wording was a deliberate choice, so did that mean she was seeing more in this relationship than he was offering?

Ridiculous, she told herself. *You've known this man less than two weeks!*

'Do you want some breakfast?' she asked. 'I think there are some pastries in the kitchen... if Felicity hasn't eaten them all.'

'Thank you.'

Brooke went to the kitchen and found a bag with one pastry left. She put it on a plate and went back to the table to find Armand switching on his phone. As the screen came to life it showed missed calls and messages, and as Brooke craned to see, he moved it out of her way and turned it face down on the table.

'I will be busy today,' he said.

'That's OK,' Brooke replied, trying not to let him see how rattled she was. 'I'll be busy too. Busy every day at the market, eh?'

'Yes,' he said, but his answering smile seemed distracted. 'Then I'm sure you want to hurry to open.'

'Will I see you tonight? I'm not asking because I expect it; I'm only asking so I know... I'm not expecting you to give up every evening for me.'

'Perhaps,' he said.

'Right... well, let me know when you can. I might spend some time with Felicity if not... feels as if we hardly see each other these days. We do, of course, but we're always working or bolting a meal to go somewhere else. We haven't actually talked, you know. Like just spent time together. I feel like I might be neglecting her.'

'But she goes out with her new friend?'

'Yes, but... well, I don't feel I'm giving her enough attention. She means a lot to me; she's always been there for me. She's the most important person in my life.'

'To have a friend like that must be wonderful.'

'It is,' Brooke said. 'You have to take care of those people, don't you, if you want to keep them?'

He nodded slowly. 'I'm sure you must.'

'Is that like you and Jean-Luc?'

'We are friends, but... I have only known him since I came to Paris. I don't think it is the same as for you and Felicity.'

'Oh. Well—'

He dropped the half-eaten pastry onto his plate and got up. 'Forgive me, but I must get dressed.'

Brooke's forehead creased as he went into the bedroom.

That wasn't weird at all.

. . .

Armand didn't accompany them to the Jardin des Tuileries like he usually did as part of their new routine, but bade them farewell a few stops earlier saying he needed to see somebody about work. But he seemed distracted and not at all like the man who'd knocked on Brooke's door the night before with champagne and a passion hot enough to melt the ice forming on the trees of Paris that morning. Felicity didn't seem to notice anything untoward, and so Brooke decided that maybe he was merely preoccupied with thoughts of his new script and the new pressures that came from Pascal's agreement and tried not to see anything in it other than that.

When they arrived at the market, a crowd was gathered around their stall.

'They're keen,' Felicity said. 'We don't usually have people waiting for us to open. Are we having a sale I don't know about?'

Brooke frowned. But as they made their way through, the reason became horribly clear.

'What the...'

Brooke stared at the scene in mute shock. The chalet had been daubed in paint. And not just a little, but absolutely covered so that barely a scrap of wood was visible. It had been thrown in temper, it seemed, and had splashed over the surrounding paving, and there were words painted in other spaces, huge letters across every wall. The decorations they'd hung all over the front had been destroyed too, baubles stamped on and smashed, tinsel and garlands ripped down.

'What...? I don't understand.'

There was no understanding, no words to describe the confusion of feelings racing around Brooke's head as she looked at the carnage. She turned to the crowd of people staring and whispering, and saw that while some obviously felt pity, others seemed to regard them with suspicion. And then Brooke noticed that no other chalet had been touched. Theirs, and theirs alone, had been targeted.

'This is personal!' Brooke said in a thick voice as she fought tears.

'Apparently so,' Felicity replied through gritted teeth, steel in her voice. 'Though God knows what we've done to anyone here that would make them want to do this.'

Brooke moved forward and the small crowd parted to let her through. She picked up a smashed bauble.

They'd worked hard to be here and had made an effort to be a part of the market community, to be good trading neighbours, to fit in. They'd come knowing they'd be seen as outsiders and had tried hard to change that perception by being open and friendly. Even after all that, did someone here hate them that much?

Her eyes were drawn back to the wording. She ran a finger across one of the letters. The paint was dry. How long had it been here? She turned to Felicity with a silent question.

'You don't want to know what it says.' Felicity's tone was grim. 'It's not exactly a glowing review of our services.'

'What does that mean?'

'Well, some of the insults even I don't know, and I speak French... but they all seem to be variations on a theme.'

'Which is? Come on, Felicity, I'm a grown woman. Tell me what they are.'

'English bitch, home-wrecker, she'll get what's coming to her... that sort of thing.'

Even though she'd expected something along those lines, Brooke still blanched to hear the nature of the insults. 'Should we call the police?'

'I'll do it. You see if you can get some hot water to make a start on cleaning it up.'

While Brooke headed to an area of the markets where she thought she might be able to get the kind of supplies they were going to need, Felicity took photos of the damage. Brooke didn't want those sorts of images on her phone – she felt sullied and tarnished at the very sight of them, knowing the words that Felicity wouldn't even translate fully for her were directed at them. But she did take out her phone as she walked, still fighting back tears, and called Armand. What she needed now was some reassurance of only the kind his steady presence could bring. She needed to be held in strong arms and to be told everything would be alright, that she and Felicity had a friend in Paris still, even if it was just the one.

But he didn't pick up. She put the phone away. So it was Brooke and Felicity against the world? Well, it had been that way before, and they'd do it again if they had to.

Brooke was scrubbing savagely at a splatter of red paint while Felicity was speaking to a market official. The water in the bucket was almost boiling and the bristles sharp, and Brooke hadn't been able to find rubber gloves, but in a strange way the pain felt good. It felt like fighting back.

She'd called Armand twice more, but he hadn't picked up and there hadn't been time to worry about it. Jean-Luc had come to their aid with some stronger cleaning products than they'd been able to get at the market supply depot, and someone had been to erect a barrier around their stall as they cleaned. This was a family place, the official who'd directed the work had said, and that sort of offensive language would not be tolerated, let alone be displayed for all to see. Their chalet would not be seen by any member of the public until every scrap had gone. Not only that, they would not be allowed to open again until it had been restored to exactly the same state as when they'd first arrived, and even then, Felicity didn't know if they'd be allowed to continue trading until Christmas. People were suspicious and Brooke could imagine what they were thinking: Were the

English women troublemakers? What had caused this? Surely
they'd wronged someone to bring this kind of misfortune upon
themselves? She had to admit, she'd be thinking the same thing,
only she had a candidate in mind, the only person she could
think of who was less than happy about their arrival because, it
seemed, even though Armand wouldn't fully admit it to Brooke,
she wanted Armand for herself. And that person was Lisette.

Felicity pushed through a gap in the barrier.

'He's still insisting we've broken market rules by not taking
the proper care of our chalet,' she said.

Brooke paused, pushing a stray hair from her face. 'What?
But it's not our fault!'

'I know. I told him that, but he says we're ultimately responsible for it and it's our lookout. However it got this way, he's
basically saying it *is* our fault.'

Brooke slapped her scrubbing brush into the bucket and
then attacked the wall again. 'This is bullshit!' she growled. 'It's
not fair! Have you called Fabien?'

'That was the first call I made. He's going to see what he can
do, but I think even he might struggle with this. He asked me
who might have done it or why we thought it might have
happened but I told him I really couldn't say. I think he might
have found that hard to believe.'

'I don't blame him. Think... is there anyone we might know
who'd do this sort of thing? We've hardly been in Paris long
enough to piss anyone off this much, surely?'

Felicity didn't reply – she simply grabbed a spare brush and
rolled up her sleeves. Brooke turned to her.

'OK,' Brooke said in a dull voice, 'I see where you're going
with this and it's crossed my mind too. You're thinking Lisette?'

'Partly,' she said.

'Only partly? I can't think of anyone else it might be, can
you?'

'Well,' Felicity began slowly, 'it could be totally unconnected but you were right about Manon. She has a girlfriend, and pretty long-term, so far as I can tell.'

'And you think she might have done this and not Lisette? Because, I assume, she found out you and Manon were spending time together?'

'I don't know. I don't know enough about her to decide what I think. Manon says they have an open relationship and they're both cool about it. I don't know what to think.'

'Maybe it's only Manon who thinks their relationship is open. Maybe her girlfriend isn't so happy about it? Have you asked her?'

'Manon? No! What am I supposed to say? Excuse me, Manon, but is your girlfriend a crazy psycho who vandalises Christmas stalls with death threats and slurs?'

'You need to speak to her,' Brooke said flatly.

'I'm not having that conversation with her. If you had to ask Armand about Lisette, would you be able to?'

'Yes, I would, but it's not the same in our case. He's not with Lisette now.'

'Wouldn't stop her from hating you so much she'd do something like this. She wants him back – she must do, why else would she be lurking around watching where you go?'

'She's...' Brooke paused. Armand had been open about his history with Lisette and how she'd refused to let go of their relationship when he'd ended it. Surely if Lisette posed any kind of danger Armand would have warned her about that too?

Felicity stopped scrubbing. 'You said yourself you feel like he has secrets. Who's to say the relationship with Lisette is as over as he says it is?'

'That was before I knew him like I know him now; he wouldn't lie about something like that.'

Felicity stared hard at her. 'So you have sex a few times and suddenly he's totally trustworthy?'

'What does that mean?'

'I think you know. If I have to ask Manon, then it's only right you talk to him too.'

'If you must know,' Brooke said coldly, 'I've tried calling him this morning and he's not picking up.'

'Fancy...' Felicity said, starting on a new section of wall.

Brooke glanced over at her. For the first time in all their years of friendship she was experiencing an emotion she'd never felt about Felicity before. Right at that moment, she hated her.

'Well, we'll soon know who's right and who needs to give a grovelling apology,' Felicity added tartly. 'Someone is going through the CCTV footage from last night to see if they can identify the culprit. With a bit of luck we'll know before the end of the week. Whether that will save our stall is another matter – let's hope they don't decide to kick us out anyway before then.'

Fabien hadn't been able to speak to the person he'd needed and there had been no news about the CCTV footage. By early evening Brooke and Felicity had cleaned most of the paint from the walls, but a lot had sunk right through into the wood so that outlines and stubborn stains still remained. Brooke didn't know what could be done about that other than stripping the varnish, sanding the wood down and repainting. That was a job the market official would not allow them to do. Felicity had practically begged, but had been told there was a regulation handyman who serviced the markets and that it was his job. But he had a packed schedule and charged a lot more than Brooke and Felicity would spend doing it themselves.

Other than necessary communication about the chalet or to arrange fresh cleaning supplies, Brooke and Felicity barely spoke. Brooke felt wretched about it now, her initial ire at Felicity subsiding. She'd had time to cool down and to think, and now she just wanted her friend back. God knew she needed an ally right now – they both did. But with Felicity still ignoring her, it felt as if the whole world was against her. Especially with Armand not taking her calls or answering her texts.

As Felicity went off to get some coffee Brooke unlocked the chalet and went inside. With the shutters down and the barrier still hiding it from the rest of the market, it was dark. Beyond those walls the other traders were spreading Christmas cheer, doing brisk trade and making a living. That was all she and Felicity had wanted.

Thankfully, the damage on the outside hadn't penetrated through to the inside – at least not too much. As she switched on the light she could see that there was some seepage at corners where the paint had crept in and the odd item had been affected, but it wasn't too bad. Small mercies, she told herself as she looked around. They'd worked so long and so hard to make all this stuff that she didn't know what she would have done if that had been destroyed too.

Picking up a crocheted teddy, she sat on the floor, held it to her chest and started to cry.

Later that evening Brooke went back to the apartment alone while Felicity went to see her cousin to brainstorm ideas that may yet save them, though Brooke could tell her heart wasn't in it. Felicity had hinted several times that she was thinking of packing the whole thing in and going home. And if she was being brutally honest, part of Brooke wished for the same thing. What was the point in delaying the inevitable? The market officials would ask them to leave before long anyway, and they'd probably get charged a huge chunk of the money they'd earned here so far for the repair of the chalet, whether they stayed or went. Not to mention that right now they were entering the busiest part of the season, a time where they were forced into closure until the handyman could come to them and do the work that would allow them to reopen. It seemed hopeless, however Brooke looked at it.

Perhaps she could bear it if she thought she still had Armand, but she was beginning to see a pattern emerging as far as he was concerned. Whenever she needed him, whenever she felt uncertain of his intentions and needed reassurance, that's when he would disappear.

All day she'd waited for a call and there had been nothing. Perhaps the muse had struck, as Jean-Luc once said it did, to send him into isolation while he wrote, but surely even then he looked at his phone once in a while? He must have seen her messages? Did he really think so little of her? Had she just been an idle distraction that he was now bored of? She couldn't – wouldn't – believe this was the man she was certain she'd been falling for, but what other explanation could there be?

Switching off her phone, Felicity still out, Brooke went to bed. Perhaps she would wake in the morning to find this had all been a ridiculous nightmare.

CHAPTER TWENTY-TWO

There seemed little point in getting up the following day. The apartment was cold and the stall was to remain shut for the foreseeable future, they'd done about as much cleaning as they could, and there was no Felicity to laugh and joke with because her friend was still very obviously mad at her.

Brooke lay in bed and stared up at the ceiling. How could a day change so much? A day ago she'd been happy. A day ago she'd had a thriving business, a best friend she loved and an exciting new romance, and Armand had been celebrating his success with her.

At little after ten there was a tap at her door.

Felicity pushed it open a crack and peered in. 'You're awake then?'

Brooke sat up.

'I just came to tell you I spoke to Manon.' Felicity pushed open the door and came in. She was already dressed, and Brooke guessed she'd been out that morning. Perhaps she'd been to see Manon in person, or maybe she'd been down to the stall.

'You didn't have to do that,' Brooke said. 'It was wrong of me to ask... I shouldn't have put you in that position, I'm sorry.'

'I'm sorry too. I didn't mean to get all defensive with you.'

'I hated that I lost it too. I'm the one who should be grovelling here.'

Felicity gave the most fleeting smile, but it was strained and barely there at all. Brooke hated to see the face that was usually so full of humour and mischief looking so beaten. 'Should we go to the stall to see what's happening?'

Brooke sighed. 'Is there any point? There's nothing we can do there right now. They'll phone, won't they? The market people will call us when they have more news about any of it?'

'They said they would, but you know what these local government types are like. And I expect they're busy with a lot more than just us; I doubt we're high on their list of priorities.'

Brooke hugged her knees to her chest. 'I don't know if I can face it. I feel as if everyone is looking at us and silently judging us, wondering what we did wrong.'

'We've done nothing wrong! Nobody is judging us, I promise. I've talked to some of the other vendors this morning and they've all been lovely. They have a ton of sympathy for us.'

'But I bet not a single one would say they saw anything if they were asked.'

'They wouldn't have done anyway. Whoever trashed our chalet did it in the dead of night; it's the only way they could have got away with it. Think, Boo, the market is open until 11 p.m. and then you need to add time for people to pack up and do the cleaning – that would take some of the bars into the early hours for sure.'

'I suppose so.'

'There's no use in speculating until we hear more about the security tapes.'

'Which they'll take forever to look at.'

Felicity's smile was a little more positive now. 'Not if Fabien has anything to do with it.' She nudged Brooke. 'Come on – get up. I've made you an omelette.'

'I'm not hungry.'

'Yes you are. And whether we like it or not we need to talk. We have to make contingency plans for whatever might come next, and we have to decide what we want to do, and that's not going to happen if you stay hidden in your blanket fort until January.'

Brooke fell back onto the bed with a sigh. 'I suppose you're right. I don't even know where to start, but I suppose that doesn't mean we don't have to. Keep my omelette warm; I'll be there in a tick.'

'Hello?'

Felicity picked up her phone and took the call. They'd been finishing their omelettes as it came through. If Felicity's brisk tone was anything to go by, it wasn't a personal but professional call, and she spoke in French.

Brooke made a start on tidying the table, keeping one eye on Felicity as her expression darkened. After a few minutes she thanked the caller and hung up.

'Who was that?' Brooke asked.

'Someone from the market. They've looked at the CCTV footage.'

'Already?'

'Yes.' Felicity gave a faint smile. 'Funny how they were all over it once Fabien got involved, isn't it? Apparently they've got a clear image of the culprit and the police have been informed.'

'Who?'

Felicity shook her head. 'They won't say. I suppose they don't know at this point anyway, and even if they did they probably couldn't tell us.'

'One person?'

'I don't know, but from the way the guy talked about it, I think so.'

Brooke put the plates down and dropped back into the chair. 'This is so frustrating!'

'You're telling me. Just so you know, Manon spoke to Valerie and says she was as shocked as us. I don't think we're going to find our answer with Manon's girlfriend.'

'I never thought we would really. I was clutching at straws. I'm beginning to think I know where our answer lies – I just didn't want to believe it.'

'Still no word from Armand?'

Brooke shook her head.

'Knob,' Felicity said. 'I'm sorry, Boo. I should never have encouraged you to go out with him.'

'You didn't make me sleep with him – that was all my doing. I know how to pick them, don't I? I don't think I should be allowed out on my own to places where men are anymore.'

'You'd think he'd at least send a short text after what you've told him,' Felicity said.

'Yes,' Brooke replied flatly. 'You would.'

Felicity's phone began to ring again. Thank goodness some-body was getting calls, Brooke thought bitterly.

'Hold that thought,' Felicity said as she answered it. 'Hey, Fab, thanks for hurrying the market people along... uh huh... yep... OK, let me know what you find out.' She ended the call and turned to Brooke. 'Fab says he's going to speak to his mate at the main police department and see what he can find out. He mentioned something about swift justice, but I'm going to pretend I didn't hear that. It's all a bit *Godfather*, isn't it? More likely he'll find out if they know who it is and tell us in case we know them – Fab likes to play gangster but his bark is worse than his bite.'

'Will they tell him? Don't they have some kind of rules on confidentiality?'

'Probably, but Fab can be very persuasive. I reckon as well, they have so much crime going on they're probably glad to let him have a sharp word with the culprit and close the case. I mean, you were mugged, and police came to take a statement, but you've never heard a thing about it since. They've got more serious crime to worry about than the petty stuff that happens on the street every day.'

Brooke got up and collected the plates again. 'I suppose you're right about that. Maybe we'll never find out for sure who did it.'

'Maybe not. It'll bug me to know they got away with it, but some things are just like that, aren't they? Want a hand there?'

'No, it's OK, you cooked. It's a bright day today – why don't you go out and enjoy it? You deserve a break.'

'So do you. Come with me. We'll grab a coffee somewhere – far away from Jardin des Tuileries – and we'll talk properly.'

Brooke considered refusing for a moment, but then remembered how desperately she'd wanted normal relations with Felicity to resume. Here was the perfect chance. So she nodded. 'Give me half an hour to finish cleaning and change out of these clothes, then we'll get going.'

They found a coffee shop not far from Sacré-Cœur. It was dowdy and a bit dated, but it was comfortable and at least there would be no danger of anyone they knew being in there. The coffee was good, despite the decor, and the windows offered great views of the basilica's gleaming white domes.

'I'm not ready to give up either,' Felicity said over her espresso, 'But we're not earning at all right now and we're still paying expenses.'

'Would we even be able to just drop the stall and go home? Aren't we under contract? They'd still take rent even if we weren't there? They're taking rent now and we're not even allowed to open!'

'Maybe, but that way we'd cut our losses. We wouldn't be

spending so much on food and eating out, and we could maybe wriggle out of our contracts on the apartment and the lock-up. Besides, I bet Fab could help us if it came to that.'

Brooke sighed. 'Do you want to go home? I suppose, really, that's the only question that matters.'

'I don't know. I didn't think so, but I don't know what else to do. I'm finding it frustrating and, frankly, boring, waiting around for things to get going again. At least at home we could be doing something useful. I've got my mum sending out our internet orders, don't forget, and I'm sure she'd appreciate the help. It's got to be better than sitting on our arses here waiting for... well, I don't even know. Just waiting.'

Brooke was silent for a minute. 'Why don't you go home?' she said finally. 'I'll wait around here.'

'Because you don't speak French.'

'I speak a little. I could ask Manon for help, right? You think she would?'

'You could ask Armand.'

'If I ever see him again,' Brooke replied darkly. 'And I'm not even sure I want to.'

'I wouldn't blame you for that. I'm not happy about the idea of leaving you behind. We're in this together. We go together or we stay together.'

'Maybe this once we'll have to work apart for the good of the team. You won't be a million miles away, a few hours on the Eurostar at most. If I need you, you could be here the same day. It wouldn't be that bad.'

Brooke's phone pinged the arrival of a text and she snatched it from the table. But the message wasn't from Armand, as she'd hoped. It wasn't from anyone she knew – at any rate, the number wasn't stored in her phone.

Go back to England! Stay away from Armand! He is mine and you cannot have him!

Brooke paled. She turned the screen to Felicity.

'Shit!' Felicity breathed. 'Well, I think we have our culprit, don't you?'

'Lisette?'

'It has to be, right? Who else is that obsessed with Armand?'

'I was scared that it might be. How do I even start to deal with this?'

'You go to the police and tell them. Show them that text for a start – she's dug her own grave right there.'

'But Armand—'

'Stop trying to protect him and think of yourself! Where is he now? She's doing this and he's nowhere! He's certainly not doing anything to stop it, as far as I can see!'

'I suppose you're right. I don't understand it. I mean, I know they were once close, but if he knows about this how can he not try to stop her?'

'Maybe he doesn't know.'

'Then how does she have my number? How does she know I've been seeing him?'

'That means nothing. You gave her your number on the night of the mugging. Just because she's never used it, doesn't mean she didn't keep it.'

'I suppose she didn't call because that would have meant giving me news about Armand.'

'Exactly. And you two haven't been discreet about your affair, have you? You've seen her around – chances are she's seen *both* of you around.'

'Means, motive... what about opportunity?'

Felicity lifted her cup to her lips. 'Seriously? She couldn't have just got up in the middle of the night with a tin of paint and snuck into the market? It's not exactly Fort Knox. I'd say opportunity was a given. You have to take this to the police – you don't have a choice.'

'You just said they wouldn't be bothered.'

'No, but if this escalates then it's important they have something on record.'

Brooke stared at her. 'Escalates? How can it get any worse than it is?'

'You tell me,' Felicity said, sipping her coffee.

'OK,' Brooke said finally. 'I'll report it. Will you come with me?'

'Of course I will.'

'I should let Armand know too.'

'Why?'

'Well, the police might want to talk to him; I think it's only fair to warn him.'

'And give him time to concoct some story that gets her off the hook or makes him look innocent? No, you don't say a word. If the police take him by surprise, they might actually get the truth, which is more than you seem to be getting right now.'

Brooke opened her mouth to reply when another message came through.

'Armand!' she said, glancing up at Felicity. 'He wants to know if I'm free. Says he's at the market stall and wants to know where we are.'

'I'd have thought it was obvious we weren't going to be there considering you told him what happened. Or has he ignored all those texts?'

'Maybe he didn't realise we'd actually be closed down, or he thought we'd be there sorting things out.'

Felicity rolled her eyes. 'Is he seriously expecting a date in these circumstances?'

'I don't think that's what he wants,' Brooke said, reading the message again. 'Sounds more serious than that.'

'Maybe he's found out what his ex has done?' Felicity sat up, more attentive now. 'Tell him where we are – he has some explaining to do!'

CHAPTER TWENTY-THREE

Armand seemed flustered as he entered the coffee shop. Locating their table with one brief sweep of the room, he strode over but didn't sit down.

'I am sorry, Brooke,' he said. 'I have been—'

'Working?' Brooke said wearily. 'Struck by the muse? Detained? Something you have to do? What other excuses do I get? Let me think...'

'Trying to save a friend,' he said. 'An old friend who has got into trouble... But I think you know something about that. I have seen that your chalet is all locked up. Jean-Luc told me about the insults painted on it.'

'So it was Lisette?' Felicity cut in. 'What has she done to deserve your help? You ought to be turning her in to the police.'

'She says she is innocent.'

'Yeah, right, well she would,' Felicity scoffed. 'Have you seen the text message she sent to Brooke?'

Armand looked from her to Brooke in some confusion. 'A text?'

'Yes. Sorry, Armand. I don't know what you're doing to save her, but I don't think it's working.'

'I don't understand... may I see it?'

Brooke opened her phone and showed him the screen. He seemed to lose three shades from his complexion. Brooke felt sorry for his obvious shock, but reminded herself that she was the wronged party here.

'Can we speak?' he asked.

'Go ahead.' Brooke gestured to a spare seat.

'Perhaps somewhere away from here?'

'Felicity is involved in this as well – you can talk to both of us.'

'But she is not involved in all of it... she is not involved in *us*...'

Felicity sighed and waved them away. 'Don't mind me – it's not like I'm anyone important or affected by any of this.'

'You're sure you don't mind?' Brooke asked, sensing that she had no choice but to go with Armand. He might not open up as they needed him to unless he was alone with her.

'I'll order another coffee and wait here. And if you're longer than that, you'll find me at the apartment.'

Armand took Brooke to a cosy bar around the corner from where they'd left Felicity. In any other circumstances, its low brick ceilings, wooden bar and warm-toned lighting might have seemed romantic, but Brooke was beginning to see that moments of romance with Armand were scarce, opportunely snatched ones. And for every moment of romance, there was an equal and opposite moment of uncertainty or confusion. It seemed that in order to have one, Brooke would have to take the other, and she still wasn't sure if she could deal with that.

A waitress placed a drink in front of each of them. Armand had ordered neat brandy, while Brooke had settled for a light beer. It seemed to be one more indicator of their situation.

'I have told you about Lisette,' he began.

'Yes,' Brooke said. 'You have.'

Why did she get the feeling things were about to go south? But she resolved not to speak her own thoughts or let him know their plans to report Lisette until he had told the story he clearly needed to tell. He wanted to give her the truth and she wanted to hear it.

'I have not told you everything.'

'Hmm. I don't suppose you thought it was any of my business at first – I get that. But something has changed?'

'Lisette and I were friends as children. Our grandparents are neighbours in Burgundy, and our grandfathers served in the army together. We have known one another for a long time. As we grew, we said we would marry each other, the way children do, you know?'

'I know. So that's how you ended up together? I can understand that. But you're not together now, are you? I mean, you told me it was over...'

'I did and it is the truth.'

'Then I don't see a problem with us... Is there a problem? Why does Lisette think it's a problem? She said you belong to her.'

'Years ago we were engaged to be married. We were young. I was foolish and I was pressured by our families who loved the idea of us being together. I liked her, I thought I was happy, but it wasn't love. We continued for a while, then I came to Paris, and after some time here I ended the engagement. She followed me here to persuade me I had made a mistake, and she never went home, no matter how many times I told her I could not love her.'

'Well, I'm glad you're telling me this now but I wish you'd told me before. It might have saved a lot of heartache. Armand, I don't know if you understand how serious this all is. Felicity and

I... this could ruin us. Our business is hanging by a thread. We sank almost everything into coming here, and Lisette, in a fit of pique or jealousy, came and destroyed everything in a matter of hours. We've been discussing whether we ought to go home early and forget the stall.'

'I am so sorry. I do not know what to say. I didn't realise things were so bad.'

'You didn't ask. I sent you messages to say there was trouble. I needed you but you weren't there.'

'Lisette came to me. She knew about us. She was angry – I was afraid of what she would do. I wanted to take her home to Burgundy – I was distracted with that. I did it to protect her but also you.'

'You were choosing her over me.'

'No—'

'But if you'd been straight with me, maybe I could have helped. I would have at least understood, instead of feeling abandoned and in the dark and not knowing how you felt about me. I still don't know how you feel about me. Did any of our time together mean anything to you?'

'Of course!'

'And yet you chose your unhinged ex over me.'

'You must understand, she is a very complicated woman. I have struggled to keep control of the things she does in Paris ever since she arrived.'

'Doesn't she have a job here? A house? Surely there are things keeping her busy, things that require reasonable behaviour? Is it really that bad? How is she even living here if she only came to follow you?'

'She worked for a television station. I helped her to find a job and a flat, because she told me she had not come to Paris to follow me, but to find excitement and a new life. But then I realised she was lying and she had come to follow me, but I still hoped, in time, that her new life with an exciting job would make her forget that I was the reason she came to Paris. I hoped she would find lots of friends and a new romance and forget about me, so I continued to help her.'

'That worked out well then,' Brooke said, her voice dripping with sarcasm. 'I don't think I've ever heard such muddled logic in my life.'

'She was fired from the television station last week,' he replied ruefully. 'I have given her money, but...'

'Wouldn't it have been better not to give her money? I guess you maybe want to help because of your past but isn't that just encouraging the fantasy that you still love her? Or *do* you still love her? Is there more I need to know? Please be straight with me, Armand – surely I deserve that much. Do you still love Lisette?'

'I love her as someone I once was very close to. I do not love her the way...' He paused and then shook his head. 'I care that she is safe, that she can eat and she has somewhere to live.'

'As far as I can see you're helping her to stay in Paris where she can ruin your life good and proper. Sometimes what seems the cruellest thing is actually a kindness. You have to stop helping her and then maybe she'll realise it's over and move on. While you're doing all this stuff you're keeping her hopes alive and it will only be harder on her when she eventually realises that you're not going to take her back.'

'You are right. I was hopeful that she would go home, once she understood that there would be no marriage, but...'

'But she's still here. What about your families? Could they help?'

'I cannot tell them all that happens – it would make them too sad.'

Brooke paused as she reached for her beer. 'I think you might have to.'

'Perhaps, but that is not why I needed to speak to you. I wanted to warn you, but I see I am too late.'

'Afraid so.'

They lapsed into silence, until he spoke again a few moments later.

'I understand if you do not want to see me again.'

'I can't deny I've thought about it. I only wish you'd told me all this before.'

'I am sorry.' He stiffened in his seat, and for a second Brooke wondered if he might leap up and shake her, but he settled again.

'You know we have to take this to the police.'

'You do not know for sure Lisette is responsible,' he said, clearly trying to keep his tone level.

'It doesn't look great for her, though, does it? This text message, for a start – pretty incriminating. And the police already have CCTV images. If we give them Lisette's name, all they have to do is see if the person on the tapes matches her photo. I'm certain it will.'

'You do not understand – Lisette is troubled but she would never do what happened to your stall. She says brave things but she is a scared little girl inside.'

'Armand, who else could it be?'

'I do not know, but I know Lisette and this is not her.'

Brooke's expression hardened. Why was he being so stubborn about this when it was as clear as day to anyone else? 'Why are you so stuck on defending her?'

'I am not defending her, but I understand her. She is a part of my past. She needs help, not police.'

'I felt like she'd been following me around, you know. For a while now.'

'Then you also kept secrets. If you had told me that, I would have been able to speak to her long before she caused trouble.'

'So it's my fault now?'

'I did not say that!'

'But *she's* done all these things, and *you've* kept her craziness from *me*... I'm the only person who's actually done nothing wrong and I'm the last person being shown any consideration here!'

'That is not true, Brooke. I have been with her, I have been helping her so that I could protect you! I have done everything to persuade her to return to Burgundy so that she would be far away from you, from us, because I—'

'How did she find out about us?' Brooke cut in.

Armand let out a frustrated sigh. 'Jean-Luc told me she'd been to the crêpe van to ask about you. Jean-Luc told her nothing, but she is no fool. We both guessed that she might cause trouble.'

'So Jean-Luc might have warned me too.'

'He did as I asked. I did not want to... I was afraid you would not want to see me if you knew about Lisette. Jean-Luc has only been a good friend since I arrived in Paris – he bears no blame. He is the only person here who knows the situation. If people found out... I would rather keep this private. I would not want people to say bad things about Lisette.'

Brooke paused. Perhaps he also didn't want people knowing about Lisette for the sake of his career, and while she could understand that, she couldn't decide if that made his motives worse or better. As things were now, however, it seemed a moot point. 'You didn't want people to say bad things about Lisette? Isn't she the one causing all the trouble?'

'It is not her fault.'

'It certainly doesn't sound like anyone else's.'

'Mine, perhaps,' he said sadly, 'for letting her believe that we would marry one day.'

'You were young! Young people make mistakes! If everyone who promised to marry kept those promises there would be a lot of unhappy people in the world. Sometimes, you figure out too late that it isn't right. It hurts, but it's better to find out sooner rather than later... take it from me, I know.'

'I handled it badly. I allowed her to stay in Paris when I should have made her return to Burgundy. If there is any blame, it is mine. I wasn't truthful with you or Lisette, and the blame for that is mine too.'

Brooke was distracted for a moment by a couple sitting at a nearby table. They looked very young and very in love, and she recognised the shadow of envy in herself as she watched them cuddle up. Wasn't that how she'd imagined, despite all her common sense, she and Armand might end up? How stupid of her. Perhaps common sense was the only faculty she could rely on these days – it was certainly serving her better than her feelings. Perhaps she ought to start listening to common sense more often.

'I suppose, if we're taking blame,' she continued, 'neither was I. I just didn't want to be that troublemaker and I was afraid it might ruin what we had. Looking back, that was pretty stupid.'

'I felt the same. I thought if I told you about Lisette you would think the situation too complicated and you would not want to see me.'

'Well, I guess that's kind of happened in the end, hasn't it?'

'You do not want to see me again?'

'I don't know how we can do anything else but end it? I know how much you want to protect Lisette, but I have to take this to the police. Catching the culprit and getting it sorted out quickly could be the only way to save our business, and I'm sure you wouldn't want to see me after I give the authorities Lisette's name. I'm sure you'll hate me, but I have to do this – I have to protect the life I had before you, the life I'll need to go back to long after I leave Paris and you're a distant memory. You must understand that?'

'Please, let me deal with it. Let me spare our families the pain of seeing her in trouble. Let me at least try. We have not known each other for long but I know you are a good woman, and I have shown that I try to be a good man? I hope so. I did my best to protect you from her. I know, I should have ended things with you and that would have been the best way, but I am human and I couldn't. Already, after only a few days, I cared too much. Or perhaps I did not care enough. Perhaps a good man who cared would have sacrificed his own happiness for yours.'

'Armand, I don't doubt for a minute that you're a good man. I don't doubt you did what you thought was right, but you must understand I'm doing exactly the same. You want to protect Lisette and I want to do the same for Felicity. This is her future too, her livelihood, and she didn't ask for any of this. So, you see, I'm the same. I have to put someone else's needs before mine. I have to choose, and I choose my oldest friend, who has stuck by me through every hardship I have ever endured, the person I know as well as I know myself, the person who will never let me down. Can you honestly say all those things about Lisette? You have history with her, you may care for her and you may want to protect her, but can you say with your hand on your heart she is more deserving of protection than Felicity is?'

'Brooke, I—'

'You can't, can you? We might have had something, and this makes me sadder than I can say, but something has got to give in this situation, and I'm afraid that something has to be us. It can't be anything else.'

'I understand,' he said after a moment's pause. He reached for his brandy, drank the rest, then got up and left.

Brooke found Felicity at the coffee shop where she'd left her.

'That was quicker than I thought it would be,' she said, looking up as Brooke sat heavily at her table.

'Hmm.'

'What happened? Want to talk about it?'

'Not really. It's over with Armand.'

'Sorry.'

'It's OK. It was never going to last anyway. Have you nearly finished that coffee? I just want to go to the police station and get the rest of this horrible business over and done with.'

CHAPTER TWENTY-FOUR

Brooke read the text message again. No caller ID, just an unknown number and a sinister message. It had to be Lisette, but she'd been second-guessing at every turn since they'd shown it to the police. What if they'd made a mistake? What if things weren't as they seemed?

Felicity had been more certain. There was no way it could have been anyone else – the message even mentioned Armand by name. And if Lisette was capable of sending that, then it had to be her who was responsible for the damage to their chalet – who else hated them that much? Who else had been so open about it? She'd more or less proved her own guilt.

They were back at the apartment now, watching TV. They'd ordered Chinese food, and the remains of it had been left on the table, both of them feeling too miserable and lazy to bother cleaning it up. Nobody else was going to see it, Brooke reasoned – it could wait until morning. Manon had messaged wanting to see Felicity, but Felicity refused to leave Brooke alone. Brooke was grateful for the company, but hated feeling she was holding her friend back. She'd made some protests that she didn't need to be babysat, but Felicity hadn't swallowed that for a minute.

Her mind had returned often to that last conversation with Armand. She shouldn't have cared. He'd hardly been reliable, had not always told her the whole truth, and had chosen to defend a woman who had gone out of her way to ruin Brooke's life, and yet, she did care. She cared about the way they'd left things, and she hated that he'd walked away without even looking back. In more feverish dreams she'd imagined they had some sort of future; she'd almost fancied he loved her – she knew she was on her way to loving him.

Perhaps she was the mad one, not Lisette. Hadn't she badly misjudged her relationship with Johnny too? Perhaps she was incapable of recognising any relationship for what it actually was? In which case, her future looked very bleak indeed. How would she ever be able to trust her feelings about any man? Perhaps it was just as well she'd chosen to save her livelihood and her friendship with Felicity because, in the end, those things might well be all she had.

'I might go to bed,' Felicity said, flicking through the channels. 'There's nothing on.'

'Already? It's not even ten.'

'I know but I'm a bit tired.'

'And we still need to talk. We've sort of skirted around stuff, but we do need to make plans, especially as we've reported Lisette now. Maybe things at the market will move quicker and we might have to decide whether we stay or go.'

'I know...' Felicity was leaning on a cushion, her legs stretched out along the length of the sofa, while Brooke was curled in an armchair. She turned to look at her now. 'What do you want to do?'

'I don't know.'

'You don't know? You just said we needed to sort it out. I

thought you might be leaning one way or another before we began.'

'I suppose... my head says stay. But my heart says I've had enough. Things have become too weird here.'

'You're afraid you might bump into Armand again?'

'More afraid I might bump into Lisette!'

'Don't think you can fool me. I don't think you're that scared of her. This is about not wanting to see him.'

'It's both. But I suppose going home would mean you can't see Manon again.'

'I'm sure she could hop on a ferry and come to England if she wanted to, so I wouldn't say I'd never see her again.'

'But would she?'

'I doubt it. It's not her style, is it? I could come here though.'

'Does it bother you?' Brooke asked.

'What?'

'That she had a girlfriend when she started to flirt like mad with you?'

'A bit, I suppose, but then she never promised everlasting love. I knew it was all nothing more than messing around for her. I went into it with my eyes open.'

'Unlike me, who made a total tit of myself.'

'You didn't. Whatever else he did, Armand cared for you; it was obvious.'

'Was it?'

'I think so. You must have been able to tell.'

'With my track record? I don't think I'd have been able to tell if he'd had "I love Brooke" tattooed on his forehead.'

Felicity smiled and then stretched. 'Right, is our chat done then?'

'I know – you're tired. I suppose it can wait until the morning.'

'I might go to the market tomorrow to see if anything has happened. The repair guy might have been without anyone bothering to let us know, and we might be sitting around for nothing.'

'I'll go with you.'

'And Fab wants to take us to dinner again. I think he feels sorry for us.'

Brooke groaned. 'It's nice of him but I don't think I can do another ridiculously posh restaurant.'

'But he's trying to be nice. Come on – let's indulge him.'

'I suppose I do owe him that much. But see if you can persuade him to do a burger bar or something.'

Felicity laughed. 'Yeah, right, because that's totally Fabien's scene. Aye, aye...' she added as her phone began to ring. 'Speak of the devil... this is him. Hey, Fab!'

Brooke grabbed the remote control while Felicity was on the phone, and with the sound on mute so as not to disturb her friend, she flicked through the channels to see if there was anything that might occupy her before she went to bed.

Pausing on a beautifully shot movie, she wondered if it might be another of Pascal's, or even the beginning of the one she'd only caught the end of a few nights ago. Maybe with the beginning and the end, even watched in the wrong order, she could piece together the story, and Pascal was hugely watchable, whether you understood what was going on or not.

But then she noticed the identification line beneath that told the viewer what channel and what feature they were watching, and she froze.

La Lune est Rouge.

Of course it would be. Someone up there was having a massive laugh at her expense. She was about to change the channel when she heard Felicity say goodbye to Fabien.

'Boo, he's done it!'

'Done what?'

'He's managed to get an image from the CCTV – don't ask how – and he's sending it now to see if we know her. I mean, I don't think it's going to take Mensa membership to guess whose picture is going to come through, but... right,' she added as a notification came through and she opened the file. 'Here it is...' She peered closely and then looked up at Brooke, but the colour had suddenly drained from her face.

'Let me see!' Brooke said impatiently.

Felicity turned the phone to show her.

'It doesn't look like Lisette,' Brooke said doubtfully. She glanced up at Felicity. 'Who is it?'

'We've stirred up a right hornet's nest here,' Felicity said in a weak voice. 'Manon's girlfriend must be one hell of an actor, because this is her!'

Brooke had barely slept, but she got up anyway and joined Felicity for breakfast, ready to head to the market as they'd planned. They'd decided not to tell anyone else that they knew who the perpetrator of the vandalism was because they weren't supposed to know yet and they didn't want to get Fabien in trouble, but they were both desperate to, if only for very different reasons. Brooke wanted to clear Lisette's name with the police, but Felicity reminded her that the security footage would have done that without Brooke's interference, and that regardless of Lisette's innocence in that case, she'd still sent Brooke a threatening text message. She also wanted to speak to Armand and explain everything and to apologise for not trusting his judgement, but Felicity had told her that wasn't wise either. And as she couldn't go to Manon before the police had been to see Valerie, her girlfriend, then Brooke couldn't go to Armand either.

'I can't believe I've been taken for such a mug!' Felicity said as they boarded the metro. 'I feel like an absolute tool!'

'You couldn't have known. Even Manon was taken in. She vouched for Valerie and I'm sure she believed her. Even I'm struggling to believe that the sweet-looking girl I saw her with outside the bakery that morning is capable of doing what she did to our chalet. You can't blame yourself.'

'And we said all that stuff to Armand.'

'Yes, but as you quite rightly said to me, he still needed to know. Lisette needs to be told that she can't behave like she does either.'

'It's my fault you dumped him. If I hadn't been so adamant that Valerie had nothing to do with—'

'Stop beating yourself up. It was my choice to end things with Armand. None of this is your fault and there's no point in taking blame for something out of your control. For now, all we can do is sit tight and wait to see what happens, and focus our efforts on the things we can influence.'

'Which is precisely zero things.'

Brooke shot her a sideways glance as she moved along the seat to allow an old man to sit down. 'It's not like you to admit defeat so readily.'

'It's not like me to be such an idiot either.'

'Oh, yes, that's definitely my territory,' Brooke said with a small smile. 'Well, I appreciate you giving me a break from that.'

The train doors opened and a school party poured in, children of about seven or eight chatting and laughing and raising the volume of the carriage so that it was now impossible to have a discreet conversation because the only way to be heard over the din was to shout even louder. But Brooke enjoyed the distraction from her own woes. They were all so cute and so excited to be there. They spoke so fast over one another it was impossible to catch the thread of a single conversation, while they showed each other toys and gaming cards or pretend rings and necklaces. Brooke could hardly remember how it felt to be so carefree; she was sure it must have been nice. What she wouldn't give for a time machine right now so that she could go back to the time when all she worried about was saving up for the newest Barbie.

The walkways of Jardin des Tuileries were busier than Brooke had seen them since the market had opened. While it was nice to see so many happy faces enjoying the atmosphere, it also reminded her of just how much business they were missing out on and what a disaster this trip had turned out to be. They'd come to Paris to have an adventure – but they'd overlooked the fact that not all adventures are fun.

She said hello to a few of the vendors they'd got to know during their time on the stall, and most of them seemed very pleased to see her, waving back or calling after her health if they didn't have a customer. Brooke had wondered if Felicity had been exaggerating about that to make her feel better, but perhaps not. It was nice to know their absence had been noted, even nicer to know that people were glad to have her and Felicity back. Not that they were exactly back. She wasn't sure coming to stare glumly at the barrier still preventing them from opening their chalet counted as being back.

Her attention was caught by Jean-Luc, who smiled and waved from his crêpe van. Brooke wasn't sure how to react. He wasn't behaving like a man who'd had to deal with his friend being dumped by her, and Armand must have told him. Perhaps, given that Jean-Luc also knew Lisette's history, he wasn't about to judge Brooke too harshly. She hoped not – Jean-Luc had been kind to them and she'd hate to think she'd managed to alienate him too.

But then Felicity's hand closed around her arm.

'Boo!' she gasped. 'Look!'

Brooke turned around. Although it was obscured by the heaving crowds, she could see their chalet – no barriers obscuring it from view, completely restored.

'It's fixed?' She turned to Felicity, confusion etched into her features. 'I mean, it's amazing, but how?'

As they went to inspect, a few more vendors said hello and looked very pleased with themselves.

'Do you think this is Fabien's doing?' Brooke asked.

'I don't know, maybe. He's good, but he didn't say anything about it on the phone last night and he's not one to be shy about stuff like this. I think if he'd had a hand in it he would have said.'

'Then who?'

Jean-Luc came over. After greeting them both, he spoke to Felicity for a few minutes, beaming the whole time and gesturing towards the other stalls. Then Felicity reached to hug him before he went back to his van.

'What did he say?' Brooke asked. 'What's going on?'

'Well, apparently all the vendors called for an emergency meeting and said they didn't like the way we were being treated. And the market people were like, "Tough, those are the rules." So the traders got together and decided they weren't having this, and so they got a petition together to demand that the repair men do our chalet straight away and that we must be allowed to open again. They said if we were sent home it wouldn't be good for Anglo-French relations and they'd tell all the British newspapers about it!'

'So the other vendors did this?' Brooke asked wonderingly, looking around to see people still watching and smiling at them.

'Yes!'

'That's... that's amazing! I don't know what to say! How do we thank them for something so huge? I mean, you can't just go around saying thanks, like they just lent us a cup of sugar.'

'That's probably all they want,' Felicity said. 'We'd have done it, wouldn't we? If it had been someone else here, we'd have fought for them.'

'I suppose so. But this is different.'

'How? Because we're not French?'

'You are.'

Felicity frowned. 'You know what I mean. Here, we're all the same. I'll tell you one thing,' she added as she got the keys out of her pocket and opened up the chalet. 'I think it would be taking the piss a bit now if we buggered off back to England after all this effort on our behalf. It looks as if we're staying for the rest of the market season after all!'

CHAPTER TWENTY-FIVE

Armand had made no attempt to contact Brooke. She supposed he must have heard about the reopening of their stall, and she'd messaged him to say she'd been wrong about Lisette after Valerie had been arrested, but although he'd sent a simple thank you for admitting she was wrong, that was it. That had been three days ago, three days filled with long opening hours and busy shifts as she and Felicity tried to recoup the money they'd lost while they'd been forced to stay closed.

It had been snowing heavily all morning. They'd been as busy as ever, which was good, because it stopped Brooke from staring into space and thinking about how she'd cocked things up with Armand at every opportunity. He must hate her now, and perhaps with good reason. She hadn't trusted him or his instincts. He'd asked her to be patient, to allow him to sort things in his own way, and she'd trampled over his request and gone straight to the police, and now Lisette had been questioned and cautioned and her family had found out the truth. At least, that was what Jean-Luc had told Felicity, and Brooke had no reason to doubt his account. He didn't know what Lisette planned to do next, but he was sure she'd stay away from the markets, and as far as Brooke could tell, she had – there had been no staring faces in the crowd since it all came out.

She'd just sent a family on their way with a set of earrings and a necklace, which she'd sold to them while Felicity went to get drinks, when her friend returned with two cups. But she seemed agitated.

'Hang on a tick,' she said, putting the cups down on the counter and rushing to open the door of the chalet. 'I need to tell you something.'

A moment later she was inside and she put the shutter down.

'What are you doing?' Brooke asked with a deep frown as the chalet was plunged into gloom. 'It's the middle of the day!'

'I know – it's only for a second. I don't know what to do with this information, but I think you need to know it anyway and I can't have us being disturbed, not while I'm trying to tell you.'

'Can't it wait until later?'

'Depends if you want to make it for a four o'clock train or not.'

'What?'

'Armand is leaving Paris.'

'He is?'

'He's going to Burgundy.'

'Oh, well his family is there. And Lisette's. Maybe he's taking her home.'

Felicity shook her head impatiently. 'No, she's not going. She's not even speaking to Armand – blames him for her family ripping into her. I mean, who knows how long the silent treatment will last with a nutter like her. But that's not important. He's going back to Burgundy. For good.'

'But his work—'

'Pascal ditched his new film!'

Brooke's mouth fell open. 'She's not doing it?'

'No, pulled out right as they were starting to approach potential backers. Now she's gone, nobody wants to finance it. Armand is devastated.'

'Nobody? But he won prizes for his last one!'

'Yes, but it's all about stars, isn't it? People will see that she pulled out and think that's a bad sign. Nobody will touch it now.'

'Someone must want to invest, surely?'

Felicity shrugged.

'I feel for him, but what am I supposed to do?'

'I don't know, but I thought I ought to tell you.'

'He hasn't spoken to me since we broke up,' Brooke said.

'Because he thought you didn't want him to.'

'What? Who told you that?'

'Jean-Luc.'

'Did he tell you all this other stuff?'

'Yes, a minute ago.'

Brooke rubbed at her temples for a moment. There was so much information being fired at her right now and even one nugget of it might ordinarily be too big to take in all at once. Yet, there was no time to process it now. 'And yet he only just thought to say anything to us? How long has he known?'

'He went to see Armand last night for a farewell drink. He tried to talk him out of leaving. I think, honestly, Jean-Luc is sort of hoping that you might be able to stop him from going.'

'Me? He's not going to stay in Paris for me!'

'That's not the impression Jean-Luc gets.'

Brooke blew out a long breath. 'I thought things had calmed down, and now this.'

'So what are you going to do?'

'What the hell am I supposed to do?'

'You tell me.'

'Well... nothing. I mean, if he's made his mind up and even Jean-Luc couldn't change it, what can I do?'

Felicity folded her arms. 'You're going to do nothing? You're not even going to call him to find out what's going on? You're just going to let him go?'

'I'll only make things worse – isn't that what I always do?'

Felicity clamped her hands onto her hips. 'God, pass me the tiny violin, would you? Is that going to be your excuse for everything from now on? "Oh I won't bother doing anything at all because I'm bound to make it worse."'

'He's better off without me. He said how much he misses home – probably better off there too.'

'He's not better off without you and you're not better off without him! All you've done for the past three days is look mournful and sigh. It's bloody painful. And he's crazy about you. He told Jean-Luc he can't stop thinking about how he mucked it up. I mean, I don't know why he told Jean-Luc and not you, apart from the fact that he probably did it knowing Jean-Luc would tell me and that I'd tell you and hoping secretly that you would go to the station and stop him from leaving because he's too chicken to face you and tell you himself. If you want my opinion you're both as bad as each other – that's how I know you're definitely meant to be together!'

'He said all that?'

'Not all that, obviously. He wouldn't have said the last bit, but he definitely said the first bit about being crazy about you.'

'Well, maybe if you'd told me that bit first I might have felt differently!'

'So you're going to call him?'

'Do you think I should?'

'Are you insane?' Felicity cried. 'Why would you not?'

Brooke grinned, seized by a sudden recklessness, and then scrambled in her handbag for her phone. Maybe Felicity was right, and even if she was wrong, maybe there was nothing to lose by trying. If she didn't, would she regret it for the rest of her life?

She dialled Armand's number and waited for him to pick up. But it rang out.

'Oh, typical!' Brooke snapped. 'Same old Armand! The minute I make an effort, he's not answering my calls!'

'Maybe he hasn't heard his phone. If he's in a cab or at the station already it might be noisy. Text him.'

'But if he can't hear it ringing then he won't hear that come through either.'

'But he'll be able to read it when he notices he has a message.'

'Yeah, halfway to Burgundy! And if he can read that then he can also see a missed call from me.' Brooke put her phone away. 'Four, you said?'

'The train, yeah, that's what Jean-Luc said.'

'Which station?'

'Gare de l'Est.'

'How far is that from here?'

'No clue.'

'Useful...' Brooke got her phone out again and opened the maps page. 'OK, metro is seventeen minutes on a good day, but today is heaving and I have to get to the metro station first. It's going to be close.'

'You're going after him?'

'Looks like it.'

Felicity grinned. 'It's like *Crocodile Dundee*!'

'I'm not running in my bare feet – it's bloody freezing! You'd better be right about this.'

'I am. And what have you got to lose? You already feel like a tit whether you try or not, so you might as well.'

'Thanks for that. What if he's not interested in picking up with me again?'

'Then you let him go and you never have to see him again because he'll be in Burgundy and you'll be back in England in a few weeks. Nobody but you and him will be any the wiser.'

As Felicity opened the shutters, Brooke bolted from the chalet. The ground was slippery, thick with a layer of snow turned to slush by the feet of shoppers. The market staff were spreading the area with a constant round of grit, but it was never enough to keep it clear. Progress was made more difficult still by the sea of people in her way, coming from all directions, and the snow falling from the sky in flakes as big as saucers. The metro station wasn't far from the markets, but today it might as well have been miles.

Finally she rushed down to the platforms, looking desperately at maps for the right train, but once she'd worked it out she was unable to get on the one that was standing ready to go and had to wait because it was too full, leaving her stamping her feet and overheating in clothes that were meant to be worn outdoors while she waited for the next one.

Seventeen minutes on a good day – this was definitely not a good day. And what was she supposed to do if she did make it? Did she think Armand was just going to turn around and change his mind? But maybe Felicity was right – maybe she had to try. Maybe if she didn't, she'd spend a life living with the regret of never knowing what the answer might have been. It felt like a do-or-die moment and anything beyond this would be too late; the timing would be off, things would have moved on, they'd be in different places and quickly become different people. Silly, but that felt like the truth of it.

With an uncharacteristic ruthlessness, Brooke pushed onto the next train. She stood, crushed on all sides by other passengers and hotter than ever in her huge coat, watching carefully for the stop. There was a change, and more jostling and she just about made the connection before the doors closed.

A few minutes later they were at the station and she sprinted up to the concourse. There were vast boards full of departures hanging above. She stopped briefly to try and work out where Armand's train might be leaving from but quickly decided that there was no time to read through all of them.

'*Pardon, monsieur... le train..* Burgundy... um, Dijon?' she asked a guard breathlessly.

Was it Dijon she needed? Hadn't Armand once told her his family lived in a village outside Burgundy's capital? So surely he'd be getting the train to Dijon?

Frustratingly, the guard didn't seem to know. He took a tablet from a satchel and started to consult it. She glanced up at the huge station clock. Ten to four – she was going to miss him. She'd come this close and now she was going to miss him because she couldn't find the platform!

While the guard consulted his lists, Brooke tried to call Armand again. This time he picked up.

'Brooke?'

He sounded confused. She supposed she could see why.

'What platform are you on?'

'What?'

'What platform are you on? I'm at the station – I'm trying to find you!'

'You are at the station? The train station?'

'No, the Finland Station! Yes, I'm at the train station!'

'At Gare de l'Est?'

'*Yes!* Armand, are you on the platform waiting for your train?'

'Yes, but how did you...?

'Jean-Luc, but it doesn't matter. Wait for me – don't get on the train! I'll come to you, so which platform do I need?'

She left the guard to his searching and dashed for the barriers, bobbing up and down on her toes, trying to see past the crowds of travellers for a glimpse of him. And then she saw a man in a long woollen coat, speaking on his phone and pulling a suitcase, walking away from the platforms and back towards the barriers.

'I see you!' she said, waving for his attention. 'I can see you! I'm here!'

She watched him stop on the marbled concourse and scan the crowds. 'I can hear you but I cannot... ah!'

Despite everything, he smiled, and she couldn't help but relax into a smile too. He began to walk, his pace hastening with every step. She was struck by the sudden urge to run to him and leap into his arms, like they did in films. But in films there was never a ticket barrier, miserable-looking train guards and a sea of people in the way.

'Brooke?' he said. He halted at the other side of the barrier and set his case down. 'Why have you come?'

She gave a wild shrug. She felt wild and slightly out of control. Why was she here? She'd fought her way over with barely a second thought as to what the real reason was. All she'd been able to think about was stopping him from boarding that train. Beyond that, she had nothing, no rational explanation at all.

'I don't know,' she said truthfully. 'Jean-Luc told us you were going home.'

'Yes, I am.'

'For good?'

'I have thought about it, yes.'

'But why?'

He shook his head slowly. 'I have done what I need to do in Paris. It is time.'

'Don't give me that,' she said. 'Nobody just decides they'll leave the city they've built their life in without good reason, and I know you have yours. What happened with Pascal?'

'You heard about that?' he asked with a tone of faint surprise – and perhaps some worry too. Recalling what Felicity had said about investors, it was reasonable to assume that he wouldn't want that news travelling any further than it had to.

'I haven't told anyone else,' she said. 'But maybe if you don't want me to hear stuff, stop telling Jean-Luc? Him and Felicity are a right pair of gossips when they're together. So what happened?'

'She changed her mind,' he said flatly.

'Just like that?'

'She is a movie star – she can do whatever she likes.'

'So nothing to do with a sneaky agent who probably got a higher-paying project lined up and wanted her to do that?'

'Perhaps. That is the business.'

She reached for his hand and gave it a squeeze. 'You'll find someone else to be your Agnes – I know you will.'

His vague frown became a small smile. 'So you came to Gare de L'Est only to say that?'

'Among other things.'

'What are the other things?'

'Firstly, I don't think you should go to Burgundy.'

'You don't?' he asked.

Now, she was certain she could see amusement in his eyes and wasn't sure whether she ought to be annoyed or not. Here she was, doing her utmost to save him from himself, and he was finding it funny? She tried to look grave.

'No,' she said.

'Why do you say that?'

'Because...' she began, reaching for the right reason. 'Because... because... Because you still haven't shown me the Louvre or Versailles or the Musée d'Orsay or the Pompidou Centre and I need to see those things!'

'You can see those things if I am not here,' he said, that irritating look of amusement growing.

'But I wouldn't be seeing them with you! It wouldn't be the same!'

'I thought you were going back to England.'

'We are... I mean we were... Didn't Jean-Luc tell you the stall was repaired and open again?'

'Yes, but—'

'Then why would we go back to England? I mean, now? We will have to, soon, but not yet, not until the markets are over.'

'I thought... when we last spoke...'

'I know I said that. I know I was hard and cruel, and I'm sorry. I'm more sorry than I can say that I didn't give you a chance to make things right. I thought that only I could do that and only I had the right to. I was selfish, thinking of my own situation and not yours.'

He shook his head. 'You were protecting your friend, as I was mine.'

'I didn't trust you enough. I thought Lisette had done something unforgivable and I couldn't understand why you'd defend her, but I get it now. You believed her, and I should have had more faith in your judgement. After all, you know her better than anyone and you'd have known what she was capable of. I'm sorry about that too. But, Armand, if you'd only picked up the phone and spoken to me, I'd have told you that much sooner. We wouldn't be here now, in this situation.'

'I am sorry I did not understand how important the stall is to you and how upset you were to see it destroyed. Even if I knew it was not Lisette's fault, I should have understood that you only asked me about her because you were trying to make sense of how it happened. You did not want it to happen again and you thought if the police caught Lisette... I should have been more patient... And I thought many times about calling you.'

'I wish you had,' Brooke said, her tone now regretful. 'Seems like we've missed out on so much time we could have been doing more fun things than wishing we'd figured this out sooner.'

He smiled. 'Perhaps.'

'So you'll stay?' she asked, giving him her most hopeful, appealing look. But this seemed to banish his amusement and he looked only sadder now.

'I have failed in Paris. There is nothing here for me. Home is where I can at least be happy if not successful.'

'What, one poxy actress changes her mind about your film and you've failed? Well, I don't know what to say about that, except that it really doesn't seem like the Armand I thought I knew.'

'It is much more than that. I cannot be all the things people need me to be here in Paris. At home, I do not need to be a great man – I can be Armand, and that is enough. Perhaps the real Armand is not the one you thought you had met here.'

'*I* don't want you to be a great man,' she said. 'Armand is enough for me too. The real one. Try it! Let's see how we get along!'

'I think I already know that. It is why I loved to be with you. You did not care about my talent or my connections; you did not care for money or status – you were happy to be my friend and sometimes my lover.'

'I liked the lover bit quite a lot actually,' Brooke said with a slow smile. 'I especially miss that bit.'

'So do I.'

'Then why go? OK, go if you must, but give it some time. Stay... for me? Stay in Paris until it's time for me to leave? Does it matter if you go now or then? Isn't it worth waiting for a couple more weeks to find out if we really had something?'

'What if we *do* have something?'

'Then I guess we could talk again. And if we don't, we've had a good time finding out, right? Even you can't deny we'd have a good time – we'd have a great time. You can go back to that little place in Burgundy I can't pronounce and I can go back to Ely, and we'll have some nice memories to take with us.'

He regarded her carefully for a moment. 'This is a lot of effort for some nice memories.'

'Oh, I'm totally expecting a lot of sex too.'

Armand gave the warmest smile. Had she done it? Had she finally cracked him? 'You are funny,' he said.

Brooke pretended to frown. 'You've said that before and I'm still not sure if it's a compliment or not.'

'It is,' he said. 'When I see you I want to smile. Always. Every time.'

'You do that to me too,' she said softly.

He leant in, and for a moment she thought he might take her into his arms. But then he simply smiled down at her. 'What should I do, Brooke?'

'You're not going to get on that train.'

He glanced towards the platforms, clearly torn. And then he looked back with a silent question.

'No,' she said, 'you're really not. It's five past four; you've missed it.'

He stared up at the huge station clock. And then he laughed.

'Then,' he said, leaning over the barrier now to kiss her, 'I suppose that is that.'

EPILOGUE

In the shadow of Ely Cathedral, Brooke waited. She'd waited there many times, in all weathers, but never like this. Today was sunny and bright and warm for early May. The stone of the cathedral seemed to have an ivory glow. It seemed only right that they'd have good weather; Brooke felt somehow she'd earned it.

Felicity wore a long, fitted black dress, which was the only colour she'd tolerate, and Manon wore a white tailored suit. She'd flown in from Paris that morning, and despite her unpredictable, tempestuous nature during the time they'd known each other, Manon would always be an important player in this story and Brooke had been glad to see her. Plus, Felicity had been pretty glad too, and if she was happy then so was Brooke. The fact that Manon had brought a man with her hadn't seemed to dampen Felicity's enthusiasm too much, though Brooke really didn't want to think about that scenario.

Brooke's gown was silk and lace, with gossamer-thin sleeves and an empire line bodice. Second-hand vintage, of course, something she'd brought back from her last visit to Paris a month ago. Far more expensive than she'd budgeted for, but she'd decided she was only doing this once and so why not have the dress she really wanted?

It had been springtime in Paris and the city had looked very different from the first time she'd seen it. In fact, it looked different every time she visited, as if it became a completely new place each week. That had been eighteen months before. A lot had happened in eighteen months, both in Paris and at home. She'd found love, for a start, something she'd given up on entirely.

Brooke's family wasn't all that big, but they were all here: Mum, Dad, half-brother Nate. They'd mingled enthusiastically with their French counterparts and everyone had coped admirably with the language barrier. No matter what their real feelings about Brooke might be, her new French relatives had been nothing but kind and supportive and she loved them for that, because she understood that this was not the life they'd wished Armand to choose.

In the end, she hadn't needed to worry about bumping into Lisette either. Armand's ex had sought professional help, at the insistence of both families, and seemed to be far more at peace with her new situation now. The last time Armand had mentioned her was to tell Brooke that she'd gone to Cannes to start a new job helping to promote the film festival. Brooke had a feeling that Armand had secretly helped to facilitate this, as he had done with her job in Paris at the television station, but he'd never said it outright, and she'd never asked. She'd simply assumed that Lisette's new start had been his doing, and that it could only be good for everyone involved, and she certainly couldn't be angry about his efforts, because if it was his doing, it only served to reinforce her firm belief that he was a good and kind man who would never see anyone suffer, no matter what they'd done to him.

None of that mattered today anyway. Brooke had stood in the shadow of this cathedral so many times watching others get their happy endings and now it was her turn. Not that she thought for a moment that marriage was the only possible happy ending, but it was one she'd always known would suit her when the right man came into her life. It was nothing to do with reliance or patriarchy or social obligation or any of those other arguments against matrimony – it was simply about a promise. It was the promise that mattered to Brooke. A promise that a couple would always be there for one another.

Of course, Brooke was nothing if not a woman of contradictions. While she wanted the dress and the cathedral and the promise, she didn't care for the right order of things. She didn't want a father to give her away because she was nobody's to give. She gave herself, and she chose whether she did that alone or with the support of the best friend a woman could have, the only person, other than her husband-to-be who had ever truly known and understood her. And so she walked to the great wooden doors with Felicity and they went down the aisle together as friends. If not for Felicity, this day would never have come, and so it was only right that she played the starring role.

And there was Armand, waiting at the end of her walk, handsome in his suit, his green eyes full of love as he greeted her with a broad smile. He looked so proud to see her and she wondered if her heart could take much more. After eighteen months of back and forth between her home and his, they were finally here, ready to be together all the time, ready to make the promise. Sometimes getting here had felt like a battle, and sometimes it had been like a dream, but it had never been dull and it had always felt like it meant something important, like this time would be different. The page was about to turn for Brooke, the start of her new story, and she couldn't wait to see what happened next.

A LETTER FROM TILLY

I want to say a huge thank you for choosing to read *Christmas in Paris*. If you did enjoy it, and want to keep up to date with all my latest releases, just sign up at the following link. Your email address will never be shared and you can unsubscribe at any time.

www.bookouture.com/tilly-tennant

I'm so excited to share *Christmas in Paris* with you. Writing it certainly had me longing for winter walks along the Seine, drinking mulled wine and eating chocolatey crêpes, even though outside my window there was a British summer!

I hope you enjoyed *Christmas in Paris*, and if you did I would be very grateful if you could write a review. I'd love to hear what you think, and it makes such a difference helping new readers to discover one of my books for the first time.

I love hearing from my readers – you can get in touch on my Facebook page, through Twitter, Goodreads or my website.

Thank you!

Tilly

KEEP IN TOUCH WITH TILLY

https://tillytennant.com

facebook.com/TillyTennant

twitter.com/TillyTenWriter

ACKNOWLEDGEMENTS

I say this every time I come to write acknowledgements for a new book, but it's true: the list of people who have offered help and encouragement on my writing journey so far really is endless, and it would take a novel in itself to mention them all. I'd try to list everyone here, regardless, but I know that I'd fail miserably and miss out someone who is really very important. I just want to say that my heartfelt gratitude goes out to each and every one of you, whose involvement, whether small or large, has been invaluable and appreciated more than I can express.

It goes without saying that my family bear the brunt of my authorly mood swings, but when the dust has settled, I'll always appreciate their love, patience and support. The world is hectic right now, and it seems to be a strange and difficult time for pretty much everyone on the planet, so I'm seriously thankful to have my writing to escape into. My family and friends understand better than anyone how much I need that space, and they love me enough to enable it, even when it puts them out. I have no words to express fully how grateful and blessed that makes me feel.

I also want to mention the many good friends I have made and since kept at Staffordshire University. It's been ten years since I graduated with a degree in English and creative writing, but hardly a day goes by when I don't think fondly of my time there.

Nowadays, I have to thank the remarkable team at Bookouture for their continued support, patience and amazing publishing flair, particularly Lydia Vassar-Smith – my incredible and long-suffering editor – Kim Nash, Noelle Holten, Sarah Hardy, Peta Nightingale, Alexandra Holmes and Jessie Botterill. I know I'll have forgotten someone else at Bookouture who I ought to be thanking, but I hope they'll forgive me. Their belief, able assistance and encouragement mean the world to me. I truly believe I have the best team an author could ask for.

My friend, Kath Hickton, always gets an honourable mention for putting up with me since primary school, and Louise Coquio deserves a medal for getting me through university and suffering me ever since – likewise her lovely family. I also have to thank Mel Sherratt, who is as generous with her time and advice as she is talented, someone who is always there to cheer on her fellow authors. She did so much to help me in the early days of my career that I don't think I'll ever be able to thank her as much as she deserves.

I'd also like to shout out to Holly Martin, Tracy Bloom, Emma Davies, Jack Croxall, Carol Wyer, Angie Marsons, Sue Watson, Bella Osborne, Christie Barlow and Jaimie Admans: not only brilliant authors in their own right but hugely supportive of others. My Bookouture colleagues are all incredible of course, unfailing and generous in their support of fellow authors – life would be a lot duller without the gang!

I have to thank all the brilliant and dedicated book bloggers (there are so many of you but you know who you are!) and readers, and anyone else who has championed my work, reviewed it, shared it or simply told me that they liked it. Every one of those actions is priceless and you are all very special people. Some of you I am even proud to call friends now – and I'm looking at you in particular, Kerry Ann Parsons and Steph Lawrence!

Last but not least, I'd like to give a special mention to my lovely agent Hannah Todd and the incredible team at the

Madeleine Milburn Literary, TV & Film Agency, especially Madeleine herself, Liv Maidment and Rachel Yeoh, who always have my back.

Made in the USA
Monee, IL
28 October 2022

16747573R00194